Life is a diamond and on it miracles happen.

...and my father was there

I0610460

a novel

Noah McCaffrey

Glory Road Books

Published by Glory Road Books

www.GloryRoadBooks.com

ISBN: 978-1-7323963-2-6

Library of Congress Control Number: 2018946747

Cover photograph (front): Library of Congress, Prints & Photographs Division, George Grantham Bain Collection, members of the 1914 "Miracle Braves"

Cover photograph (back): "Nig" Clarke, 1911, Public Domain

For the mothers and wives who fight to hold their families together…

ACKNOWLEDGEMENTS
(Names mentioned below are not meant as endorsements of this book)

I'd like to personally thank all of colorful and interesting characters from baseball's past and present who have made baseball "America's pastime," and those who have chronicled the game since its inception—the writers, radio and television commentators, the analysts, and the number crunchers and historians from SABR, Retro-Sheet, and Baseball-Reference who spend their time finding new and interesting ways every year to count, calculate, and share insights about this beloved game. In addition, I'd like to thank the archivists. Without the myriad of archived newspaper articles, sports and score pages, and baseball guides from the early 1900s, this book would not have been possible.

I'd like to say a special thank you to John Thorn—preeminent baseball historian, author, and publisher—for taking a few minutes out of his busy schedule to answer some of my publishing questions. Also to author David O. Stewart, thank you for your tips on writing historical fiction. To Scott Crawford, Director of Operations, Canadian Baseball Hall of Fame, and to Adam Stephens, Chair of the Canadian Baseball Hall of Fame, I'm truly grateful for your willingness to read this book in its advance stages.

On a personal note, I'd like to thank my father for teaching me to play the game, and for the times we had playing catch together. Those moments have never left my heart. To my friends, John Ames and Eddie Ewell (pastor and amateur baseball historian), thanks for your insights. To God—without You I'd be but dust on this earth. Finally, to my beloved Jenny—thank you for your love, support, and patience.

PROLOGUE

T *he Great War* in Europe took my father from us at the end of
       1917. He ended up in France, fighting the Kaiser from cold
muddy trenches carved into barbed-wire-laden, smoke covered
battlefields. He and his Army unit must have been overwhelmed
because the country sent my father home to us ten months later,
bloodied and broken—just one of nine men from his unit to
survive their last battle. A *stupor* they called it, his mind asleep and
his sinew locked in tense turmoil, the result they said of a blast
injury to the back of his head. He could eat, but only if we fed him;
stand, but only if we supported him. His brown eyes were lifeless
but for a distant stare, his scarred face only a reflection of the man
he once was. His name was Laird Allen Young II and before the
war—*he played baseball.*

1

CHAPTER ONE

I got my love for the game playing streetball as a kid, and from reading about big-league greats in monthly editions of *Baseball Magazine* and the *Sporting Life*. My mother, a tough and slender outspoken woman who no matter where she lived could never leave her Texas breeding behind, had a tremendous influence on my becoming a professional ballplayer. Most boys go to the ballpark with their dads, but it was Mom who took me. And she knew the game too—better than most men. That's because my father had played for the Boston Braves. She figured if baseball was going to be his mistress she might as well get to know her too. But my mother never did anything halfway. She became a student of the game, then an expert on it. Mom could spit out stats faster than the tickertape could spit out paper, sling averages and percentages faster than politicians could spew lies.

With that in mind, it was no surprise that my birth would be forever tied to baseball. I was born October 13, 1914, the day the Boston Braves swept the Philadelphia Athletics to win the World Series. They called it "The Miracle"—not my birth but the sweep—because going into July that year the Braves were in last place; but as fate would have it, they mounted a remarkable comeback to win the National League pennant—and they won it with a ten game lead over the next best team. Going on to a four-game sweep of the Athletics in the World Series, well, what else could you call it but a miracle? Mom likes to tell the story of how

3

she had the delivery nurse feed her live updates from the game via the telephone during delivery. She says she was struggling to "get me out" up until the fifth inning, while the score was still a 1-1 tie, but in the bottom of the fifth, when Johnny Evers hit a two-out, two-run single to break the tie, she sat up suddenly and shouted, "That's giving it to 'em, Johnny Boy!" And that's when I "popped out of the dugout."

My father was on that team but missed the game to be at the hospital with my mother, whom team manager George Stallings had affectionately dubbed, "Mother." I say affectionately because Stallings appreciated my mother's baseball knowledge, and he also found her Texas twang amusing. The fellas on the team just thought of her as one of the guys. In appreciation of her, they presented her with a game-four ball, autographed by each member of the team. As a boy I admired that autographed World Series ball so often that my mother eventually gave it to me, a gesture I couldn't fully appreciate until much later—but I'll get to that in a bit.

When I was a young boy, just a waist-high, blue-eyed towhead in kiddie jeans, sneakers, and my father's Braves ball cap—which was too big for my little head and constantly falling over my eyes— my mother would catch for me. She started out at about ten feet from me when I was barely able to pick up the ball, and when my throwing motion resembled an awkward toddler swatting flies away from his right ear. As I aged and gained more power and accuracy, she scooted back until finally she couldn't handle my speed any longer, her slender working hands still ladylike and no match for a hard fastball, even with the glove on. It didn't matter anyway because my father's condition gradually worsened until he became her fulltime commitment. Carl, a kind and compassionate black man she'd hired to help out with things, would sometimes grab the catcher's mitt and let me hurl a few in his direction, I think because he felt sorry for me at times. I had no brothers or sisters, and any

4

friends I may have had lived miles away in town; my father, well, he wasn't even able to communicate with me let alone play catch. Mostly, though, I'd practice pitching alone behind the barn, which wasn't but a pop fly's distance from the front door of our house.

I had a pretty good setup—a pail full of baseballs, three stacked hay bales with a strike zone painted on them serving as my backstop, a 17-inch block of wood making for home plate, and two batter's boxes, one on either side of the plate, that I'd carved with my shoe. A few wheelbarrows of pasture dirt and I had myself a pitcher's mound, its round peak exactly ten inches above the flat surface of home plate, and a two-foot piece of 2 X 6 lumber anchored exactly 60 feet 6 inches away from the back-edge of home plate made for a good rubber, though before I was strong enough I had to pitch from a closer distance to home plate. All that was needed were some batters, but my fertile imagination took care of that. It seems every famous big leaguer of our time stepped into my batter's box when I took that mound, and of course I got every one of them out. I'd be on that mound, imagining the game announcer saying over the scratchy ballpark loudspeaker—

"First up for The Greats is The Babe, sporting his Yankee pinstripes with pride, his cocky eye on the young upstart from Lynn, Massachusetts, Laird Allen Young the third, who's stepping in once again for his injured war hero father, 'Al' Young."

Of course, my father wasn't a pitcher, but I liked the idea of playing for my war-hero father.

"The Boston Braves took a chance on this sixteen-year-old phenom," the announcer says, "but it's proven a solid bet with Laird coming off his one hundred thirty-eighth straight perfect game against The Greats. Today he's hoping for his one hundred thirty-ninth. The Babe steps into the batter's box as Laird takes his position on the mound, rear foot on the rubber, front leg out for support, body bent at the waist with his glove tucked in tight to his torso, his head forward and eyes steady like an eagle on the catcher's fingers calling for the curve."

Being so good, I shake off the catcher's signal; I'm my own man, after all. I've done my homework on all these batters and I know their preferences and weaknesses.

"Looks like Laird wants to show Babe his fastball instead of his curve. Babe grins, extends his bat to centerfield as if to say, 'Kiss it goodbye, kid,' then leans in for the pitch, taking a couple of practice swings."

I wind up, pausing briefly when my body is completely straight up and down, giving Babe a snicker.

"And here it comes! The ball is screaming down the pipe! It hits the sweet spot of the catcher's mitt before Babe can even blink! 'Steeeeee-a-rike one!' the umpire calls." A minute later, "'Steeeeee-a-rike two!' That's two fastballs in a row. Surely The Babe won't let him get away with a third. The catcher calls for the curve but once again Laird shakes him off. If Laird has his way The Babe's going down on fastballs."

I wind up and again taunt The Babe with that familiar snicker before hurling the ball toward home plate.

"*Crack!* The Babe hits a line drive straight back at Laird on the mound!"

Of course I catch the ball—behind my back, just to humiliate The Babe.

"Can you believe that, folks? Unbelievable! Laird tips his cap to the adoring crowd. This kid is amazing! Next up is Rogers Hornsby. This guy can hit, folks."

But like The Babe, Hornsby's gone in three. Honus Wagner is next to go down. Then Heinie Groh is sent packing, his downcast face looking like his wife just kicked him out. Tris Speaker, Goose Goslin, George Gibson—all go down without making contact. And that's the way it goes through nine. I'm on a roll—unhittable.

"Last up," the announcer says, "is the immortal Ty Cobb, a man who looks determined to shut this rookie down, to put this thumb-sucking weasel in his place. 'Steeeee-a-rike one!...two!... three!' Can you believe that folks! Whose sucking his thumb now, Mr. Cobb?"

I lift my hands in victory as Cobb breaks the bat over his thigh in frustration!

Nobody threw as many perfect games as I did those days behind the barn. My mother would sometimes come out to get me for dinner and I'd be on my mound preparing to throw. I'd ask her to wait and she'd ask me which all-star I was facing at that moment. I'd tell her the name and she'd start rattling off their hitting statistics, including their career or prior season batting averages and home runs. I'd tell her, "No problem. I can take him," and that's how it would go. I never lost a single game behind that barn, never even gave up a hit. Too bad it never went like that in real games.

One pitch I was particularly fond of but had no talent for throwing was my knuckleball. A knuckleball when properly pitched has no spin and sort of just floats unpredictably in to the plate, at such a slow speed the red and black or red and blue seams on the baseball are visible. Most batters are way ahead of it, or under or over it, swinging like fools at air. And that's what mine would do *when it worked*. But most of the time it didn't. I found the baseball hard to hold by the knuckles—having to curl my fat and calloused fingers under, only my fingertips touching the ball—so sometimes when I would try to throw it, the ball would end up nowhere near the plate. Once, during one of my minor league games for the Hartford Bees, I accidentally threw the ball straight to the second baseman during my wind up, who was playing the bag because the base runner had a big lead. The ball just slipped out of my hand during my arm's rotation—just slipped out halfway through. My second baseman fielded it by instinct, but with a look of bewilderment. The base runner was caught out in no-man's land between second and third bases and eventually tagged out. The umpires spent five minutes in conference trying to figure out if they should call it a balk and let the runner advance to third base, or call him out. Another time the ball slipped out on my rotation and went up in the air above my head; I just caught it right there, acting like nothing happened, trying not to let the laughs get to me. Another time my knuckleball sailed into the visiting team's dugout, hitting their manager in the head and causing a bench-clearing brawl. It got so bad one season that while playing bush league ball my coach banned me from throwing knuckleballs; threatened to kick me off the team if I even *thought* of throwing one more.

Though my father and I share the same name, people just called him "Al." I'm the third Laird Allen Young, my grandfather being the first. When my father left for Europe he was a brawny, twenty-three-year-old man, a bench player for the Braves, husband to a devoted wife and mother. When he returned, his body and mind were seemingly frozen, as if forever locked at the point and time of his injury—forever an invalid. Time has loosened his leg muscles allowing him to stand when assisted, but his arm muscles are constantly constricted, keeping his fingers clinched into fists and his arms bent at his side like greedy gnarled branches unwilling to surrender their fruit. His jaw muscles seem loose and unaffected, though, as if God knew he'd need to eat to survive. But the saddest thing is that he can't talk. To this day I cannot recall ever having heard my father's voice, though I must have when I was just a toddler, before he left. It's one of the great disappointments in my life. I sometimes sit and wonder what he would have sounded like. Would his tone have been deep? I can't imagine it being too high. He was too big and strong for that. Did he speak with authority, or was his tenor more unassuming? What was his laugh like? You can tell a lot about a man by his laugh. To hear my father laugh—just once—that would be something to remember. And there are times, if I'm being honest, when I wonder why the tender mercies of God didn't befall my father—why God didn't see fit to take the whole man rather than just choice pieces.

These are the things I've wondered about my father—things I'm too *afraid* to ask others, those who knew him before the war. There are other things I'd like to know too but am afraid to ask, like how he played the game. I'm told he played shortstop. I've always liked shortstop. You've got to be good to play short. But what made my father good? Was it his glove? Being quick off the ball—quick to second for the double play to first? Did he bat right or left? Hit the long-ball or go for base hits? Did he take the catcher's lip when he stood in the batter's box or did he give it back, like me? And there's one other thing I'd like to know, something personal and unrelated to the game. I'd like to know if my father was afraid, if he feared for his life—for us—when the country sent him to war. But only he could tell me that.

There is one memory I have of him that I cling to in my heart, when things start to get me down. It's Christmas time because I can see our tree, big and full, its lustrous green needles and sap-stained trunk giving off a strong pine scent, the metallic orbs and colorful ornaments cast aglow by the lamps lighting our home, ours one of the first in the area to have electricity. And it's the night my father left for the Army because he's in uniform, the olive green dress uniform complimenting his tanned skin and dark hair. He's sitting on the log-framed sofa with me on his lap, Mom rocking in a chair nearby, her pretty face stained by glistening tears as she admires us both. In my small little curious hands is his black-billed army-green cap, and I'm picking at the silver insignia above the bill. My father motions for my mother to come sit with us. She comes over, leans in close, laying her head against his chest. He kisses her on top of her head and then does the same to me before looking off, at what I don't know, something only he can see, I guess—*the future maybe.* All I see on his rugged face is the worry. That's it; there's nothing more. It started out as the vague recollection of a three year old, but time has filled in the details. That memory is all I can recollect of him as a whole man. Or it was—*until mom gave me the tin box.*

CHAPTER TWO

It was a cold Sunday in November when mother drove out from Boston to see me. I'd been living in Hartford, Connecticut since the Boston Braves signed me to a minor league contract. That was in 1938. They had a single-A club there—The Hartford Bees of the Eastern League—and they needed a good closer. I'd always been a starting pitcher and didn't quite like the idea of closing, but what could I do? No other clubs had come calling. Besides, the Boston Braves were my father's team—my mother's team; turning them down, even one of their farm clubs, well, that would have been a *nightmare*. Eventually, the manager saw my potential and made me one of his starters, but it took a while.

The house we lived in was nice—a blue two-story Victorian, the kind with wood siding, lots of white-trimmed windows, and a big wraparound porch—but it was much more expensive than my miniscule minor league salary could afford. In fact, my pay was so little that during the off-season I had to work down at the mill, stacking lumber onto railcars. Still, work at the mill didn't add enough to my income to pay the mortgage and other bills, so my entrepreneurial wife Janie started a part-time pie-making business. At first she just made pies for a couple local restaurants, but once word got out how good her pies were, her business multiplied. Soon she found herself delivering pies and other pastries to restaurants and markets miles away—so many that we had to add a second oven in our basement.

11

When my mother arrived that Sunday in November, she found me at the side yard raking leaves under three tall maple trees that grew adjacent to our home. In summer, the shade those trees provided was like leaping into a cool stream after a long hot trek through the desert. But in the fall, I found the leaves they shed to be more like a bothersome neighbor who wouldn't go away.

"Hello, Laird," Mother said, her voice softer than usual. "How are you, Son?" I looked up to find her standing there but nervously looking off, nibbling her lower lip.

"Fine. Didn't see you come up."

"Beautiful day, isn't it?" She had on her Sunday dress—a light-colored patterned garment with big black buttons down the front, one that draped her slender figure to just below the knees. And she had a knitted burgundy shawl draped over her shoulders, her arms crossed at the chest, holding something close to her heart.

"Yes, a beautiful day to rake these cursed leaves." I laid the rake down to hug her, kissing her cheek before asking, "What brings you out this far? Everything okay?"

"Fine. Everything's fine," she said, but then that was her standard answer whenever things weren't fine. We walked up the steps to the porch—a railed behemoth that seemed to engulf the entire perimeter of the house—but when I opened the screen door to let her inside, she said, "Please, would you mind, Laird, if we sat outside for a bit? I've always loved the fall, the brisk Atlantic air…the changing colors. Reminds me of…"

When she couldn't find the right words I knew something serious was on her mind. "What is it, Mom? What's the matter?"

We sat together on the wooden porch swing she—and my father in her words—had given us as a housewarming gift.

"This is nice," she said in reference to the swing. "Use it often?"

"We sit out here sometimes, sure."

"How's Janie?"

"Janie's good. Busy. Out making deliveries somewhere."

"And the baby?"

"Good, I guess. In the last trimester now. Getting close."

"Janie must be getting big."

"Yes, but it looks beautiful on her."

Smiling to herself, "She's such a pretty young woman. Are you excited about becoming a father?"

"Are you excited about becoming a grandmother?" I asked with a grin.

"Yes, of course, though I could do without the title. I'm going to spoil her madly, you know?" she said with a laugh.

"Might be a boy. Ever think of that?"

"Impossible." After she said that she looked away, like a lonely white swan does while drifting on a still dark pond.

"What's the matter, Mom?"

"Oh, you know—"

"What's that?" I asked, spotting the tin box on her lap.

She hesitated before saying, "It belongs to your father. He wants you to have it."

I took a moment to consider what she had just said. *My father wants me to have it.* "He just up and told you this? The man hasn't spoken in twenty-five years, Mom. He can't write, either. So how do you know he *wants* me to have it?"

"Why do you hate him so much? What has he ever done to you?"

"Nothing. That's just it. He hasn't done a thing to me or for me."

"That's not true. Your father has done a lot for you. You're just too blind to see it."

"Like what? Tell me?"

"Like giving you life."

"That doesn't count."

She scoffed. "Doesn't count? You wouldn't be here if it wasn't for him, but okay. Like giving you his good name, and a love of baseball. Like going to every one of your games growing up. How many father's go to every game?"

"He didn't *go* to each of my games. You *took* him to every one of my games. There's a big difference. He was there, but he just sat there, that same blank lifeless stare, drooling all over himself. He was there but he wasn't seeing me play. He wasn't seeing a thing. Come on, Mom. Be honest. You really—"

"Why you ungrateful, insensitive fool! How do you know he didn't see a thing? How do you know, Laird? Are you in his head? It just might be he sees everything! It just might be he hears everything, all the rotten things you say about him!"

"I know, I know. I'm a weed. A parasite in your grand imaginary garden."

"And I'll tell you something. There are days…there are times when I look into his face…into his eyes…and I can see him. He's in there. He's in there looking back at me, begging to get out, and it breaks my heart—just rips me apart." She began to sob, swiping at the tears with prideful hands before turning her face away.

A long silence settled in between us while I searched for something meaningful to say. Placing a caring hand on her leg, I said, "I know you love him, Mom—I do. But he's making you miserable."

"Can you really be this heartless? Are you my son? You can't be *his* son because your father is a good and decent man."

"*Was,* Mom. *Was.*"

"And he hasn't made my life miserable," she said, scoffing. "You know nothing about what you father gives me. In fact, you know nothing about the man at all. You're too concerned with yourself to ever try and find out—too afraid. That's why whenever any of us try to tell you something about him you turn away or leave the room. Too afraid to let us tell you what a fine man he was—and still is. Then you might learn you actually have a heart.

Then you might have to care about the man—*your father.* And caring hurts sometimes."

"Mom—"

"I'll tell you this about your father—he was no coward. He faced his fears. Didn't run. You...I don't know. But then that's my fault, I guess. I coddled you. Protected you too much. Fought your battles for you. Felt sorry for you that you didn't have the same kind of dad as your friends. And you want to know why I *took* your father to every one of your baseball games? For *him,* not you. For *him,* Laird. Your father loves the game of baseball. And he loves you."

"Okay!" Her words hurt, mostly because she was right. "Enough!"

"Taking him to your games...I thought if anything could bring him out of his sleep it would be that...watching *you* play *his* beloved game. Bring you out of your sleep too. Maybe by playing the game in front of him you'd see you two have the bond of baseball, gain some semblance of a traditional father-son experience. No, Laird, you can't toss the ball around with him. I'm sorry for that. But you can share the game itself because you've both experienced playing it. You can't talk about it, no, not right now. But maybe one day. That's why we stayed in Boston—why we never went home to Texas. That's why we're still here. Because I'm still hoping that one day, in God's good time, that your love for your father will one day reveal itself, and that when it does...when your love pours out on him...that it will free your father from his bondage—both of you from your bondage. But I can see now that it'll never happen. I can see now I've been a fool."

"Okay!" I shouted before settling again. "Okay. I got it. I'm no good."

"No, that's not true. You have good in you, Son. You do. I've seen it. I've seen the way you love Janie. How much you adore her. But with your father you're different. It's like you're mad at him for

15

deserting you. But maybe he should be mad at you for deserting *him*."

"Please stop, Mom," I said, fighting back tears.

She looked off for a long bit, her words like concrete in my heart. "You want to know when your father told me he wanted you to have this?" she asked, looking back at me, lifting up the tin box. "He told me before they took him from us—before he left for the war. The night he left your father told me to give you this box if anything happened to him over there—if he never made it back," she said, holding out the box to me, her voice trembling, betraying heartbreak at a sudden revelation. "Guess he never really did come back to us, so here."

"Mom, did something happen?" I asked, concerned. "Did Dad—"

"Not yet, but some days…I don't know."

Seeing the tears in her eyes, I said, "For you to cry like this it must be serious."

"I just never know…and that scares me. That man is all I've ever known. I love him with every ounce of my soul, every cell of my being. If something happened to him…"

I slid over on the swing and held her in my arms as she wept. After a few moments she shoved off of me, stood, and then laid the tin box on my lap before walking back to the car.

"Mom, come on! Where're—"

"He said to give it to you," she hollered as she stormed across the grass, "that you'd appreciate what's inside." She opened the car door but stood looking at me for a moment. "Said he was counting on you to do the right thing with them. Don't know why, though. You haven't done *right* by your father yet."

"The right thing with what?" I called out, but she slipped into the car and sped away as if fleeing an explosion, leaving me alone—just me and my father's tin box.

I stood watching for a moment as she disappeared down the

road, the trunk of her car barely visible through the rising dust trail. I considered her words for a moment. They were harsh—cold and piercing like an arctic nor'easter—but they were well deserved. I knew I'd been a rotten son to my father but I just couldn't seem to change. There was a certain vulnerability that came with loving him and that frightened me.

A moment passed before I lifted the tin box for a closer look. The first thing I noticed was how heavy it was. Though the box only weighed a few pounds, it felt as though the weight of the world rested upon it. And the tin box was cold, much like the father-son relationship it symbolized. The box may only have been made of tin, but it might just as well have been made of gold, because what it held inside was more precious than some physical object; it held the weighty burden of a father trying to communicate with his son through time. The red paint on the outside was chipped in places, and the lid was slightly bent along the edges, but other than that the tin tobacco box had held up well. It measured about twelve inches by twelve inches in my estimation and looked to be about four inches deep. You could still read the lettering on the outer band of the lid: *Pastime Plug Tobacco—John Finzer & Bros.* And in the center of the lid was the image of a man and his Setter, bird hunting. I wanted to look inside—thought hard about it—but in the end decided to take the box into the house, put it somewhere and leave it be; let the thought of the box, it's contents, and the gesture of handing it off to me ferment a bit, like a newborn wine sipping time until palatable. But if I'm being honest, the main reason for waiting was that my heart wasn't prepared for the mystery of it. I would open the tin box when I could muster more courage. Whatever treasure lay inside meant a lot to my father. That he trusted me with it only made me *nervous*.

CHAPTER THREE

I 'd met Janie while playing bush league ball—before the Boston Braves signed me to a minor league contract with the Hartford Bees. Some guys play college ball in hopes of getting noticed by scouts, but college wasn't for me. That didn't set well with my mother, but that's the way it had to be. I wasn't book-smart like some guys, but I was game-smart. I knew the game of baseball and I knew that my future was in it. I'd have a good life one day, I was sure of that too, but it wouldn't be by way of the ivy leagues; it would be by way of the big leagues. Still, I had to prove myself and the first opportunity came with the Lynn Wildcatters, a bush league outfit from my hometown of Lynn, Massachusetts—where my parents still lived. The Wildcatters were a bunch of scrappers, always fighting and mouthing off. Guess a bit of that wore off on me over time too, like the day I met Janie—the day I went a few rounds with a bruiser from Brocton.

Janie never really cared for baseball, at least that's what she told me then. The only reason she was at the game that afternoon was because the old jalopy she was driving had broken down on the street outside the park where we were playing, a city park with a ball field anchoring it; a ratty little field with chain link fencing and splintery dugout benches—dugouts that smelled of urine and stale beer. If you were on the outside looking into our dugout, you'd have thought none of us had wiped very well after our last visit to the bathroom, with seated players leaning this way and that in an

18

odd, un-choreographed dance, picking and pulling at the butt of their knickers. It wasn't that we weren't hygienic; it was because anytime one of us slid even an inch on that rotted wooden bench we'd get a splinter up our backside, which made for a pretty grumpy set of guys. I must have pulled five long narrow slivers of wood out of my britches in the first three innings alone, slivers that scratched and poked my skin until removed. By the end of the game we'd all given up and had taken to just standing in the dugout or sitting on the ground in front of it—grassless ground that some wiseguy thought should be covered in pea-gravel, which found its way into our cleats, making it painful to walk.

If that wasn't bad enough, the pitcher's mound had a peak to it, looking more like a jagged miniature mountain than a slightly raised hill. When I'd pitch, my front foot would plant about two feet lower then my back foot, which was still on the unsecured elevated rubber. It was like stepping off a small cliff every time I threw a ball because the groundskeeper, if there was one, never thought to replace the displaced dirt after each game. The result was a deep hole on the front slope of the mound. Sometimes, rather than trying to catch myself, I'd just let myself fall over after the pitch; it was easier than trying to remain upright. Anyway, we griped and whined but it was baseball, and we were being paid to play. If splinters and rocks and crazy pitching mounds came with the money, so be it.

Since Janie had to wait for a tow truck, she decided to take in some of the game. She'd heard the joyful crowd and saw the men on the playing field and thought it looked like more fun than sitting in her broken down car. Janie told me later that she hadn't been there long when she saw me come up to the plate. Honestly, I saw her first while taking practice swings in the on-deck circle between home plate and our dugout. When I first laid eyes on Janie it was like getting punched in the face, but from the blindside; I was completely dazed. She was just sitting there in her long summer dress, on the first rung of the bleachers right beyond the chain link backstop, with her legs extended in front of her, her ankles crossed. She seemed uninterested in the goings on, her thin fingers combing through her sorrel-colored hair, which was long and flowing like a horse's mane, only fine like loomed silk. She wasn't a pinup girl, but she was pretty and wholesome looking, conservative in the way she dressed, and with a spirit that reflected outward, like the sun on a mirror—warm, bright, and not to be missed.

She also said later that I looked a little too sure of myself, chewing my gum, tapping the heels of my cleats with the bat as I walked into the batter's box, burying those same cleats into the soil for grip as I took some practice swings, staring down the pitcher at the same time, my baggy tan knickers swishing with each wiggle of my butt. What she didn't know was that I was a pitcher who could hit, and that in the first inning I had taken the opposing pitcher for a two-run double. In the forth inning I had taken him deep center for a solo home run. In the sixth I chopped a single to right, bringing in another run. When she saw me it was the ninth inning, and in my mind I was about to bury this guy—about to nail his coffin closed and spit on his tombstone. Only, he had other plans. I'd humiliated him enough and he was about to do something about it.

He was a big boy—six feet three maybe, thick boned with dark hair under his cap—and a guy I'd faced several times before. I knew him to be a proud man, one that was having a bad day. He took his place on the mound, looking menacing in his black uniform, staring down the pipe and confirming the call with the catcher by nodding. He then straightened before going into his windup, hurling a fastball—*right at my head*. Thinking about it afterward I would have done the same thing. No pitcher likes a guy taking him for four runs in a single game. But right then—laying on the ground in a dusty heap, spitting dirt from my mouth, the crowd *oohing* and pounding the chain link fence, that screaming hard fastball having just whizzed past my noggin—I wasn't sympathetic.

"Say," the masked catcher said sarcastically. "You got pretty good reflexes, kid. Saved your life right there."

I leapt to my feet and charged the mound, having the good sense to drop my bat first. A player could get suspended for charging the mound with a bat. He knew I'd be coming for him and met me halfway, his big right fist cocked high and ready to slam me with all his might. But I went in low, tackling him to the ground by his waist and throwing as many blows as I could into his ribs and belly before his teammates could pummel me. I'd been fighting for years, ever since boys began referring to my father as a "retard," and I'd learned early on that most guys go for the face first; if I came in low I had a better chance of outlasting them.

I didn't like fighting; it wasn't something I went looking for. But I didn't mind fighting if it found me. That one-minute of explosive energy—and most ball field fights were over in less than a minute—brought with it remarkable relief from stress. Though my nose might have been bloodied, my eyes blackened and body bruised, my muscles and mind would be relaxed for days after. Physically hurting people, though, that wasn't something I enjoyed; in fact, I always felt bad about it after.

Of course, my guys wanted in on the action and soon the benches cleared, the small crowd in the stands loud and approving. Even the coaches were throwing blows that day. There must have been sixty guys brawling near the mound, blood and spit and fists flying! Thankfully my father wasn't feeling well that afternoon and my mother had to take him home early. But the fracas made the papers the next day. *Malay At Mayfield Park,* I think one headline read. *Young Goes Berserk On Brocton Bomber,* another read. When my mother saw them the next morning, she called me. I always hated those calls, the ones where she told me I was an embarrassment.

After it was all over I limped out to my car. Bush league games were played anywhere in those days so a lot of the time we didn't have lockers. On those days, what we wore to the game we played in and wore home later, so I was a mess, my tan-colored uniform bloodstained and ripped—and covered in red dirt from the pitcher's mound where I'd been fighting. I never did find my cap. As I opened the driver's side door to my green 1928 Chevy pickup—a hand-me-down from the ranch—I saw a young woman out in the street, sitting on the rear bumper of her car looking bored and a bit irritated as other cars honked, forced to go around her.

I called out to her, "Hey! You all right?" When she didn't answer I walked over to her. "Miss, are you okay? You break down or something?"

That's when I realized it was the girl I'd seen in the stands, just before the brawl. She glanced up at me, gave a snort in disgust, and then turned her sights down the road, as if watching for something.

"Hey, listen," I said, "I'm not trying to pry into your business. It's just, well, it isn't safe for a lady to be sitting out here by herself, especially in the middle of traffic."

She turned her head, gave me the once over and said, "I'd be safer with you? Is that what you're saying?"

"Oh, this," I said, looking down and brushing my hands over my soiled uniform. "I guess it doesn't look too good, me being bloody and all."

"Are your games always like that? You always beat each other silly at the end?"

"The pitcher was just sore at me, that's all. I'd taken the guy deep—"

"And you were just being friendly, I suppose?"

"Listen, lady, you stand there and let a screaming fastball brush within an inch of your head—see how you react."

She turned her sights back down the road. When nothing was said for a few moments I decided to leave her alone. "Okay, Miss.

Suit yourself."

As I turned to walk back to my truck, she said with a hint of frustration in her voice, "Yes, my car broke down—my father's car, actually. You know anything about cars?"

"Not much," I said as I walked back toward her. "You waiting on a wrecker?"

"Called for one an hour ago." She stood, brushing out the creases of her ankle-length dress. "So are you okay? That looked pretty bad. You took a few punches there," she said.

"I'm fine."

She stepped in closer, her fingertips gently lifting a tuft of bloodstained blonde hair from my forehead, revealing an open gash. "That's a nasty cut."

"It's nothing," I said, tilting my head away from her hand. "Someone sucker punched me, the rat." A moment passed before I let out a laugh. "To tell you the truth, I think it might have been one of my own teammates who hit me there. So many fists being thrown at my face, I tried to get out of the way and ran right into it."

We stood there for a few minutes, laughing and talking more about things, Janie tending my wounds with a handkerchief she dabbed on her moist tongue. "Sorry about the spit. I don't have any water."

"It's fine, honestly. I appreciate your kindness. What's your name?"

"Jane Kwiatkowski."

"Gee, the Jane suits you, but we gotta work on getting you a better last name." That last bit just slipped out, like a fart in a crowded room.

Janie stopped her mending and leaned back, giving me a disapproving look. I imagined her thinking I was arrogant, a big bold heathen that needed to be put in his place. But then she laughed out loud. She's always been like that, always doing the opposite of what you think she's going to do or say. "You got a better last name you'd like to give me? That it?" she said, continuing to tend to my wounds.

"Oh, no…I didn't mean…well, Jane Iris Young does sound pretty nice,' I said, grinning.

Just then the tow truck arrived—a rusted heap of bolts with a reinforced double-strap, black canvass lift off the back, the business name on the truck doors worn off and unreadable. The driver hoped out, a gum-chewing short guy, cocky as a lone rooster in a big hen house, greasy jeans and black boots to go with his worn and cracked leather coat. His blonde mop kept falling in his face prompting him to sling it back with a hand every few minutes or so.

"Who here called for a wrecker?" he asked, walking right past us to look over the car.

"I did, sir," Janie said, sweetly, like a newly awakened child walking into the dining room to say good morning to its parents, suckling its own thumb, clinging to its little blanket for security.

"Yeah?" he asked, strutting back over to us, giving me the once over. "You look like you could use a wrecker too, pal, only the ambulance type."

"Should have seen me a few minutes ago."

"Whatever he did to you, lady, you got him back good. Like you took a brick and—"

"Just help the lady and shut your—" I stopped short when Janie gave a disapproving shake of her head. "Thank you kind sir," I said, "for your useful commentary. Now if you'd be so kind as to assist this fine maiden, get her to the garage safely, I'd appreciate it."

Janie winked. "Good save."

"Whatever you say, pal. Have this tin can hooked up in a jiffy," he said, handing Janie the invoice. "Sign here, lady."

"Oh, my father will take care of the bill."

"Maybe so but you still gotta sign this here release of liability. The company ain't responsible, and all that."

Janie signed and the guy went about hooking the car to the tow truck. I hated saying goodbye to her, and I could see her reluctance to leave as well. We were both young, just nineteen and twenty, but we could both see there was something special between us. I guess it's been that way ever since. Nine years together and I'm still mesmerized by her. We courted after that, for quite some time. We had to; I didn't have the money to get married. They paid me by the game, not an annual salary. Sometimes a player would get bonuses by the hit or strikeout, but that's it. I'm still not sure where the money to pay us came from sometimes. If we asked the manager or owner we were told our share came from ticket sales, or the hat that got passed around at most games. Still, some of us speculated about gambling among the owners. There did seem to be a lot of money changing hands in the stands during some games. Honestly though, I don't think any of us cared, as long as we got paid to play. In our minds, bush league or major league, we were *professional* ballplayers—and that meant something to us. That day, though, the hat got passed around and we all got a big payday. Seems fans like to see a good bashing. One older fellow with an oversized belly pressed a $50 bill into my palm on the way out to my car—fifty big dollars! "That should cover your medical costs," he said, letting out a hearty laugh before walking off.

I jumped around teams in the bush leagues for the next four years, living on the farm with Mom and Dad, working odd jobs to help out with the bills, helping care for Dad too—when my mother made me. But when the Braves signed me to Hartford in 1938, offering to pay me $1,100 annually, Janie and I decided to finally get married. It wasn't easy holding on that long, especially for Janie, but we managed to stay together. Now we were married, had our own house—thanks to the down payment made by her parents—and had a baby on the way. Hard to believe sometimes when I think about it. All because I got beat up and her car broke down.

CHAPTER FOUR

When Janie got home the evening of my mother's visit, I was in the garage, which doubled as a woodshop—my refuge when the world felt heavy. It was a matching detached structure that sat behind the house by about thirty feet, with a large pull-up door that enclosed one open bay big enough for a single car and a walled workbench. Most of the work I did there was hand-tooled, the way master carpenters did it in the olden days. I was no woodsmith, though; at best I was handy, making wood furniture mostly. I did keep a clean shop, though, something my grandfather impressed upon me whenever he'd come visit us from Texas. "Take care of your tools and they'll take care of you," he'd say. Pegboard paneling lined the wall above my workbench and it was there that my tools hung, each tight in formation like soldiers on a parade field, each cleaned and polished like newly minted silver dollars. I did keep two power tools, though—a jigsaw to help cut shapes and round corners, and a hand drill to drive in screws and to drill holes.

I'd always loved the smell of freshly cut lumber. That's one of the reasons I took the job down at the mill. One thing I enjoyed making, when feeling particularly low, were wooden Adirondack chairs—the relaxed, high-back kind you see on lawns and verandas. They were easy and I found something therapeutic in their making—the repetitive motion of sawing the slats to various lengths, the rhythmic sound of screws being drilled into the

27

assembled pieces, the smell of wood glue, saw dust, and sealer, and the pride in seeing and sitting in the finished chair. I'd gotten so adept at building those Adirondack chairs that I could turn out a pair in about three hours. Janie would sometimes paint the chairs bright colors before setting them out on the curb with an equally bright *For Sale* sign, the price barely enough to cover the cost of lumber and screws. Seems most of the homes on our block had my chairs in their yards. By the time Janie arrived home that evening I'd finished one pair and had started another.

"It's getting dark, honey," Janie said as she climbed from our car, which she'd just parked in front of the garage. "Why don't you turn on a light?" When I didn't respond she walked inside and switched on the light, pecking my cheek with her soft lips afterward. "There. Now you won't cut your fingers off."

"You have a good day?" I asked, halting my work to help her carry groceries inside the house, Janie as cheery as a little girl after her first day of kindergarten, gabbing the entire way.

"You know the Lewis Market out in Waterbury? That big one with the giant moose out front?"

"Um hum." I yawned, swinging open the side door to the kitchen—which had begun to rot at the bottom corners—letting her pass through first.

The kitchen of our home was square-shaped with eggshell-colored cabinets around the perimeter, both above and below the mint-colored tile countertop, with an open gap between the upper and lower cabinets. The recessed sink sat below a sliding window that opened to our backyard, and there was an island in the middle of the floor that matched the cabinets, which Janie asked me to build when we first moved in.

"They want me to supply them with fifteen assorted pies, six cakes, and ten bags of cookies each week! Isn't that wonderful!" She set her bags on the countertop and started pulling items out of the brown paper bags. "And I landed another customer in

Farmington on my way home, a small deli that wants to expand their dessert menu. Who would have ever thought, me a successful businesswoman?"

"I would have," I said, setting my bags next to hers.

"Ah, that's sweet, honey." She leaned in to kiss me.

"We sure can use the money."

"Why?" She stopped and leaned back, looking up at me with squinty eyes. "Jerry let you go? Oh, Laird. Why?"

"Got into it with one of the truck drivers. Didn't like the way I loaded his truck, I guess. Took exception. Called me a few names when I wouldn't pull everything off and restack it."

"You didn't hit him, did you? Tell me—"

"No, but probably should have, the old coot. No Janie, I politely told him if he wanted his truck reloaded, no problem. Then I yanked all those boards off onto the ground and told him to reload it himself. Then I walked off. Guess Jerry didn't think that was customer service worthy of his good name. Paid me cash out of the till and told me to get lost."

She began moving things around in one of the cupboards to make a place for the new groceries. "Why are you like that, Laird?"

"Like what?"

"Difficult. If you haven't noticed, it causes a lot of problems."

"I'm not difficult."

"See, you're doing it now."

"What? I'm just supposed to let you say that about me...lay down and let you trample me like a dirty rug?"

She gave my butt a firm pat. "So dramatic." After a moment she said, "You could always enlist. There *is* a war going—"

"No." The word came out like a bullet intended to immediately end a dispute.

"I was kidding," she said, planting her supple lips on mine, which were chapped and bleeding in one spot. "Ooh, you should put some balm on those chops, sweetie, before they scab."

"They're fine."

"Well I'm sorry, honey. I'll see if I can get more customers, up my orders with those I already have. Should get more with the holidays coming up. Might need your help though with deliveries."

Standing there, watching her move from the bags to the cabinets and back to the bags, I felt lost. "Been thinking I should quit altogether."

"Quit what? Didn't you already get fired?"

"Baseball."

"What?" Janie stopped, stunned at what she'd just heard. "You? Quitting baseball? That's like saying you aren't gonna breath anymore!"

"I'm serious. I need a better job—more money."

"You're serious? No. You can't be serious."

"What kind of guy just goes off and plays a game...a *stupid* game...letting his wife and baby starve?"

"The kind of guy that gets *paid* to play that game. It's our biggest source of income." Janie walked over and felt my forehead. "Honey, are you all right? Did you fall down—hit your head or something? As long as I've known you I've never heard you *ever* even hint at quitting baseball. I always figured you'd just die out on the mound one day and I'd get the boys to just dig a hole right there, roll you into it and I'd say goodbye. They'd replace the rubber, a reliever would come in—"

"Funny. I'm serious, Janie. How long have I been in the minors...five...six years?"

"So. You're getting paid to play, aren't you?"

"So? The war has pulled a lot of players out of the majors, reducing the league to a skeleton. They need players badly and I'm still playing in the minors. The Braves could sell my contract to another team but they don't. What does that tell you?"

"That the minors are in worse shape than the majors. That they want to keep you for themselves?"

"No—that I don't have any value. I'm not worth anything to them."

"That's the devil talking. You're a great pitcher with a lot to offer."

"Then why am I still playing for the Bees?"

"I don't know, Laird. Why don't you call management and ask them? Ask them why, if you're so bad, they haven't fired you altogether—why they still let you play."

She went over to the wall-phone and picked up the receiver.

"What are you doing?" I asked.

"Calling Doctor Thompson. Something's seriously wrong—"

"Don't be silly." I took the receiver from her hand and placed it back in place.

"Well something's not right with you," Janie said, going into the adjoining dining room and switching on the light. "First you get fired, now you want to quit baseball." Pointing to the red tin box, which rested atop the morning newspaper lying on our oval oak dinner table—another of my projects—the date on the paper, November 4, 1943, the bold headline reading, U.S. PLANES BOMB KEY GERMAN PORT OF WILHELMSHAVEN. "What's that?"

"*That* is what's wrong with me," I mumbled.

"Not the newspaper. The other thing."

"I know."

"I'm confused," Janie said.

"It's a tobacco box, Janie."

"I can see that. What's it doing here? If you tell me you've taken up smoking now I'm *really* gonna call Doc Thompson."

I shook my head. "It's not mine. Well, it is now, I guess. My mother brought it."

She got excited, her eyes searching about. "Oh, is she here? Where? I'd love to see her."

"We had an argument. She couldn't stay."

"You argued with her too? Honey, this just isn't your day."

"You can say that again."

"What'd you two argue about? Let me guess—you're dad."

I nodded. "Do you think I'm heartless?"

"Is that what she said?"

"I'm serious, Janie. Be honest. Do you think I'm heartless?"

She gave a shake of her head as if to say *no*, but then looked me straight in the eyes and said, "Sometimes. Yes, Laird, sometimes you are." She walked over to me and wrapped her arms around my waist, looking up at me with her hazel eyes. "But never with me. You're a good husband, Laird, just not the best son sometimes, maybe not the best baseball idol sometimes."

"What do you mean by that?"

"Well," she said, thinking back. "Like in September, when you guys played Wilkes-Barre. You had a bad game and were upset with yourself...walked right past a young boy holding out one of your foul balls...wanted an autograph. Remember that?"

"No."

"Of course you don't. You were too caught up in yourself to notice him. I was there waiting for you. I heard him say in the sweetest voice, 'Hi Mr. Young. Would you sign this foul ball for me?' But you stormed past him—even bumped his arm out of the way. Who does that?"

"It was a critical game, Janie! We were one game back of Utica! You wouldn't understand."

"No, I guess not. But that boy did. He said, 'That's okay, Mr. Young. Maybe you can sign it in Scranton next week?' Broke that boy's heart, but he thought enough of you to let you off the hook."

"Guess that was pretty mean," I said, pushing away from her and taking a seat at the table in front of my father's tobacco box.

Janie watched me for a moment, like a teacher taking a moment before returning to her desk, waiting to see if her rebellious pupil acts up again. When satisfied I'd been humbled, she plopped down in a chair next to me. "There are other days, honey, when things are going good for you. You're out there smiling and signing hats and cards and gloves for those boys. Chatting it up with them, tossing the ball around with them. But a man isn't judged by what he does when everything's going well. It's what he does—how he responds when everything is falling apart. That's what makes him great—or not so great."

"Where'd you hear that nonsense? My mother?"

"My father, and it's not nonsense."

"I suppose not." I picked at the edges of newspaper, considering her loving honesty. "I'll try to remember what you said. Next time I have a bad day I'll...gee, guess I did disappoint that boy. Other boys too, I suppose."

Janie gave me a smile, ran her hand affectionately up and down my back. "So, what's in the box?"

"I don't know."

"Aren't you going to open it?" she asked, reaching for the box and sliding it toward me.

"I'm afraid to, if you want to know the truth."

"Why?"

"My mother said, and I quote, 'Your father said he was counting on you to do the right thing with them.'"

"By *them* he means what's inside the box?"

"Um hum."

"Sounds serious."

"Yes."

"And you don't trust yourself to *do the right thing* with them?"

I cocked my head to the side as if to shamefully agree.

"But how will you know until you look inside and see what *them* actually is...or are...or whatever?"

Janie was right; I wouldn't know until I opened the box. And my mother was right; I *was* a coward. Part of me wondered if there was something my father saw in me as a toddler that led him to believe that I'd grow up to be the pathetic wretch that I am, and that I would need some sort of test later in life to either confirm or deny his suspicion. And that same part of me was screaming, *No! Don't do it! Don't take the bait! Play it safe! Never, never, never open that box!*

"Would you rather open it without me here? I can leave if you want."

I placed my hand on her thigh, looked at her and said, "No. You should be here."

She pecked my cheek before leaning in and resting her head on my shoulder, her eyes fixed on my calloused hands holding both sides of the lid to the mysterious red tin box. After taking a deep breath and letting it out, my hands slowly lifted the hinged lid and laid it back against the table. At first I wasn't sure what to think. The tin had gone green on the inside lid and there was the lingering scent of fresh tobacco escaping like a prisoner fleeing years of captivity. Leaning in closer we saw the note, scratched in a child's writing on a small, yellowing piece of lined paper torn from a bigger sheet. It was resting on an off-white hand towel that had been used to wrap and protect whatever lay underneath. I lifted the aging paper and held it directly under the light. The words were written in pencil, smeared a bit, but still legible.

Ennis 1902

"Ennis, nineteen o-two." Janie looked up at me, puzzled. "What do you think it means?"

I shook my head and with my other hand, opened one flap of the hand towel, then the other, to reveal eight baseballs. "I'm guessing it has something to do with these."

I laid the paper down and took one of the balls from the tin box. I looked the ball over carefully. It was dingy white with red and black double stitching, and judging by the scuffmarks on the hide, it had been used in a game—they all had been by the looks of them. There were markings on the balls, each stamped in black ink. In one place the balls were stamped *Spalding No. 1*. Underneath that, and between two rows of stitches, were the words *Official Texas League*. Underneath that but below a row of stitching was the official Spalding trademark stamp.

"Look at this, honey," I said in awe, bringing the ball closer. "This ball is what they call a *dead ball*...made with a rubber core instead of the cushioned-cork core we use today."

"Is that good?"

"Not really, but I've never seen one until now. They used them up until around nineteen o-nine. The rubber core and loosely wound insides deadened the impact between the bat and ball so the ball didn't travel as far as the ball of today. Fans didn't get to see as many home runs then as they do now, but hey, it's still baseball, right? Anyway, fans wanted more so in o-nine, I think it was, someone came up with the cushioned cork-centered ball, the kind we use today. Soon both the National League and American League were using them and you saw averages nearly double in some cases. Ty Cobb and Shoeless Joe both hit over four hundred in nineteen eleven. That's crazy!"

"Four hundred home runs each...in a single season? That is crazy!"

I laughed. "Not home runs, silly, batting average. Most guys are considered good hitters at three hundred. Four hundred for a season was unheard of back then—still rare today. That's why those guys are immortal." I shook my head as I considered those numbers. "I'd kill to hit four hundred."

"Didn't Shoeless Joe cheat? Isn't he the guy that played in those black socks all the time?"

"No, babe. He played for the White Sox, but they were *dubbed* 'The Black Sox' because in the nineteen-nineteen World Series eight guys from the White Sox...never mind. It's not important.

35

I'm just saying that these 'dead balls' are rare. Now I'm looking at eight of them. And look at this! Did you know there are one hundred and eight double stitches on a baseball, still today? If you look closely you can't tell where the first and last stitches are. They're continuous. The first and last stitches are inside. I've always wondered how they got that last stitch inside. These stitches here are red and black. That's the Spalding way. Other balls made by Reach or Rawlings have red and blue stitching." A smile came to my face as I admired the old baseball. "Amazing that this little ball has brought so much joy into kids' lives. Even today. Kids nowadays, you know, a lot of them have sad faces. Who can blame them? Their dads are away fighting the war. But ask a boy to toss this little ball around and his face lights up. He instantly forgets all his troubles. Amazing."

"Like your face?" Janie observed with a smile.

"What do you mean?"

"Look at you! You're like a little boy who just met Gabe Ruth!"

"*Babe*," I said, laughing. "*Babe* Ruth. Not Gabe, you silly goose."

"Babe...Gabe...who cares? You know what I mean. You're *happy* again."

I suppose Janie was right about that too. Something about those eight baseballs and the note made me realize how much I still wanted to be a part of the game, or perhaps how much the game was still a part of me. Maybe it was the mystery of it all, the tin box and the eights balls; maybe it was that the balls belonged to my father and that he cherished them enough to want to leave them to me; maybe it was a little or a lot of both. Either way, I wanted to know more about the balls and where they came from—what made them so special that my dad would hold onto them all this time. I picked up the scribbled note one more time and read it allowed. "Ennis, nineteen o-two...Ennis, nineteen o-two." Then something clicked in my memory. "Ennis, *Texas*, nineteen o-two."

CHAPTER FIVE

Ennis, Texas was where my father had grown up. Back then Ennis was a pocket-sized railroad town, huddled on the deep edge of Dallas' long southern shadow. "Cotton and Cows" my grandfather would answer whenever someone asked what Ennis was known for, "Cotton and cows"—*and now baseball.* Could that have been the *Ennis* scribbled on the note in Dad's tin box? Could those eight baseballs have been from Dad's childhood, from games he'd played? I wasn't even sure they had organized baseball for kids back then. Maybe they had local teams, boys from one town getting together to play boys from another nearby town. My father would have been eight years old in 1902, old enough to play fairly well, but still a little clumsy. Doubt those eight balls were homers he'd hit that season. Probably wasn't strong enough at that age to even hit a home run on a t-ball field. Whatever the case, those eight balls were special to him and I needed to find out why. There could be no asking my father directly, but perhaps my mother knew something about the baseballs. She hadn't alluded to even knowing the contents of the box, but then she was like that. The box and its contents were between father and son; Mom was just the delivery girl. Besides, she was too busy during her last visit *branding my backside.*

On most days the drive from our house in Hartford to Mom and Dad's property outside of Boston would take only a couple hours. But the day I chose to drive out, we got hit with one of our classic November snowstorms, one with flaky white plumes twirling in the wind like mini tornadoes passing on either side of the car as I drove. It made for treacherous driving in places, the asphalt and tires separated by a thin layer of compressed snow, making it feel more like gliding on grease rather than driving. If I touched the brakes in those spots the car's momentum would conspire with the frozen surface to try and lead me into roadside ditches. Our 1938 Buick Special was five years old then—gray with red leather interior, four doors, fat white walls, and a trunk back— and the car ran like a champ, hitting eighty miles per hour when Janie wasn't around. But it just wasn't built for snow. Most of the weight fell forward with the engine, keeping the traction in back light, unleashing the rear end to drift like a dog's down the snow-covered road whenever it got an inkling. Last thing we needed was for me to wreck our only car. Janie didn't get mad at much, but she'd have flipped over that! It was all we could afford at the time. Those Buick Specials were nice, but they sold for $1,047 brand new, which was too much for my minor league salary. I got it cheap though from a former teammate. He decided to dump it when the Braves called him up. Picked himself out a Cadillac—one of those two-seater jobs. Said it had more *style*. Truthfully, even if I had the money, I would have taken the Buick Special over that Cadillac. But that's me.

Between the falling snow and my drifting Buick, I nearly forgot to deliver some pies for Janie at a diner she said was on my way. It's a wonder those pies survived all the slipping and sliding of the car in the snow, but they did. The Buick had slick leather bench seats. Because of that, I put the pies in the front seat with me, so I could catch them if needed. But a fella only has two hands and with the car gliding and sliding on the slick road, and me wrestling with the wheel, one pie sort of got away from me, spinning across the seat during a particularly abrupt skid, hitting the door panel hard, the crust on top crunching up and exposing the blueberry filling in places. With a little finagling I was able to straighten the tin pan with my free hand, pushing the filling and crust back in place with my fingers. When I arrived at Jack's Place in Tolland—a busy railcar diner at the intersection of 74 and 195—it was nearly perfect again, *nearly*.

Jack's place was packed that day, a refuge I suppose for snow-weary drivers. The lines painted on the asphalt parking lot that would have been there to outline parking spaces had been covered by accumulating snow, leaving motorists free to park any which way they chose—and they did. The parking lot looked like the floor of a boy's bedroom just after he dumped his tin of miniature toy cars. And there were probably ten long-haul trucks huddled together and idling out back, black exhaust smoke polluting the air from vertical stacks. It looked like a bomb had gone off, cars covered in snow and pointing in every direction, leaving scarce room to maneuver mine. Once I did find a spot, I headed inside, bundled in a long coat, scarf around my neck, and a pie in each hand, the rock salt on the walkway crunching under my shoes.

After managing to open the front door with one of my feet, I stepped inside. The first thing that hit me was the heat, like the blast of warmth you get in your face upon opening the iron door to a wood stove. The contrast in outside and inside temperature nearly overwhelmed me. The next thing to hit me was the smell, something akin to greasy burgers and roasted chicken, sprinkled with a pinch of long-haul B.O., and garnished with a heaping helping of acrid cigarette smoke. And every light in the place was on, drawing attention to the hoard of odd trinkets and figurines resting on wall-mounted wooden shelves, and product promotional signs screwed to the paneling.

"Cop a squat anywhere! Someone'll be right wit'cha!" I heard someone call from the kitchen.

"Not eating!" I called back. "Just dropping off some pies!"

Jack was big fella and must have served in the navy because

when he walked out to greet me he still had on his white sailor's cap, half cocked on his bald head. And he must have been both owner and cook because he wore a white apron, which had a mosaic of stains—ketchup, mustard, something green, but mostly varying shades of golden grease. Under the apron he wore denim pants and a white t-shirt, the sleeves rolled up to reveal jackhammer arms, one hammering bicep bearing a side tattoo that read: *Check out these guns!* He looked me over as he wiped his hands on his apron. "How's dat pretty wife of yours?"

"Good," I said, my head bobbing up and down, eyes looking off awkwardly.

"Why'd she send you? I was kinda lookin' forward to—"

"Busy," I blurted out, afraid of what would come out of his mouth next. "Baking."

"She bakes good—like she looks."

"Yeah...um..." I said, handing him the first two pies, one at a time. "These two are cherry."

"How many you bring? I ordered five."

"I brought five, just like you ordered. I'll just run out and get the others. Be right back."

When I brought the next two in I didn't wait for more commentary. I just handed them to Jack, smiled, and hurried back out to the car for the last pie—the damaged pie. As I reached for that pie on the seat, I muttered to myself, "I'm gonna be wearing this pie in a minute. Blueberry coat...blueberry shoes...blueberry face." I closed the car door and once more gingerly made my way across the snow covered parking lot and walkway, trying my best not to slip and damage the pie further, holding my breath so as not to breathe in the noxious truck exhaust.

When I got inside I heard Jack call out to one of the other cooks behind the counter, "Hey, Reggie, take that burger out to table ten, will ya? I gotta deal with this guy."

Deal with this guy? Uh oh. I swallowed hard before stepping forward and placing the pie into his thick calloused hands. "That's it," I said, throwing up my hands. "Five pies. Five wonderful pies…baked good…by my good looking wife."

He looked down at the blueberry pie for a long moment, and then looked up at me with a twisted grin. "Hey. This pie all right? I mean…it don't look right."

"Yep. Blueberry."

"I can see dat. But ain't the blueberries supposed to be *inside* the crust?"

"Oh that. That's because…well, you see…this is a new kind of blueberry pie. It's called a blueberry crumble. You know—*crumble*," I said, making a swirling motion with my index finger over the pie. "Right there's the crumble."

Jack looked at me hard and long before pursing his lips and nodding.

"Okay, then," I said, rushing toward the door. "I'll be seeing you,"

"Hey, bub!" Jack called out. "Hey!" He called out to a trucker near the door. "Stop that guy!"

This is it! He's about to slam that pie into my face—or one of his big fists! I thought as the burly trucker stood blocking my path, still chewing his food. I turned to face Jack once more. "Hey, I'm sorry for—"

"Ain't you gonna want no payment for these here pies?" he blurted out.

"Oh, that," I said, walking back to him. "Of course. My wife would kill me if I came home without the money."

He reached into the till and pulled out some bills. "Just saved your life, pal. Don't that deserve some sort a discount?"

"Uh…how much we talking?"

Scoffing and slapping the cash into my outstretched palm, he said, "It was a joke." To an old man at the bar huddling over his steaming bowl of chowder, Jack said, "Get a load of this guy. So uptight." Speaking to me again, "Hey, tell your pretty wife I'll take five more next week—and no more blueberry crumble. My customers want a slice, not a pile."

"Sure thing. I'll tell her. A slice, not a pile." After that I hightailed it out there, wondering how the heck I get myself into these things

CHAPTER SIX

Mom and Dad's property—my home growing up—measured a little over twenty-two acres, small by ranching standards, but big enough to give Mom and Dad some semblance of their prior lives in Texas. Dad had grown up on a ranch in Ennis, helping run things while his father was away, him being an itinerant preacher. They'd kept about forty head of cattle on their three hundred acres, some chickens for their eggs, and a dozen or so goats to keep the weeds under control. They'd reserved ten acres for cotton, which I'm told my father hated picking, and another ten for assorted vegetables like corn and potatoes. A shallow well provided good water for the house and an underground spring kept the stock tanks full. When things got particularly hot and humid, Grandmother said they'd go "swimming with the cows."

The Texas ranch operated somewhere between breakeven and halleluiah, depending largely on the weather that year; but to my grandparents, having the ranch was never about the money. To them, the lifestyle was more important. Living off the land, honoring God by working hard with the hands he'd given them—like the apostle Paul commanded in the Good Book—that's what mattered. Grandmother liked to relate faith to farming, planting and sowing and all that. When I'd spend time with her as a boy, she'd say things like, "The corn won't grow unless you plant it, and neither will faith." She'd say, "A small seed goes into the ground dead, but if you nourish it, that seed will be reborn and rise to nourish *you.*" Another favorite of hers was, "Picking cotton's like flirting with temptation. Do it often enough and eventually you'll get stung," referring to the stinging Pack Saddle worm that loves to feed on cotton leaves.

Mom was raised on a neighboring Texas ranch. Her father bred Morgan horses for the Army. He did that until 1909 when he caught the diphtheria and died. Her mother tried to carry on the business but died three years later, just days after my mother and father married. My parents had known each other since toddlerhood. Mom liked to joke that she'd loved my dad "since he had brown in his britches." I guess that's what my mother meant during her visit when she said my father is *all she's ever known.* They were just eighteen when they married. Grandmother said my parents would have married sooner if Mom's mother would have consented, but she wouldn't; to her, eighteen was young enough.

The house on Mom and Dad's property in Lynn was a modest log cabin—just three bedrooms and a big open area made up of a family room and fireplace, a kitchen area with wood-burning stove, and an adjoining area for eating meals. Mom wasn't big on decorating. The walls were just the interior version of the outside, brown logs with sand-colored chinking in between. One thing my mother did keep on display was a lot of photographs of my father before the war, which on most visits I'd avoid, as I would a cluster of honeybees bent on keeping me honest. Getting too close to their honeysuckle could result in painful emotional welts! The roof of the cabin was shake shingle, weathered and covered with moss in spots, and steep in pitch to help the snow slide off. But it seldom did. The rough-sawn shake seemed to grab hold of the snow, and during days of continuous snowfall, we'd sometimes hear the roof creaking under the heavy load. But it never caved in on us.

Dad fenced the property right away and built a four-stall barn; that was before I was ever born. The property had good pasture and fed the livestock we kept. We had a couple horses—Morgans of course, like Mom's parents raised. "If Morgans were good enough for the Army and Calvary," Mom would say, "Then they're good enough for us." They did the heavy work. And on average we'd have four to five Hereford cows, and a few steers. We had one bull, a burly beast with an ill temperament. Herefords, by and large, are gentle bovines—beautiful too with their dark red hides, their white heads and flanks. But for Shooter—that's what we called our bull—being gentle just didn't suit. Couldn't get near the cows with him around; had to separate him out first. Otherwise he'd try to impale you with one of his short horns. Luckily his horns were naturally turned downward so when he did make contact it didn't break the skin—*only bones*. Anyway, we'd sell two steers or heifers per year for cash income, which we would then use to buy back processed beef as needed, since we didn't have freezers in those days to store our own beef. If Shooter did his job—and he usually did since he was never short on bullets— there'd be two or three calves to replace them.

We had a sweet old Jersey cow named Meg who supplied the milk; kept her in the barn with the horses. And there were a dozen or so chickens running around that provided plenty of eggs. We even had a small garden where Mom grew potatoes and other vegetables. To supplement Dad's $100 per month disability pension, Mom would sell the extra milk and eggs. It wasn't much, but taken together, the sale of two steers per year, the daily sale of extra milk and eggs, and the money from Dad's pension, we had just enough to get us through the depression.

They'd only moved out to Lynn, Massachusetts so Mom could be close to Dad when he played for the Boston Braves, a few years before he went to War. Some scout had seen him play in a Texas League game somewhere. Said Dad was the best shortstop and hitter he'd seen in years. Signed him right there. Said he hadn't seen such a well-rounded player since Johnny Evers, a keen second baseman whom the Braves had just picked up from Chicago. A few weeks later my parents were on a train heading north, bound for Boston and big city life. That was in 1913.

Dad finished out the last two games of the '13 season with the team, but sat backup on the bench to veteran shortstop Rabbit Maranville, who'd not missed a game since taking over for Art Bues on Easter Sunday. Maranville was part of the 1914 Boston Braves team that won the World Series the day of my birth; so was my father. He'd played the entire '14 season with the Braves, though he rarely got off the bench. The only time my father saw playing time was as a pinch hitter or when someone got injured. Still, they might have put him in during the World Series, especially when in just sixteen at-bats that season—I was told by my mother—he batted .338, driving in five runs and even taking Babe Adams of the Pittsburg Pirates for a home run to deep center during one game. That was no small feat against a pitcher who earlier in the season had pitched twenty-one straight innings against the Giants—not allowing a single walk—and who, just a year earlier, had won twenty games.

So you never know, they might have put my father in a World Series game. Coaches are sentimental; they care about their players and want to see them succeed. But my father chose instead to go be with mother at the hospital when he heard she'd gone into labor with me. I guess that says something about his character. But missing a chance to play in the *World Series—with the Boston Braves?* I don't know. I'm not sure I would have done the same thing, even for my own wife and child. I'd like to think I would have, but even now I don't know. My dad made a choice. The series ended that night. He played for the Braves the next three seasons but they never made it back to the World Series. At the close of 1917 my father went to war. When he came home in 1918, he was half-dead and unable to suit up again. Was missing his chance to play in the World Series the right decision? I just didn't know.

When the season ended that October back in 1913, my parents

went searching for property with a home on it, settling in the rural community of Lynn, some ten miles north of Boston. Thinking about it now, that's all I really knew about my father's baseball days. Somewhere along the way I'd put up an emotional wall and stopped asking—stopped listening. But now I was on my way to their home to do just that—to ask my mother questions about my father, and to listen.

Mom met me out front when I arrived. I parked where I always had, on the dirt drive between the house and barn—a dilapidating structure made of aging rough-sawn wood, the pitched roof sagging on the windward side like a partially melted candle. I could just make out the tan heads and black manes of Buck and Shiloh, the old buckskin horses Mom kept. They'd always seemed to enjoy the cool weather rushing over their faces as they gnawed their hay; but they did not like the rain and snow and cold on their hindquarters, which were always backed into the covered stalls and out of the elements. The snow had stopped falling but my mother was still bundled up against the lingering chill. By then she had traded her long dresses and flats for more practical denim pants and boots, except on Sundays when dresses were still proper. And I could just make out a thick gray sweater under the long blue overcoat and red neck-scarf she had on.

The minute I opened the driver's side door of my Buick, the warm inside air began to mix with the cold outside air causing the windows to fog. When I stood, my exhaled breaths crystalized into small visible puffs of condensate, each flowing over me with every forward step I took around the car. The soil under my feet, once a muddy mess of compressed footprints with pushed up edges, had now frozen into hardened divots, making the ground feel rocky and uneven beneath my shoes. And it only took a few moments for my body's core to suck the warm blood out of my hands, back toward my heart and vital organs where its warmth was needed most. I cupped my hands together and blew warm into them as I stumbled about, the smell of horse manure and hay hanging on the air I breathed.

"Hi, Laird," Mom said, hugging me before leading me toward the front door. "Come inside before you catch cold. You're always underdressed for cold weather. Don't you have a coat? Look at you. Just a flannel shirt."

"Coat's in the trunk. Got blueberry pie filling on it," I answered after slipping on a patch of ice and nearly falling. "Look at me. You'd think I just learned to walk or something."

"Blueberry pie filling? How'd—"

"Delivering Janie's pies. Tell you about it later." I opened the front door and followed my mother inside. The rustic cabin felt warm, the raging fire in the fireplace being held up by the draft flowing into the flue, its orange and white teeth sharp and as hot as forged steel. Mom had the wood stove going in the dining room for extra heat, a full teakettle with the lid open boiling on top of it. Mom always said the fireplace and stove sucked the moisture from the room, so to put moisture back into the air she kept an open kettle boiling. Something passed down from her own mother, I think. "Where's Dad?"

"In the study, looking out the window. He likes it there," she said, opening a kitchen cupboard to retrieve a couple of mugs. "How about some hot chocolate?"

How she knew my father liked anything was a mystery. His expression rarely changed. He was like one of those bronze or marble busts you see in museums, his hollow eyes and emaciated face set for eternity. "Hot chocolate sounds good. Where's Carl?"

"Sent him over to Paulson's for a few things. Dinner stuff."

Paulson's was the local market, just up the road and only a stone's throw from the North Atlantic. It wasn't a large market, but it had a good selection of meats and cheeses and vegetables, and the owners bought eggs from Mom twice a week.

"Yeah? How's he doing?" I asked, making my way over to the

front of the fire, turning and warming my backside.

"Getting older, like the rest of us. Just turned sixty-one. Hard to believe."

"That old? How long's he been here now? Must be twenty…twenty-five years."

"Since your father came home from the war. Carl's a good man. He's helped me out so much over the years." A moment passed before she added, "God holds a special place in heaven for people like Carl."

"And a special place in hell for guys like me."

"Not true, Laird."

After warming myself for a bit I took a seat at the small round dinner table just off the kitchen, admiring her as she poured steaming water into the mugs. She'd thinned over the years, the way a old pair of jeans wears away on the thighs when washed and worn too much, leaving only bare threads to cover the body. "I'm worried about you, Mom. You don't look good."

She snapped her head around in my direction. "Surely I taught you better manners than that!" She came over and took a seat at the table with me, sliding my mug of hot chocolate over to me. "Here, put this in your mouth to shut it up."

"I'm just saying you're too skinny. Look at you, nothing but bones. You're clothes don't fit anymore. They just hang on you— there to mask the carnage."

"Don't overstate things. That's just age."

"No it's not just age. Are you getting enough to eat? I know things are tight, having to pay Carl and all. You need money?"

At that she let out a sarcastic laugh, "Oh that's priceless," she said, her eyes shooting me a condescending glance over the rim of her mug as she sipped her hot chocolate. "Why? You got some you can spare?"

It was an intentional jab to shut me up. Mom knew we were poor and that I wasn't providing adequately for Janie and me. "No, guess I don't. But if you need some I'll figure something out. You've gotta eat, Mom. Can't just feed Dad and Carl."

"Son, why're you so concerned all of a sudden about things here?" I just shrugged and looked off. "We've made it this far, your father and I—Carl too. We're not living high on the hog but we ain't eatin' the pig's slop either. Now where's my sweet daughter-in-law? You couldn't bring her?"

"Thought about it. She wanted to come. Just thought it was best to come alone this time—have a talk about some things."

She nodded. "Well, before we get to talking, go say good morning to your father. He loves it when you come."

I sighed. "Oh. Okay. Maybe he can tell me where he's been for the last twenty-five years—tell me about the contents of the tin box."

"Don't you do that, Laird! Don't you do that!" A few moments passed before she shook my rudeness off. "Now go say hello before my boot impales itself in your butt." She then gave a wave of her hand. "Scoot, buckaroo, and make it more than *hello* this time."

I took a deep breath before standing and walking toward the study, the way a shy boy does, hands in his pockets and arms stiff, head cocked and shoulders hunched, taking small detours on his way to talk to a crush for the first time. Mom just called it the study; really though, it was my old bedroom, the bed removed to make room for several large bookshelves. Mom read more than anybody I'd ever met. Dickens, Austen, Dostoevsky, Hans Christen Andersen, and all the other great storytellers were on those shelves. Books about cattle, horses, and other livestock too. Larger books on art lay flat and stacked on shelves like pancakes, the kind with oversized portraits of paintings and sculptures. And all the world's greatest thinkers stood binding to binding like an army of intellectuals parading for the common folk. But mostly, there were *lots* of publications on baseball—decades of yearly editions of reference books like *Spalding's Official Base Ball Guide, Reach's Official American League Base Ball Guide,* and *Wright & Ditson's Base Ball Guide,* just to name a few, as well as decades of monthly subscriptions to *Baseball Magazine* and *The Sporting* Life, which stood vertical on the shelf like hundreds of slender bamboo reeds packed in tight to support each other. Even the works of Shakespeare occupied a corner of one shelf, though I had a hard time imagining my mother reading Hamlet with that Texas drawl. "To impale or not to impale; that is the question."

When I got to the doorway of the study, Dad was there in his wheelchair, just as mother said—his chair a wooden contraption with a high back and wire-spoke metal rims—looking out the window, his blank face reflecting back to him off the inside pane.

"Hi, Dad," I said, reluctantly stepping inside the room from behind him. "How are you?" As usual there was nothing—no response. I stepped up beside him and took a seat on a sturdy side table, looking off, out the same window as my father. "Boy it's cold today. You been outside yet? No, I guess you haven't. Well, trust me—it's cold. I see you've still got old Meg. She's a sweet old gal. I remember milking her twice a day, everyday. Remember that? It was like Meg and I were dating, only not as perverse as that just sounded." I struggled to find something meaningful to say to a man who seemed unable to understand. Then something slipped out of my heart that I'd never known was in there. "Oh, Dad, " I said, looking down at my feet. "I wish you could talk to me. I wish...I wish we could just, I don't know, throw a ball around...play catch sometime...take in a game together...share a laugh or two."

Right then I heard a noise behind me, which sounded like sniffling. I stood and turned to find my mother leaning against the bedroom doorjamb, mug in one hand, the other hand wiping the tears from her cheeks. I'm not sure why but seeing her there made me angry, as though I'd been violated somehow. I walked straight past her and out to the barn and the horses. A few minutes later there she was, laying my father's heavy coat and scarf over the stall door I was slumped over, twenty years of frustration rushing through my head like raging river rapids.

"Put this on before you catch your death."

I put the coat on as directed, slamming my hands down into the pockets and taking a few steps away from her, my back turned. "I hate this."

"Hate what?"

"This—coming here."

"Then why come?"

"I don't know. Compelled, I guess, like a sick fascination that has to be satisfied."

"What do you mean?"

Turning to her. "I mean I stay away as long as I can, block his memory from my mind as long as I can…but then I wonder…then I start to wonder if maybe he's getting better…if maybe there's a chance this time…a chance we could…I don't know."

"He loves you, Laird—"

"See! There you go again with that wishful thinking! Drives me nuts!"

"He can't tell you himself, no. But he loves you, Laird. If you could have seen him the night he left for Europe—for the war. He was so torn up inside. He held you the entire night."

"I know. I remember."

"You remember? How? You were just three years old."

"I don't know but I do. He held me and I held his cap. I don't know but I do."

"That's right," she said, thinking back. "You did hold his cap. Amazing you can remember that."

"That's it, though. I've nothing else to hold onto but images of an invalid." I shook my head, beginning to weep but trying to fight it. "You know, some nights…some nights I have this recurring dream. Dad's laying on the ground in pieces—a leg over here, a leg there, arms…" I shook my head. "His eyes are wide open, battle shocked, and he utters with his last breath, 'Remember me, Son. Remember me.' It's sick! I'm sick!"

"I'm very sorry you're so tormented, Son. I never knew."

I just shook my head and wiped my tears. "It's not something I go around telling people."

"Does Janie know?"

"No, and I don't want her to know."

"Laird, anytime you'd like to know more about your father, please ask me. There's so much I've been waiting to share with you."

"Waiting?"

"Yes, Son. You haven't exactly been a willing participant in conversations about him."

"Like what? Give me something…something else I can hang onto because I need something besides," I said, waving my hand back toward the house and my wheelchair-bound father, "besides that."

"Okay, let's see. Your father hated school, just like you. The two of you had that in common. But unlike you, he seldom thought of himself. He did his studies, as he did everything, because others were counting on him to do them. Your father had a profound sense of duty."

I nodded, in an inward fashion, as if accepting what she'd just told me as truth. "What else?"

"He was a lousy driver," she said with a grin. "Too curious about everything around him to pay attention. He was good with money…and he used to sing to himself a lot."

Once again I nodded without comment.

"You want to know something else?" She asked.

"Sure. Pitch it in."

"You sure you want to hear it? It'll sting a little."

"Yep," I said, one hand on my hip, the other motioning for her to give it to me.

"Remember how I told you your father was all torn up inside the night he left? Want to know why?"

"Sure."

"Because he was never drafted. Your father volunteered to go to war. He saw other boys being yanked from their families and it ate at him until he couldn't stand it anymore and went down to enlist."

My mouth dropped open. "He *enlisted?* But what about you?" I could feel my blood getting hot. "What about me? Did he ever stop to think what his *sense of duty* would do to me?"

"Yes, Laird, he did. He agonized over it, over the thought of leaving you and me—never coming back, not seeing us again."

"Then why? And don't tell me I need to ask him or I'll shoot myself."

"He said that in the end his decision came down to one thing—that he wouldn't have been able to live with himself if he'd let other boys die alone out there...for him...so he could stay home and play baseball, stay home in the loving arms of his wife and child."

I shook my head. "I wouldn't have done that. No way."

"I know, Laird," she said, pulling a folded sheet of paper from her coat pocket and holding it out to me.

"How would you know? What's that?"

"A copy of your draft notice."

I snatched it from her hand in anger. "How'd you get this?"

"Bob Paulson. You remember him—owns the market down the road. Sits on the draft board. Said you came to see him."

"That's right. What of it?"

"Said you told him you couldn't honor your draft notice because your father needed you. Asked me if it was true. Did you tell him that?"

At that moment a warm flush washed over my face. "Maybe."

"Oh, Laird."

"What'd you tell him?"

"Well, I didn't lie for you if that's what you think. I simply said, 'If that's what Laird told you then that's what he told you.'"

"You act like you want me to go to war—to get myself killed! Do you want me to come back like Dad?"

"No, Son, that is not what I want. Lord knows I couldn't survive such heartache. But you using your father as an excuse to get out of going is a new low for you."

"Well, sorry to disappoint you, Mother dear. Sorry I'm not the perfect man like your husband."

"He wasn't perfect, Laird. He had his flaws like any of us. But he had honor and a humility you'd never comprehend."

"Duty?"

"That's right, Laird—*duty*."

"Great. Anything else you want to tell me. You've already broken my heart. Might as well crush it."

"Just this…his last words going out the door were," she starting to sob, "were, 'Tell my son I'm sorry.'"

I buried my face in my hands; when I lowered them Mother was gone. A moment later I was on the barn floor in a heap, crying into the straw, twenty-five years of tears flowing over my face, the horses looking down on me with pity. When I finally regained control of my emotions, I went inside to ask about the tin box and its contents—the reason for my visit in the first place. The conversation was short. My mother said she'd never looked inside the box, that it wasn't her place. She said my father had never made mention of the box until the night he handed it to her, the night he said, "Tell my son I'm sorry." She said if I wanted to know what *Ennis 1902* meant, then I'd need to ask someone who'd lived with my father in Ennis during 1902—*my grandfather*.

CHAPTER SEVEN

J anie wasn't happy about my impromptu trip to Ennis, Texas.

"Laird, I'm glad you're excited about these baseballs...about them belonging to your father, but we can't afford this," Janie said the next morning as she wrote out a new shopping list in the kitchen, checking the cabinets for things needed.

"I've got the cash still in my wallet...my payout from the mill. That'll get me a round-trip ticket by train."

"We need that money for other things, Laird."

"Like what?"

"Like everything—bills, baby stuff, food, gas for the car so I can make my deliveries."

"So I have to sacrifice everything for your business?"

"That's not what I said—not all of it, anyway."

"The bills are paid. You just bought groceries. The car is full of gas. And the baby isn't due for nearly two months."

"No, Laird."

"Don't tell me 'no,' Janie. You're not my boss."

"No, Laird, you're right. Nobody's your boss. You don't like bosses. Laird does his own thing. Laird's his own man...and he's so good at it his wife has to work to help support him."

"That's a low blow, Janie. I provide for you and your business—mostly."

"Do you? Do you really?"

I thought about it for a long moment. "No, I guess I don't

provide enough. I guess I'm a failure, but I'm trying not to be…and this trip is part of that effort."

Janie shook her head. "Okay. Do what you want. You will anyway."

"It's important to me, Janie," I said, reaching out for her.

"Go," she said, pulling away and grabbing her coat off the nearby rack, slipping her arms into the sleeves and shooting me an angry glance.

"Janie, please, I have to do this. I don't know exactly why. I only know that I do."

She stopped and looked at me for a moment before giving me a pursed lip smile of approval and kiss on my cheek. "Okay. I'll support you on this. But when you get home we need to figure something else out for extra income." She reached into my front pant pocket and pulled out the car keys.

"No, because you're going to be so successful in your business they'll be calling you 'The Pie Queen of America' and we'll be rich."

"Keep dreaming, honey," she said as she walked out the door, laughing. "Keep dreaming."

MOM AND JANIE saw me off at South Station in Boston, a grand neoclassical structure anchoring the intersection of Atlantic Avenue and Summer Street. The tall, sand-colored brick front curved around the corner at greater than ninety degrees and looked more like a house of parliament with its array of windows, columns, and its mighty crown. It was a busy hub, the dull noise from locomotives battling for supremacy against the shrill caw of a loudspeaker spewing movements and destinations of every train, and the collective utterances of thousands of hurrying ticket holders. And the fresh air coming in off the sea was being choked and polluted by engine exhaust. Most of the people were bundled up against the cold and there were uniformed soldiers and Marines clustered in places—young men most of them—waiting to be shipped off to Europe or the Pacific, their faces and laughs full of life that might soon be lost.

Seeing those boys made me think of my own cowardice—about my father. I wondered if he might have left from this very station, gathered with fellow countrymen awaiting their train to sudden death or disfigurement abroad. *Be more respectful,* I heard my conscience say. *These men have a sense of honor and duty you don't possess.* Just then a young soldier, maybe nineteen years old, his face pure and bright, caught me gazing at him. When I looked into his eyes I could see the anxiety—the fear. It was the first time I'd ever noticed that these young men were as afraid of war as me, only they weren't cowards. Their country needed them and they were answering the call, despite being afraid. When he nodded kindly to me, I nearly broke down in tears. Only my pride kept the water from draining down my cheeks. I swallowed hard, nodded in return to the brave young soldier, and then turned away toward the ticket counter.

The ticket agent was an old fellow, fat with a silver beard and flush cheeks, with a jolly laugh and disposition—the spitting image of Santa Claus, but without the red suit. I mentioned as much to the man and we all had a good laugh about it. His name badge read Mr. Smith, a rather lazy alias for Kris Kringle I told him, but he assured me his name really was Smith. Said he'd been with the railroad nearly forty years and could remember when trains coming out of and going into Texas were the favorite marks for bandits. Told me to "keep my pistols loaded and my eye sharp." That made me laugh.

The trip by train from Boston to Dallas would be about 1,800 miles and would take approximately three and a half days I was told, thanks to the latest model streamliner taking me there—a purple and silver locomotive with yellow trim and ten passenger cars hitching a ride. Janie would stay and keep my mother company at her place for a couple days before heading home to fill her bakery orders. Mom loved Janie and welcomed any time together with her, though I'd always seen them as opposite eggs, my mother being hardboiled and my wife being a fluffy scramble. Still, the thought of them being together part of the time gave me comfort since I'd be gone for close to two weeks and Janie was eight months pregnant. I never much liked leaving Janie behind; seems I was always doing that, one of the downsides to being a professional baseball player. Since that first day we met—when Janie had broken down on the street in front of my baseball game—I've felt the need to watch over her, to protect her. Sometimes Janie would surprise me and show up at an away game, when the games weren't too far from home. Seems I always had a good game when she did that.

"Tell your grandparents we are well and say hello," Mom said, hugging me and giving me a coach's pat on the butt. "On your way. Tell them next year we're coming to Texas for Christmas."

"Okay, skipper," I said with a grin.

"And here," Mother said, handing me an old book. "For your journey."

I started to read the title but she stopped me and reiterated firmly, "For your journey."

Janie slid under my arm and wrapped her arms tightly around my waist, hiding her teary eyes in my chest. "None of that," I said, lifting her face to look up at me. "Don't you know the best way to ruin a beautiful portrait is to get water on it?"

Janie stood on her toes to kiss my face in multiple places. "I know you have to do this but I'll miss you."

"You could have come if I hadn't lost my job. We'd of have had the money then."

"If you were still working you wouldn't be free to go," she said, kissing my lips and imitating my mother by giving me her version of coach's pat on the butt.

"You're supposed to pat it, not squeeze it," I whispered.

"One of the privileges of being your wife. Now go. It's for the best."

The train blew its bellowing horn and the conductors hollered in unison from the platform, "All aboard!" each standing near a passenger car stairway in their dark blue conductor's uniforms with matching caps, stamping tickets as passengers stepped aboard.

I scooped up the tin box and grabbed my bag, gave Janie another quick kiss, and then climbed the steps into one of the passenger cars, which on the inside seemed quite luxurious with its varnished maple walls, lush burgundy carpet, etched glass panels, and green leather cushions. I found a seat near a window that I was able to lower, allowing me to lean out and wave goodbye. As the train began to roll, Janie rushed up to the window, running alongside as I leaned down as far as possible without falling out, trying awkwardly and unsuccessfully to connect our lips one last time. A few moments later she'd become just a tiny figure waving in the distance.

Since I was going so far I was assigned a sleeping birth, a cozy little economy class compartment with nothing but a bed, pillow, and curtain. Above me was another birth assigned to a rather large man. Each time he moved or rolled in his bed the wooden bottom creaked—so bad it seemed as though he'd come crashing down on me at any moment. My compartment did have a sliding window, which allowed me to take in the sights and fresh air along the way. It was quite refreshing, really, the way the cool air washed across my face at speed, whisking tufts of hair into little warring strands, and the way the fragrant forests and flowered prairies aroused memories of Janie fresh out of the bath.

When I wasn't lying on my bunk I'd walk the long string of cars, the air being choked by swirling cigar and cigarette smoke. I'd look at the people—businessmen in suits reading large newspapers, manicured ladies in outrageous hats gossiping among themselves, others just common folk with common children, on their way to a better life I thought.

The afternoon of the second day we stopped to resupply in Harrisonburg, Virginia, a small outpost with an outdoor platform and station. I'd been walking the cars again and was returning to my assigned car when I saw a kid dressed in rags and wearing a newsboy cap reaching into my sleeping birth. I stopped to watch from afar as he pulled the tin box from my bunk to admire it. He couldn't have been but nine or ten years old and his small hands fumbled with the box.

"Careful with that, kid," I said, stepping closer.

My voice startled him and he looked at me with round fearful eyes, placing the tin box back down on the bunk. "Gee, I'm sorry, mister. I didn't mean any harm."

"Sure, kid. I know. Just curious, right?"

"Honest. It's just, I've never seen a box like that before...with a dog and all on it."

"You a passenger on this train, kid?" I asked, picking up the box and holding it out to him.

"No, sir."

"Take a look, but be careful."

He looked up at me, unsure.

"It's okay, boy. Go ahead." He took the box from my hands, set it down on the bed and admired it for a moment. "Not a passenger? You must work for the railroad, then."

"No, sir," he said, shame washing over his innocent face.

"Then why are you here? Must be some reason you came aboard."

He hesitated, wiped his hands on his ragged overalls, then confessed, "Just looking for food, mister. I'm sorry."

For such a young boy, he was well spoken and well mannered. He started to move backward like he was about to flee. "Wait, Son.

It's okay. Here…" I reached into my coat pocket and retrieved a candy bar I'd just bought an hour earlier. "I was saving this for later but now I'd like you to have it."

"That's awfully nice, mister, but I don't have any money to pay you for it."

"It's a gift. Here, take it." The young boy snatched the chocolate bar from my hand and gobbled it down in just a few minutes. "Hungry, huh?"

"Yes, sir," he said with a mouthful, smiling at me now.

"When's the last time you ate?"

"Yesterday morning, I think."

"That's tough. Where're your parents."

"Don't have any."

His words stuck in my heart. *No parents.* "Have a seat," I said, sitting on the bed and patting the mattress with my hand. He sat next to me, his feet dangling, "Look at this." I opened the lid to the tin box and when he saw the baseballs his little face lit up.

"Gee! That's swell, mister!"

"Here," I said, handing him one of the baseballs. "Look at this. This ball is from nineteen o-two. Can you believe that?"

"Nineteen…that's when they had dinosaurs!"

I couldn't help laughing. "Almost. You a baseball fan? Got a team you like?"

"Don't know much about baseball, except I like to play it."

"Me too. How old are you, boy?"

"Eight—just last week."

The more this young lad spoke the more my heart broke for him. "You telling me the truth, kid—no parents? Where's your mother?"

He handed the baseball back to me, his head hanging low. "She died a couple months ago…from the polio."

"Gee, that's tough, kid. What about your dad?"

"He's buried in North Africa, they said."

"Who said?"

"The soldiers that came to our house last year."

"Your father died in the war?"

He nodded.

"You don't have any grandparents or relatives?"

"I have an aunt in Ohio. She's supposed to come for me."

"When?"

The boy shrugged.

"So you've been on your own for two months...since your mother...?"

"Yes, sir," he said, as softly as a kitten's meow.

"Well where do you sleep?"

"I find places. Most nights I sleep in Saint Anthony's church."

"On a pew?"

"Father Patrick doesn't mind. He gives me food and blankets. I'm supposed to stay there I think until my aunt comes. But Father Patrick has been away." There was a brief pause. "Father Michael isn't as nice."

"He's filling in for Father Patrick?"

"Um hmm."

"This priest booted you from the church?" I asked, my blood beginning to percolate like hot coffee. "That doesn't seem very Christian of him."

He stood and looked at me. "Well, I'd better get off the train. I appreciate your kindness, sir. I won't forget."

"Wait a minute, kid," I said, standing and stuffing the tin box under my pillow, placing my suitcase on top of that before closing the curtain. "Let me walk you back to Saint Anthony's."

"It's okay, mister. I'll be okay."

"I want to."

Just then a porter, a black man with an intellectual's face and beard came up to us. "Pardon me, young man, but you aren't supposed to be on this train. I've told you before."

"It's okay. He's a friend of mine. Say, how long is our stop here?"

"Be moving on in about three hours, just after we're loaded and re-supplied."

"Thank you. Let's go, kid," I said, leading the young boy off the train and across the concrete platform. The day had brought with it blue skies and a strong breeze, which stirred up smells of oil and hot metal coming from the train, the air brisk and cool on the cheeks, the warmth of the sun being felt at every windbreak. And there was a new determined manner in my step, perhaps too determined because my little companion seemed to have trouble keeping up.

"Where are we going so fast, mister?"

"To see someone who isn't so nice. What's you name?"

"Billy. William if my mother was still around."

That made me laugh. "I know what you mean, Billy. My name is Laird Allen Young the third."

"Nice to know you, Mr. Young the third."

"Just call me Laird." I pointed to a nearby building with spires. "Is that the place?"

"That's Saint Anthony's, yes. But gee, mister, I don't want any trouble."

"Oh, it's no trouble," I said as I led him up the concrete steps of a gothic looking church, one with tall spires, saintly figurines carved into the stone facade, and large hand-carved wooden doors. "In fact, it's going to be a real pleasure."

I flung open the doors and we stepped inside. It was a typical Catholic church with rows of wooden pews, ornate architecture, and a large crucifix hanging below a set of stained glass windows, just behind the center pulpit. And there was a robed man lighting candles up front. "That him—Father Michael?" I asked walking toward the man, the young boy in tow. Before Billy could answer I blurted out, "Hey! You Father Michael?"

I'd obviously startled the man because he swirled around suddenly. "Yes, I'm Father Michael. I didn't know anybody was here."

"Of course you didn't," I said, coming to a stop just a few feet from him. "You the guy who told this boy to beat it?"

"I told him he could no longer sleep here, that's correct."

"You told him he could no longer sleep here?"

"That's correct? What's this all about?"

"You threw this little eight year old orphan boy out on the street? Why?"

"I did not throw him out on the street as you say. I merely suggested he find other sleeping arrangements."

"Other sleeping arrangements?"

"That's right. This is a house of God, not a hotel or dormitory."

"Do you know that guy hanging up there?" I pointed to the crucifix on the wall.

"What?"

"The guy up on that cross? I was told he loved children and would never cast them off like dirty clothes too soiled for God's house."

"Sir, I hardly think you are the one to tell me my business."

"I *will* tell you because you need an education, and if I wasn't a God-fearing man myself...well, on most days...okay, today anyway...I'd take that white collar of yours and, well, let's just say it wouldn't be pretty."

"Perhaps I'd better go get the police," Father Michael said, taking a few hurried steps toward the door.

"Stay right there, padre. Father Patrick is your boss, correct?"

"Yes, but he has put me in charge of his flock in his absence."

"Well you're not tending them very well. Father Patrick was particularly fond of this little sheep here—told by this boy's aunt to look after him until she arrived from Ohio. He fed this little boy, gave him a bed, just like Jesus would have done. Do you think you're more knowledgeable…more righteous than Father Patrick…than Jesus?"

"No, of course not."

"Then what gives?" There was a long awkward silence as Father Michael fumbled for something to say that would justify his actions. "Look, I can see that you've simply made a mistake. It's understandable. We're all sinners after all." I thought to myself, *And I'm the biggest of them all.* "But I'm a forgiving man, which is why I'm going to let you redeem yourself to my friend here. Tonight and every night until Father Patrick returns from wherever he is, or until this boy's aunt arrives to collect him, you will gladly let my friend Billy here, a cherished lamb in God's sight, sleep on a church pew." I stepped in closer to Father Michael and inconspicuously pressed twenty hard-earned dollars into his palm. "You will feed him three good meals a day, bathe him, and buy him a new set of clothes. In two weeks time I will stop in and confirm with my young friend here that you have indeed reformed your ways and been both gracious and kind to him. If so, I will leave you to God's work. If not, well, let us not envision such an ungodly scene." My hypocrisy sickened me but it had to be done.

After clearing his throat, Father Michael said, "Yes, of course. One must continually look for ways to reform oneself."

"Good," I said with a forced, condescending smile. "Thank you and God bless you." I then kneeled down and said my farewell to Billy. "I'm awfully sorry I couldn't do more for you, Billy. It's just, well, I'm on my way to Texas, then back to Connecticut where I live with my wife. You understand."

"Yes, sir," he said, but his face was downcast.

"I'll see you again, Billy."

His face flashed bright like a light bulb. "Promise?"

I looked into his hopeful eyes and just couldn't confirm what I'd said. "I'll try. Now you be good for Father Michael." I stood and walked toward the door, turning at some point for one last look at the young boy who'd just pierced my cold heart. Just as I pushed the door open I heard Billy call out.

"I'll be seeing you, Laird! I'll be seeing you!"

I hesitated for a moment, considering whether I should go back for him, but then beat a quick escape back to the train. Somewhere along the way I said a short prayer for that boy. "Father, please take care of Billy. If you have any heart at all, take care of him."

FROM HARRISONBURG, VIRGINIA, the train took us south to the Tennessee border, where it turned due west toward Memphis and the lower Mississippi River. Seeing the "Mighty Mississippi" below me for the first time led me to wonder what life was like for Mark Twain, the author of two of my favorite books, *Tom Sawyer* and *The Adventures of Huckleberry Finn*—both required reading in high school. I wondered what it must have felt like when Mark Twain—then Samuel Clemens—captained his wooden rafts and later his riverboat down this long and obese waterway, what Tom Sawyer and Huckleberry Finn would have felt if they'd truly set out to raft this grand and muddy lady in search of adventure and independence, laughter their constant companion. I saw myself, not as a minor-league baseball player, but as a shirtless and rebellious, joy-filled boy in ragged denim overalls, my pant-legs rolled up to reveal my boney ankles and dirty bare feet, wrestling with the rudder of my handmade log raft as I steered it over a treacherous part of the river, a piece of straw I'd plucked from my limp hat stuck between my cheek and gum, the sky a happy blue, the water a swirling brown, the smell of stale mud and fresh fish being churned up by the large paddlewheel of a passing steamboat, a bushy-haired Mark Twain giving me a wink and wave from the wheelhouse as it passed.

Suddenly the river was behind us, Arkansas and Texas ahead. Soon I'd arrive in Ennis. Soon I'd see my beloved grandparents again and be able to ask the questions I'd come so far to ask. Soon I'd find out where the eight baseballs came from, their significance to the game, and why they were so important to my father.

CHAPTER EIGHT

My grandparents met me at the station in Dallas, which was a little more than an hour's drive from their home in Ennis, Texas. Grandfather was a soft-spoken rail of a man, tall like a tree, boney in the face with deep-set eyes, a look more suitable for a mortician than for an itinerant preacher. But there was nothing sinister or threatening in his manner, only humility and a profound sense of inner peace. Whatever gratuity was afforded him in the course of his travels he put back into God's work, often to his own detriment. Grandmother, a petite and gentle soul, understood and supported him in any way she could, often travelling with him, ensuring, as she put it, that he got a good meal daily. In the early days—the days when my father was just a boy—my grandfather would travel alone by horse, calling on the good country folk and shoring them up in their faith; but these days, he made his rounds in an old rusty pickup truck, the same one they'd brought to collect me from the station. It rattled and shook going down the road—"Character," Grandmother said—but it ran and rolled just fine. The three of us in that small and noisy cab, though, made for uncomfortable travelling. I suppose that's why we held most of our conversation until we arrived at their home.

They lived in a small house suited to their thrift, the exterior wall cladding a dry-stacked limestone, with lots of windows for ventilation and natural light. There were just two modest bedrooms, and a larger open room made up of the eating area, a kitchen with a four-plate wood-burning cook stove, one my grandmother refused to trade for a modern oven, and a family area with a large fireplace. The fireplace had been constructed from the same stone used to form the structure of the house, all except the mantle, which was a simple slab of birch, barely visible under an array of framed family photographs, most of which were in black and white. Colorful hand-braided rugs covered much of the home's wood flooring, and the walls were adorned with Grandmother's embroidered hangings, some with garden scenes and animals, some with notable Bible verses. And in the air hung the aroma of freshly baked bread mingled with sweet apple pie, the scent of burnt wood from a fire long gone out still lingering. Theirs was rustic living, but it felt more like a home than anyplace I'd ever been. Inside was a palpable warmth, one that came not from the fireplace, but rather from the heart, born out of love for one another, love for humanity, and love for God.

"You can stow your things here," Grandmother said, opening the door to my father's old bedroom. "The bed isn't much, but it's the best we can do for now."

"It'll be fine, Grandma. Thank you." I set my suitcase down in the center of the floor, the tin box still in my hands as I contemplated the room my father had slept in as a boy. I'd bunked here many times over the years, but this time things seemed different. I'd never really opened my heart to my father's childhood before that moment. Perhaps it was the tin box and its contents; surely that played into my feelings. It was here, in this house, that my father put those eight baseballs into the tobacco box he wanted me to have. And that box was why I'd come so far.

"Come out to the kitchen," Grandmother said, hooking her arm in mine and leaning her head against my shoulder like a lovesick schoolgirl. "Let me dote over you for awhile, feed you some of that apple pie you smell. Put a little cinnamon in it like my mama used to do. That's the secret, you know?"

I took a seat at the dinner table while she cut me a big slice of pie, herself a small piece. She came and sat near me, waiting with anticipation for me to take my first bite. "Umm," I said. "Even better than Janie's. But don't tell her I said that."

She smiled. "Thank you, child. Thank you for that."

It was then that I noticed how old she had gotten, the creases on her face bending and deepening with her smile, time having lightly marked her skin in places, every hair on her head the same shade of silver. When my grandfather came through the door with an armful of chopped wood, I left my grandmother to go help him. He struggled to close the door behind him with his booted-foot while maintaining control of the stack, one log falling from the top into my quick hands. "Let me take some of that, Grandpa."

"Very kind of you, Laird," he said, handing off the stack before turning to latch the door. "Seems my arms aren't as strong as they used to be."

"But your mind is, lover," Grandmother said, always offering encouragement. "And it's your mind that won me over."

"Then I best not be losing that now. Wouldn't want you finding your way over to that young buck next door—the professor."

"Sounds like a scandal brewing," I said, grinning.

"Don't you mind your grandfather, Laird. That young buck he's speaking of is ninety-two years old and has the constitution of a cooked noodle. But I suppose he has been after my hand for years."

"A heathen if there ever was one," my grandfather said, warming his hands by the fire, shooting me a wink. "What news have you of your mother? Is she faring well?"

"She's fine, at least that's what she tells me. Said to send you her love and to tell you next Christmas we'll be coming here."

"Glorious!" My grandmother said, clasping her hands together. "I'm so thrilled!"

"And what of Janie and the baby?" Grandfather asked.

"Both are well. The baby's coming along. Janie's busy making a profit off of Grandma's patented pie recipes."

"Tell her she's free to use any recipe she wants," Grandmother said. "And God bless her if she's making money from them. That's delightful."

"And your father? Is he well?"

"That's the reason I'm here, honestly."

"Oh no! Has something happened?" my grandmother asked.

"Come, come, boy. Out with it," my grandfather added.

"No, nothing bad has happened. Dad's still the same."

"Thank goodness," Grandmother said. "For a moment, I thought maybe…"

"No, but he gave me something, rather, he gave it to Mom to give to me…long ago." I rushed off to the bedroom, returning a moment later with the red tin tobacco box. "I was hoping you might be able to tell me something about it."

Grandfather took the box from me, looking it over as if trying to solve some mystery in his mind. He ambled over to the dinner table to sit—recollecting. "I've seen this tobacco box before. Why, I think it was mine. Yes, I'm certain of it. Kept it in the barn. Kept loose hardware in it. How did you say you came by it?"

"Mother gave it to me. She said it belonged to Dad. She said that when he left for the war he told her if anything should happen to him she was to give it to me, that I'd know what to do with them—what's inside."

Grandpa gave me a look, like a child looking at his parents, unsure as to whether or not he should stick his hand in the cookie jar even though he'd been given permission. I nodded for him to go ahead and after a brief hesitation he opened the lid, revealing the note I'd placed back on top of the towel covering the baseballs. He picked up the piece of paper and read it. "Ennis, nineteen o-two."

I reached over and unfolded the towel, revealing the eight aged baseballs. Then I watched my grandfather's reaction. He seemed a bit stunned, raising a hand to cover his mouth. "No. Could these really be? No. They can't be." He removed the hand from over his mouth and reached for one of the baseballs, shimmers of light reflecting off his curious eyes, illuminating the joy washing over his face. "I can't believe it!"

"What is it, dear?" Grandmother asked.

"Quick," Granddad said to her. "Find my glasses." He glanced at me before returning his sight to the baseballs in the box, peering at them from above like a mad scientist does his experiment. "I just can't believe...it seems impossible!"

While my grandmother searched for his spectacles, I asked, "Have you seen these baseballs before, Grandpa?"

"I believe so, yes." Just then Grandmother returned with his glasses. Placing them on his nose, he said. "But I'll know for sure in a moment." With his glasses on he examined the baseball in his hand, searching for something only he thought should be there, something that would confirm his suspicions. He rotated the ball with his gnarled, spotted fingers until he finally saw it. "There! There it is! Yes! Oh, my!"

I leaned in close to see if I could see what he had found. "I don't understand."

"Here, boy! See this mark—in faded ink?" he asked, pointing to a small speck. "Here, take my glasses."

I held his glasses up to my eyes and scrutinized the ball. There it was. I'd looked over these balls many times since being given them and hadn't see it until now. It was small, but with the glasses I could clearly see it. "It's the number eight."

"That's right. And if I'm correct each of these balls will have a number leading down to the number one. I know because I was there when he marked them. He marked them with the pen I used to write my sermons. It was in my saddlebag that day."

"Dad?"

"Yes, Laird. You're father marked each of these balls so he'd remember in what order they were hit—what order he retrieved them in."

"Order? But where'd they come from?"

Rubbing the baseballs with his hands, he said, "From a professional baseball game played on June fifteenth, nineteen o-two, here in Ennis, Texas."

"So Dad didn't hit these balls? Were they foul balls he shagged?"

"No, boy, better than that. These are the eight home run balls Jay Justin Clarke hit that day."

"Eight home runs in a single game?" I asked. "Come on. No way."

"It's true, Laird. He was the catcher for Corsicana Oil City, and your father was there to see it."

"You're not kidding? Eight home runs in a single game? How come I've never heard about this?"

"I don't rightly know, Grandson, but it happened. These baseballs prove it. I'm stunned your father saved them all these years."

I picked up one of the balls, rubbed it in my hands to warm it like a good pitcher would, gave it a toss, then asked, "So these are the eight balls? The eight home run balls?"

"Yes. It was a strange game. The score was fifty-one to three, if you can believe that."

"Now I know you're fooling me. That's a football score, not baseball."

"I was there, too, don't forget. It was fifty-one to three, Corsicana Oil City over the Texarkana Casketmakers. Look it up when you get home. I'm sure it's in one of those big baseball reference books your mother keeps. The score was so high partly because the field was short, a bandbox I think you players call it, with the fence down the first base line angled in, making the right field fence shorter than the rest—that and because the Corsicana team was so good at hitting. Seemed everybody from Corsicana homered that day, but that fella Clarke just kept placing his hits over that shorter right field fence. Just amazing accuracy."

"If everybody was homering, how'd my dad know which balls were the eight homers hit by Clarke?"

"Because after the fourth one he—"

"Started numbering them," I said, finishing his sentence.

"The game wasn't supposed to be played in Ennis. It was a Sunday and in Corsicana games were prohibited on Sunday because of 'blue laws.' So they moved the game here. Factories and shops each had their own baseball teams back then and they needed someplace to compete against each other. That was their field."

"I've heard about those corporate teams. Some were pretty good."

"I remember that day now like it was this morning, though I honestly haven't given it much thought until seeing these balls again. It was a humid day...and particularly hot, me being in my black Sunday suit and all. The only thing providing relief was my brimmed hat. And it was the only Sunday I'd ever played hooky from preaching. I remember the smell of grilled hotdogs in the air. I never could resist a good frankfurter so I purchased one from a vendor. Mustard, I've found, makes it go down easier. Well, all the boys in town were excited about the game and many were shagging balls, some like your father over the outfield fence, catching home run balls, other boys running up and down the sparse stands to catch fouls. Must have been a hundred shirtless farm kids in overalls, many without shoes, sprinting here and there." He smiled as he recollected. "There was a man pushing a cart around—hired by the league. He gave flavored shaved-ice cones to each kid that returned a ball. But your dad, I reckon he sensed something special was taking place that day with Clarke's multiple home runs, so he held onto those balls. If another boy shagged a Clarke home run ball, your father would trade the boy two home run balls hit by other players. Those boys got two for one, so they didn't mind the exchange."

"Pretty smart for an eight year old kid. Probably worth a pretty penny these balls."

"But he was always that way, your father," said Grandmother. "He was always keen about such things. Always thinking ahead."

As we talked about that day in 1902, I realized that for the first time I actually longed to hear more about my father—about his life as a boy, as a man, and as a ballplayer. I felt new affections for my father I hadn't experienced, and they didn't scare me.

Remembering fondly, Grandfather added, "That was the first organized baseball game your father had ever seen. Can you believe that?"

I shook my head.

"But after, on the way home, he leaned over my shoulder in the saddle—we'd ridden old Woodrow to the game, a horse we'd bought from your mother's folks, your young father riding the rump, his pockets full of baseballs. Well, with a conviction I'll never forget, your father declared, 'When I grow up, Pop, I'll make my living playing baseball!'"

"What'd you say to that?" I asked with a smile.

"What I've always said to boys with big dreams. 'If God wills it, let it be so.'"

THAT NIGHT, AS I lay asleep in my father's childhood bed, my mind took to dreaming—only this dream wasn't the nightmare I'd told my mother about in her barn. This dream was different, somewhere between a nightmare and a revelation, like when a fella tells you that it's wrong to make moves on his favorite girl, right after he cracks you in the nose.

In my dream, I was in the wheelhouse of a steamboat, fighting the wheel as the giant paddlewheel propelled me down an old river, the river getting rougher and the weather more tumultuous as we flowed along. There was an explosion to port, water raining down on the boat, eventually subsiding to reveal a raft drifting with a young, unconscious and bloodied soldier lying on it, reaching a hand upward as he cried, "Tell my son I'm sorry! Tell him!" I countered and slammed the wheel to starboard, trying to avoid him, when suddenly I saw a small dredger working the underlying sandbar to stern, my mother at the controls and saying to me as I fought to keep from running into her, "He loves you, Laird. He loves it when you come to visit." I steered clear, but then there was that boy, Billy, adrift on a log, shivering and cold, struggling to stay afloat. But as I looked closer, Billy's face morphed into my own and I screamed out, "No! I helped that boy! I didn't pass him by! I helped him!" Then Janie appeared on the foredeck like a hologram, her dark dress and pale face drenched by pouring rain. "You're just not the best son sometimes, Laird." Panic set in and I called out to Janie as my mother joined her. "It's not my fault! He enlisted! I love my father! I do! I promise!" Suddenly the weather settled, the way it had calmed instantly for Jesus when the apostles cried out to him in the boat. Suddenly the sun broke clear of the clouds and light and warmth filled my wheelhouse.

Just then the bedroom light flicked on and I sat up to find my grandfather walking toward me. "Everything okay, Laird?"

I threw my legs over the side of the bed, planting my bare feet on the floor, my hands rubbing the sleep from my eyes. "Yes, Grandpa. Just a dream—a silly dream, is all."

He was robed, his pajamas underneath, lined slippers on his feet. And he had a pipe in his boney hand, packing tobacco in the bowl as he pulled a chair alongside the bed. "Feel like talking about it?" he asked, striking a match on the bedframe to light his pipe, puffing a few times to make sure the tobacco was lit before extinguishing the match with a quick shake.

"No," I said. "I'm fine."

"Your mother says the same, but I've learned things are rarely fine when she says that."

"I've learned that too."

"This room holds a lot of memories for me." He looked around, admiring some of my father's things that still lay about, others still hanging on the walls. "You see those flattened pennies there on the shelf."

I nodded and went to retrieve a couple. There were twelve in all. "What happened to them?"

"The train got 'em. Your father liked to lay a penny on the tracks each time we rode old Woodrow into town. On the way back we'd look to see if the penny was still there. If not then we knew it'd been run over by a train. We'd search about, sometimes up to a hundred yards away, until we found that penny. Then we'd look at the shape. Each penny turned out differently after being smashed by a heavy locomotive. We'd take turns thinking of things the new flattened penny looked like."

"Only twelve?"

"Well, a penny in those days was good money—these days, not so much. But mostly, in our house anyway, every penny we had was a gift from the Lord. To waste it that way didn't seem right."

"But you let Dad waste twelve pennies," I said, grinning. "You're not afraid of being cast into the lake?"

Grandfather laughed behind the smoke of his pipe. "We serve a merciful God, Grandson. Besides, I actually let your father smash twenty-four. He sold the other twelve to the boys at school, two good pennies for one flat penny. We broke even."

Now I was laughing. I'd always admired my grandfather's dry humor and dignified mischief. He enjoyed a good time as much as any man, but he did that within set boundaries. He stood firm on his convictions and faith, but never seemed to lord them over anybody. He simply offered both to the world, like a trusted pair of helping hands. He left it up to the individual to accept those hands or not.

"Do you miss him, Grandpa?"

"Your father?" he asked, his eyes shifting my way as he inhaled on his pipe. "Oh, yes. Very much."

"I do too. But I've never really known him. How can I miss somebody I've never known, Grandpa?"

He looked up toward the ceiling—toward heaven maybe—giving my question some thought. "I'm told, by women who've had the misfortune to miscarry a child, that they often find themselves missing the child they never met—years later even. It's understandable, really. Though the child lived in the mother's womb biologically, it lived also, perhaps more so, in the mother's heart. That's where hope is stored—the hope of what is and what will be. The child may be gone but the heart won't let go of the hope, only now it's for what might have been. Perhaps it's like that for you, Laird. Perhaps your heart is clinging to the hope of what might have been."

His words were rich and deep and true. "Grandpa, how'd you get to be so wise?"

He just smiled, "I'm only wise when your grandmother allows me to be. Right now she's sleeping."

"No, I'm serious, Grandpa. You're the wisest man I know."

With the humility of a man not comfortable with praise, he said, "Well, thank you, Laird. If I am wise it is because God made me so. But thank you."

"Sometimes I hate him," I said, looking off. "Not God, though I get confused by that too. Dad."

"I know, Grandson. It must be very hard for you at times."

"Then I hate myself for hating him. He didn't do anything to me, but then he did a lot to me. Can you understand?"

He nodded, inhaling on his pipe.

"I look at him...in that wheelchair...tense...his mind gone...it makes me mad one minute then sad the next. What do I do with that?"

"Well, let's start with why it makes you mad."

"Because he abandoned me."

"Would you have rather he let his friends fight and die alone over there?"

"Friends? You mean his fellow soldiers?"

"Them too, but I mean Joey and Hal Mitchell, two boys he'd gone to high school with here in Ennis, neither of whom made it home by the way. Rube Bressler, friend and pitcher for the Philadelphia Athletics."

"Dad knew Bressler? Good ace, not so good with the bat though. Won a Series with Cincinnati didn't he—1919?"

"Possibly. I'm afraid I don't possess your mind for things." He gave the conversation more thought as he toked on his pipe. "Fred Tyler, brother of Lefty Tyler, teammates of your father's, who incidentally came right over to be with your Dad at the hospital after Game Four of the World Series, along with Rube, the night you were being born…men who, when you were young you used to call 'uncle.' Fred and Lefty lived in Boston and helped your mother quite a bit after your father came home. Each of those boys meant a lot to your father, and each was headed to Europe and the war."

"But what about me, Grandpa? I needed him here. Didn't he know that? Mom said he did but enlisted anyway. He *enlisted*—went voluntarily."

"I know, Son. But your father—"

"I know—'Duty.'"

"It was more than that, Laird. Your father…he was a bit like me, I suppose…quiet. He internalized things. But he was unique. His heart was big, Laird, and he felt things for people others might not have. He *let* himself love people…strangers, men, women, children. I remember one time, when your father was about thirteen years of age, he got word that Butch Olsen's mother had passed away from a severe case of influenza. He flew out the door of the house, no shoes on, running through our cotton field, leaping our fence into your mother's property, running full speed through an irritated herd of horses, scattering them as he ran, no concern at all for his own safety. By the time he arrived at Butch's place his feet were a bloody mess. Now, all this might not be out of the ordinary, except that Butch Olsen used to pound on your father at school—a big boy with bad manners, if I don't mind saying so. Still, God had given your father a heart for that boy in that moment and he ran to his aide. That's not a trait you often find in men."

I nodded, a bit proud.

"Oh, I'm not just saying these things because he's my son. I'm merely offering them as an explanation of sorts as to why he *had* to go fight beside his friends. Those boys...they only had each other over there, at least in your father's mind. And he would never let his friends go to fight—possibly die—without him. You had your mother, and he trusted you with her more than anybody else. Those boys, though...they'd be facing an army of men trying to kill them, and that just didn't set well with your Dad. What would you have done, Laird? You ballplayers seem to get yourselves into scraps on the field. Would you let your friends and teammates brawl without going to help them—just sit it out on the bench?"

I thought about his question for a moment, remembering a game where my third baseman, Bags Wheeler, got intentionally cleated in the leg by a runner sliding into third, how Bags was hurt bad, his leg cut open at the shin, how I first ran to his aid from the mound but upon seeing the gash turned and walloped the runner. "No, I guess I couldn't do that. Mom said he wouldn't have been able to live with himself with other boys over there dying while he stayed here and played baseball, home safe with his wife and son. She didn't tell me, though, that the boys she mentioned were his friends."

"Did you let her get that far?"

"Guess not. Why didn't anybody tell me this when I was young? Might have made a difference you know."

"Whenever we tried to tell you about him you shutdown."

"You don't know what it's like to have him at your games…to have an invalid for a father."

"No, but I know what it's like to have an invalid for a son…and it's hard. Seeing him in that condition, knowing he once ran like a wild stallion, it's not easy. That why you fight so much…on the ball field growing up…at school?"

"Well it hurts when someone calls him a 'retard,' you know. Not easy for me to let that go."

"Have you treated your father like anything more than a 'retard,' as you so colorfully put it?"

"I didn't call him that name. Other boys did. I hate that name." I thought about his question. It hit hard, like a fastball high and inside to the ribs. "No, I guess I didn't treat him much better. But I defended him. That's something, isn't it?"

"You mean, 'I can beat up my brother but you better not touch him.' That sort of thing?"

"Grandpa—"

"Laird, why not let go of the anger?"

"I'm trying. I really am trying."

"Give it to God. Let him deal with it. You just concentrate on finding love for your father in your heart. He's in there. And when you do you might find life easier going."

A moment passed before I lifted the tin box from the floor and removed one of the eight baseballs. "Dad told Mom that I'd know what to do with these—that he knew I'd do the right thing with them. What do you think he meant?"

He shook his head, "I do not know, Grandson. What do you think your father wanted done with them?"

"I'm not sure. Maybe sell them. Use the money for Mom. I'm sure these eight balls are worth a small fortune to a collector."

"That's a thought. But could your father have foreseen that? Does your mother need the money?"

"Hard to say. She doesn't talk about money with me. But I'm concerned about her. She's very thin. I don't think she eats sometimes."

"Worry can sometimes do that to a person. I'll talk to her."

"What happened to Clarke—the guy who hit these eight home runs? Did he play in the big leagues anywhere? Hard to believe a feat like that could go unnoticed by scouts."

"I think he played for several big league outfits...the Cleveland Naps, Detroit Tigers, a couple others I think."

"Wait a minute!" I said, excited and sitting forward on the bed, like a kid who'd just got a crazy idea. "Clarke...Jay Justin Clarke...they called him "Nig" I think. Yeah!"

"A not so flattering nickname, I'm told."

"Yeah! He played with the Naps! Caught a perfect game for Addie Joss in 1908, I think!"

"You sure have a memory for baseball."

"A little bit of Mom coming through. Yeah, I've heard of this guy, Clarke. That perfect game he caught for Joss in 2008...one of the greatest pitching duals ever, they say. Wish I could have seen it. Big Ed Walsh of the Chicago White Sox went into that game with thirty-nine wins! Can you believe that?"

"Is that good? I don't know about these things."

"That's incredible! Joss himself had a fantastic year going into that game with 24 wins. There were only a few games left in the season when that game was played and Chicago and Cleveland were within one game of each other for the pennant. It was an important game and both those guys pitched their hearts out. Walsh they say struck out fifteen batters! That's crazy that the Sox still lost the game. But Joss pitched *perfect*. Twenty up, twenty down…and Nig Clarke called his pitches from behind the plate. That's saying something about both Joss and Clarke."

"Sounds like an exciting game."

"Some say Clarke was the first catcher to wear shin guards."

"Well, I'm not sure whatever happened to him after his baseball days. I'm sure if you asked around you could find out more. Wherever he went though, I'm sure that game on that day in 1902 went with him. Eight home runs and a score of fifty-one to three…that's hard for some to believe. Might not believe it myself it we weren't there." He stood, patting my shoulder before walking toward the door. "Your grandmother will be awake soon, don't want her to catch me in here being wise," he said, turning with a grin. "Get some sleep, Laird."

"I love you, Grandpa," I said, rising and walking over to him in the doorway, reaching in to hug him like a schoolboy who just found out his best friend died. The gesture was as much foreign to my character as it was an unstoppable impulse.

"What's this?" he asked, patting my back as I held him. "Looks like you've got more of your father in you than you realized."

"Maybe so."

"I love you too, Grandson. Now get some sleep. I've got something special I want to show you in the morning."

After he left I laid on the bed in the dark, the blue light of the full moon casting into the room through the window, the flattened pennies on the shelf radiating their warmth and luster like twelve little copper angels watching over me. In that moment I offered my anger to God, as nervous and unsure as a dirty homeless man seeking a handout at a private black-tie only club, the women as polished as fine crystal, the men like tailored penguins sporting bushy gray muttonchops and puffing fat Cuban cigars, the stiff doorman with the upturned nose stopping me before I can enter. That's how I felt, honestly, like I had no place approaching God. He had a place for ingrates like me and it was hot and violent and untamed by morality; it was an ugly place—one I suddenly feared.

Nothing miraculous transpired after my little prayer. I felt no different than before, except maybe like my ship had finally been freed from a tangled mooring. Anger, I was discovering, was a heavy burden to bear. Carrying it around was like wearing a solid lead helmet on my head; by the end of each day my neck was stiff and sore, and any joy I might have had was gone. And love for others cannot fully develop in a heart filled with anger and resentment; that heart is too centered on itself. That too I was learning—from a father who seemed to be teaching me through others.

What's this? Looks like you've got more of your father in you than you realize.

Maybe I do, Grandpa. Maybe I do.

CHAPTER NINE

The aroma of fried egg and gently burnt toast wafted into the bedroom to stir me awake the following morning, but it was the smell and pop of sizzling bacon in a cast iron skillet that lifted my body out of bed, like a magician's levitating assistant rising horizontally under a blanket, then rotating during the trick to land feet first on the ground. I reckon sizzling bacon is the greatest smell on earth. I'd bet if you took a skillet into a cemetery, built a small fire and started frying up some bacon in that skillet, I'd bet you'd soon see dead bodies bursting forth from the earth, gasping and reaching for you like submerged swimmers fighting their way up to fresh air, each decaying body suddenly alive, salivating from exposed skulls as they move in to sit near you at your fire, hands out, begging for that bacon!

"Morning, Grandma," I said before yawning, trying unsuccessfully to compress my hair, which was as spiked as a frightened girl's in one of those cheap horror flicks. "That for me?"

"Of course, and for your grandfather," she said, joyfully.

The clock on the wall said 7:15 but she was already dressed for the day, having shunned her robe and nightgown for riding clothes, her jeans stuffed into a worn pair of suede cowgirl boots, a flannel shirt tucked into her jeans at the waist, a brown leather belt adorned with etched silver conchos and a matching silver belt buckle holding the ensemble together. Funny, I never took my grandmother for a country girl, though I should have expected such, her and my grandfather being owners of a Texas ranch. I'd always seen her in dresses and sweaters and things, graying hair manicured and off the shoulders, delicate as a spring flower on a kitchen windowsill, her spirit just as bright.

"Where's Grandpa?"

"He'll be along in a moment."

I took a seat at the breakfast table, already set with placemats and silverware, condiments of butter, ketchup, and hot sauce, half-empty salt and pepper shakers slipped into slots cut into the transom of an old toy tractor, painted green and yellow and about the size of a soup bowl. "This is great! Where'd you get it?"

She brought two steaming plates of breakfast food to the table, setting one before me, the other in my grandfather's spot. "That toy tractor belonged to your father. Bought it for him to play with when he was just knee high to ol' Bess, our dairy cow. He was so anxious to work, to help your granddad out around the ranch, but he was just too small at the time. He loved that tractor. Wore it plum out the first year. The wheels fell off and your grandpa had to do some mending. But a year later your father lost interest in the toy tractor. I suppose he'd outgrown it. Thought about donating the tractor to some other family but just couldn't bring myself to part with it. So I set the toy tractor aside until I could find another use for it. Now it's a useful table ornament."

"Pretty ingenious."

"She's a creative one, your grandmother," my grandfather said, carefully taking his seat at the table next to me.

"You all right, Grandpa? Looks like you're moving slowly this morning."

"Just the old lumbago acting up. Comes and goes, like gas, only without the quick relief."

That made me laugh. "Want some coffee or juice, Grandpa?" I asked, just as my grandmother brought him both.

"I've got it. You boys eat."

"Been married to your grandmother for half a century. At this point she knows what I'm thinking before I do."

I couldn't help but admire them together. They reminded me of two bookends, a matching set that held everything within their grasp together. Take away one and the other wouldn't be able to function fully.

"Come and join us, dear," Grandfather said, sprinkling a little salt on his fried egg. "Let us pray together and offer thanks for this blessed bounty." Grandmother slid into her seat beside her husband, her petite and aged hands joining his and mine across the table as we bowed our heads. "Heavenly Father, we are truly thankful for this time of fellowship together, for the provision you've placed before us this day. Let us savor them with thoughts of you in our hearts. Amen."

"Amen," my grandmother and I said simultaneously.

"Umm," I said, biting into a strip of cooked bacon. "Delicious. Extra crispy, just the way I like it."

"I know," grandmother said proudly.

"Not me," Grandpa said, taking hold of a limp and greasy slice and sucking it into his mouth. "Like mine to slither into my mouth, like a snake trying to make a quick escape."

"That's gross, Grandpa."

"To each his own, boy. To each his own."

"You're already dressed, Grandma. Going into town?"

"No. We're going riding."

"You and me?"

"Um hmm, right after you help me muck the stalls." I rolled my eyes. "Won't kill you to help out."

"But I didn't bring any—"

"Already thought of that. If you look in your father's closet you'll find some of his clothes. They're old, moth-ridden some of them, but you look the same fit, except maybe his boots. Your father had a big foot. He left the clothes when he and your mother shipped off to Boston. Said he wanted new clothes to go with his new life in the city."

"Odd since he and Mom ended up buying and living on twenty-two acres in rural Lynn."

"I guess you can't hit a home run if you don't take a swing," she said smiling.

"Did you just use a baseball analogy, Grandma?"

"I may be a yokel, but that doesn't mean I can't communicate in your vernacular."

"Any biddy can cluck, but that don't make her a genuine hen," my grandfather said with a chuckle.

Grandmother fired off a sanctimonious glance at her husband, one coated in affection but loaded with buckshot.

"You coming with us, Grandpa? Riding, I mean?"

"No," Grandmother said like a coyote toying with its prey. "Your grandfather has graciously volunteered to do the dishes."

I looked over at my grandfather who just winked at me, scooping up some egg yoke with his toast. "Like I said, Grandson, she knows my thoughts before I even think them."

THE RIDE OUT across the open range felt invigorating, the two thousand pound well-bred thunderbolt beneath me, the click and clack of hooves nipping small rocks and limestone filling my ears as we rode, the gentle rocking as soothing as lying in a hammock under a shady tree in summer. White pillowy condensate polluted the blue sky we found ourselves under, the browning terrain rolling like swells from an endless sea, with some of the valleys harboring seasonal creeks that slithered over and around rocks like dark fluid snakes on the prowl. Our horizon was unobstructed, except for fencing that sectioned off the distant hills, and a few well-placed oak trees, proudly standing erect upon various peaks, their gnarled wooden branches stretched out wide as if declaring, "This is our world."

"That was you mother's place, there," My grandmother said, pointing off to the west as we rode south along a perimeter fence, my grandmother making mental notes of breaks in the barbed wire that needed repair. Pointing to a leaning fence post, she said, "Cow did that. They like to scratch their backs and sides against the wire. Too heavy for it, though. Seems there's always something to repair on a ranch. Not sure how much longer we'll be able to keep it up."

"Can't you hire somebody—a ranch hand? Thought you had some?"

"We do, but they're seasonal mostly, and the ones we hire permanent are cowboys that don't seem to understand the word—hardworking boys that drift like tumbleweeds in the wind."

"That's too bad." I could see the worry plaguing my grandmother's face as she lumbered lazily in the saddle, her body in complete submission to the movement of the horse she rode. "Wish I could help."

As if she had been setting me up for it, my grandmother reined her horse to a stop, reaching over to stop my horse as well, saying, "Think you might like this place someday, Laird?"

"What do you mean?"

"I mean, your grandfather and I have talked and, well, we were thinking this might make a good home for all of you...after we go...after you finish your baseball."

"'After you go?'"

"Do I have to say it?"

"You mean...? Ah, don't talk like that, Grandma."

"I'm serious, Laird. It's a lot of work," she said, motioning with her arm, "all of this, but it's hard to beat the splendor of it. Look at it, Laird. Just look. Have you ever seen such beauty? It's like God painted it himself."

"Grandpa would say God did."

"If we left it to you, would you keep it...work it...live on it like we have? It'll grow on you over time, the way a stray dog does when it makes its way into your life. You never wanted the pitiful thing, but you can't turn your back on it either. You start to feed it, look after it, and then one day, years later, you realize this beast you never wanted has become your constant companion…the kind of friend that's always willing to give its love in gratitude, the kind of friend you can trust…the kind that never leaves you when things get tough."

There was an awkwardness that fell between us like a large boulder blocking a path between two granite faces. I looked off for a moment, trying to find the words to say. "Is this why you brought me out here this morning, Grandma?"

"No, I honestly hadn't planned on asking you yet. But as things go sometimes, a moment presents itself and—"

"Do I have to answer you now? Can I discuss this with Janie?"

"Of course. You both have to want this or it won't work. But there's one thing, Laird, and it may affect your decision. We want you *all* to live here—you, Janie, your future children." She waited a bit before dropping the bomb on me. "And your mother and father."

I nodded to myself. Of course that would be part of the deal.

"We've got some money saved. We'll build another house for you and Janie—give you some privacy. It won't have all the latest gadgets, but it'll be a good home if you make it one. Your mother and father can have our house."

"You act like you know the date and time of your passing."

"I don't mean to give that impression, Laird, but when a person sees the twilight approaching, well, it feels better knowing those you're about to leave behind will be provided for…that they'll be all right."

"Why not sell the place and give Mom the money. She could put Dad in a good facility where they could look after him twenty-four hours per day. Wouldn't that be better?"

I could tell by the way she dropped her head and rode on without me that I'd disappointed her with my question. "Wait! I didn't say I was going to do that!" I galloped up to her. "I was just exploring different options."

"Your mother would never do that—one of the many things I love about her."

"I know, Grandma. Honestly, I wouldn't want that either."

She looked at me, searching my face with her eyes, looking for any trace of dishonesty. When she was satisfied with my sincerity, she smiled. "Thank you, Laird. It gives me great comfort knowing that."

WE ARRIVED BACK at the ranch house to find my grandfather feeding reeled film through a movie projector he had resting on a small foldup table in the center of the family room, the front propped up with a few books, the lens pointing at a white sheet he'd hung above the mantle of their smoldering fireplace, the smell of breakfast still hanging on the air. He had the curtains closed and only the kitchen light on behind him.

"What's this?" I asked, tossing my coat over the back of a leather chair kept close to the fireplace for those cold Texas nights.

"This is the surprise I spoke of last night, if I can ever get this to feed. Ah, there she goes." The film entered from the front just below where the feeder reel hung, then sprinted out the back and all over the floor, causing my grandfather to panic momentarily.

I leapt to his aid, switching the unit to neutral. "There you go. Now just find the end and wind it on the rear spool until the slack is gone."

"Thank you. This modern technology baffles me. Take a seat in that chair. I've been waiting for the right time to show you this film—when I thought you could handle it." He had my interest the way a magician captivates small children sitting before him on a floor. "It's newsreel of your father...taking batting and fielding practice before a game against Saint Louis."

"No kidding? Wow!" I leaned forward in the chair, resting my elbows on my knees, anxiously awaiting the first visual frame of the game and my father in motion—running, walking, and talking, the way he was before being imprisoned in his mental shell and wheelchair. Grandfather switched on the projector and the perforated film began clicking as it rolled through the feeder gears, followed a moment later by black and white flickering images on the hanging white sheet, images of ballplayers in knickers, strutting about with bats and gloves.

"There was no sound in those days, mind you," Grandfather said, "but I think you'll enjoy this."

My eyes searched closely for the first sign of my father. "What year is this?"

"It's from the first game ever played at the new Braves Field—August eighteenth, I think, nineteen fifteen."

"Look at these guys!" Two ballplayers stood next to each other, hamming it up for the camera, both from the Braves, both dressed in light colored uniforms with knickers for trousers, short-sleeved shirts with buttons down the front, dark pinstripes on both sides of the buttons, creating an inch-wide strip travelling up the front, around the neck, and back down the front. The word "BRAVES" was stitched across the chest in big letters with a single capital "B" on their pale ball caps, just above the dark colored bills. "That's Butch Schmidt on the left. First baseman. Seen pictures of him in *Baseball Magazine*. And that's Johnny Evers on the right. Hall-of-Famer, now. He owned second base back then. Picture of them both up in the Braves' clubhouse."

Next there were a couple minutes of footage showing two other Braves players tossing the ball back and forth.

"I'm told there were forty six thousand fans there that day to commemorate their new stadium," my grandfather said, now standing beside the projector, his arm wrapped around the waist of his beloved wife, both smiling almost as big as me.

"Where'd you get this?" I asked as images of the stands and fans showed, most of the men in suits and Fedoras or straw boaters, with hoards of kids in newsboy caps and T-shirts squeezing between them like weeds forcing their way up between tightly packed rows of monochrome tulips. After that the footage cut to a lone batter in the box, taking batting practice and making solid contact with every ball pitched, his swing fluid and graceful, like a hawk soaring and circling on a rising thermal, his prey below fully sighted all the while.

"I wrote to the owner of the Braves shortly after your father returned home from Europe, asking if he had any playing footage of your father. He sent me this."

Leaning in for a closer look at the batter, his back to the camera. "Wait. Is that—"

"Yes, Laird," Grandmother said, soft as an angel's whisper. "That's him. That's your father."

It's hard to describe what I felt at that moment—seeing my father in motion for the first time, standing and setting himself firmly in the batter's box, in uniform and swinging a bat, sending balls sailing out of the frame. Even though his back was still to the camera, it seemed as though my heart had stopped beating in my chest and had somehow lodged itself in my ears, the rhythmic thumping all I could hear, except the imaginary *Crack!* I heard every time his wooden bat struck the hard ball. When the newsreel cut to show my father batting from the front, my father smiling big at the camera and firing off a wink just before smacking one out of the park, I could hardly contain my emotion. Tears began to fill my eyes.

"There he goes," Grandmother said, "Batting those chocolate dollops."

"'Chocolate Dollops?'" I asked. "What are you talking about?"

"Something Edith, your mother's mother said to me one night when we were chaperoning a local dance down at the hall. Your mother and father were dancing hand in hand, already so much in love. They must have been in their early teens then. I said to her, 'My boy sure has eyes for your daughter.' And she said, 'The feeling is mutual, I can tell you that. I overheard Em,' That's what she called your mother, short for Emily of course. 'I overheard Em tell one of her girlfriends that Laird's brown eyes are like buttery swirls of chocolate, two dollops begging to be eaten.' We laughed for a moment. I, said, 'Oh the things young girls say sometimes.' And she said, 'It gets worse. Em said Laird's smile is like a bright sliver of moon bursting through the clouds, like hope after a long spell of gloom, his brown flowing hair as inviting as the Texas hills in spring. It's all that reading she does, I'm telling you!'"

I heard and smiled at what'd she'd just told me, but my eyes were fixed on the screen. "Hard to imagine Mother talking like that—her so hardened now by life."

The sight of my father, happy and swinging and standing on his own, filled me with tearful joy—a joy soon pushed aside by a sickening feeling in my belly, caused by the realization that what I was seeing was past and not present. That is what he *was*—a handsome, athletic, heroic figure—before his injury. Seeing him on screen, in uniform and so happy and full of life made my father's current state seem all the more tragic.

"He was beautiful," my grandmother said, removing a handkerchief from her pocket to wipe the tears.

"Yes, he was," I agreed.

"Still is," Grandfather pointed out.

I found myself nodding in agreement. "That's about as perfect a swing as I've seen. Fully extended, power off the back leg, good follow-through."

Then the footage cut to my father at shortstop fielding some grounders, each time throwing or tossing the ball quickly to Johnny

Evers at second who then hurled the ball to Schmidt at first."

"Young to Evers to Schmidt. Good combination," I said, "Dad's quick on and off the ball. Look how he hops just before the bat contacts the ball. Helps him spring in the direction of the ball when he lands."

"I've always wondered why they didn't play him more in the three and a half years he was there," my grandfather said.

"Two words," I said, still watching the screen, which now showed a group of men, my father included, playfully doing tricks as they tossed the ball around, like seals nosing a beach ball back and forth in a circus. "Rabbit Maranville, all-star shortstop with a good bat. Future Hall-of-Famer for sure."

"How do you know all of this, Grandson?" my grandmother asked.

"Mom. She knows everything. Haven't you heard?" When they laughed, I said, "Seriously. She does. Nobody knows more about the Boston Braves than her, especially during the period Dad played. And she doesn't mind telling you that either."

Just then, on screen, Evers and Maranville sandwiched my father between them, my dad acting helpless, a couple of St. Louis Cardinal players in the background poking fun. "Look at these guys. You gotta love this...the innocence of it all...just grownup kids playing a child's game. Amazing."

Suddenly the sheet went white again to the sound of the film's end smacking the projector each time it rotated loose on the reel, sounding like a playing card clipped to the front fork of a bicycle, the card slapping the spokes of the spinning wheel. Seeing those images disappear was like losing my eyesight while standing before God. I just sat there in a sort of shell shock, staring up at the white sheet, only not seeing it.

"Are you all right, Laird," my grandfather asked, switching off the projector and placing a gentle hand on my shoulder.

I nodded. "Thank you for showing me that, Grandpa."

When I stood my grandmother slid in beside me. "There's so much of him in you." I shook my head. "There is, Laird. You just aren't seeing it yet. But we see it, more and more every time you come visit."

"Sure wish you could stay beyond tomorrow, Grandson," my grandfather said, taking down the hanging sheet that served us well as a screen. "Been nice having you around."

"I wish I could too, but if I'm not home by Thanksgiving Janie will disown me."

"Doubt that," Grandmother said.

"Say, why don't you two come back with me? Yeah, that would be terrific! Mom and Janie would be over the moon!"

"Wish we could, but we've got the horses and animals. And the mill is sending a crew to harvest our cotton next month," Grandmother said. "Somebody has to be here."

"Isn't there anybody that can look after this place so you can come with me?"

"I don't know," my grandfather said, scratching at the morning stubble on his chin, giving my invitation serious thought. "Let me make a few inquiries. Might be somebody."

My grandmother's face lit up like a candle glowing in the night. "Do you really think we could, honey? My, my! That would be marvelous—seeing your mother and Janie again. Oh, and the baby! Wouldn't that be wonderful if Janie delivered while we were there? Our first great grandchild!"

"Well don't count on that," I said. "I don't think she's due until late December."

"These doctors, they think they're like weathermen, predicting childbirth like it's a coming rainstorm. What do they know?"

"I'll take a drive out and see Henry Wells. His boy Frank...you know the one. He helped us out for two summers during high school. I think he's still around. If not maybe Henry himself." My grandmother held out my grandfather's coat as he slipped one arm after the other into the sleeves before heading for the front door. "I'll see what I can do." In the doorway, the blue horizon as his backdrop, he proclaimed, "No, I'll do better than that. I'll make it happen."

CHAPTER TEN

The sleeping berth allotted my grandparents by the railroad resembled a very small hotel suite, complete with an undersized sink for washing, a cozy bench seat next to a grand single pane window, one that when the scenery passed at full speed gave the impression of being at the cinema, your point of view that of the fleeing robber being chased by police. And a larger than normal single bed folded down lengthwise from the wall, a bed big enough for two people if they loved each other enough. My economy berth, on the other hand, could have been the same one I had on the trip down to Texas; it looked that similar—just a bed, a curtain, and a window. Didn't bother me any; I'd had worse on the road with the team. Many times we just slept in our seats, still in our travelling clothes, wadded coats or travel bags making for bumpy pillows, hats resting over our faces to block out the light, our bodies and minds exhausted from continuous weeks of playing and travelling away from home.

My grandparents were excited about the spontaneous trip to see their son and daughter-in-law—as well as Janie—their faces awash with joy overflowing, their steps light like people half their age, their eyes brimming with anticipation. Train travel from Texas to Massachusetts was no small affair for folks in their seventies. I suppose that's why they'd only made the trip four times in my twenty-nine years of life, their last journey being five years earlier. Mother and I had made the trip from Boston to Ennis four times as well over the years, bringing my father along with us, and Carl, so I guess we were even in effort. Still, I was glad they were planning on staying through Christmas. That'd give them enough time to recover before the long trip back home. Strange how I'd never given any thought to my grandparents nearing the end of their lives. I suppose I'd taken for granted that they'd always be there for me—for my mother and father. But ever since my grandmother asked about my willingness to accept their homestead *when the time comes*, their mortality had been buzzing about my mind like a pesky fly does your plate of food at a picnic. It was hard to imagine a day when they'd become only a bouquet of fond memories.

We spent much of the first two days of travel together, seated in one of the many passenger cars, either in a section of four seats where two seats faced the other two, with a large side window for viewing, or at a table for four in one of the dining cars, all the while watching the green ranchlands of eastern Texas bid us good afternoon, the thundering skies of Arkansas put us to bed, and the warm sun and rolling forests of western Tennessee kiss us good morning. The night of the second evening, as our train rode the border between northern Tennessee and southern Kentucky—the Appalachian Mountains on either side of us—and while we dined on something resembling baked chicken but tasting more like roasted rat, I noticed a familiar fella walking the aisle toward us, a tall confident man in a spiffy suit, with a fedora in hand and a folded newspaper under one arm, a smile and low "Hello" for every passenger that looked his way. Turns out he recognized me too because he extended a hand and said, "How ya doin', slugger? Been awhile."

"Hey Max!" I said, rising and nervously shaking his hand, wondering to myself if his offering of peace was just a distraction to keep me from seeing his left fist coming at my face. "How you been? Still pitching for Brocton?

"No. Gave up professional ball a few years back."

"No kiddin'! Wow! Never imagined that! Here, have a seat," I said, motioning with my arm for him to slide in next to my spot, directly across the table from my grandparents.

"Okay, but only for a few minutes. My girl starts to wonder if I don't make it back in a *reasonable* amount of time." His manner reminded me of a greasy worm that squirms when held for too long.

"Max, these are my grandparents—from Texas."

He reached across and shook my grandfather's hand, then rose as best he could behind the table to kiss my grandmother's hand, causing her to blush. "Nice to meet you, Grandparents from Texas. Max Trotter. Pleased to know ya."

"Max and I played the bush leagues together."

"Oh? Were you teammates?" Grandmother asked.

"No!" Max and I said simultaneously, as if we wouldn't be caught dead together, prompting a curious look from both my grandparents.

"No, your grandson took me for three runs one game—"

"Four, I think it was," I reminded him.

"Whatever," Max said to me out of the corner of his mouth. "Laird here made a fool of me one day during a game in Lynn. Of course, he couldn't stop there. He then had to pulverize me with his knuckles, breaking three of my ribs in the process."

"Gee, Max, I'm awfully sorry about that. Three ribs, huh?" I said, a sick pride rising inside me.

"And I'm awfully sorry for throwing the fastball at your noggin."

"You didn't?" My grandmother said, aghast.

"Oh, I missed. Don't you worry. I'd never intentionally mess up your grandson's pretty boy looks.

"Three ribs?" I asked again, more to myself this time.

"That's right, handsome. Aren't you proud?" Max said.

"Kind of," I muttered.

"Laird!" Grandmother said. "Really!"

"Just fooling, Grandma. Say, Max, if you aren't playing anymore, where're you at these days?"

"I didn't say I wasn't playing anymore, just not playing professionally. Been playing for Johnson's Mill—where I work."

"In Hartford?"

"That's the place. They've got a corporate team. Local stuff."

"Yeah, now that I think of it. Some of those corporate guys are pretty good, I've heard. How you holding up?"

"Doin' alright. Work in their sales department...pitch a few games each month. If I win the boss'll kick me a bonus. It works."

"How ya fixed for dough?" I asked, leaning over to reach into my back pocket, acting like I had some dough to give.

He placed a hand on my pocket arm. "No need to feel guilty, pal, so put away the sugar. If I could have taken your head off that day I would have. Believe me. No, thanks anyway. Sales are good. Like taking candy from a baby, honestly. No, this sales stuff isn't bad. Pretty easy with my chops. Even got a sweetheart pressuring me for a ring. How'r you doin'? Heard you're with the Braves now."

"One of their minor league affiliates—the Hartford Bees."

"That's right. I do seem to recall catching a couple games. You didn't do so hot in those games, if I recall correctly. O-for-four in one game I saw. Gave up nine runs too. Such a shame." Max said, his own sick pride betraying him. "Oh, I forgot to tell you. They found one of your stray knuckleballs floating in Boston Harbor last week." He scratched his oily head. "oddest thing."

"Very funny."

"Anyway," he said, flicking his hand as if shooing me away, "Off with ya. My gal's probably loading her gun about now."

I slid out of my seat, allowing him to stand. "Mr. and Mrs. Grandparents from Texas, it's been a pleasure. Laird, it was nice chatting with you again. I wish you all the best in your future battles."

Max then bowed before us, took a few steps backward, and with the swish of his hat, turned and trotted for a distant door, like a Musketeer having just addressed the King.

THAT EVENING, WHILE standing in the aisle of my sleeping car just in front of my berth, the curtain pulled back and my hands ruffling through my bag, which rested on my mattress, the car abruptly swayed as the train made a sweeping turn away from Tennessee and northward toward Virginia. The jolt caused my bag to flip on its side and me to have to grab hold of the bunk rail above mine to brace myself. When I turned the bag upright again, there lay the book Mother had handed me upon leaving Boston. I'd forgotten about it until that moment. I looked over the massive brown, leather bound book the way one would a completely foreign object never before seen. The book was old but distinguished looking, the scuffed leather a burnt sienna and imprinted with a floral design, worn at the edges, the title framed in gold-leaf, which across the front read, *Tennyson,* and on the spine read, *Tennyson's Poems.* The loose binding and dented corners led me to believe that my mother, and others before her, had read this 700-page antiquity often. Upon thumbing through the pages I discovered their cream color had begun to brown to a color resembling hot tea splashed with milk, their accompanying illustrations, once colorful sketches, now dull like distant rainbows. The book even smelled old, like an historic home coated in dust or an aged red wine that had spent its adolescence in an oak barrel. I'd never been much of a reader, but as books go, it was quite impressive and inviting.

I found myself moments later reclining on my bunk, curtain closed, window cracked open to allow whiffs of Virginia Pine into the compartment, my fingers flipping through the pages of the book, poems with titles like *The Lady of Shalott, Locksley Hall, Morte d'Arthur,* passing quickly before my eyes, *The Princess* and another named simply, *Maud* following close behind. But the one my eyes and fingers stopped upon that first night of reading had the heading *Ulysses*, which took up three pages and seemed to be about the mythical Greek hero, Ulysses, fighting against discontentment, old age, and time, the desire to continue exploring still in his heart. The first time through it left my senses dry and parched, like having just trekked days through the scorching Sahara without water. But after several readings I found myself intrigued and sympathetic to Ulysses' plight.

> *How dull it is to pause, to make an end,*
> *To rust unburnish'd, not to shine in use!*
> *As tho' to breathe were life! Life piled on life*
> *Were all too little, and of one to me*
> *Little Remains: but every hour is saved*
> *From that eternal silence, something more,*
> *A bringer of new things…*

Those words resonated within me, the thought of my grandparents chasing heaven, making perhaps one last journey to a faraway place—to one last *something more, a bringer of new things;* thoughts of my father enclosed by the words, *How dull it is to pause, to make an end, to rust unburnish'd.* But there was another verse that stirred my soul, this time with reflections of my mother:

> *Tho' much is taken, much abides; and tho'*
> *We are not now that strength which in old days*
> *Moved earth and heaven, that which we are, we are;*
> *One equal temper of heroic hearts,*
> *Made weak by time and fate, but strong in will*

To strive, to seek, to find, and not to yield.

If those words ever described anybody, they described my dear mother, her resolute spirit defying her weakening body, her heroic heart standing fast against fate. I read those last three lines again:

One equal temper of heroic hearts,
Made weak by time and fate, but strong in will
To strive, to seek, to find, and not to yield.

I laid the book open upon my chest and closed my eyes, meditating on those last lines. In that moment, at rest on my bunk, Tennyson's poignant lyric within me, I realized how much I loved my mother—for who she was, and whom she refused to become. She would never surrender my father willingly; never accept that his infirmity had made him worthless. To my dear mother, to her that sees beyond the injustice, to that stalwart, unbreakable heroine who constantly lays hold the flickering flames of hope, to her it is always, *Tho' much is taken, much abides*

CHAPTER ELEVEN

When I woke the third day, it was with a start, as though I'd missed something very important during my sleep. Suddenly I realized that we might have passed Harrisonburg and little Billy during the night. I slipped my feet into a worn set of Cole Haan dress shoes, tucking my button down shirt into my suit trousers with only one hand as I ran down the corridor of the sleeping car in search of a conductor, straight past my grandparents—who scooted to the side to let me pass, a concerned look on their creased faces—all the while trying unsuccessfully to don my suit jacket without bumping into things, finger-combing my hair simultaneously.

"Have we already passed through Harrisonburg?" I asked the conductor I'd located three cars up toward the engine. He was a short slender man in a blue suit and matching cap, fortyish, his face pocked by childhood acne, stubble kept on the jaw and neck to hide a bad case of razor bumps. Despite those blemishes, he had a kind face, his dark round eyes wide and attentive.

"No, sir. Should be passing through in say..." He looked at his watch, "eighteen minutes."

"Thank goodness. Thought I'd missed it. Thank you." I turned and started walking back to my train car when what he'd said hit me like a knuckleball to the head. "Wait," I said, walking back to the man. "Did you say 'pass through'?"

"Yes, sir."

"You mean we aren't stopping there to resupply like before?"

"Harrisonburg is only a resupply point on the southbound leg, sir. Northbound stops in Winchester, Virginia, another hour up the tracks."

My gut suddenly turned within me, the way it does when I'm about to regurgitate my lunch. I hadn't decided until we boarded the train back in Ennis that I'd stop and check on Billy. Something in me told me his aunt would never come for him. She'd left him on his own for two months already. Something must have happened to her. Why else would she not come? And I knew the boy's heart was breaking over the loss of his parents, that he was alone and scared and yearning for some semblance of that love his parents had given him while alive. That's why I didn't promise him I'd be back, only that I'd try—one of the reasons anyway, the other being that familiar fear of caring. But every time I thought of that young boy, the way he came aboard the train in search of food, his clothes tattered, his good manners not yet corrupted by hardened street life, his sweet voice crying out, "I'll see you again, Laird!" a tenderness I never knew I possessed would swell within me, like a warm Caribbean tide lapping at my conscience, beckoning me to wade in.

Just then my grandparents joined us.

"Laird," Grandfather said, "Is everything okay?"

"Sir," I said to the conductor, desperation in my voice. "Is there any way, any way whatsoever this train could stop in Harrisonburg?"

He shook his head, smiling sympathetically. "I'm sorry, sir. We have a schedule to keep. Passengers are depending on us to reach—"

"I understand—I do. But I just need twenty minutes."

"Sir, I wish we could help you but it isn't possible."

"Laird," my grandfather interjected, "What's this all about?"

"A little boy." Once again to the conductor, I begged,

"Fifteen…just fifteen minutes to run and do something very important."

"Sir…" He didn't know what else to say.

"Can you at least ask the engineer—the driver?"

"I can try, sir, but I know he'll say no."

"Please. Tell him it's important. Tell him there's a little boy—an orphan boy who'll be crushed if I don't show up. Will you tell him that? I'm sure he'll understand."

Reluctantly, the conductor turned and headed for the engine.

"Who is this boy, Grandson?" my grandmother asked, perplexed.

"A boy I met on the train out. He came aboard looking for food. A young kid, frightened and alone."

"Well, where are his parents?" Grandfather asked.

"Dead."

"Oh, that's a shame," Grandmother said, her hands joined over her heart. "Poor boy."

"Where is he now?" Grandfather asked.

"I'm not sure. I'm hoping at Saint Anthony's with Father Michael, where I left him."

"What do you intend to do with this boy, Laird?"

"Just check on him. Show him somebody cares about him. Let him know he's not alone."

Just then the conductor returned. With a cock of his head, he said, "Okay. You'll have twelve minutes. That's how much we're ahead of schedule at the moment."

"Thank you, so much!" I grabbed the man's hand and shook it enthusiastically.

"I've been instructed to caution you that if you are not back within twelve minutes we will leave without you. So if there's any question about it, you might want to take your bag with you."

"I'll be back. Thank you. Thank you, so much."

As promised, the train came to a stop in Harrisonburg, Virginia and I was allowed to depart—the only one allowed. I ran as fast as I could in my slick-souled dress shoes, sliding into the corners and accelerating out—the way a champion driver does his dirt-track racecar—until I found myself standing on the steps of Saint Anthony's, stopping briefly at the sudden realization of what I was about to do—let myself care. But when I entered through the large wooden doors, I found no one inside—no Billy, no Father Michael. I searched the pews thinking Billy may be asleep on one of them, but I found no sign of him. My heart sank as I turned back up the aisle and out the front doors, standing on the steps and scratching my head. Just then I heard voices—young boys—coming from around the corner, toward the back of Saint Anthony's. I followed the sound to find a group of boys playing baseball in an overgrown field, their catcher none other than Father Michael. I walked toward them when I heard the most wonderful words come from centerfield.

"Laird!" Billy hollered, running toward me. The game stopped and Father Michael, still in his black religious clothes, rose from behind home plate to remove his catcher's mask and watch our reunion. "I knew you'd come! They didn't believe me," Billy said, leaping into my arms and catching me by surprise. "But I knew you'd come back!"

I held the boy in my arms, awkwardly, the way a new father holds his baby for the first time, his small legs wrapped around my waist, his small arms around my neck, his small head on my shoulder. "That's great, kid. Great to see you again." I put him down at my feet, his head coming to just above my navel. "How ya been, kid?"

"Fine! Father Michael's been teaching us baseball!"

I addressed Father Michael who now stood beside us, as well as sixteen other boys, some teenagers. "You did this?"

"I've been reformed," he said with a grin. "It's been fun, actually."

"Wow! It's a miracle! This is great! Where'd these boys come from?"

"Seems helping Billy inspired me."

"All these boys sleep with you at the church?"

"Not all, but a few. Most live locally."

I glanced down at Billy before asking Father Michael, "His aunt never showed up, huh?"

Father Michael pursed his lips and shook his head.

"No word at all from her?"

"None."

"Well, do you have a phone number for her? Anything?"

"Just an address. Number 15, Gosford Lane, Cincinnati, Ohio."

"Have you tried writing to her?"

"Father Michael did a while back. No word yet."

I sighed. "Well, the mail's slow sometimes. Maybe you'll hear something soon." I could tell by the way he bent his lips that he wasn't expecting a response. "You think I could have a few minutes with Billy? My train leaves in about," looking at my watch, "eight minutes."

"As you wish," Father Michael said, raising a hand next to his head and rotating his hand as if rounding them up. "Boys, let's play ball!"

The boys followed Father Michael back to the field while Billy and I strolled off to the side. "So you've got it good here, now?"

"It's okay."

"Well you've got friends now…baseball…a place to sleep. That's pretty good, isn't it?" I asked but knew nothing would ever replace loving parents to an orphaned child.

"Yeah," Billy said, looking down, kicking at the dirt with his Converse. "It's okay. Why do you have to leave?"

"Oh, well, my wife, she's waiting for me back in Connecticut. I've been gone for two weeks. She's pregnant."

"She's going to have a baby?" Billy asked, excited at first before turning sullen. "Is it a boy?"

"I don't know. We have to wait and see."

"Do you want a boy?"

"Well, sure. What father wouldn't want a son to...look, kid...I know things are hard for you right now, but you hang in there. Don't let this world beat you." I checked my watch, before lifting Billy's face by his chin with my fingers, tears staining his cheeks. "Ah, don't do that, little fella. Please. I can't leave you this way, crying and all." I looked in the direction of the unseen train upon hearing the horn blow. "Billy," I said, kneeling to look him in the eyes. "I have to go, Son. The train's calling me. I'll try to come back and see you."

"No you won't. You'll forget about me when you have your baby."

"Kid, you're breaking my heart here." I wiped his tears.

"It's okay, Laird." He wiped his sniffling nose. "It's okay."

When he said that, I thought about the story Janie had told me, about how I bumped that little boy holding out one of my foul balls for an autograph, how he let me off the hook by saying, "It's okay, Laird. Maybe you can sign it next week in Scranton." I looked over Billy's shoulder at Father Michael far off, beginning to panic knowing full well the train and my grandparents were about to leave without me. I stood and grabbed Billy's hand, calling out, "Father Michael!"

He rose from his squat behind home plate and looked at me, raising his catcher's mask onto the top of his head. "Yes, Mister Young?"

"You mind if I borrow Billy here for a while—for the holidays?"

"But how will you get him back?"

I glanced down at Billy's bright face, a smile big and white, like an elephant's tusk. Then I turned toward the train, walking briskly, calling back over my shoulder, "I don't know! I'll figure something out! I'll call you!" Then to Billy, I said, "Quick. Run inside and get your bag before the train leaves without us."

Billy ran into the church by way of the backdoor, reappearing a few minutes later at a full gallop and dragging a duffle that seemed too heavy for his eight-year-old arms. I went to help, taking up his bag, then slinging Billy up and onto my back by his arms, making sure his legs and arms were wrapped around me tightly before I ran like a deer toward the angry bellowing horn in the distance, my mind stuck on one disturbing thought: What do I tell my grandparents? *What do I tell Janie?*

AT DINNER THAT night, little Billy stole the show, captivating my grandparents the way one of their newborn frolicking foals might do as it joyfully leapt and bounced about, having just learned what legs were for, Billy's good manners on full display like a blinking neon sign. He'd even asked me earlier if he could freshen up before eating. "Does this train have a bathroom? Mother said I should always wash my hands before eating. And to never wear my hat at the table. She said a good boy presents himself for dinner like a gentleman."

How many times had I sat down to eat with dirty hands? Plenty. But he was right and I followed his lead, washing up and combing my hair before dinner—like a gentleman.

"Tell me, Billy," Grandmother said enthusiastically, "Have you ever been to Boston?"

"Boston?" he said, more like a question. "No, ma'am. Is it a fun place?"

"Oh, it's delightful if you like big cities. Wonderfully tall buildings, the Atlantic ocean, Museums, historical sites."

"Delightfully wonderful traffic, noise, and crime," Grandfather added.

"Don't listen to him, Billy. The city is what you make of it, just like anywhere else," Grandmother reached across the table to give Billy's hand a pat. "You'll see."

"Don't forget Fenway and Braves Field," I offered with a wink. "The only history little Billy here needs."

"You and baseball," Grandmother said. "There's more to life, you know?"

Glancing down at Billy, I said, "I'm beginning to see that."

"Can we go see a baseball game?" Billy asked, excitedly.

"Sorry, pal. It's the off-season. But maybe we can swing by Braves Field sometime. See what kind of trouble we can get into."

"That would be swell!" Billy said with a mouthful of steak, before placing a hand over his mouth. "Sorry."

"Have you ever seen a more polite boy?" Grandmother asked. "Your parents must have been fine people."

The thought of Billy's future fell upon us like a dreary fog, resulting in us sitting silent for a long moment.

"What's your full name, Billy?" my grandfather asked.

Without hesitation, he answered, "William Bradford Sunday, sir."

"William Bradford Sunday? That's quite a famous name, young man, did you know that?"

"Yes, sir," Billy said matter-of-factly. "William Bradford came to America on the Mayflower."

"Indeed," Grandfather said, somewhat taken aback. "He was a very important man to this country. How is it you came to be named after him?"

"My mother, she said we're related on her side."

"Is that so? Well, now, you don't say."

"He was my very great grandfather—but more greats than that. Dad said it's not true, though."

"Well, let's say it is. That's something to be proud of, William, or do you prefer Billy?"

"Billy, please. Mom used to call me William, mostly when she

113

got mad."

"Billy it is. And how about that name 'Sunday'? How'd you come by that one?"

"My dad."

"I see. So you call yourself Billy Sunday, then?"

"Yes, sir."

"Well, now, Billy Sunday is a famous name too. Did you know that?"

"It is?"

"Indeed. Billy Sunday is a respected man—a well-known travelling evangelist."

"Evanga-is?"

"A travelling preacher. You should know that, Laird. He was once a professional baseball player."

"It's a sin to lie, Grandpa, especially to little boys. You of all people should know that," I said.

"It's true! Played for the Chicago White-Stockings."

"When? What position?"

"Eighteen eighties. Played centerfield, I think."

"Billy Sunday? Billy Sunday the evangelist, the guy who holds those big tent revivals? He played centerfield for the Chicago White Stockings? Get out."

"Look it up if you don't believe me. Better yet, ask your mother."

"My, my," Grandmother said. "We're in the presence of American royalty!"

"I am?" Billy asked, proud as an altar boy who just spiked the holy water.

I bowed from my seat. "At your service, M'Lord."

Later that evening we retired to my bunk. The conductor said children under ten years of age were allowed to ride for free, but Billy would have to share my bunk because all the sleeping berths were taken. I didn't mind, though. Billy was about as thin as a pencil and only about four feet tall. How much space could he take up? At first we sat on the bed, our legs and feet in the aisle, taking stock of Billy's sparse possessions, which he'd dumped on the mattress between us, the dull brown top-blanket now peppered with colorful keepsakes and clothes. It's amazing to me what a young boy finds important enough to keep. There was the flat newsboy hat he was fond of wearing away from the dinner table; another pair of jeans that looked small enough to be my keychain; and three pair of crew socks, because Billy's father told him, "It's the feet that move the man, so take care of them." There was a pencil with teeth marks up and down the shaft; a yo-yo with a looped knot at the end of the unrolled string; some small stones, the flat kind you skim off the water's surface; a baseball and kid's leather glove, the sweet spot of the glove beaten into a dark brown; a few pieces of rock candy of varying colors, each with pocket lint stuck to it; a chrome coach's whistle attached to an olive green cotton lanyard; a man's gold watch, which I assumed belonged to his father; and a women's hairpin, a fancy long-toothed type made from tortoise shell, no doubt an heirloom from his beloved mother. And there were three cherished baseball cards, each inserted into a form-fitting clear plastic sleeve.

The top card was from 1937, what they call a four-in-one, an amazing card that had the images of four prominent New York Yankees—Lou Gehrig, Tony Lazzeri, Vernon Gomez, and Joe DiMaggio. "Say, kid, if you're a Yankee fan I'm gonna have to take you back to Saint Anthony's." Underneath that card was a 1939 rookie card for Ted Williams, left fielder for the Boston Red Sox, swinging the bat and wearing number nine. "Okay! Now we're talking! Had me scared there for a minute. I bring a Yankee fan home to my mother and whew! I'm a goner!" Billy looked confused. "What's this last card? Hey! Harlond Clift! Great find, kid! All-Star third baseman for the Saint Louis Browns! Where'd you get these, Billy?"

"They were my dad's."

"Oh," I said, like a deflated balloon.

"It's okay."

"Well, your father sure knew his baseball cards. Was he a big fan of the game?"

"Not really. He just liked collecting things."

"Yeah? Like what?"

"I don't know," he said, looking down at his swinging legs and feet. "Just things."

"Do you have anymore baseball cards?"

"The landlord took them. Mom owed him money."

"Oh. The landlord took everything?" I could feel my blood percolating again but took a deep breath, then exhaled long and slow to calm myself.

"Um hum, except these cards…and the watch and Mom's pin. I hid those."

"Good for you, kid."

I could see he'd had enough of that sort of talk, so I stood, collected his things back into his bag, then tossed it on the foot of the bed, in the corner and out of the way. "Time for bed, young man. Scoot," I said, motioning him to slide onto the mattress, closest to the window. He did just that, laying his head on my pillow, his arms back behind his head, staring up at the top bunk like Huck Finn daydreaming on a riverbank, the only thing missing the piece of straw in his mouth. "Hey, what gives? I'm sleeping here too, you know. And that's my pillow."

Billy giggled and lowered his arms to his side, allowing me to slide in next to him, my inside arm now serving as his pillow. "Why'd you come back for me?" he asked all of sudden.

"Oh, well, I wanted to see you is all. See how you were getting on with Father Michael. What? You didn't think I would." That last bit I said knowing full well I'd had my own doubts at one time.

"No, I knew you would."

"Oh yeah? What makes you say that?"

"Because you have a good face," Billy said, giving a quick glance backward and up at me, smiling.

"Phew! Nobody ever accused me of *that* before."

"Well I think so," he said, now looking off, holding my arm as he lay next to me.

"Thanks, kid. Thanks a lot. Say, do you like poetry?"

He let out a loud giggle, the scoffing high-pitched kind that says, "Don't be stupid."

"No? Well humor me." I reached for Tennyson's book of poems resting on the windowsill of the compartment, opening it before flicking on the small reading lamp located above our heads. "This is good stuff. I mean it."

"Okay."

So that night, the night before I would have to face my mother and my wife, answer questions about Billy and why he was there, I read him Tennyson; I read him Tennyson's *The Charge Of The Light Brigade,* all the while wondering, once again, how in the world I get myself into these things!

CHAPTER TWELVE

Janie's first reaction upon seeing me reach back for Billy, lifting the eight-year-old lamb from the high train steps down to the concrete platform, was one of joyful surprise. She glanced down at Billy, then up at me with a curious smile before kneeling down to greet my young charge, my grandparents still aboard the train waiting for their cue, my mother standing off a bit to give Janie and me a private minute together.

"Well hello there, little man," Janie said, giving a pat on Billy's backward newsboy hat. "What's your name?"

"Billy Sunday," he answered, shyly.

"Why that's a fine name! Are you lost Billy Sunday?"

Billy looked up at me for help answering.

"Not exactly," I said, still holding Billy's hand in mine as Janie rose to my level again, her smile fading, her head cocked to the side like a kitten that's just heard a sound it doesn't understand.

"Not exactly?"

"He's here to spend the holidays with us." I studied her eyes to see if they'd betray her feelings at that moment, but nothing. She had her game face on, eyes fixed and steady on her opponent as he showed his cards. "He's an orphan."

I imagined her thinking me a fool, a pathetic, confused imbecile who in trying to make this boy's life a little better just made ours worse. I imagined her thinking, *I love this man but if I had a gun right now I'd shoot him! Take the insurance money and find me someone with a real job and a real brain!* If she was thinking that, though, she didn't let on.

Leaning down, the smile returning to her face and her hand extended in friendship, Janie said to Billy, "Well I for one am delighted you'll be joining us, Billy." He took her hand and she wrapped her other around it. "It'll be so nice to have some intelligent conversation for a change." That last bit she said glancing up at me out of the corner of her eye.

Just then my mother stepped up, her hands clasped in front at the waist of her long skirt, her sweater off and draped over them. "Hello, Son. Welcome back," she said, kissing my cheek before looking down at Billy, who now held my hand and Janie's. "You've multiplied since you left."

"This is Billy. He's going to spend the holidays with us."

"I heard. Looks like you went searching for answers but found your heart instead," she said with a wry grin. "Just call me Grandma, Billy."

I shook my head as if to say, "No, don't confuse him." She just laughed, though.

Her 'Grandma' comment reminded me that my grandparents were still on the train. "Oh, I'll be right back. I left something important on the train." I rushed back toward the steps of the train car we'd exited minutes earlier.

"Where're you from, Billy Sunday?" I heard my mother ask.

"Harrisonburg, Virginia, ma'am."

"Anything good we should know about that comes from Harrisonburg?"

"Me!" he said with a big smile. That made Mom and Janie laugh.

A moment later I was helping my grandparents down the passenger car steps and onto the platform. Billy pointed and said, "See what we brought you?"

They both turned and when they saw my grandparents they

rushed over, their faces falling on my grandparents' necks like burping babies, Mom weeping like a willow.

"What? But how?" Mom asked.

"It was Laird's idea," Grandmother said, wiping her wet eyes. "I'm so glad he thought to ask us along."

"Me too," Mom said, giving me an approving glance. "Seems he's full of surprises lately."

"You've got to watch that boy, Emily," Grandfather said before giving me a wink. "He's a crafty one. Always into mischief."

"Laird," Janie said, moving in close to me but hesitating before grabbing hold of me and burying her head in my chest. "I just don't understand you sometimes. One minute you're—"

"Heartless?"

"Sorry. But then you're so kind at other times."

"Are you mad?"

"No," Janie said, looking up at me with misty eyes. "Not mad. Happy. Confused a little too, I guess. But not mad."

"It's just until I can find his aunt—Billy, I mean."

"We can talk about him later. I'm just glad you're home."

BY THE TIME we arrived at our home in Hartford, night had fallen, its heavenly face beautifully plagued by a million twinkling freckles, the white iridescent moon straight above us. Both Billy and Janie were asleep in the front seat, Janie using her sweater as a blanket and resting her head against the passenger door, Billy with his little legs bent on the seat resting his head against Janie. I sat idling in the driveway for a long moment, secretly admiring them both, telling myself that though we looked like a family, we weren't; that Billy wasn't ours and would only be with us a short time. I didn't like the idea of giving him up to his aunt, but I'd have to when the time came; could Janie? Right then Billy was more like a visiting cousin to her, but in a short time he'd have her heart the way he had mine. Then what?

"All right, kids, we're home." I opened my door and the interior light flicked on, eliciting a disapproving groan from Janie. "I know but there's a big soft bed upstairs waiting for you." I helped Janie from the car then grabbed Billy—still asleep—and slung him over my shoulder, the way a fireman does a hose. After closing the car door and starting toward the house, I asked, "Where do you want to put Billy?"

"In the room next to ours," she said. "That way we'll be close by if he needs something. It's a big house. He could lose his way and get scared."

"Good thinkin', Lincoln."

Janie propped herself against the doorway of the spare room as I laid the young buck gently on the bed. He was a stomach sleeper just like me, one leg bent and one arm out, like one of those chalk outlines you see on the street at a murder scene. He was also a drooler, as evidenced by the wet spot on my shoulder, where his head had been. I unfurled the quilt at the foot of the bed and laid it over him, leaving his outstretched arm and shoulders exposed. I stood for a moment at his bedside, admiring the little guy when Janie said from the doorway, "Cute kid. Now what?"

"I don't know," I said, joining her in the doorway.

Janie walked away and into our bedroom. When I followed a few moments later she was already fetal on the bed, looking like a big egg with her hands clasped together under her head, legs pulled up close to her very pregnant belly, her bare feet crossed at the toes, her pink-painted toenails on full display.

I took off my coat, laying it over her as I kissed her warm cheek. As I walked toward the door she said, still in her fetal position, "I hope you *do* know what you're doing, Laird."

I went and sat next to her on the bed. "Just trying to give him the attention and love he deserves. Isn't that what you wanted me to do?"

Janie turned her head slightly to look up at me from the corner of her eyes. "Signing a boy's foul ball after a game is a lot different then bringing the boy home to live with us."

"I know. I know."

"Do you, Laird? You know that boy's going to develop affections—*we're* going to develop affections. That's a lot of affection that'll be crushed when his aunt shows up and takes him away."

I nodded in agreement. Billy was a good kid, sweet and easy to like, easy to love too, I suppose. It would be hard to let him go, but I would do my duty when the time came. I just hoped they could all forgive me. I placed my hand on her shoulder and then said, "Goodnight, beautiful."

"Um hmm," was all she said.

I went out to the car to retrieve our bags, which I dropped just inside the door upon my return, following my nose afterward—which had picked up the faint smell of freshly baked cherry pie—and found a whole pie resting on the countertop, still in the pie tin, its crust vented and golden brown, red cherry filling oozing out the vent slots. A moment later I had a quarter of that pie on a plate and was shoveling it into my mouth at the dining room table, the fingers of my free hand flipping through the two weeks of mail Janie had stacked on the table. The electric bill, water bill, and gas bill greeted me first, followed by several postcard-sized advertisements, one for a new diaper service in town, which I set aside figuring we'd soon be giving them a call. Underneath the stack lay the one-inch thick Sears catalogue, which Janie and I both liked. I flipped through the pages briefly when I noticed a letter resting against the flowered centerpiece on the table. Upon closer look I could see it was addressed to Laird Allen Young III—and it was from the County Draft Board.

I laid the letter down, took a couple more mouthfuls of pie, then shoved the plate away to take up the letter again, staring at it suspiciously like I would a gun I'd just found lying in the street, nobody around but me. At that moment a few thoughts went through my head, like bullets from that gun I'd just found in the street. The worst that could happen would be that the Draft Board denied my appeal and were shipping me off to war, where I would die or come home missing a few appendages. The best that could happen would be that they approved my appeal for some other reason than the one I'd given them. The bittersweet pill would be that the Draft Board granted my appeal on the basis of my cowardly excuse—that my father, the man I'd resented and so callously shunned my entire life, now needed my help. Next thing I knew my fingers were opening the letter.

Dear Mr. Young:

This letter is to notify you that after careful deliberation, the Essex County Draft Board has granted a deferment of induction under the classification 3-A, Men with Dependents-Invalid Parent. (See the enclosed NOTICE OF CLASSIFICATION card, which must be carried on your person at all times.) You are required by law to report changes in your status. Failure to notify this board of changes to your situation could result in criminal prosecution.

Sincerely,
Essex County Draft Board...

There was great relief that came in reading that letter, but also tears, not of gratitude but of shame. No, I did not want to go to war where I could die and leave my future child fatherless, or worse, come home an invalid like my father. Very few of those boys over there fighting in Europe or the Pacific wanted to go either, but they went. Their country called and they answered. Many were afraid but they answered. I ran and in the process shamed myself, my wife and mother, and worse, my father, whom I'd used as my excuse. That sudden realization weighed heavier on me than the fear of going, something I hadn't expected.

"Honey," Janie called sleepily from the top of stairs. "Are you coming to bed?"

"Be right there." I collected up the letter and hid it in my bag—inside the red tin box, atop the eight precious baseballs my father had bequeathed me, the sacrilege of that act completely lost on me as I headed up the stairs to my nice comfortable bed next to my loving wife in the safety of my own home.

CHAPTER THIRTEEN

When I woke the next morning I found Billy sitting on the bed licking his fingers and trying to press standing tufts of hair back into place, still dressed from the night before, his shoeless feet dangling off the side of the bed.

"Hi'ya, sport," I said from the doorway, my flannel pajama bottoms being pushed low on my hips as I scratched my upper buttocks, my own hair looking like I'd just freed it from the vacuum cleaner. "You okay?"

"I wasn't sure if it was okay to leave the room," he said, looking as hesitant as a fawn on its own in the forest for the very first time.

I walked over and sat next to him on the bed. "Billy, I don't know what your life was like before, and I'm sure this must all be pretty frightening for you, being here in this strange house with people you hardly know, but I want you to understand that while you're here this is your home, okay?"

Billy nodded and gave me a smile.

"You can stay in this room next to ours. Hang your pictures. Make it your own. It's your room now. Get comfortable." I smiled back. "Now how about you and I go down and make breakfast for Janic?"

He jumped up and nodded enthusiastically. "Can we?"

"Do you know how to cook?"

Billy shook his head, the look on his face saying "Uh oh."

"We'll figure it out together, then," I said, my arm around his back as I led him through the door and down the stairs to the kitchen, where we proceeded to make pancakes with chopped strawberries on top, and crispy strips of bacon to go with them. We'd planned on taking it up to Janie in bed but she surprised us by sneaking into the kitchen just as we topped off the pancakes with strawberries.

"What's this?" she asked, peeking her head around the cabinets for a look at what we were up to at the kitchen island. "Smells delicious!"

"Janie, we were just bringing this up to you. Now you've ruined it."

"Surprise!" Billy shouted, jumping and hopping like a sugar-loaded kangaroo.

"You're so sweet, Billy! Thank you!" Janie placed her hands over her mouth.

"Do you like pancakes?" Billy asked.

"I love them," she answered, swiping a strawberry off the top and nibbling it, her eyes wide at the sight of flour splashed across the countertop, the bowl still containing pancake batter, the skillet of bacon grease still popping atop the lit burner, which Janie turned off. "Does breakfast come with you guys doing the dishes or is that another surprise I have in store?"

"Billy has volunteered to do the dishes."

"Huh?" Billy said.

"I'm kidding. I'll do them."

Right then Janie saw her cherry pie. "Laird Allen Young! You ate my pie!"

"So. I thought that's why you made it." Billy looked at me and I shrugged.

"Not for you! For the Millers up the street! June paid me to bake her one for their Thanksgiving dinner, you dope!"

"Oops."

"Ugh. Okay. I still have time to bake them another," she said, pulling ingredients from the cupboards and refrigerator, shoving our breakfast dishes into the sink with one swipe of her arm.

"What about your breakfast? It'll get cold."

"You guys eat it."

"You don't want your pancakes," Billy said, more surprised than dejected.

"I do, sweetie." Janie knelt down and kissed his cheek. "And I'm so happy you made them for me. But my *husband*, whom I love more than anything right now, sort of put me in a pinch. Understand?"

Billy nodded.

"Great!" Janie stood and shooed us toward the dining room, handing us the plate of pancakes and bacon and a couple of forks. "Now if you two will leave me to it, I'll get this pie baked and delivered, hopefully leaving enough time for me to prepare the food we'll be taking to your mother's this afternoon."

I fed Billy a forkful of pancakes while still standing, much to his delight. "Would have been nice just to have stayed at her house last night," I said, biting into a crispy strip of bacon. "Not enough room, though, not with my grandparents there."

"Well it's worth the inconvenience. Inviting your grandparents back—actually getting them to come all this way—you made your mother and me very happy...and your father."

Despite my new desire to learn more about my father and his previous life before his head injury, it still bothered me when Mom and Janie spoke as though he could convey his own feelings—tell us what he was thinking. Perhaps they were picking up on something I wasn't capable of hearing or seeing, like that sixth sense men say that women have, the sense that knows when something bad is about to happen, or something good, or the sense that tells them what you're thinking before you actually think it, as my grandfather playfully says. Whatever it was, whatever they thought they were seeing or sensing, to me it was still an illusion brought on by wishful thinking, their imaginations spinning threads of hope into a tapestry more pleasant to their mind's eye. The reality was much uglier. My father could not talk. He could not speak. He could not feed himself. He could not bathe himself, stand on his own, nor take himself anywhere on his own. His body had atrophied to the point that his skin clung to his bones like Saran Wrap under his clothes, betrayed only by his sunken cheeks and deep shadowy eye sockets, which made his face appear overly chiseled and elongated and old. That was the harsh reality both Janie and my mother suppressed, the way an afflicted adult does a tragic event from childhood, one too terrible to remember, too terrible to face over and over, every single day for the rest of their life.

Even then, I admired them both for their ability to see beyond my father's surface, beyond the decaying façade, seeing with their hearts instead of with those bitter truth tellers called eyes, communicating with my father through some alternative realm provided by God. I wondered why God hadn't seen fit to provide me that ability, that access to my father's thoughts and feelings. But then maybe he had. Wasn't I learning more about my father through the eight baseballs he'd given me? Wasn't God revealing to me more about the man and his feelings, his thoughts and ideals, through eight red and black-stitched, horsehide balls? And wasn't my father communicating directly to me through them? Wasn't he trying to teach me how to be a good man, a good husband, a good father? It sure felt that way; it honestly did.

AFTER BREAKFAST I took Billy outside to show him around. We lived in South Windsor, just above East Hartford and not far from Vinton's Millpond, a popular recreation area. Directly across from our house, on the other side of the street, lay the

Podunk River, a small ambling tributary of the larger Connecticut River that sashayed through downtown like a giant anaconda flaunting its girth. We walked over to the grassy bank of the Podunk, which at that time of the morning seemed to be fast asleep, just a dark green pane of glass lying flat and framed on two sides with grassy shore, the ends being pulled and stretched toward the east and west horizons like a single piece of taffy being fought over by two bickering children.

Underneath a large Red Maple I taught Billy how to skim rocks off the glassy river. At first he hardly got a single hop from his flat stones; they just plopped and sunk to the bottom. But I taught him it was all in the angle of the arm and shoulder, and in the action of the wrist. Guiding his shoulder and arm through the motion without throwing, he was able to see that the throwing motion should be more sidearm, the upper torso coming down a bit at the side with the throw making it so the release was on a similar plane as the water's surface. I then demonstrated, getting my stone to skip four times before sinking, impressing Billy to no end. He then tried it, hurling his stone sidearm and low, just as I'd taught him, getting two good skips from his stone before it disappeared underwater.

"That a boy!" I said, proudly.

"Let me try another! I'm sure I can get more this time!" Billy hurled his stone and this time got three short skips across the liquid glass. "See!"

"You're a natural. Pretty soon you'll be taking my spot with the Bees."

Billy giggled. "They don't let eight year old boys pitch in the majors. Even I know that."

"Minors," I corrected. "I don't know, Billy. Stranger things have happened. Though I think you'd have a hard time getting the ball to home plate. But hey, you could bounce your pitches in. The batters would just stand there dumbfounded. You'd strike 'em all out. Call you Billy 'The Bouncer' Sunday." I chuckled. "Wouldn't that be something?"

"Okay, but only if I can play for the Yankees."

He said it and took off running, with me fast on his heels acting like I was going to string him up. "Why you trader! I'll get you for that!"

I chased Billy back to our house and the garage, where he plopped down in one of the two Adirondack chairs I'd made before leaving for Ennis, Texas, their yellow pine arms, legs, and reclined bodies still unpainted and as naked as newborn twins. "Say, these are neat!" Billy said, laying back with a smile on his flushed face, his legs three inches off the ground, swinging like weighted wrecking balls. "I've never seen chairs like these. Where'd they come from? China?"

I laughed. "No, nothing as grand as that, kid. I made them myself, here in this garage."

"No foolin'?"

"Honest as a prisoner before the parole board."

"Is that honest?"

"No, I guess not," I said with a laugh. "Not always. But I am telling the truth," I said, rising and opening the garage door to show him my shop, a half-finished chair resting on the floor near my workbench. "See. Here's another I've been working on."

"Wow! Can this one be mine?"

"Sure. Why not?"

"Thank you! That's swell," Billy said, running his fingers over the chair's skeleton as he walked around it. "What's that?" he asked, pointing to a two-foot long, two-inch thick rough-sawn slab of pink Sitka Spruce lying on the bench, the bark still clinging to the edges. He walked over to get a closer look as I held it up, the surface partially carved, a nearby photo of Janie serving as the inspiration.

"What do you think?"

"Is that your wife?"

"Well, not yet, but I hope it will be soon. It's supposed to be a surprise for her birthday next week."

"How did you do this?" he asked, his curious fingers tracing Janie's carved face.

"With these." I pulled a rolled tool belt from the upper shelf and unrolled it on the bench before him, pulling out one of the chisels. "I just go slow and hopefully when it's finished it'll look like Janie and not Winnie-the-Pooh. I work on this when I'm feeling good. I build the chairs when I'm feeling...not so good."

He counted up the chairs before saying, "You must feel not so good a lot! Look at all these chairs!"

I had to smile. "Perhaps you're right."

Billy looked once again at the wood carving of Janie. "You're an artist!"

"Nobody ever accused me of that before. No, I'm just someone who loves his wife and wants to do something special for her."

"I'm an artist. Well, I want to be."

"Yeah? Got any drawings?"

"Not anymore...but I used to draw a lot."

One thing I noticed about Billy when he spoke was that his recollections were punctuated by "used to," and that bothered me.

"See," Billy went on, now pacing the garage, looking down at his feet that kicked at imaginary rocks. "I used to have this small sketch book. I kept it right here." He patted his right rear pants pocket. "My mom...she said to fill it with memories because memories can flutter away like butterflies, taking their beauty with them. She said if I didn't capture them somehow I'd lose sight of them."

"Your mother must have been a wise woman, Billy. You must miss her a lot."

"Yeah," he said, as emotionless as a nail.

"What happened to your sketch book?"

131

"Some kids beat me up and took it."

I shook my head to myself. "I'm sorry, Billy. I hope you got some licks in on the dirty rats." I found myself gritting my teeth in anger at the injustice of it all. "Forget that last part. It's not good to fight. Not unless you have to."

'That's what my dad said. He said try to walk away. If they won't let me, give it all I've got until I *can* walk away. Don't hurt anyone more than I have to—and never start it."

I nodded, thinking about my own immoral pugilistic tendencies. "I'll try to remember that too. Come on," I said, my hand around his shoulder. "Better get cleaned up for Thanksgiving dinner later."

"At Grandma's house?" he asked.

"You'd better just call her Ms. Emily."

"But she said—"

"I know what she said, but trust me, kid. *Not* a good idea."

CHAPTER FOURTEEN

We arrived at my parent's house later that afternoon to find my grandmother hard at work in the kitchen, whipping up a heaping bowl of mashed potatoes, steam rising from the top around a large scoop of melting butter. Next to her on the counter sat a large oven-baked, golden brown turkey being basted with its own juice by my grandfather, its aroma so delicious my stomach began to growl like a lion calling its pride home. In addition to the turkey and mashed potatoes, my mother and grandparents had made a plate of freshly baked dinner rolls, a mound of sweet cranberry sauce so big it rose above the rim of the bowl it was in by nearly two inches, yellowy-white cream corn, gravy with bits of turkey mixed in, long green asparagus, and Grandmother's creamy homemade butter. Somewhere amongst that feast hid one of Janie's apple-cherry pies, just crying out to be eaten. It was a feast prepared for a king, but one being fed to paupers. During the meal we chattered like chipmunks, catching each other up on our lives, and we ate like ravenous wolves two weeks deprived of a meal.

Carl joined us and helped tend to my father at the head of the table, all the while sharing stories of his life as a Mississippi sharecropper, prior to coming to work for us. The creases on Carl's dark face told their own stories, the creases on his forehead and at the corner of his eyes telling stories of hard work under the scorching southern sun, those on his cheeks telling stories of happier times, of laughing with family and friends around the fire, and of playing his harmonica, or "harp" as he called it, on the sagging wooden porch of his family's ramshackle cabin. Carl had always been a hard worker and his solid build showed it. But he walked with a slight limp, the result he said of a beating he'd taken from a drunken father while trying to defend his mother. He was just seventeen at the time and managed to hold off his bigger father for a time, but eventually Carl went down from a hard blow to the head. While on the ground his father stomped on the side of his leg, at the knee where some crucial ligaments were located. His leg eventually healed, but in a way that kept him from fully extending that leg. Carl said he bore no grudge against his father, and I believe it; that's just the type of man Carl was, a kind and forgiving sort to whom no offense could stick. His beard and curly hair had changed color over the years to a mixture of gray and black that seemed to suit him.

After dinner, when my distended belly threatened to expel the buttons from my jeans and shirt, my mother and I retreated to the study to discuss what I'd uncovered during my trip to Ennis, Texas. I'd brought the tin box with me and opened it, showing my mother the contents for the first time.

"These eight baseballs, I found out, are from a game played in Ennis, Texas on June fifteenth, nineteen o-two...between Corsicana Oil City and the Texarkana Casketmakers. During that game, the catcher for Corsicana hit, get this, eight home runs— eight home runs in a single game. Can you believe that?"

My mother picked up one of the baseballs, looking it over the way a detective would a suspected murder weapon. "And your father was there?"

"And my father was there."

"Wow. That's impressive."

"His name was Jay Justin Clarke. Played later for—"

"The Cleveland Naps," Mom said before I could finish.

"Caught a perfect game for Addie Joss in o-eight."

"That's the guy."

"The Naps called him 'Nig' Clarke, I think. Ty Cobb put Clarke on his best catchers list, though he had quite a few passed balls in his career if I remember correctly. Still, hard to argue with Ty Cobb and Addie Joss. And your father was there? These balls here?"

"Yep. Grandpa was there too. Said Dad shagged all eight of Clarke's home runs that day."

"Eight home runs by one player in one game," she pondered. "How'd the rest of team do?"

"The score was a ridiculous fifty-one to three. Everybody on the Corsicana squad was banking 'em that day. Grandpa said the right field fence was quite a bit shorter than the others and that's where Clarke put all his."

"Even if the fence was short, putting eight balls in the same spot in one game, home run or not, that's incredible hitting, don't you think? How many times did Clarke bat that day?"

"Grandpa recollects eight."

"Eight homers in eight at bats—eight hits in eight at bats. That's amazing."

I nodded in agreement.

"You say this game was played June fifteenth, nineteen o-two?" she asked, going over to the bookshelf and taking out *Spalding's Official Base Ball Guide of 1903,* before sitting again to flip through the pages. "This should say something about it." After a minute or so, she stopped on a page and scrolled down with her finger, as if her finger had eyes and was searching for a clue to its existence. "Here," she said, beginning to read the text.

Six clubs began the Texas League season of nineteen o-two on April twenty-sixth...

"Yada, yada," she said, her finger skimming ahead a couple lines before reading from the text again.

The schedule was made up to include games from April twentieth to September fifteenth, but the season's play had not progressed far before the Corsicana club obtained such a commanding lead in the race that the league at the close of the June campaign had to make a double season of it, the record of the first season's standing as follows…

She shook her head and motioned for me to look down on the page to where her finger pointed. "Look at this. Says of their sixty-six games played to that point, Corsicana had won fifty-seven of them, losing only nine games. That's incredible! That's a winning percentage of eight sixty-four!"

"That can't be right," I said, looking at her with a perplexed look on my face.

"You mean like eight home runs hit by the same player in one game? Corsicana was twenty-two games ahead of Dallas, the second place team. No wonder the league made them play a longer season."

"That's crazy! I'd have loved to play on that team!"

"Who wouldn't have?" My mother read on, as intrigued as I'd ever seen her.

The record of the Corsicana club of the league up to July, nineteen o-two, was one unprecedented in professional club annals.

"I should say so."

"Says the second season of the league ended August thirty-first with only four clubs. Looks like the two last place teams, Waco and Sherman, which must have been the Texarkana club, retired early."

"Must have been pretty humiliating for them, especially Texarkana. I couldn't imagine us getting whooped fifty-one to three. I'd have changed my name to John Jones and disappeared into obscurity."

"Looks like Corsicana didn't do quite as well against those remaining teams." She scoffed and grinned before saying, "They only finished those last forty-four games with a six eighty-two winning percentage, six games up on Dallas who was once again the bride's maid."

"The 'Miracle Braves' of fourteen only had a winning percentage of six fourteen."

"You can't compare the majors to the minors like that, but I get your point. Corsicana dominated. Must have been deep at all positions. Either that or nobody got hurt."

"Does it say anything about the game of June fifteenth, where Clarke hit the eight homers?"

She scanned the page, flipped the next few pages just to be sure. "No. Nothing."

"Strange. You think they'd mention at least something about the high score—about Clarke's eight home runs."

"They didn't have radio and television in those days so I guess information travelled slower. Still, somebody would have written somebody else about it." She closed the book. "Give me some time to do a little more digging."

"This is fascinating stuff. I'd have never even heard of Corsicana or that game without Dad's baseballs."

"Seems to me I've heard something about Clarke before, not just the perfect game he caught for Addie Joss, but something I think from your father. Seems to me he'd mentioned Clarke to me, maybe in one of his letters from France—from the war." She rose and headed toward the door, tapping her chin in thought, as if sending a Morse code message to her memory asking for help. "You go sit with your father on the porch, let me search through his old letters. I'm sure he mentioned Clarke in one of them."

My mother had the memory and constitution of a mule. If she

said my father had mentioned Clarke before in one of his letters, he did. What Dad said about him though remained to be seen.

WHEN I WENT outside to join my father, the immense carmine sun had just begun to settle beyond the distant horizon, like a wooden ship ablaze and descending to Davey Jones' Locker, its scarlet halo rippling across the heavens toward us, losing pigment until the wispy clouds above us were awash in amethyst and lavender. The entire property—trees, fences, barn and pastures—seemed to be blushing.

"Have you ever witnessed such splendor, Grandson?" my grandfather asked, his time-stricken face turned toward heaven in awe as he smoked his pipe. "It's truly remarkable."

"Indeed." I answered, stepping out to the edge of the porch, hands in my pockets to warm them against the evening chill, my eyes scanning the Master's canvas like a humble and adoring student. I turned back toward grandfather, who sat legs crossed on the porch bench, smoking his pipe, my father's wheelchair pulled alongside. I thought about us, about the three generations of men present, how we shared the same full name—Laird Allen Young— how we shared the same features, each with a strong chin and chiseled nose, the only things different our eye and hair color.

"How are you, Dad?" I placed a hand on his shoulder, turning around to watch the sunset with him, Janie and Billy chasing chickens in the yonder pen, Grandma and Carl leaning on the fence, laughing with Billy and Janie who laughed at themselves, at their inability to catch even one of the spirited birds.

"It's perfect, isn't it?" Grandfather admitted.

"Almost."

My grandfather knew what I meant and gave me a warm smile. "I love you, Grandson."

His words seemed to get caught in my throat, causing it to

tighten, my eyelids fighting to hold back tears. "I know," I muttered. "Thank you."

A few moments later, the entire chicken-chasing crew returned, Janie and Billy panting like horses returning from a long ride.

"That was fun," Janie said, kissing my cheek before taking a seat on the wooden porch rail, helping Billy up to sit next to her. I joined them as we now faced everybody else.

"I knew another young boy that used to have trouble catching chickens," grandmother said, patting my arm.

"Easier with a gun," I said.

"That's not the point, Grandson, is it?"

"No, ma'am. Guess not," I said laughing.

"Thank you."

My grandmother sat next to Grandfather on the bench just as Mother came out though the door, her cheeks stained by tears and eyes red. She had in her hands a stack of letters.

"Are you okay, Ms. Emily," Billy asked.

Mom laughed at herself. "Yes, I'm fine. A woman has to cry sometimes to release all those emotions she builds up. Otherwise she might one day explode." She held up the letters. "From your father," she said, leaning down to kiss his dry lips. "The best writer I know."

My grandparents scooted over on the bench, allowing Mother to sit close to Father.

"You found the reference to Clarke, I take it."

She nodded, pulling one particular letter from the pile, the envelope already opened and discolored by time, stamped with circular red and black ink, the postal marks of numerous countries the letter had to travel through to arrive in her mailbox. We all watched her as she slipped the letter from the envelope, swallowing hard as she unfolded it. "I'll try to get through this first part without, well, without exploding." She placed a gentle hand on my father's arm, which was tucked in close to his body, as it always was, only the elbow touching the armrest. His eyes stared off ahead, those too as they always had, only for the first time I seemed to notice a glimmer of emotion in his dark eyes, one of melancholy, like a man who dreaded returning to a painful place. "Here we go."

My Dearest Em,

How lost I am without you. I'm always so confident when you're around me, but here in this place, I realize how utterly weak I am, how dependent upon you I've been, and how dependent I am right now upon God's mercy. I am afraid, Em.

I immediately choked up upon hearing those words. I'd wanted to know for so long if he was afraid and there it was, from his own hand, and it broke my heart—it seemed to break every heart listening.

I'm not proud to say that to you, my beloved and cherished wife, but it's true, and if I cannot be truthful in this moment, in this place that sits on death's doorstep, then what good is my writing? I am not permitted to tell you where we are, but the enemy hems us in on three sides. We are entrenched so deep that I sometimes feel as though we are sitting on top of hell. If it weren't so bitterly cold and damp and muddy I'd be sure of it. But all is not lost, Em. I fight beside some of the bravest men God has ever created. We are a force, Em, a reckoning to be feared. The Germans outnumber us by some estimates seven to one, but each one of us in spirit is worth seven of them in the flesh. That makes the odds even and if they are even then they are in our favor.

My grandfather wiped his eyes, nodding simultaneously. "That sounds just like my boy."

Did I tell you, Em, about my arrival in Brest, our disembarkation point in France? Things run together and I cannot remember if I've told you this story, but we were in Brest for a few days awaiting orders and preparing our gear. Suddenly some guys from the Marines and Army got a game going, a real baseball game in France during the war! I couldn't believe it! A few of my guys from the 4th Infantry and I walked over to watch. They had wagons and trucks bumper to bumper for an outfield fence. It was great! That's when I noticed Nig Clarke, a ballplayer I'd idolized as a boy, only then he went by his real name, Jay. How he ended up in Brest, France and the war I don't know, but there he was walking up to the plate in his Marine trousers and undershirt like it was just a random day in his life, guys stacked four or five deep watching along the sidelines, some loudmouth on the mound, who I later discovered was Butch McAllister. He was a starter for Detroit back home. He called himself "Big Mac." Well, Clarke took some cuts at a few pitches and grounded out. The pitcher unloaded obscenities on Clarke. It seemed unfair so I stepped out onto the field, took Clarke's bat from him and asked him to wait so we could talk. I told him I had something of his that I wanted to return but that it was back in the States.

My mother shifted her teary eyes up from the letter briefly to make contact with mine, as if to say, "Here's what you've been looking for."

Then I hollered out to McAllister to put up or shut up. I stepped into the batter's box, pointed my bat to right field, calling my shot, then took a few practice swings, him laughing all the while. A minute later the ball sailed over right field fence.

"Right field?" I said to my mother and grandfather—to Janie. "He was thinking of Clarke's eight home runs over right field fence in nineteen o-two. He was paying tribute to Clarke."

I turned to Clarke and said, "Ennis." He smiled and started to come over to me, but just then we got our orders and had to go. I had so much I wanted to tell him but didn't get the chance. But I met him; I met my boyhood idol and I played baseball in France, during the war. That is something I one day hope to tell my son, that I played baseball with Jay Clarke of the nineteen o-two Corsicana team, in France during The Great War.

Well, my dearest, I must close for now. Please know that you are walking here beside me, your hand in mine, your courage leading me on. You are like the warm sun to me, as real and fragrant to me here as a meadow of wildflowers. I know you today as I knew you then, the night I left you behind.

Just then I saw it: My father unfurled the fingers in the hand connected to the arm my mother had hold of, stretching them out as if trying to grab something. Then he made a grunt, looking as though he was trying desperately to rotate his head, his blink-less eyes now moist, as if about to cry. "Did you see that?" I stood up.

Give my son a kiss for me. I long for the day when I can hold you both again in my arms.
Yours,
Laird

Walking over to my father, I said again, the others still wiping their tears. "Did you see that? Look! Mom, look at Dad's fingers—his eyes! It's like he's trying to get to you but can't!"

Everybody stood to see what I was seeing, my mother squatting before her beloved husband. She moved her hand cautiously toward his outstretched fingers, which were straining as if being held back. When her hand was within reach of his, his fingers clinched around them. I started sobbing. "Dad, are you…are you in there? Are you trying to talk to us?"

Right then a tear rolled down his cheek and he shook—ever so slightly—in his chair. My mother dropped to her knees, took his face in her hands, and as gently as a feather brushed against the skin, kissed his eyes, following his tears down to his lips, which she kissed repeatedly, saying in between, "Oh, my dear husband. My dear, dear, dear husband."

"Remarkable," Grandmother said, stunned, her hand over her mouth and eyes wet.

"A miracle," Grandfather added, one hand on Mother's shoulder, the other wiping his tears with a handkerchief. "An honest and true Miracle."

Well, we hugged each other, thankful for the blessed moment God had just given us, one born of an enduring love. Our miracle didn't last long, but it was as real as the spectacular sunset we'd witnessed and the Thanksgiving dinner we'd all shared.

"Is he broken, Ms. Emily?" Billy asked, walking up beside my mother, who still knelt before my father.

Mom giggled and hugged him. "No, baby. He's not broken, just misunderstood. *Very* misunderstood." Mother rose to her feet, stiff from age, my father's fingers still gripping hers, though by that point he seemed to have returned to his stupor, his fingers clinging involuntarily. "That was the last letter I got from him. Of course, now we know where he was when he wrote that beautiful letter— on the Western Front, in the Argonne Forest, part of *The Grand Offensive* that took the lives of over twenty-six thousand American men."

"The human spirit wasn't meant to experience such horrors," Janie said, wrapping her arms around me and burying her sweet face in my chest, the lilac-scent of Janie's shampoo still in her hair, which felt like threads of silk under my rough chin.

"Well said, dear," Grandfather commented. "The greed of kings and queens and tyrants has been the source of heartache for so many, but perhaps none have suffered more than the ones sent to fight their battles."

"Indeed." I kissed my wife's head before nodding. "Indeed."

"Yet none so deserving of honor than those sent to defend against that greed and tyranny," Mother countered, leaning down to kiss my father's head, holding her lips there for a long moment, as if taking in his very essence, as if waiting for her moist affection to penetrate to my father's soul.

"No, child," Grandfather said. "We mustn't forget that."

"Duty," I said, my eyes fixed on my mother who turned her eyes to mine, searching my inner being for any sign of contempt, begging the question: "Did you mean that?" When I gave her a nod, she smiled, an ever-faint beam of approval that said, "Now you understand, Son."

CHAPTER FIFTEEN

Grandmother told me later—when they all came the following week for Janie's birthday—that in the days following Thanksgiving, my mother had tried desperately to recreate the miracle, reading all my father's war letters aloud to him. When she failed to elicit any further emotional response from my father, she sank into a temporary despondency, the elation she'd felt when he'd reached for her disappearing like the white smoke that masks a magician's trick. Grandfather reminded her that though the moment she'd had with my father on Thanksgiving was as fleeting as a dream, her heart could cling to it as tightly as her husband's hand had clung to hers, and that the hope and faith she'd had for so long, the kind that believed she would one day have her husband back—the man she'd known before the war—had not disappointed her thus far. He encouraged her to keep believing, to let that miraculous moment lift her spirit higher, not to let its passing bring her down.

When I heard that, I imagined my mother recalling something similar she'd told me when I was a young boy, regarding a dog I'd had for only a short time, a stout and curly stray that had wondered onto our property, staying and playing with me for a few weeks before disappearing again and leaving me heartbroken. One day she found me standing on our dirt driveway, waiting for my four-legged friend to return, my face downcast. She asked, "What's the matter?"

I said, "He's gone."

"Yes, I know."

"But I don't want him to go. He was my friend."

"It's hard to lose somebody you love, Son," she said, "but would you have rather not had that joyful time with him?"

I answered, "No."

She said, "Then perhaps you should be thankful for the joy he brought you while he was here."

"But I'm worried about him, Mom."

She put her arm around me and said, both of us looking down the road, wondering I suppose where he went, "I know, boy. I know."

I believe now that my mother was speaking to herself, not me, reminding herself to be thankful for the joy my father had already brought her, and I believe she still worried about him. I suppose she always has and always will. That's what love does.

The week leading up to Janie's birthday, Billy and I spent most of our time in the wood shop, me carving my birthday gift to Janie, Billy learning to carve on a piece of scrap redwood he'd found in the bin. Several times I stopped and looked at my work, at Janie's wooden image, and each time I told myself: *Don't be a sap! Run to the store right now and buy her something that won't make her puke, that won't make her want to punch your lights out, something sweet like perfume or something that truly shows your appreciation for her, like diamonds or pearls. Seriously, who carves their wife's face into a block of wood? Not a husband that wants to live very long.* Each time, though, Billy would say, "You really are an artist! It looks just like her!" He said it so often his words lost their credibility. I thought he was just stroking my ego the way he might pet a cat or something—just before the dog eats it.

The night before Janie's birthday, Hartford got hit with an arctic blast that sent temperatures plummeting to eight degrees Fahrenheit. Any exposed water pipes froze, like the pipe to our outdoor water spigot, which rose two feet out of the ground near the garage. Upon awakening the next morning I peeked outside from our upper bedroom window to check the weather, the sky gray and overcast, frost laying like a sheer-white blanket over the dormant grass and fallen leaves, the frost like long Band-Aids stuck to the top edges of forlorn branches—and an ice fountain where the spigot had been, a tall arching band of frozen water that looked more like the urine stream of a relieved garden gnome.

"Are you kidding me?" I said in disgust.

Janie stirred under the covers, the only skin visible that on her half-covered face. "What's the matter, honey? Someone steal the car?"

"Pipe froze."

"To the car? That's weird."

I slipped out of my pajama bottoms and quickly into my jeans, shivering against the chill, the hardwood floor searing cold to my bare feet. Pulling off my shirt and searching the dresser drawer for an undershirt, I said, "Fire must have gone out too."

"That poor car. No wonder the pipe froze to it," Janie muttered.

"Not the car's fire, you goose, the house fire." I pulled the white undershirt on and then reached under the bed for my Georgia work boots and heavy cotton socks, which were stuffed inside my boots like wads of newspaper. Then I walked over to the closet and grabbed a button down flannel shirt and my wool pea coat before heading for the door.

Janie suddenly sat up in bed, like a corpse that just realized the casket was open. "The house is on fire?"

I scoffed. "No, Janie. There's no fire. Go back to sleep."

She let out a sigh before falling like a tree back onto the mattress, rolling over and pulling the covers over her head this time.

"I'll need to shut the water off for a bit so I can fix the broken pipe."

"I thought it was just frozen to the car," she muttered from under the covers.

"Never mind." Trying to have a conversation with Janie while she was half asleep was like trying to communicate with Daffy Duck underwater—nothing but air and bubbles. "I'll be outside."

It took me about three hours to fix the broken pipe, mostly because I had to wait for the hardware store to open so I could get a threaded section of three-quarter-inch galvanized pipe, a union to connect it to the old pipe still in the ground, and another union ninety-degrees to connect the replacement spigot to the end of the pipe. My family arrived just as I was connecting the new spigot to the new pipe, Mom pulling her four-door "woody" wagon into the driveway behind our Buick. She needed a tall wagon to haul my father and his wheelchair around, but she wanted "one that had a little class, not one," as she said, "that would make her look like a milkman or a plumber." Aside from it's long square shape, which resembled a half-loaf of bread, it really was a beautiful car—the front half a pearlescent blue, the same shade covering the rear fenders, the rest of the wagon adorned with glossy wood panels consisting of natural maple trim and mahogany inserts. And that woody had so many windows that no matter where you were sitting, the abundant light made it seem like you were riding in a convertible, only without the rush of air whipping up your hair.

While Carl and Mom got my father out of the car and into his chair, Grandfather walked over to see what he could do to help.

"Need another set of hands, Grandson?" He stood there, his tall lean figure hidden behind a long gray heavy coat, the collar up to keep the chill off his neck and ears, his hands buried deep in the coat's pockets, his face flush behind the puffs of breath coming from his mouth.

"Think I've got it, Grandpa," I said, standing and stretching out my back for a moment.

"Looks like a new hose bib. Broken pipe?"

I nodded. "Fixed now—I hope." I held up crossed fingers then opened the spigot before going to the main shutoff valve at the curb and turning it on. Water began to flow out of the spigot, spitting out heaping gaps of air for the first thirty seconds or so before steadying itself to a continuous stream. "Ah, success," I said as I walked back toward the others.

Just then Janie stuck her head out the side door and called to me, "Honey, something's wrong with the water! It's not working!"

"Just turned it back on! Try it now!"

"Fine work, Laird. Always feels good to fix things myself. A sinful pride, I suppose, but I don't think it'll be held against me later," he said with a wink.

"I do enjoy fixing things, just not with frozen fingers." I blew warm air from my lungs over my red fingertips. "I can't recall it ever being this cold here in early December."

"Have you ever thought of leaving the spigot on during cold days like this...just a trickle to keep the water from freezing? Always worked for me."

"No, but I will now. Thanks."

After helping take Janie's gifts and the food my grandmother had made inside the house, I went upstairs to clean up while my grandfather got a good fire going in the fireplace. When I came back down a rising wall of orange and white flames consumed the brick opening to the fireplace, the pleasant smell of burning logs emanating with the heat the inferno gave off, the glow from the dancing flames lending some much needed life to the drab living room. My grandfather stood with his back close to the fire, his hands extended behind him as if trying to grab hold of the warmth, Billy right beside him, emulating his elderly companion's every move.

"Seems my old bones don't feel as old when they're toasty," he said to me as I descended the adjoining stairs, my hair combed and glistening, my face clean-shaven.

"My old bones too," Billy said, trying to imitate my grandfather's distinguished-sounding voice. "I prefer them toasty."

"That makes three of us," I said, rubbing my hands together for warmth, glancing around at everyone, my father in his chair, which had been rolled into the spot we'd cleared for the Christmas tree we'd be buying and decorating later. My mother and Janie sat on the loveseat next to him, each holding a cup of hot chocolate, my grandmother seated in the rocking chair she struggled to scoot closer to the fire, trying not to spill her hot tea in the process.

"Let me help you with that," Carl said, rising from the sofa to go to her aid. Grandmother stood and he slid the chair forward until she was satisfied with its position to the warm flame.

"Thank you, Carl," Grandmother said, "for being a gentleman."

"You're welcome, Mrs. Young."

"How many times have I told you, Carl? Call me Rose. You're family, for goodness sake."

"Yes, Ms. Rose." Carl returned to the sofa.

"No, Ms. Just Rose."

"You're fighting a lost cause, Rose," Mother said. "I've been trying for twenty years to get Carl to call me Emily, but he won't. It's always Ms. Emily." She gave Carl a wink and smile. "Isn't that right, Carl."

"Yes, Ms. Emily."

"Well, God love you for your manners, Carl," Grandmother said. "Lots of young men out there today that could learn a thing or two from you. Seems a lot of them have lost respect for women—for their elders too."

"So, should we open gifts and then eat?" I asked, changing the subject. "Or would you rather—"

"Let's open gifts first!" Janie said, clapping her hands lightly and close to her chest like a giddy sea lion. "Of course, you all shouldn't have, but since you did, lets!"

That made everybody laugh. I went to join Carl on the sofa, his legs crossed, the mug of cocoa he held in his hand resting on his top knee.

Mom presented her gift first, wrapped in a medium-sized round box. "From us," she said to Janie as she handed it to her, patting my father's knee simultaneously. "It's a hat."

"That sort of takes the surprise out of it, Mom, if you tell her."

"Well, it's pretty obvious, isn't it? It is a hat box, after all."

Janie smiled excitedly, shrugging her slender shoulders before slipping the lid off. "I love hats. Besides. I still don't know what type it is." When she saw the hat, Janie said gleefully, "Oh it's so pretty!" She lifted the hat from the cylindrical box, careful not to damage its contoured shape. "What a lovely cloche hat! And so soft!" she exclaimed, caressing the grey felt fabric dome and matching felt flower with her thin fingers. "It's very fashionable, Emily. Thank you."

Janie stood to hug my mother and to try on the hat. I've never known about such things, but Janie knew just how to wear that style of hat, her long hair tucked up and under, the hat slightly cocked on the head, the flower side hanging lower with the narrow brim curved slightly down, the plain side higher with the brim curved slightly upward. Once Janie was satisfied with the fit, she struck a model's pose, slightly bent at the waist, her hands on her knees, head turned to flash a wink and kiss.

"You look lovely!" my grandmother said. "Just lovely!"

"I love it, Emily," Janie said, carefully lifting the hat from her head, shaking her hair free to brush across her back, the way a mare's mane does when she tosses her head, whinnying her mate closer.

Billy leapt to his feet and said, "Here!" his small, extended hands holding an even smaller box, wrapped only with a string tied in a bow, his smile wide and exaggerated. "And I'm not telling you what it is."

"For me?" Janie bent to accept his diminutive box, Billy placing it in both her hands the way a humble liege might place a Queen's scepter in her hands. "Oh, thank you, kind sir."

"You're welcome. Open it."

Janie pulled the string to release the knot, then opened the top flaps to reveal Billy's precious gift to her—his mother's tortoiseshell hairpin—the heirloom he prized so much. "Oh, Billy, sweetie. It's beautiful."

I honestly couldn't believe the boy's sincere and unselfish gesture.

"Do you like it?"

"I love it, but—"

"It was my mother's."

"It was? Oh, sweetie, you have such a good heart, but I can't take this from you. It wouldn't be right."

"Why not?"

"Well," she said, pausing to search for the right words. "Something like this, Billy, it's so valuable, more than you can understand right now. But later you might—"

"I want you to have it. Please." His round blue eyes were telling Janie that he'd be hurt if she didn't accept his mother's hairpin.

Janie looked at me, her eyes pleading for help, as if asking, "What do I do?" All I could do was purse my lips and raise my eyes, give a shrug of my shoulders. She looked to everybody else in the room and got no help. In one last desperate plea she looked at me again. This time I nodded.

Janie took Billy in her arms and pulled him close, the fire orange and bright behind them. "This is quite possibly the nicest gift I have ever received. I will cherish it for as long as I live, Billy. But please know, sweetie, that if you ever, for any reason, want your mother's hairpin back, I'll understand."

"Okay," Billy said, kissing her cheek and joining Carl and me on the sofa, plopping down between us.

"That was very big of you, young man," Carl said, eliciting a prideful smile from Billy.

"*Very* big of you," I added, mussing Billy's hair with my hand.

"Well, who could follow that?" Grandmother asked, tenderly.

"We had planned on sending you something," Grandfather added, his furrowed face turning a faint pink, "but then Laird came and invited us here. Things were so last minute we—"

"It's okay, Grandpa," I said. "That the two of you are here with us, that's the greatest gift you could give us."

"I agree," said Janie, going over and hugging them both. "I'm so glad you came."

"Where's your gift, Laird?" Billy asked me, as brash as a young lawyer interrogating his opponent's witness. "Are you afraid to show her?"

"No," I said. "Maybe."

"Show me what?" Janie said, creeping toward me like a tiger about to pounce on its prey, tickling my belly with her fingers to make me squirm away.

"Okay. Okay. Give me a minute. I forgot to bring it in." I slipped on my coat and hurried out the kitchen door and across the driveway to the garage, toting Janie's gift under my arm upon my return. When my grandfather saw the size of the wooden slab, he stepped away from the fire to let me pass. There in front of the fire I started the speech I'd been practicing in my head, all the while looking down at the image carved on the slab. "Sweetheart, each year I struggle with finding something worthy of your grace and goodness. This year, I decided the best thing to do was to..." Cocking my head, my eyes still on the image, on my work, "was to...was..." Just then I shook my head, slung the slab into the fire, then reached into my pocket to pull out a small necklace box covered in white felt. "I decided the best thing to do was to get you this." I flipped the box open to reveal a polished, sterling silver locket, a small, semi-flat, heart-shaped pendant with rounded edges and an inscription on the face that read: *My heart is yours...* "See."

"Laird!" Janie said, going around me and bending to try and pull the slab from the scorching fire.

"Let me get that," Grandfather said, gently moving her aside to pull the charred piece from the fire. Trying not to burn his fingers, he handed it to Janie. "Careful, it's a bit warm."

Janie shot me a disapproving glance before flipping the slab over to see the image. "Oh, honey, is that...is that supposed to be...?" She pointed to herself, the way a bashful child might when the teacher motions with her finger to come forward. She took a long look at my carving of her while I hid my face, tilting her head to the left and right, trying to get a better perspective. When she felt satisfied that she'd viewed the piece from every angle, Janie slung the slab back into the fire and snatched the box and locket from my hand. "I love it! Thank you, sweetie!"

Well, that just made Billy fall about himself with laughter, burying his head into Carl's side, who'd been sitting on the sofa quietly taking it all in. Billy's unrestrained laughter, infected by little snorts, made my mother laugh, then me, until all of us were laughing so hard that had the neighbors heard us they might have called the local asylum to have us committed.

About midday we had lunch and shared in Janie's birthday cake, an airy black and white angel food cake, tall and round with a hole in the center, a hole overflowing with freshly cut strawberries, the cake itself drizzled with vanilla frosting. Afterward, I went in search of the perfect Christmas tree, my grandfather, Carl, and Billy coming along to give their input. We took the Buick down to a tree lot in East Hartford where the rows of cut trees stood like debutantes in green hoop skirts awaiting eligible suitors. We courted them all but in the end selected a full-figured Scotch pine beauty for our bride, roping her horizontally to the roof of the Buick for the short ride home, the point forward making it look like we were toting a missile.

"It's beautiful, honey," Janie said upon seeing us bring the tree through the front doorway, "but it's so tall. Will it fit in here when we stand it up?"

Carl and I maneuvered around the furniture until we were where we could stand our lovely lady up again. "We can trim it if it doesn't," I said as Carl and Billy pushed the tree upright, my booted foot keeping the trunk from sliding. "There. It's perfect. No trimming required."

I bear-hugged the tree, lifting it and setting it in the stand, Carl hand-tightening the screws until the four screws put equal pressure on the trunk, holding the tree straight up and down. The space between the plaster ceiling and the tip of the tree seemed just enough to allow for the star.

"That is a lovely tree!" Grandmother said. "Don't you think, Emily?"

"Very nice," Mom said, glancing up while bending to put medicated drops in my father's eyes, wiping the draining excess with her thumbs. My father had developed a recent eye infection, something he seemed prone to since his condition limited his ability to blink. At that moment she caught me admiring her, nervously combing back her hair with her fingers as I stared. "What?" she asked. "Is something wrong?"

I smiled warmly, giving a barely-noticeable shake of my head. "Just watching you."

She was so good with my father. Tending to him seemed as natural to her as breathing, though I suspected it wasn't so easy at first. I imagined she had to grow into the role the way some of us grow into adulthood, one hard lesson after another. I imagined the strong face she put forward often found itself distraught and wrought with tears behind the scenes. I imagined she often felt very alone, my grandparents in Texas, her own parents deceased, me off doing my own selfish things. Though I hadn't shown much interest in helping her care for my father in the past, I now felt a growing inclination, and I felt suddenly envious of Carl, the kind-hearted man who acted more like a son to her than me, the man who had always been there to help her. I imagined her and Carl having a deep friendship, borne of respect and gratitude, a relationship whereby they shared secret pains and joys, wherein they laughed at the absurdity of life and a world gone mad over war, where she shared her disappointment with me as a son and her excitement over becoming a grandmother.

"Well stop looking at me," Mom said, standing to reposition my father's chair closer to the tree, as if he could somehow help decorate it. "It's making me nervous."

"Oh, mother. I do love you." I walked over and kissed her cheek, before helping the others pull decorations out of their respective boxes, glancing back over my shoulder to see her holding a hand to her cheek where I'd kissed her, a stunned look on her face. I smiled to myself: *I'm learning, Mother. I'm learning.*

CHAPTER SIXTEEN

That evening, with the heat of the fire warming the room, the fire's orange light softening the white incandescent light of the tall floor lamp, Janie, my grandmother and grandfather, Billy, and Carl took to decorating our Christmas tree, which we'd tucked into a corner next to the French window. Meanwhile, my mother and I sat in the adjoining dining room, the table still offering plates and bowls of tasty finger food, like assorted cheeses and crackers, sliced meats, potato chips, and leftover birthday cake, the cake but a third of its original size, the exposed portion of the plate covered in cake crumbs and smeared icing. We were discussing Jay Justin Clarke, the tin box between us on the table, the eight aged baseballs exposed and tucked in neat rows like eggs in a carton, my father wheeled in close, my mother still holding out that these recollections might trigger another miracle.

"Here's what I know," she said, recalling research she'd stored in her mind's filing cabinet. "Nig Clarke, that's what they called him mostly. Canadian born—a small town in Ontario. Amherstburg, I think. Seems he played for two minor league teams in o-two. He played four games with Littlecrock before jumping ship to play for Corsicana, which as we know had put together an ace club that year."

"Smart guy."

"No kidding. He batted left, and with Corsicana that year he had three hundred sixty-seven plate appearances, averaging three sixteen and getting a hundred and sixteen hits, eleven of those being home runs."

"Eight of those home runs during that one game in Ennis, Texas—with the shorter right field fence," I said, leaning in close, my elbow serving as a kickstand for my head, my free hand loading a cracker with sliced cheddar and roast beef and stuffing the entire thing in my mouth.

"Yeah but all the Corsicana guys put up big numbers that day. Clarke went eight for eight that day, but so did the second baseman, Alexander, and the left fielder, Pendleton. Out of Alexander's eight hits he parked three over the fence. Pendleton two. Morris the shortstop went six for eight, O'Conner the first baseman seven for eight."

"That pitcher for Texarkana must have had his head in the toilet."

"The owner insisted his son pitch, so the manager said, 'Okay, let him pitch.' Well, the score was so outrageous that its caused some doubt as to its legitimacy, primarily from people not there that day. Something about a teletype mix up. But those that were there at the game, some of the players, the scorekeeper, they attest to it, some under oath. They say the score was in fact fifty-one to three and that Clarke did pull those eight home runs over that right field fence."

"Looks like Dad was there too. These eight balls prove that."

Mom nodded. "Clarke bounced around the minors for the next few years until he moved up to the majors, landing for a brief time in Cleveland, who leant him to Detroit for a few games before bringing him back to Cleveland."

"In the same season?" I asked. "Cleveland to Detroit and back to Cleveland? Weird."

"The three games he played for Detroit, he made an impressive showing. In only seven at bats, Clarke got three hits, one of those a home run. In those three games he averaged four twenty-eight.

Guess the Naps were willing to help out Detroit with their slack catching, but not *that much*."

"That's pretty good, though three games isn't a full season. And he played catcher for those teams?"

"Yes, his entire career, except for a few games at first base with the Browns in nineteen eleven."

"Nineteen o-five was Ty Cobb's rookie year, wasn't it. He got to play with Cobb in Detroit for a few games. That's pretty nice."

"Clarke caught two games for Detroit, not sure about the third. But he finished the season with the Naps in Cleveland. Played there for the next five years before being traded to the Saint Louis Browns in nineteen eleven. His major league career overall was just average, but he did have some high points. As you know he did catch that perfect game for Addie Joss in o-eight. In nineteen o-six he played fifty-seven games and hit for three fifty-eight. Not a bad average if you ask me. In fact, Clarke tied George Stone who led all of major league baseball that season with a three fifty-eight batting average. But when you only play fifty-seven games to Stone's one fifty-four you don't get credit. Still, when I saw Clarke's numbers that year something didn't seem right because they were so impressive, so I looked at everybody's batting that season…not just their averages, but also the number and types of hits they got— singles, doubles, triples, home runs. Then I divided that by the number of at-bats each had that season. I looked at how many games each played also."

"You're not human, Mother."

She just grinned. "Wished I'd invented it but I didn't. It's a new calculation that some unemployed statistician I read about came up with. His name is Allan Roth. Calls it 'Slugging Percentage,' though nobody's buying it yet. It's got a future, though. Says a lot more about a player than just batting average."

"Sounds interesting."

"Anyway, Clarke's four eighty-six slugging percentage that year was the second-highest in Major League Baseball for players playing more than fifty games, even beating out Harry Lumley and Honus Wagner, and Lajoie who was his own manager. Stone once again took high honors with a slugging percentage of five hundred one, and once again Clarke's limited season garnered him no mention. The other guys all played over sixty percent of their respective team's games, whereas Clarke only played thirty-six percent of his team's games, so Clarke's stats don't count in rankings. But he gave those legends a run for their money, credit or no credit."

"Wow," I said, shaking my head. "Hard to believe I've never heard of this guy until now."

"He had some embarrassments too. He led the American League in passed balls twice, in o-five and o-seven. O-seven must have been a tough year for him because he also led the league in stolen bases allowed. But he did *lead* the league in defense as a catcher that year, as well as third in the league for put outs and assists, so go figure. Some things don't make sense unless you're there to see them for yourself."

"Yeah, it's hard to figure sometimes when you can't be there."

"He redeemed himself in o-eight by leading the league in caught stealing percentage. Also catching that perfect game for Joss."

"Probably why Cobb put Clarke on his best defensive catchers list."

"Anyway, in his entire major league career Clarke only hit six home runs with a career batting average of two fifty-four."

"Seems ironic since it was probably those eight home runs in one game that got the attention of scouts. But he seems to have held his own in the majors as a pretty good defensive catcher. And I don't see anything to be ashamed of with his offense either. A career two fifty-four isn't bad, not for nine seasons. Six home runs isn't great, but it proves he could hit the big parks, just not consistently. The errors he was known for—that's just baseball. We all have our moments—our weak areas."

"And say what you want about those eight home runs that day in o-two," Mother said. "He *still* went eight for eight that day— eight at bats, eight home runs. Even if the right field fence was only two hundred ten feet, even if it was shorter, as one of his teammates recalled, Clarke still hit *one thousand* that day. Still put *eight balls* over that fence *right where he wanted them to go.* That in and of itself is phenomenal hitting."

I thought about that feat for a moment. On my best day I might go four for four, and on my best day I might be able to place two of those hits exactly where I wanted it. The other hits would go where they ended up depending upon what the pitcher gave me and how far ahead, behind, below or above the ball my swing was. That previous season with Hartford I played one hundred thirty-two games, hit three o-eight with eleven home runs. Not a bad ending. But never in my wildest imagination could I envision myself coming to bat eight times in one game, and in each plate appearance putting the ball over the fence, putting the ball over the exact fence I wanted. Never, even if the fence were only one hundred forty feet away and the pitcher got them all over the plate.

"What happened to Clarke after baseball?" I asked. "Any word, beside the Marines and the war?"

"Well, I put a call into the Pittsburg Pirates' office and asked them. That was the last major league team he played for after the war, just a few games. They told me that last they heard he was married and living in River Rouge, a suburb of Detroit. They said he played in the minors for a bit before falling on hard times. The hard times they said was just a rumor, but they also said he'd taken a job as a welder's helper to make ends meet—care for his aging mother. So maybe the rumor's true." She slid a half-sheet of paper toward me on the table. "Here's his address."

"They gave it to you?"

"No, but it seems he's listed in the River Rouge phone

directory. I called the operator and she gave it to me."

"What am I supposed to do with it?" I lifted the paper and looked at it.

"You're going aren't you—to take him the baseballs?"

How could she have possibly known that? "Yes."

She smiled. "Janie know?"

"No she doesn't. How did you know I was going?"

"Your father's letter. I saw the look on your face when I read the part where he wrote, 'I told him I had something of his I wanted to return.'"

"I don't get that. Why would Dad want to return those baseballs? It's customary for fans to keep fouls and home run balls, at least nowadays."

"Yes, but the big ones, the milestones like Ruth's sixtieth home run in twenty-seven, many fans feel compelled to return those balls to the player. The player usually gives them some other piece of autographed memorabilia in exchange."

"True." I said it, but in my gut I sensed there was more to it than that. My father, if he was the man everybody said he was, had a deeper reason than just returning the "milestone" baseballs to Clarke. My hope was that by visiting Nig Clarke I might better understand the significance of returning the eight home run balls to him.

"How will you pay for the trip to Michigan? Got any money?"

"I'll figure something out." When she didn't seem convinced, I added," I have to, don't I?"

"What about the boy?" Mother asked, both of us watching Janie dote over Billy near the tree, the way a doe would her new fawn.

When I didn't answer my mother stood, placed a hand on my shoulder, then wheeled my father over to join the others around the tree, which was now adorned with delicate and colorful ornaments sparkling in the light, the tinsel glittering like slivers of hanging icicle. My grandmother and grandfather stood with arms around each other's waist watching Janie—her belly smooth and round like a half-moon under her light-colored dress—point out to Billy just where he should place a particular ornament, Carl working like a crafty cat to get the tinsel and decorations around the back of the tree at the corner of the wall. Seeing them all there together—my family, little Billy and Carl—I realized for the first time how much I'd truly been blessed.

"Laird, honey," Janie called, holding the final ornament in her hand. "Come put the star on top of the tree. We've been saving it for you."

I rose from my seat and went to them, Janie kissing my cheek and handing me the star.

"Oh! Can I do it?" Billy asked, bouncing excitedly in circles like a solid rubber ball.

"How about we do it together?" I said, handing him the star and lifting him, holding him out in front of me, his body rigid and straight, angled up like an ascending airplane, his arms over his head with the star in his hands. A few moments later Billy gently placed the star on top of the tree, the star's golden veneer glinting and flirting with the firelight the way its cousins in the sky do the moon.

Setting him back on the ground, I said with a wink, "Well, done, Billy Sunday."

"Thank you!" He glanced up at me with round eyes that revealed the joy in his heart, then reached up to slip his small hand into mine, the soft skin on his palm and fingers as tender and fragile as his spirit. As we stood there—both of us admiring the beautiful tree under his shining star, Carl playing the sweetest rendition of *Silent Night* I could ever recall hearing on a harmonica—my mind wondered how I would break the news to Billy that he would be leaving us sooner than expected, that this would not be his tree this Christmas, his home this Christmas, his family this Christmas. How, I wondered, does a man do that?

CHAPTER SEVENTEEN

B illy spent the day baking and prepping pies in the basement with Janie, her looking like Mrs. Claus in her red and furry white-trimmed Santa hat, Billy looking like an elf in his oversized green apron, one that strapped around the neck to drape his full front, and one so long he kept stepping on it when he tried to walk, both of them giggling at his predicament until he nearly dropped a hot cherry pie he was tasked with carrying to the nearby cooling shelf. That's when Janie took action, lifting the bottom corners of the apron and stuffing them into the front waist pockets, making the elf's apron hang shorter. Janie had a big order to fill by the end of the day so she had both ovens working, the basement oven and the kitchen oven. But her prep station and cooling rack, which I'd made for her out of 2 X 2s, were located in the roomier basement. That forced her to have to travel up and down the stairs regularly, something hard on the knees and back when you're a day away from nine months pregnant. She'd take steps up or down the stairway until halfway, then stop to stretch her back out, her hands on her hips, taking a few deep recovery breaths before proceeding the rest of the way. It was hard on her but with Billy's help she'd get everything done and packaged.

"When did you have the boxes made?" I asked her upon seeing Billy folding the thin white pie boxes, the word *Janie's* on the folding top, the letters a bright pink and the whole word stretched and rounded over the top half of a pie image. Laid over the pie image were the words, *Pies & Pastries*. Rounding the lower half of the pie in the same pink ink was her simple motto: *Homemade & Handmade*.

"While you were away in Texas."

"They're nice. Not cheap, I'd imagine."

"No, but necessary if I want people to take me seriously. Don't you think so, Billy?"

"Yes, ma'am."

They made a good team. Part of me, the sensible part, the part that knew Billy would be leaving soon, felt I shouldn't let the two of them bond any further. That other part of me, the one that lived in fear, said not to object to them spending time together because that would elicit questions from both Billy and Janie, questions I wasn't yet prepared to answer. So I left them on their own and went upstairs to our bedroom to get changed for my trip into downtown Hartford. After putting on my suit, a gray conservative number with matching Fedora, I went to the back of the closest where we kept our small safe, hidden under boxes of Janie's shoes, some of which had never been opened, the shoes never worn, purchased she said "just in case," whatever that meant. Janie had more shoes than Churchill Downs on race day. She never shopped like that for clothes, opting instead to mix and match to save money—probably for more shoes. "A woman just has to have the right pair of shoes!" she would tell me whenever I asked if she *really* needed another pair. They weren't flashy shoes; she wasn't a flashy person. Often they were just the same style of shoe in four or five different colors, and most of the time they were purchased on sale. But they took up a lot of space. The good thing was that robbers are lazy by nature so if ever one made their way into our house looking for our safe, they'd see our closet and all those shoes and say, "Fuhgeddaboudit!"

Once I got all the boxes moved I knelt down on all fours before the low-profile safe, a heavy black steel box bolted to the floor, carefully spinning the dial this way and that until the combination had been entered and the latch opened. Inside we'd put some emergency cash, some war bonds we had purchased to support the war effort, our $30,000 life insurance policy, our passports—which we'd never used—a precious tintype of Janie's deceased great-grandparents, and a baseball that had begun to darken to the color of a coffee stain, the inked signatures starting to fade. The baseball rested on a two-inch by two-inch, coverless claw-type stand, its inch-high trunk and three stubby fingers cut from cedar. When I pulled the baseball and its stand from the safe, the baseball rolled off the stand. If not for the fast reflex of my free hand the ball would have hit the hardwood floor, possibly scuffing the ball. Instead my hand caught it, my lungs exhaling in sudden relief.

After closing the safe and haphazardly restacking Janie's shoe boxes, I went to the end of the bed and sat, tossing my hat on the bed, admiring my most prized possession—the ball from Game Four of the 1914 World Series, signed by every member of "The Miracle Braves," my father included.

Just then Billy strolled into the bedroom and said, "Gee, that's swell! Can we play catch?"

He hopped up on the bed next to me and I showed him the ball. "Not with this one, kid. I mean Billy. I call you kid a lot, don't I? I'm sorry about that."

"It's okay. I am a kid."

"This ball we cannot play catch with, no."

"Why not?"

"Because this is a very valuable ball. It's very special. This ball is from Game Four of the nineteen fourteen World Series."

"Wow! That's swell!"

"It gets better. See these signatures," I said, lifting the ball closer to his eyes so he could get a better look. "These signatures are from famous baseball players. See right here...that's Hank Gowdy's signature—the catcher. See this one? That's the signature of Bill James, a great pitcher. And this here is Lefty Tyler's signature, another pitcher." I spun the ball until I found the signature I was looking for. Pointing to my favorite signature on the ball, I said, a bit choked up, "But this one here, this is from my father. This is his signature."

"Your father played big league baseball?"

I nodded. "Yes he did. He played for the Boston Braves. That's who all these signatures belong to—the players. They gave this signed game ball to my mother because she couldn't be at the game on account of me. I decided to be born during Game Four of the World Series."

"That's bad timing."

Laughing, I said "Yes, I guess it was. My father didn't play that game because he was at the hospital with us."

Billy thought hard about what I'd just shared with him before looking up at me. "Did your father get hurt playing baseball?"

"No, Son. The war did that to him."

"I hate war," Billy said, looking down at his feet, no doubt thinking about his own father being killed in North Africa during the war.

"Me too. Guess we have that in common."

"What are you gonna do with the ball?" He looked up at me again.

"Oh...well...I was thinking I'd...Hey, aren't you supposed to be helping Janie?"

"I guess so, but I wanted to be with you now."

"That's very nice of you, Billy," I said, standing and lifting him off the bed so he could stand on the floor. "I'll tell you what. I'm heading into town. When I get back we'll throw a ball around. Sound good?"

"That would be swell! Thanks!" Billy ran out the door and hurried down the stairs, one hand on the handrail as he hopped like a rabbit down each step, the thud growing fainter the further down he got.

I took a long look at myself in Janie's vanity mirror and didn't like what I saw, a confused man about to break two sacred covenants with himself, about to do two things he swore he would never do—sell what he viewed as the holy grail of baseballs, a 2014 World Series ball with his father's signature on it, *and enlist.*

CHAPTER EIGHTEEN

The Hartford Times had been printing newspapers since 1817 and had one of the largest circulations in the state—and it was no fan of mine, at least not their sports editor, Mel Fisher, a sanctimonious key-puncher who a couple years before, when he was just a beat reporter, had written:

The bumbling Bees of Hartford lost yet another game, due in part to that two-bit hack with a bat, Laird Young, who on his best day couldn't hit the moon if he was standing on it. Drafted for his pitching as well as his bat, Lil' Boom Boom might try using another arm to throw with because the one he's using is too busy most games throwing punches. I've said it before and I'll say it again, this kid is not his father. He's a baby in big boy clothes, a thumb-sucking tyke who needs his nose wiped and his diaper changed. This kid needs remedial training in all elements of the game, starting with class and respect. Teach the boy those things and he might have a place in professional baseball. Until then, get him out. Send him back to the family farm in Lynn where he can put his hands to better use—milking cows.

It was true what Fisher wrote about my lousy hitting that season. And in frustration I found myself arguing a lot, even with my own teammates. They understood, though; they were players. That's something Mel Fisher and other cubs in the press don't understand, the things that go through a player's head when he falls into a slump, when the season before he hit for .358, but the next he can't reach 200; how one season he wins 20 games as a pitcher with an ERA of 2.55, but the next he loses twenty with a rotten ERA of 5.87—so bad that players, fans, and reporters start to doubt his value to the club—so bad he starts to doubt *his own* value to the club.

When that happens a guy's got a thousand thoughts scrambling in his head. It's like traffic in New York City on Monday, mass congestion bogging everything down, drivers laying on their horns and pointing their fists at each other. And trying to pitch in that state of mind is like trying to take an important exam when you haven't slept in three days. You look at that catcher's mitt from the distant mound and it's like that little blurry dot you sometimes see floating on your eyeball. Trying to pitch it in there, it's like trying to thread a needle when you're drunk, and when everybody's watching you. Finally, when a player gets low enough, he reacts; it's just human nature. But like Janie had said to me: "It's what a man does when everything's falling apart that makes him great—or not so great." And I suppose that's what Mel Fisher was getting at when he called me ...*a baby in big boy clothes, a thumb-sucking tyke who needs his nose wiped and his diaper changed.* But the fighting bit, the part about my arm not throwing anything but punches, that just wasn't true. Sure I'd broken a few bats, thrown a few tantrums, but I'd only been in two fights that season, one earlier in the season when I was on the bench—when a fight on the field cleared the benches—and one in that particular game Fisher wrote about where I taunted a batter and he charged me on the mound. I just couldn't find the strike zone and was on a five game losing skid. I just got tired of guys taking me for hits and home runs. It happens.

But there I was, sitting in my car, parked on Prospect Street outside the Hartford Times building—a multistoried brick building with six green granite columns out front—about to go up to Mel Fisher's office and bow down to the demigod, to offer him the one thing I valued most in this world behind my wife—my prized autographed baseball. That thought turned my stomach. Selling that baseball to Mel Fisher was on the same level as eating rank cheese; but I guess when a fella's hungry enough, he'll eat anything.

A few minutes later I walked into The Times's newsroom, a big open area with at least fifty desks of varying dimensions split into four rows, each desk with a typewriter and chair, some desks vacant, others filled with faces staring at notes as their fingers punched keys on their typewriters, nearby ashtrays full of cigarettes and cigar butts, wisps of harsh smoke slinking along the newsroom ceiling toward two open windows on the far side of the room. There were young men and women shuttling notes from the teletypes to reporters, as well as finished articles from reporters to the editorial offices off to the side—six big offices with glass windows separating the editors from the noise of the newsroom, but still allowing the editors to see the goings on.

"I'm here to see Mel Fisher," I said to the receptionist who'd just hung up the telephone—a manicured young woman no older than twenty, with short brown hair and a pleasant phone voice.

"Um, I believe he's in a meeting. Did he know you were coming?" She twirled a pencil between her fingers.

"No, but he'll see me. Tell him 'Lil Boom Boom' is here and he has something you want."

She scrunched the skin on her forehead, her green eyes squinting at me, her head cocked. "'Lil Boom Boom?'"

"That's right. The 'sniveling tyke that needs his diaper changed.'"

"Sir, I'm not sure—"

"Just tell him. Forget it." I pushed my way through the low swinging door onto the newsroom floor, making a beeline toward the row of glass offices.

"Sir! Wait! You can't go in there!" She said, following but failing in her heels to keep up.

I checked three offices before I found the worm I'd come to

see. His back was to the door, his balding dome—shiny in the office light—the only thing visible above the high back of his swivel chair, his hands holding up an article submission his eyes were perusing.

From the doorway, I said, "How ya doing, Mel? Remember me?"

He swung around in his chair to face me, just as the receptionist arrived.

"I'm very sorry, Mr. Fisher. I tried to stop him but—"

Mel held up a hand to stop her. "It's fine, Sally. Do me a favor, though. Call down to the nursery. See if they have room for one more sniveling tot." When she looked lost, Mel said, "Leave him. He's harmless."

I stepped into his office and took a seat in front of his desk, directly across from him. "Still ruining people's lives with your lies?"

He scoffed. "I give my opinions. Sometimes they hurt."

"More like knives, if you ask me. I know. You've stuck a few in my back."

"Again, sometimes they hurt. How's your father?"

I thought about his question, nodded to myself, then answered, "Don't talk about my father. You couldn't care less about him or my family."

"Not true. Your father was a good man."

"Still is." It was like my mother had just spoken through me.

Mel nodded in agreement. "So what can I do for you, Mr. Young? I have a deadline to meet."

"Maybe I can do something for you." I squirmed in my chair, my gut telling me not to go through with it. But I knew I had to.

"Oh yeah? Like what? Last I checked you and I weren't exactly, you know, amicable. Why would you want to do anything for me?"

When I removed my hat from my lap to reveal the autographed 1914 World Series baseball being held by my left hand, Mel nearly leapt from his chair. Only the poker player in him kept his haunches down and his face emotionless. But it was his greedy, hairy hands that gave his excitement away, rubbing themselves together in front of his chest like two conspiring thieves waiting to pounce on their victim. "You have my attention."

"Thought so. Still want it?"

"You must be in a tough spot to be selling that piece of candy."

"No. I could walk out of here with this ball right now and it'd be all right with me."

"Then why sell it? Why me—a man you despise?"

"Because there's something I want that's more valuable to me. Because you want this gem and I'm gonna make you pay to get it."

"Yeah? What's more valuable to you than a World Series ball...an autographed nineteen fourteen World Series ball...one with your father's signature on it?"

"That's between me and God."

"You a religious man now, Boom Boom?"

"What do you care?"

"Normally I wouldn't, but you finding religion, spreading the gospel with your fists, that's news."

"I've had only six fights my entire professional career so stop with the pounding pugilist nonsense. Try telling your readers about my career three o-eight batting average, my career two point nine-o ERA."

"I've got your ERA at three point one five."

"Whatever. Why not tell them about my curve, how it's got more movement than any pitcher out there?"

"No, that's your knuckleball, if I recall."

"Funny. Why not tell them about my eighteen wins last season—my eleven home runs? Why not tell the truth about me instead of spewing garbage?"

"Sometimes the garbage reads better."

I scoffed at that. "Five thousand."

"You're out of your mind. Get out of here."

Without hesitating I rose and headed for the door, taking the jewel he wanted with me.

"Wait!" He said just as I got to the doorway, rising from his desk and waving me over to a wall-mounted bookshelf with only two shelves and locking glass doors. "See that old ball glove there? See how it's small and flimsy—the leather dark brown?" I nodded. "That glove belonged to 'Big Ed' Delehanty, 1888, when he played for the Philadelphia Quakers. Autographed too, right there," he said pointing as I leaned in for a closer look. The writing was small and black—hard to see against the dark brown leather—but the signature was there all right. "I paid three hundred dollars for that relic. See that autographed bat there, in the center of the top shelf?" I nodded again. "The very first Honus Wagner engraved, Louisville Slugger bat ever produced—from nineteen o-five and signed by 'The Flying Dutchman' himself. How much do you think I paid for that?"

With pursed lips, I answered, "Four hundred. Maybe Five."

"Six hundred clams. See that ball there? That ball's signed by Ty Cobb. It's from the game he played May fifth, nineteen twenty-five, the day he hit three home runs, a double, and two singles for a total of sixteen runs—a record that still stands. Twelve hundred dollars. That ball there, it's from game three of the infamous nineteen-nineteen World Series."

"The Black Sox."

"That's right. It's signed by Shoeless Joe Jackson. I paid twenty-two hundred dollars for that piece of sugar. People thought I was crazy. And that space there, that's for the rock of all rocks, Babe Ruth's record-setting sixtieth home run of the nineteen twenty-seven season. That's where it'll go if I can ever get Truly Warner to sell it to me. I offered him four grand for that gem. Now you want me to pay five for your ball?"

"That's right."

"Why would I want to do that?"

"Because it irks you that a weasel like me has it. Because you've been trying to figure a way to lift it off me ever since you heard I had it. Because it's the only autographed baseball actually used in game four of the nineteen fourteen World Series...signed by every member of that team, including Stallings the manager. Because twenty to thirty years from now this ball's going to be worth twice that. But mostly because you need to satisfy your ego—to be able to tell people *you* own it."

There was a long silence between us, like two gunslingers facing off in the middle of a dusty Tombstone street, their fingers teasing the ivory heels of their six-shooters, each eyeing the other like sly cats, each waiting for the other to flinch.

"Two thousand," he said, plopping back down in his chair, throwing his crossed legs up onto his desk, his hands behind his balding head, his beady eyes fixed on mine.

"Five."

"Three and I'll even give you a nice write up at the beginning of next season, if you give me something nice to write about."

"Four and a half, and you can keep your nice write up."

He looked me over like a man unsure if he should call the police or cooperate with the guy robbing him. "Four, but I'll be sharpening my knives."

I shot him a sarcastic grin. "Done." He dropped his feet and leaned in to grab the ball from me, but I pulled it back. "Your dirty hands can soil it *after* I have the money."

His hands disappeared under his desk, fiddled for a few minutes with what I figured was his safe, then reappeared above the desk, handing me a stack of bills. "How'd you know I wasn't reaching for my gun?"

I laughed. "You don't own a gun. They don't issue gun permits to rats like you."

He smiled and nodded. "Count it."

I thumbed through the bills, all fifty dollar notes. When satisfied, I handed over my most cherished possession, feeling like I'd just sold-out my father, mother, Janie, and myself. And I couldn't help thinking I'd sold out the 1914 "Miracle Braves," who'd thought so much of my mother that they wanted to give her an autographed game ball. Even then I knew it was the right thing to do. The end would justify the means—that's what I kept telling myself.

After I'd finished with Mel Fisher I walked about 300 yards up Prospect Street to the local Army recruiting station, my approved draft deferment in my wallet, right next to Mel Fisher's four grand. It wasn't hard to find the recruiting station because, as I approached, Uncle Sam pointed directly at me from the red, white, and blue sidewalk poster out front, his wavy silver hair streaming from underneath a white top hat with a star-spangled blue band around it, his white breast and red bowtie visible under his blue lapelled coat, his voice exclaiming in big, bold, red and black print, "I want you for U. S. Army!" It was stapled to a two-sided poster board made of plywood, the upside down V type, the kind that has a hinge on top and small chain connecting the two angled sides near the bottom so they don't do the splits and fall flat.

The building wasn't much to look at; just a two-story cinderblock building painted beige, with a wide metal door doused in Army green—that flat olive color one shade up from dirt. But then, most military architecture falls short on style I've learned. And the interior wasn't any better. The interior walls were the same cinderblock and the same beige, the only furniture a large metal desk with an equally large and sturdy sergeant sitting behind it. And about twenty chairs lined the walls, several filled by civilians like me, each with a clipboard and pencil, filling out enlistment paperwork, I presumed. Lastly, two plain and un-shaded light fixtures hung from the ceiling, each suspended by a single cord. Honestly, the place was about as plain and sterile as a hospital ward hallway, the smell of layered floor wax overpowering my sinuses.

"What can I do for you, mack?" The sergeant asked, his body facing me as I approached his desk directly in front, his eyes never looking up from the form he was filling out on a desktop void of anything else but a half-full mug of black coffee and a stack of gray metal trays for filing forms.

"Um, yes, sir. I'd...um..."

"Spit it out, mack. I'm busy here."

"I'm here to enlist."

"Yeah," he said, his eyes giving me a glance before continuing with his paperwork. "Why us? Why not the Navy?"

"What?"

"I mean you look like a Navy guy to me."

"Oh yeah? How's that?"

Glancing up at me again, this time his eyes giving me the once over before looking back down at his form. "I'm saying you look more equipped to swab decks than to fight. We're a fighting force."

"Seems to me the Navy's been doing a lot of fighting, especially in the Pacific."

"True, and they battle hard, just not hand-to-hand. They have Marines for that."

I scoffed at his assumption of me. A few minutes ago I was in Mel Fisher's office defending against his claim that I fight too much, now I was standing in front of a guy who thought I was too soft to fight. The whole thing seemed ironic. "Listen, Sergeant," I said, leaning down to rest my hands on his desk, purposefully putting my face closer so he would hear me. "I've got no problem fighting. In fact, on my worst day I could take you apart."

Right then he dropped his pen and stood up behind his desk, hands on his waist, iron jaw clinched, his dark eyes squinted and pointed right at mine. "Is that so?"

I straightened up, took a deeper breath than normal, then continued with my line of thinking. "Yes it is, so save your intimidation tactics for somebody else."

The sergeant came around his desk and stood nose to nose with me, so close I could smell the coffee on his breath, the cigarette he'd been smoking earlier on his clothes, and the pomade he used on his hair to keep his crew cut polished. "I say you're a cupcake. I say you've got milk in those veins of yours. I say when the fighting starts you'll go as limp as a wet noodle. We don't have room for cupcakes or noodles in this man's Army."

I refused to break eye contact with him, though I could sense other eyes on me as well, those of the civilian men there to enlist, those seated in the chairs along the walls filling out their paperwork. "Think what you want, but I'm here to enlist in the Army—*your* army. If you refuse to do it I'll find somebody else, someone with more brain than brawn."

"All right. No problem, pal. The old man can always use a boy to shine his shoes."

"You've been doing that just fine. I'm here to join the Fourth Infantry, to carry a weapon, to fight, in battle, on the front lines of who knows where, on Hitler's front lawn if that's where it takes me."

He walked around me, his eyes looking me over, up and down, like a butcher would look over a side of beef. "You want to be in the Fourth, in the 'Ivy Division?' Why? There's a lot of history there. Ever hear about what they did in the first war—the battle of Meuse-Argonne? The entire regiment received the French War Cross for gallantry."

"I know."

"Really? How would someone like you know something like that?"

"Because my father was there."

That got his respect. "Oh, yeah? Your father fought in the Battle of Meuse-Argonne? What phase?"

"Both. He was there for both offensives."

The sergeant nodded his respect. "Did he make it home?"

"Yes, but severely wounded."

He nodded again, looking me over once more. "What's your name, soldier?"

"Young. Laird Allen Young...the third."

"Okay, Mr. Young. Good job. You'll do." He returned to his chair, reached into one of the desk trays to retrieve a clipboard pre-loaded with the correct forms. Handing it to me, he said, "Fill these out—everything. I don't want to see any blank spaces. You have a question, ask me. And don't make any mistakes or you start over. Savvy?"

"Savvy." I said, taking the clipboard from him.

"Take a seat over there with the rest of the guys. Come back up when you're finished."

I took a seat between two boys who couldn't have been older than nineteen, making me feel like their father, my being twenty-nine years of age. Both watched me as I sat, both green-eyed and baby-faced, one still with pimples, the other with a small scar on his chin. I gathered they were brothers, possibly twins, though I figured with enough difference in features that they'd have trouble fooling their mother the way some twins try to do. The boy to the left of me leaned over to say, "He did that to all of us...a test, I guess."

The boy on my other side added, "But you gave it back to him better than us. I hope we can be that brave when the time comes, you know, later."

I thought about his words. I thought about the 'later' he spoke of—the hand-to-hand combat that might befall us in battle. "I hope I can too." That was all I said. That was all I *could* say, because at that moment I suddenly feared for those two boys, for their mother, for all the boys fighting in the war and all of their mothers. I thought about what Billy had said when remembering his father, that he hated war, about how I'd agreed with him, that I hated it too. In that moment, right there in that room, in that recruiting station with all the others set to do their duty, right there the reality of what we were about to undertake hit me—it hit me so hard it hurt my stomach, so hard that it nearly took the wind out of me— the reality that we would each be fighting for our country, each fighting and killing other human beings in defense against tyranny, and if need be, die doing it. In that moment, in that room, I got my first *real* taste of something I'd taste again soon—*fear.*

CHAPTER NINETEEN

I arrived home to find Janie in a panic, meeting me outside as I pulled the car into the driveway. She had cleaned herself up after baking and seemed dressed to go out somewhere, her hair as pretty as I'd ever seen it, her dress pressed, her feet wearing "the right pair of shoes." Before I could even step from the car she started in on me.

"Laird, honey, where have you been? I'm late." She took the keys from my hand and hurried back toward the front door.

"Late for what?" I asked, following.

"I have a big delivery to make, remember?" She flung the screen door open, stepping inside to let the door slam in my face.

"Janie, I'm sorry. I completely forgot."

"We need a second car, Laird." Janie had all of her pies laid out on the counter, packaged and ready to go. "Billy, sweetie, would you mind helping me load the car?"

"Okay," he said, his speech barely coherent, his fists rubbing his eyes, his body having just risen from the sofa where he'd been napping.

I started to help but Janie tried to put me off with a raised hand.

"Nope. We've got it, honey. You've obviously got other things on your mind." Even in her anger she tried to be polite. Janie headed back toward the front door, Billy following, both with their hands full of pies.

I grabbed some pies anyway and followed out to the car. "I said

I was sorry, Janie. What else do you want me to say?"

"Nothing. I just thought you'd take my work a little more seriously."

"You think I don't? I'm sorry you feel that way but I've done my best to support you in this business. I'm proud of you actually. It takes courage to be an entrepreneuter."

"The word is entrepreneur, Laird. Entre-pre-neur."

"Fine. A businesswoman. I think it's great."

"Then maybe you should act like it." She placed her pies carefully in the trunk, then Billy's, then mine.

"What? That's not fair."

"Well it's certainly not a priority with you, though all things considered, it should be."

"What does that mean?"

"You got fired, remember? We spend all your yearly salary during the season. We don't save any for the off-season. That means we need the money I earn from baking. Now do you understand?"

Her words hurt, but they were true. Our financial troubles were my fault. "Sorry. Sorry I'm such a loser, Janie. You deserve better, you're right."

"I don't want better. I just want you to think of someone other than yourself sometimes."

She stomped back to the house for more pies, Billy opting to remain outside until Janie and I had our say.

"Oh really? How about bringing my grandparents back with me from Texas? Was that selfish of me?"

"No, but the trip to Texas was given our financial issues. You took a trip to Texas, spent one hundred dollars we didn't have on a round-trip train ride, all for what? Baseballs?"

"You know it was about more than that, Janie? Now who's not supporting who?" When Janie didn't answer, I said, "How about that boy out there? Did I think of myself with him?"

"Yes, you did!"

"What? You're kidding, right?"

She stopped in the kitchen and turned to face me. "No. You brought a boy home without asking me first. You didn't think about my feelings at all."

"Well you sure seem to be getting on well with him."

"He's a child, Laird. A sweet, sensitive child. What's not to get along with?"

"I know. A boy whose parents died and who needed some joy in his life."

"I know you meant well, honey. I do. But he wants to stay with us. He asked me this morning. I nearly cried."

I thought about that for a moment. I'd always figured that could happen. Billy was vulnerable and scared to be alone. What eight-year-old orphan having to scavenge for food wouldn't be? But I hadn't thought about the probability of that happening. And I hadn't thought about how my own feelings might develop, how I might come to want him to stay, to not go live with his aunt. I'd certainly felt those inclinations since his arrival. Teaching him to skip stones, carve wood, watching him with Janie decorating the tree, I could see he was a good fit for our family. Not only *could* I see Billy as a member of our family, I'd begun to hope for it. "Well, he'll be leaving soon."

"I know. After Christmas."

"No, sooner."

That came as a shock to her. "What do you mean? What did you do, Laird?"

"I'm taking him to his aunt's in Ohio, on my way to River Rouge, Michigan."

"What? But when? What's in River Rouge, Michigan?"

"Nig Clarke."

"You must be kidding?"

"No, I'm not. I know what my father wants me to do with

183

those eight baseballs. I've known since Thanksgiving, when my mother read my father's letter."

"You're saying your father wants you to return those baseballs to Clarke in Michigan, over twelve hundred miles from here?" When I nodded, she said, "Laird, I'm pregnant. I could deliver any day now."

"You're not due for a few weeks I thought. If you're worried about it I can fly."

"Yes, but the baby could come sooner. Besides, we're broke. Remember? We can barely pay the bills."

Just then I pulled the four grand out of my wallet and fanned the bills out on the countertop before her, not saying a word, just watching for her reaction.

"Where did that come from?" The question had its origin in utter shock. She picked up the money, held it up to the light to make sure the money was real before laying it back on the counter, looking at it like it might be diseased or laced with poison. "What did you do to get that money, Laird? Be honest. If you're in trouble—"

"I sold my baseball."

"Your baseball? The one in our safe? Your father's *World Series* baseball? Oh, honey. Why?"

"To pay for the trip—and for other things."

Still stunned, Janie asked, "What other things?"

"Everything, Janie. You said it yourself. We need more money. Now we've got it. I'll take two hundred with me, another two hundred to give to Billy's aunt—to help care for him. You can have the rest. Open a real bakery."

She shook her head. "No, Laird. I need you here."

"Janie, I have to go."

"They're just baseballs!" Pointing to her distended belly, "This is a baby! Which is more important to you?"

"It's not a choice for me. When I accepted those eight

baseballs, it was the same as making a promise to my father. Don't you see that? Besides, something good is going to come of all of this. I don't know what it is, but I feel it. Something good will come of this."

"Well, when are you going on this journey?"

"If it's okay with you I'd like to leave tomorrow."

"But why so soon? Why do you have to go now? Why not go after Christmas?"

That's when I pulled the new induction letter from my pocket, hesitating before handing it to her. "Because I won't be here after Christmas."

"But…" Her eyes scanned the document and when she saw the words *Order To Report For Induction*, she looked up at me, horrified. "You've enlisted?" I nodded but remained silent. "But you had a deferment."

"How'd you know about that?"

"I saw the draft notice when it came, Laird. I'm not stupid. Most of the men around here have gotten them. But I figured since you didn't report then you must have gotten a deferment."

"Why didn't you say something?"

"Well I was hoping you would. I'm your wife after all."

"They granted me the deferment because I told the draft board my father needed me. I lied and I just couldn't bring myself to tell you."

"It says here you're to report for induction December twenty sixth of this year, nineteen forty three. How could you do this, Laird—to us? To the baby and me? To Billy?"

"I don't know."

"You don't know? That's all you've got for me?"

"Janie," I said, as tender as a father speaking to his hurt daughter, stepping in close to try and hold her. "I had to. My conscience couldn't bear it any longer, the shame I've felt over using my father as an excuse to get out of going to war. Other men have to go. They don't have an excuse, and most wouldn't use one anyway."

She pushed away, turning her teary eyes from me. "Well you've done it now. There's no going back from this, Laird. You know that, right?"

I stepped up behind her, placing my hands gently on her shoulders, pulling her back into me so I could wrap my arms around her, her head under my chin.

"Do you know what branch," she asked, "or do they tell you that after induction?"

"The Army. Fourth Infantry—my father's unit."

"Infantry? Couldn't they have made you a cook or something, for the rear commanders?"

"I asked for infantry, Janie. I need to know."

"Need to know what? What it's like to be killed?" She turned to face me, her cheeks wet, her worried eyes red. "What it's like to lose an arm, a leg, your mind? Is that what you need to know, Laird?" She buried her head in my chest, trying to hide from it all.

"I need to know what my father had to face going over there."

She looked up at me again. "That's why you're going to war, to possibly die? So you can know what your father had to face over there? Newsflash, Laird! He faced other men trying to shoot him, kill him, keep him from coming home to his wife and child! That's what he faced!"

"You forgot one thing. My father also had to face himself—his fears. He was afraid, Janie. You heard him say it himself in that letter of his Mom read. But he chose to go anyway. He had to because he had to be able to look at himself in the mirror without disgust, and he couldn't have done that had he stayed home and let other men do the fighting and dying."

"Ugh! That word—*Dying.* I'm so scared, honey."

"I know. Me too."

She laid her head against my chest and we held each other for a long while in the kitchen, her belly—our baby—between us. I imagined her wondering at that moment what would happen if I didn't came home alive, if she had to bury me and raise our little girl or boy on her own. Could she make it on her own? How would she survive, make a living, feed our child? I'd known Janie to be a confident woman, capable of many things, but at that moment she seemed as helpless and as blind as a hatchling in a nest perched high upon a treacherous cliff.

"I can't even imagine life without you," she muttered, her nose runny, her tears soaking through my shirt. "You're so much a part of me."

"I've been away before, on road trips with the team."

"This is different. Then I knew you'd be home eventually. Now…this…it's not the same. It's all so…uncertain."

"I'll come back to you, Janie."

"How do you know?"

"It's difficult to explain, but something tells me I will."

"Let's hope so." Janie pulled away from me to examine herself in the glass pane of one of our upper cabinets, trying to see how bad she looked after crying. "Now look at me. I'm a mess. My eyes are puffy and face flush."

I kissed her moist lips, her face being held by my hands. "I've never seen you more beautiful."

"Now you're a liar. Keep it going, honey. You're batting a thousand."

"Can I come in now?" Billy said, popping his head inside the front door. "It's getting cold out here."

"Come, sweetie," Janie said, motioning with her hand. Billy came and she hugged him. "I want to thank you for all your help today. I couldn't have done it without you."

"That's okay. I had fun." He looked up at me, a big grin on his face. "Can we play catch now?"

"That's right," I said, snapping my fingers. "I did promise you

187

we'd toss the ball around when I got home. Run and get your glove, sport." Billy bolted up the stairs. "And get mine too! It's in the closet in my room! But watch out for the shoes! A fella could get killed in that closet!"

"Very funny," Janie said. "Can't believe you sold your baseball. Can't believe any of this, really."

"I know. Hard for me to believe too."

"What do you think your mother will say? Think she'll be mad?"

"I think she'll understand."

"I can't find your glove!" Billy hollered from upstairs.

"On the top shelf, to the right!"

A moment passed before he called down, "I see it but I can't reach it." By the intermittent thumping noise coming from the ceiling above us, it sounded like Billy was jumping and trying to grab the glove.

"Be right up!"

"I'd better get going," Janie said, the last two pies balancing in her hands as she headed for the front door.

"Let me get the door for you."

"He'll be crushed—Billy. You know that don't you?" I nodded. "How will you tell him?"

"Think I'll just wait until we're there, standing in front of his aunt's house."

"That seems pretty mean to me."

"Would it be better to tell him now and ruin the rest of his time here, have him sulking and crying? Wouldn't it be better just to let him enjoy himself a little longer?"

"Maybe you're right." She kissed my cheek. "When he asked if he could stay with us forever it got me thinking. I thought, yes, Laird would like that. I'd like it too. Our baby would have a brother to grow up with, to play with, to laugh and cry with. And Billy wouldn't be alone anymore. He'd be loved again. Guess it wasn't in

God's plan." On that she walked out, got in the car, and drove away.

Just then I heard a muffled crash and thud coming from our bedroom. Figuring Billy had fallen, I dashed up the stairs to find him splayed out on his back in the closet, a bunch of crushed shoeboxes underneath him, stray shoes that were once in their boxes now scattered about, my baseball glove lying on the bedroom floor a few feet away.

"Well aren't you a sight? Are you hurt?"

He giggled, sounding like a goat. "No."

"Well I'm glad somebody finally got some use out of all those shoes." I extended my hand to help him up. "Don't worry, kid. She won't notice."

Brushing himself off, he said, "That was fun!"

"At least you got my glove down." I picked up glove and felt around the upper shelf until I found a baseball to go with it, then we headed downstairs and outside. There we played catch and I taught Billy the fundamentals of fielding grounders and fly balls.

"Try to get in front of the ball," I told him after throwing him a ground ball. "Then drop your knee to the ground in front of you, turning your down leg across your body a bit so the ball can't get under you if you miss with your glove. Keep your glove on the ground, and always keep your eye on the ball." That last part I stressed again. "Watch the ball all the way into your glove. Don't get ahead of yourself and start looking to see how close the runner is to the base. You'll miss the ball if you do that. Field it first, then throw it."

"Okay," was all he said.

His technique was a bit clumsy but I expected that at his age; he was only eight years old, after all. A few times he fell over trying to stop quickly and set his knee the way I'd showed him, but soon he had it down. There was a certain pride that came from teaching him something and watching him try to grasp it and make it his own, like what a teacher must feel when her young student solves a complicated math problem. It'd given me a glimpse of fatherhood, a sight I found pleasant to the soul, a sight I thought I'd like to see more often.

After throwing him some grounders we switched to fly balls. "Again, never take your eye off the ball. Find it in the air as soon as you can, run to meet it based on its trajectory, then catch it in your glove, but with the help of your other hand, like this." I showed him how to use his free hand to help keep the ball in his glove when the ball makes impact. "Bring that hand over the opening of the glove the second that ball reaches the glove or the ball's likely to pop out."

"What's trajectory?"

"The angle and direction of flight. The path the ball is taking. What you're doing is trying to get an idea of where the ball will land so you can be there waiting. Understand?"

"I think so. If the ball is going that way I run the same way."

"Correct."

"But everybody knows that."

I smiled. "You'd be surprised, kid. Believe me. I've seen ballplayers defy all logic. The ball gets hit one way but they run in the opposite direction. You're left scratching your head, wondering what they think they saw. It happens."

"I sure hope I don't do that."

I put my arm around him and we turned toward the house. "Me too, Billy. You don't want *that* picture showing up in the papers. Trust me." I said it knowing I'd done it myself. "That would be embarrassing."

CHAPTER TWENTY

B illy was over the moon about flying. He didn't care where we were going; didn't even ask. He told me he'd always wanted to fly, that his father used to have an old leather flying helmet he would let Billy wear around the house sometimes, pretending he was an airplane with his arms wide open and voice revving like an engine. To be honest, I'd never flown before either so I shared in his excitement, though with just a tinge of anxiety to accompany it. Janie on the other hand wasn't so thrilled. She'd never trusted airplanes, though she'd never flown. Still, whenever news broke about an airline accident Janie would say, "Lead weights weren't meant to fly." I'd remind her that airplanes weren't made out of lead and that they were designed specifically for flight, but those words would just shatter against the rock that was her head in such moments.

"What should I bring?" Billy asked, looking at me as I leaned against his dresser, all his possessions—his ball glove, his father's watch and baseball cards, the new clothes we had purchased to replace his old—all laid out on the bed, evenly spaced in three rows like checkers on a board at the start of a game, his scrunched duffle nearby, one hand holding it open, the other hand ready to start tossing things inside.

Janie leaned arms folded against the doorjamb. When I gave her a glance to see if she had any suggestions, she simply raised her eyebrows and twisted her lips before looking away.

"Tell you what, sport," I said. "Why don't you bring it all? Shouldn't take up much room. Besides, who knows what we might need—what type of mischief we might get into?" I shot Billy a wink and then watched as Janie backed out of the doorway, arms still crossed as she walked away. I imagined her thinking me once again heartless, a selfish man about to break another boy's spirit, only this wasn't about an unsigned autograph; this was about broken trust, about a child who was counting on me to care for him and protect him, to tell him the truth. In my mind I was doing just that by delivering him to his aunt in Ohio—his next of kin— but in my heart I felt more like I was about to betray him, to dump him off on somebody who, up until that moment, hadn't seemed too keen on taking him, somebody that may not give him as much love as we could.

"Good idea! If I bring my glove, maybe we can play catch with Mr. Clarke!"

"I'm sure he'd love to throw the ball around with you."

"That would be swell!" He began stuffing his things into the duffle while I headed to my room to pack.

I'd told Billy we were going to deliver the eight baseballs to Clarke, but I didn't tell him where, just that it required a day's flight on an airplane. It would be hard to imagine a child of his age knowing his geography and the proximity of Ohio to Michigan; it would be even harder to image he could make the connection that we were going to his aunt's also. Still, I wasn't taking any chances. We'd catch an American Airlines flight out of New Haven Municipal Airport, fly to Philadelphia where we'd layover for a few hours before flying on to Detroit. After delivering the baseballs we'd get a hotel room, then fly out the next morning from Detroit to Cincinnati. I'd fly home from there by way of Philadelphia again. My sincere hope was that Billy would not come out of this hating me. I supposed I would do enough of that myself. And I figured Janie would get a few subtle jabs in also. She'd hinted that she wanted Billy to stay. She'd also hinted that I was doing the wrong thing by not telling him where we were going, that only I would be coming back home. When my chosen path failed, she'd be there to politely remind me how heartless I'd been.

The anxious part of me prompted a study of the plane we'd be taking, not that it'd help much if the plane went down. Still, knowing a little about the plane would help calm my nerves. American Airlines used mostly Douglas DC-3s, I'd read—a 21-seat passenger aircraft with a cruising speed of 207 miles per hour and a range of 1,500 miles. It was a polished aluminum plane with lots of windows and two prop-engines, one mounted under each wing, and was said to be very comfortable for passengers on long flights. We would soon see.

Janie drove us to New Haven Municipal Airport, which on that day—without bad weather or traffic—took only 45 minutes. New Haven had only one terminal and it wasn't particularly crowded that day, perhaps 50 people, some being passengers, some there like Janie to see their friends or family members off, a little girl with a red ribbon in her golden hair laying at the feet of one couple, propping herself up on her elbows to color in a book, doing her best not to mess up her pretty white dress. And there were porters and ticket agents moving about doing their jobs. The terminal seemed almost entirely made of glass on the runway side of the building, with many onlookers like us standing close to watch intermittent flights takeoff and land, the service crews tending to three passenger planes moored on the concrete runway within a hundred yards of the terminal.

"One day we'll all be travelling by airplane," I said. "Trains will be obsolete. Passenger trains, anyway."

"Well if so," Janie said, "We'll be travelling separately—you by plane, me by car."

"There's always the bus."

"Ugh. Cross-country by bus? No thanks."

"American Airlines flight twenty-four to Philadelphia will now begin boarding at gate number two," a woman politely cawed over the terminal loudspeaker. "Those passengers needing assistance with boarding, please see the gate attendant. Again, American Airlines flight twenty-four to Philadelphia will now begin boarding at gate number two. Thank you and thank you for flying with American."

"That's us," I said, my eyes scanning our tickets while I picked up my bag, motioning with my chin for Billy to pick up his.

"Are you excited about your flight?" Janie said to Billy, doing her best to put a smile on her sad face, tickling his waist and causing him to leap forward giggling. "Wish I was going with you."

"Me too," I said, putting my arm around her and kissing her cheek as we walked toward the nearby gate.

"You do? Why didn't you ask me then?"

"Because you're very pregnant. Can you even fly in your condition?"

"I don't really know. Probably not, but it would have been nice if you'd asked."

"Janie, I'm sorry. Seems I'm always messing things up between us."

"No, not always," she said, stopping at the gate to kiss my lips. "Just sometimes."

"I'll do better. I promise."

"When?" she whispered in my ear. "When you get back from abandoning Billy? Or when you get back from abandoning me to go fight in the war?"

"That's not fair and you know it," I whispered back.

Janie smiled up at me before kneeling to give Billy a hug goodbye, her eyes teary, reflecting the light. "I'm going to miss you, Billy Sunday."

"It's okay. I'll only be gone for a little while," he said, his head over Janie's shoulder, her arms holding onto him a little longer than she might otherwise.

"Well," she said, leaning back to look at his innocent face. "I still think you should know that you are an amazing boy, and you are going to do amazing things in this world. I just know it. Until we see each other again, Billy, you remember that you have a permanent place right here." Janie pointed to her heart, tears starting to trickle down her pale cheeks. Pointing to his heart, she added, "And you make sure you keep me right there, okay? Always."

"Okay, Janie. I will." He looked up at me with eyes as eager as a greyhound's, one waiting for the gate to open so he can chase the rabbit. "Can we go on the plane now?"

I kissed Janie's forehead, then found her wet eyes and kissed each before looking into them. "I love you, Janie."

"Me too," she muttered, her hands intentionally covering her face as they wiped her eyes. "See you in a few days."

We walked to the gate and as I handed the agent our tickets—Billy smiling up at her like the cat that just ate her pet mouse—I watched Janie walk away, still wiping her eyes, still, I imagined, disappointed in me.

A moment later we were seated in two high-back upholstered chairs that were mounted side-by-side, Billy sitting in the window seat, me in the aisle seat. Across and facing us were two elderly women, both wearing black and white habits, both nuns of one order or another.

"Hello, sisters!" Billy said. "This is my first time flying! I'm excited!"

"Well, hello to you, young man," the nun closest to the window said. "This is not our first flight, but we are very excited too."

"My name's Billy. Billy Sunday. What's yours?"

"Billy," I said, "I don't think you—"

"No, no," the nun in the aisle seat said. "It's perfectly fine. Don't stop the boy. If he wants to be polite and introduce himself, it's only right that we do the same in return. I am Sister Helen."

"And I am Sister Catherine," the other nun near the window said. "And who is this fine young man with you, Billy Sunday?"

"Laird Allen Young the third," Billy offered.

I laughed. "Yes. But please, just Laird—and no Mister Young. That's for my father."

"Okay. Laird it is," Sister Helen said.

"Are the two of you related somehow?"

"Not yet," Billy blurted out before I could answer. "But maybe soon."

I pursed my lips and shook my head slightly. They seemed to understand and changed the subject.

"Did you know you have quite the famous name, Billy Sunday?" Sister Helen asked.

"Yes, sister. My real name is William Bradford Sunday. I'm named after a founding father of this country, and Billy Sunday is an evang-a-ist."

"Well, now!" Sister Catherine exclaimed, glancing over at Sister Helen. "Isn't that something?"

"I have a lot to live up to," Billy said, matter-of-factly, stretching his torso in the seat to stare out the window at the propellers, which had begun to turn. "Look!"

I looked through the window over Billy's shoulder. "Here we go. Won't be long now before we're in the air."

"Soaring the heavens," Sister Catherine added, her eyes closed, imagining fondly.

"Close, anyway," Sister Helen said, patting her friend's arm. "Sister Catherine is a romantic, you see."

With her eyes still closed and head slightly up toward the "heavens," her hands clasped over her heart, Sister Catherine quoted, "How wondrously they rise, above the smooth green pastures, into the azure skies!"

"Henry Van Dyke. 'The Heavenly Hills of Holland.' " Sister

Helen said. "But he was speaking of the rising hills, not the rising airplanes."

"One sees what one sees," Sister Catherine mused.

"Sinful. Just sinful," Sister Helen said, patting her friend's arm once more. "But there is always hope, my sister. Always hope."

My lips couldn't help but smile at the two nuns who seemed very fond of each other. They weren't at all like what I'd often imagined—self-afflicted orthodox creatures void of any sense of humor or happiness, offering themselves wholly to The Almighty, bondservants to "The King of Kings."

"Please check your seatbelts," the attendant said as she passed, looking down at our laps to make sure our hands did as told. "We'll be departing shortly."

Suddenly the plane jerked forward and we were rolling, the propellers humming loudly, the terminal growing smaller out the window as we moved to the end of the runway, holding for takeoff until the "all clear" was given. Billy pushed himself firmly against the back of his seat, his hands gripping the armrests, his head forward but eyes still watching out the window.

"Scared?" I asked.

"Um hmm." But he was grinning, so excited he might have rocketed out of his seat if it weren't for the lap belt holding him in place.

"Me, too."

Next thing we knew we were increasing speed, the plane rattling, the engines screaming, the ride becoming bumpier and bumpier, the scenery moving past us quicker and quicker, until without warning the nose of the airplane lifted high, the rear following it up until the rattling and bumps ceased, the only sound the engines.

"That was swell!" Billy said, now straining to see the descending earth out the window.

I decided to hang on to the armrests a little longer. To me, our fate could change at any moment and I wanted to be ready, which I figured to be laughable since if we did crash, they'd still find my dead body; I'd just be clinching the disconnected armrests in my fists, the rest of my seat a mile away.

WHEN WE LANDED in Detroit it was four in the afternoon and Billy and I were as relaxed as playing kittens. We'd lifted off and landed twice by then and were now experienced fliers. Detroit City Airport, like Philadelphia's, had much more real estate to navigate, from the numerous runways to the numerous terminals, to the congested streets out front of the terminal. Most of Detroit's automotive manufacturing plants had been converted to produce airplanes and vehicles specific to the war effort, so Detroit City Airport, as well as Detroit Metro Airport—also called Romulus Field—were sharing runways with the military. With that came a massive influx of domestic immigrants to fill the higher paying production jobs, as well as streams of military personnel and equipment, making Detroit's already congested streets worse. Hordes of tall industrial stacks blotted out the horizon like a hundred smoking gun barrels pointed at the sky, their condensate and pollutants choking the air and giving it a burnt rubber smell, each cluster of stacks protected by high factory walls and large iron gates, with passage through the gates permitted only by guards. And each factory had fields of parked cars around it.

River Rouge was an industrialized suburb of Detroit, approximately 30 minutes downriver. Ford's River Rouge plant occupied a large portion of real estate and skyline in the city, as did several shipbuilding and steel manufacturing plants. For those like Nig Clarke who lived in River Rouge, it must have seemed like they were just sediment in the fuel tank of the big, angry, loud machine engulfing them—a machine with a bad case of smelly gas.

Clarke's modest tract home sat just *two* blocks from the river, on a street that cowered under the tall red brick walls of the Ford plant, the sound of machines stamping out sheet metal heard in the distance, the early evening sun giving the polluted sky an agouti appearance, the smell of paint and burnt steel falling on us like invisible rain as we walked up the concrete walk, the large wraparound porch the only thing between us and the wide front door—between Nig Clarke and I finally meeting.

"Is this where he lives?" Billy asked, dropping his duffle and stopping to look about.

I compared the address written on the paper my mother gave me to the numbers nailed to a post at the front porch. "I think so. Same address."

"Is he poor?"

"I don't know. It's not polite to ask, so don't."

"Okay."

A few moments later we were standing at the front door, my knuckles up but frozen, unable to knock on the door.

"What's the matter?" Billy asked, looking up at me. When he didn't get an answer he yanked on my coat. "Why don't you knock?"

Billy leaned in to knock but I stopped him. "No. Wait."

"For what?"

I took a deep breath of the caustic air. "I just need to think for a minute about what I'm going to say to him."

"Just say, 'Hi, Mr. Clarke. My name is Laird Allen Young the third and I have your balls."

"I can't...you can't just say, 'I have your balls,'" I said, laughing, thankful for how innocently children state the obvious. "That doesn't even sound right. He might punch me in the nose."

"Well, you gotta say something, right?"

"I know, I know. Just wait a minute."

I took another deep breath, raised my hand to knock, but stopped short of knocking when I heard a man's voice behind us.

"Can I help you fellas with something?" The question wasn't gruff or confrontational; it was more the polite inquiry of a friend. Billy and I turned to see a fit, middle-aged man about five foot eight inches tall, wearing soiled jeans, work boots, a flannel shirt, and a lined jean jacket, his salt and pepper hair mussed and sweaty, his hardhat under one arm, a gray lunch-pail being held by the handle at his thigh. "Are you fellas lost?"

"No, sir!" Billy said, extending his small hand. "We're here to see you!"

The man shook Billy's hand but seemed confused, and also amused by Billy's confidence.

"If you're Nig Clarke," I added, extending my hand also.

"Say, fella," he said, stepping in close to whisper. "Just call me Jay, not Nig."

"I apologize. I didn't mean to offended you. I thought—"

"Don't misunderstand me. I'm okay with players and people calling me 'Nig.' Never seemed to bother me any. But my wife, see, she don't like it, okay? She hears it and phew! You know what I mean?"

"Yes, sir. I do."

"So you fellas are here to see me?" Clarke asked, passing by us to reach for the front door handle.

"Yes, Mr. Clarke," Billy started, "We have—"

"Something to give you," I finished. "My name is Laird Young. This here is Billy."

"Something to give me?"

"Yes, sir," I said. "Is there a place we can sit and talk? This could take a while. But, hey, if this is a bad time we can come back in the morning."

"No, no. Just let me okay it with the misses. She helps take care of my mother who lives with us. Tires her out some days. Plus I'd like to clean up. Won't take long. These welders at the steel plant keep me running."

He opened the door and stepped inside, adding just before he shut the door, "Excuse me."

Nig Clarke—Jay—wasn't at all what I'd expected. The image I had in my mind was of Jay Justin Clarke, the brazen young catcher that could rile Ty Cobb; not Jay Justin Clark, the blue-collar welder's helper with the soft-spoken voice and gentleman's manner. I somehow figured him to be larger-than-life and immortal, still wearing his catcher's mask and shin guards; not mid-sized and aging, wearing a hardhat and work boots.

"He seems nice," Billy said, taking a seat on the front steps, looking up at the factory that seemed to be peeking over the wall at us from across the street. "What do they make there?"

"Cars, I think?" I sat next to him on the steps. "Fords."

"My father liked Buicks. He used to say they were bricks with wheels—whatever that means."

"I like Buicks too."

"Do you think they'll ever make a flying car?"

"Maybe...someday, I suppose."

"Then we could fly here in our car."

"With the nuns?"

Billy giggled. "They were nice."

"You think everybody's nice, don't you?"

He thought about my question for a moment. "My mother used to say that everybody deserves a chance to be nice. She said everybody has nice in them. Some people are just hurting and take it out on others. She said not to repay meanness with more meanness. She said if I'm nice, most people will be nice back. That's a lot to remember, but I try."

I smiled and looked off. "Seems to me you're doing all right."

"Do you want a boy or a girl?"

"Hmm. I don't know. I suppose I'd be happy with a girl or a boy."

"With a boy you can play catch, and sports, and fish, and ride bicycles. But what can you do with a girl?"

"Lots of things. All those things you just mentioned a girl can do. Why? You don't like girls?"

"I like girls. I just can't find any use for them. I know they make good nuns and moms when they're grown up, but as girls, what good are they?"

"The world would be an awfully dull place without girls, Billy. Why, without girls I don't think we'd ever learn how deeply we can love, or how beautiful a butterfly is, or how colorful and fragrant a flower is, or how wonderful perfume smells behind an ear, or what the heart is capable of, or what tenderness feels like, or what tears are for, or how powerful and delightful a kiss can be. Fathers wouldn't know about pigtails, or what laps are for."

Billy giggled. "Where I come from you could get beat up talking like that."

"Where I come from too," I said with a laugh. "But one day Billy, in the not so distant future, you're going to learn why God made girls, and believe me, brother, it'll be a beautiful, awful, delightful, awakening."

"How can something be awful and delightful?"

"You'll see."

Just then the door squeaked open and we leapt to our feet, turning to see Clarke in the doorway, his face washed and hair slicked back, his clothes changed, the aroma of roast beef and potatoes escaping from inside the house. "Sorry for the wait, fellas. I'll bet you're both hungry. Come on in. Please."

"Oh, we didn't mean to interrupt your dinner. Maybe we should just come back tomorrow."

"No, please. We'd like you to join us."

"It smells really good!" Billy said.

Clarke leaned down and whispered to him. "I'll let you in on a secret, Billy. It's even better than it smells."

"We're very grateful," I said with a nod, passing by him as he held the door open, my bag in my hand at my side, Billy in front of me, his duffle slung over his shoulder, his eyes scanning the interior like a patron at a museum.

"Where's all the baseball stuff?" Billy asked.

Like Billy, I'd expected to see baseball paraphernalia strewn about like dirty clothes—old jerseys and caps lying about, photographs of Clarke with greats like Ruth and Cy Young, Ty Cobb and Wagner, but there wasn't *anything*.

"You like baseball?" Clarke asked Billy.

"Yes, sir," Billy said. "I like it a lot! Laird's been teaching me."

"We both like baseball. That's why we've come."

"Yeah?" Clarke said. "Well, let's eat first, then we can talk baseball. I'll even show you where I keep all my 'baseball stuff.' Sound good?"

"That would be great," I said, struck by the thought that Clarke didn't even ask what it was about, didn't think for a moment that we might be deranged fans coming to his home for some sort of reckoning; he didn't seem to care. He simply welcomed us into his home, welcomed us at his dinner table, gracious in every respect. We'd come to visit him and that was all the reason he needed, though I suspected his wife might have liked some advance notice.

Clarke led us into the cozy dining room where his aged mother was already seated at the oval table, one made from mahogany, with a mahogany pedestal and clawed foot, the tabletop partially covered by a white cloth resembling a doily, as well as dinner plates, glasses and silverware arranged similarly before each of the five matching chairs, the sixth chair up against the wall, one of its wooden legs broken and laying underneath. Next to his mother stood a small black dog with a fluffy coat and curled tail, a tail that wagged faster than high-speed windshield wipers, the dog's dark eyes and smile cheerful, waiting it seemed for its share of that delightfully smelling dinner, part of which was already on the table.

"Have a seat, fellas," Clarke said, pulling out two chairs directly across from his mother. "Won't be but a minute." Clarke disappeared through a swinging door that I figured led to the kitchen.

"Hello," I said to his mother. She smiled politely but didn't say a word. She was a tiny woman, which I figured partially accounted for Clarke's mid-sized frame, reasoning that his father must have been somewhat taller, putting Clarke somewhere in the middle. The skin on her face had been loosened and wrinkled by time, her hair a bright silver, pulled up at the bottom into a bun, the color of her eyes obscured by spidery red veins and sagging eyelids. She sat leaning forward with her arms tight to her body and hands under the table to fight off the chill.

Just then her little dog came around and leapt onto Billy's lap, giving him a joyful start. "Well, hello!" Billy said, petting the dog's soft coat. "What's your name?"

"That's Molly," Clarke's mother said. "She's a Shih Tzu."

I reached over to pet the dog. "Nice to meet you, Molly."

"Molly, off!" Clarke's wife said as she came through the swinging door, one hand struggling to support the heavy plate of partially sliced roast beef, the other carrying a large bowl of skinned and baked potatoes, their outsides buttered and golden. Clarke followed his wife with a pitcher of milk and a bowl of what appeared to be asparagus.

"I hope you gentlemen are hungry," Mrs. Clarke said, setting the dishes in the center of the table. "If I'd known you were coming I'd have prepared a nice dessert."

"This is wonderful, thank you," I said.

"I'm so hungry I could eat it all!" Billy said.

"Fellas, this is my wife, Mary. And this is my mother. You've met Molly. Mary, this is Laird Young and his son, Billy."

"No, not my son, but a very special friend of our family."

"Well I'm pleased to meet you both," Mary said, taking her seat at one end of the table, tucking her long skirt under her as she sat, primping her chocolate-colored hair—also in a bun—and dabbing her face with her folded cloth napkin. "Please excuse my appearance. It's hot in the kitchen."

"There's nothing to excuse," I said. "You look lovely."

Mary blushed. "Well aren't you nice? That's very sweet. You must be married."

"Yes, ma'am."

Clarke reached for the plate of roast beef but Mary rebuked her husband with a stern glare. "Shall we say grace, then?" Mary asked. We joined hands and Mary said a brief prayer. "Thank you Father for this food and for the fellowship of friends. May they both be a blessing to us. Amen."

"Amen," the rest of us said in unison.

"Dig in, fellas," Clarke said as he laid a slice of roast beef on his mother's plate, then three slices on his own before handing the plate off to me. "So where are you from? I'm picking up maybe New England in your accent."

I nodded. "I grew up outside of Boston—a town called Lynn. Been out that way?"

"Plenty. Faced the Sox more times than I care to mention."

"That's right. I forgot. The Naps were in the American League."

"Faced the Braves a couple times, too, when I played with Philly. But that was near the end of my big league days…nineteen-nineteen."

"Playing the Red Sox you must have had to face Cy Young sometimes."

He nodded, his mouth full of food but talking anyway. "Yeah, Cy was a right guy. One of the best pitchers ever to play."

"Get any hits off him?"

"I took him for a few bases," he said, humbly. "But he could make that ball dance. Sometimes you just stood there thinking, 'What just happened?' He was that good."

"You were good, too, though."

He cocked his head. "Thank you. That means a lot that you'd say that. But some guys are so special—so gifted. They're in a league by themselves. Know what I mean? Like Cobb and Wagner, Grover Cleveland Alexander, Ruth and Hornsby, and that's just a few. And 'The Grey Eagle,' Tris Speaker. Can't forget him."

"But you had to play against them *all*. You held your own against the very best. One reporter for *The Plain Dealer* wrote in nineteen ten, 'When he wants to be, Clarke is the best catcher in the American League.' In o-six your three fifty-eight batting average tied George Stone's who led all of Major League Baseball. You didn't get any credit because you only played fifty-seven games. That same year your slugging percentage of—"

"My what?" Clarke asked, his voice muffled by the fork still in his mouth.

"Slugging percentage...some new statistic my mother came across and likes...takes into account the number of each type of hit you got divided by your at-bats."

"Your mother?"

"Yep. Anyway, your slugging percentage of four eighty-six was second highest in the majors, beating even Honus Wagner, Harry Lumley, Nap Lajoie. Again you didn't get credit. In o-seven, though you let a bunch of guys steal on you, you *still* led the American League in defense as a catcher, and you were third in putouts and assists. In o-eight you led the league in caught stealing percentage, and you caught the perfect game for Addie Joss. All those things say something about you as a player. You were good, at least good enough to last nine years in the majors against the best who ever played."

"Thank you. You sure know the game."

I laughed. "My mother. She eats baseball statistics for breakfast."

"You're mistaken about Ruth, though. I never played against

him. You ever play—professionally, I mean?"

"The minors," I said, nodding as I ate. "You're a fine cook, Mrs. Clarke. It's very good."

"It's delicious!" Billy said, smiling with a mouthful of food.

"Thank you, boys," Mary said.

"The minors? What club?"

"The Hartford Bees, a Boston Braves affiliate."

"Yeah? That's great! What position?"

"Pitcher. Tried to put me at third once but it didn't suit."

"You good?"

I laughed. "That depends on who you ask."

"I'm asking you," he said with a grin. "Don't be modest. What's your ERA? What's your best pitch?"

"High twos, pretty good curve. My fastball's got some speed too...pretty accurate."

"That's real good. Say, I hear the majors are strapped right now, lots of guys getting drafted or volunteering to go fight the war. Maybe the Braves will call you up."

"Doubtful, but maybe."

"Can you hit?"

"I do alright. I'm hitting about three hundred, three fifteen, somewhere in there."

"That's pretty good. I think it could happen."

"You came all the way from Hartford to see my husband?" Mary asked. "Must be very important."

"Yes, ma'am."

"We have something we need to give him," Billy added. "Some balls."

"Yeah?" Clarke asked. "Balls? For me?"

"My father, he...it was a long time ago. It'll take awhile to explain."

"Did I know you father?"

"Yes, well, you met him once...in France...the war."

"Your father was in the Marines?"

"The Army—Fourth Infantry. You two met briefly in Brest, where he disembarked."

"Hmm. What was your father's name?"

"Same as mine. Laird Allen Young, but people just called him 'Al.' Some called him 'Big Al,' but mostly just 'Al.'"

Trying to bring my father's face to mind, he said, "I'm sorry, Laird, but I don't seem to recall meeting anybody by that name."

"It was during a baseball game. Some guy was mouthing off to you from the mound. My father shut him up."

"Wait! Was your father...was he the guy that...yes! He hit a ball over the right field fence...called it first too...then turned to me and said, 'Ennis.' Told the guy he'd take him for eight base hits too!"

"I didn't know about the eight base hits."

"No? Well, let me tell you about that. This guy on the mound, some rookie pro pitcher I'd never heard of but who'd heard of me, he pitches to me and I hit a grounder to the third baseman for an out. I'm walking back to the bench and this guy's yelling from the mound, 'You're nothin', Clarke! Nothin'! Eight for eight? Are you kiddin' me? You couldn't go eight for eight if my little sister was pitching!' I didn't care much and kept walking, but your dad walks up and takes my bat from me, says to the guy on the mound, 'I'll take that challenge! Eight base hits in eight at bats! Let's go!' The guy must have been a genuine idiot because he walks over and says to your father, 'But my sister ain't here.'" We all laughed at that. "Your dad says, 'Not your sister. Eight for eight against *you*. Come on.' The guy laughs it off and says, 'This I gotta see.' Your dad says, 'Give me three outs. Three outs and I'll take you for eight hits, all of them to right field, and one will be a home run.' The guy says, 'You're on, moron. Let's go.' He walks to the mound and your father turns to me before getting in the batters box...says, 'I have something of yours, Mister Clarke, that I want to return. I'll find you when this war is over, when we're stateside again.' I didn't think much of it except it was strange how he referred to me as Mister Clark."

"He respected you," I said, noticing Mary leaning in listening intently. "Did he get the eight hits?"

"Boy did he! It was really something to see! He dropped the first three in the gap between right and center, between infield and outfield. When the outfielders shifted in shallow, your father dropped the next one in deep, over their heads. The next he put over the wall. That's when he turned to me and said, "Ennis!" The outfielders shifted deep and your father dropped three more in the gap. Now your dad's got them all confused and that big mouth pitcher flustered. The pitcher tells his infielders to play deep, but they play too deep. Your father sees it and of course, drops a bunt, straight down the first base line, just fair. Caught everybody looking for another fly. Well your father runs like a spooked deer down to first, that pitcher racing for the ball that was still rolling just in front of your father, not too far from the bag, the first baseman trying to get back to first base to help out. Your father and the pitcher got to the ball about the same time. The pitcher tries to tag your father out but your dad takes a couple long steps to avoid the tag, planting his foot on first base in the process."

"That must have been something to see," I said, a proud smile on my face.

"Never seen anything like it in all my days! Those boys there, all those soldiers and Marines and Sailors watching, officers and enlisted men, they all just went crazy! Especially when your dad laid down that bunt!"

"But he didn't take all eight to right field."

"Who cares? That was better!" Clarke clasped his hands together, reliving in his mind the excitement he'd felt that very day in Brest. "He was the first hero of the war—for a lot of us anyway. That scene did more for moral than anything else. Anyway, before your dad and I could talk he and the guys he came with got called away. I looked for him later that day but couldn't find him. They said his unit shipped out to help with some big offensive."

"Meuse-Argonne," I said.

"When I got home from the war I would sometimes look on the field at the ballplayers, looking for your father's face. I figured a guy who could hit that good had to be in the majors somewhere. But I never found him."

"He played for the Boston Braves—shortstop. But that was before the war."

He shook his head. "I knew he just had to be a pro player! I knew it! How is he? Did he make it back from the war okay?"

"No, he got hurt pretty bad."

That took the life out of our conversation. "I'm truly sorry to hear that, Laird. Truly sorry."

My throat tightened and I found myself fighting back tears. "Yeah, but he made it home alive. I guess that's what matters most."

"What happened to him?" Clarke asked, leaning in, very concerned and interested.

"Jay, please," Mary said. "It's not polite to—"

"It's fine. It's okay. He suffered a head injury from a shell that exploded near him. Shattered the back of his skull. They pieced it back together but it left him in a stupor. He requires fulltime care now."

I saw some water welling in Clarke's eyes. He swallowed hard before asking, "Is there anything I can do? Anything? I'd be happy to?"

"I'm not sure there's anything any of us can do at this point. He's been like that for the past twenty-five years. But thank you. That's very kind of you to offer."

After that we ate in silence, finishing the fine meal Mary had made for us before Clarke, Billy, and I retired to a room Clarke called his "room of memories." This was where he kept all his baseball memorabilia. On the wall were several old jerseys, hung on hangers attached to the wall by a single nail—a Naps jersey with a swathe of blood across the belly.

"Look at that!" Billy said, pointing to the bloody jersey. "What happened?"

"That's Cobb's blood, not mine. That's why I kept it. Nap Lajoie took it out of my salary, though, the cheapskate."

"What happened?" I asked, mildly amused.

"Ty tried to steal home on me. He came in hard but I shut him down. Catchers don't like it when a fella tries to steal home on them. We tussled a bit on the ground, but I held the ball. He got called out and got a bloody nose in the process."

"You punched Ty Cobb?"

"No. No, I wouldn't do that to him. He and I were friends...well, as much as you can be friends and still be competitors. We met when Cleveland leant me to Detroit for a few games in nineteen o-six. We were both rookies and got on well. He could really make me laugh, that guy. No, Cobb barreled into me rather than sliding. That's how the blood got there." Clarke laughed, recalling in his mind. "Led with his face instead of his arms. His face hit my hip and gut so hard it knocked the wind out of me and nearly broke his nose. As I went flying I grabbed onto him and we both landed in a heap on the ground. He was mad. Some things were said between us, but the boys separated us. After the game he was signing autographs near their dugout, his nose as big as an egg. Ty was like that. His legs could be broken but he'd still meet with fans after the game. Anyway, I went over to ask him if he was okay. He saw my bloody shirt and knowing it was his blood, he took his pen and wrote," Clarke pointed to some small writing just over the swathe of blood. "'Next time it'll be your blood.' Didn't sign it because that's not why he did it. But that's his writing—his blood too." He giggled to himself.

"He was a great player, for sure, but I've heard about his legendary temper."

"Cobb was the greatest player I've ever faced, and I've faced some great ones, like Eddie Collins. Collins could hit. And he could steal bases. Used to annoy me how many times he got me. Eddie Collins was with the Athletics when they got beat in fourteen by the 'Miracle Braves.'"

"The day I was born."

"No kidding? That's one birthday your mother won't forget!" He chuckled to himself. "But Cobb...as great as he was, and like I said, he was the greatest player I ever saw...he was still the easiest to rile...just a passionate guy. Whenever I was catching and he'd come up to bat, I'd flick dirt on his shoes while he was standing in the batters box waiting for the pitch. It'd drive him mad sometimes, especially if he was having an off day. One time he extended his bat to me while I squatted there and using the tip, he shoved me backward and over onto my back. The crowd loved it. That's how we were. He roughed me up once over a meal, when I admitted the umps got a few calls wrong at the plate when he tried to score on me...when they called him out instead of safe. Got upset, said I cost him some runs off his record. But other than that we had a good relationship."

"You see him a lot now that you live in Detroit?"

"Sometimes I'll bump into him, when he's in town for some event. He's moved on, back to Atlanta, last I heard. Once he stopped by the house when he was out this way. Came and saw me a couple times when I was in the Marines stateside. He liked the Marines. Had a lot of respect for them. But no, I'm married and have to care for my mother. And I work at the mill helping the welders there. Those things keep me busy. Baseball's just a memory now. But I'll try to catch a game now and then, especially when the Red Sox come to town. I like to watch that Ted Williams fellow. He interests me. Good player. But that's another player caught up in the war effort. He volunteered, though, right?"

"I think so."

"Anyway, these other things probably wouldn't mean much to most people…just things others have given to me or a ball I felt like keeping, like this one here. Cy Young beaned me with this ball, right here," he said, putting the ball against his left ribcage. "Hurt worse than the time a stray pitch split my finger down to the bone. Thought my ribs were broken but they weren't. But I stood there at the plate for a few minutes, bent to the side and cringing, holding my ribs. That's when I saw the ball still on the ground, resting against my shoe. So I grabbed it and handed it to Lajoie who'd come out to check on me. Told him to keep it for me." Clarke smiled to himself as he remembered that day. "That guy was still pitching in his forties! Can you believe that? Cy came over to Cleveland his final year. I caught a couple games for him, one in April of nineteen ten, against Cobb and Detroit, one day after I caught Addie Joss' second no-hitter, that one against the White Sox. Fun game, the one I caught for Cy. I got two hits that day but we still lost. Cy got a hit too. He had a tough year, but gave it his all to the end. That game probably doesn't mean much to most people but it was one of the highlights of my career. Shoeless Joe Jackson was on our team that year, though he didn't arrive until July. Nice fella, Joe…great player, too. Shame what happened to him."

"You were pretty old by the time you retired too."

"Yeah. I played into my forties also, but I finished in the minors."

"You finished with MVP honors, though."

"How do you know all of this stuff about me?"

"Like I said, my mother."

"No, there's more to it than that. You do all this research on me, come all this way…there has to be a reason."

I nodded. The moment had come to return my father's prized baseballs to the man who'd hit them, but in my heart I didn't want to. They'd brought me so far in my relationship with my father—and my mother—that to let them go now seemed unfair somehow. But that was just the selfish side of me resurfacing. "You're right, Mr. Clark."

"Please, just Jay."

I reached into my bag and retrieved the red tobacco box. Holding it out to him, I said, "These are why I've come so far."

"Why *we've* come so far," Billy reminded me.

"*We've*," I conceded. "Why we've come so far."

Clarke eyed the box for a moment the way a tiger might gaze upon a suspected trap, body still, its mind working through the different scenarios. "This is for me?"

"Yes, sir, but not 'for you.' They belong to you. My father wanted me to return them."

Clarke opened the box, and just as I had, saw the folded towel covering the baseballs, with the note on top reading: *Ennis 1902.* He picked up the note. "It's starting to brown up."

"It's been in there for a long time. My father wrote it when he was just eight years old…forty-one years ago."

Clarke unfurled the towel. When he saw the eight aged baseballs, I could see he'd made the connection in his mind. "Are you telling me…are you saying that these here eight baseballs…that these are the eight home run balls I hit with Corsicana that day in nineteen o-two?"

I couldn't bring myself to speak, so I nodded, my heart caught up in my throat.

He lifted one of the baseballs out of the tin box, placed it under his nose, leaving the ball there for a long moment, his eyes closed, his exhaled nasal breath echoing off the ball's surface, sounding like a panting horse after a long run. I imagined him taking himself back to Ennis, Texas, June 15, 1902, *Oil City* stitched across his jersey as he struts to the plate for the eighth and final time, staring down the weary opposing pitcher about to be taken for his fifty-first run, Clarke's cleated feet scratching the dirt and setting themselves for the pitch, his bat coming around to pull and lift the ball once more over the right field fence, this last home run barely clearing the wall, his trot now familiar to the adoring crowd, his exuberant teammates welcoming the eight-for-eight player to home plate where he plants his feet before leaping into their grabbing arms. When Clarke's eyes opened again, he lowered the ball from his face, tossing it in his hand and watching it travel up and down—a big smile on his lips. "You know they don't make balls like this anymore?"

"I know," I said.

"These balls from the dead-ball era have a different smell than the cork-centered balls of today. It's the rubber inside. Smells like leather gloves after unloading tires all day. Never thought I'd smell it again, to be honest. The loosely wound rubber gave them a slightly spongy feel. Didn't travel as far off the bat so you had to play small ball, try and place your hits better. Probably sounds corny to you, I guess, but I miss those days." He took hold of another ball, then another, holding all three up to the light. "I played half my career in the dead-ball era."

"My father marked them in the order you hit them. That's how we know they're yours. My grandfather was there that day too. He watched my father shagging your home runs beyond the short right field fence."

"You know, that's all some people want to remember about that game...some of the writers, I mean...that the fence in back of right field was only two hundred ten feet, one hundred forty if you go by what my former teammate Walter Morris recalled recently to *The Sporting News*."

I nodded. "Well, whether a short fence or long fence, two ten or one forty, you still put eight baseballs in the same spot for eight home runs in eight at-bats. That's saying something about your hitting that day. And you knocked in sixteen RBIs doing it."

"See, it doesn't bother me about the distance of the fence and all that. But sometimes it just seems a fella has it in for you and no matter what you do, he isn't going to print the good stuff. Know what I mean?"

"I know exactly what you mean."

"And that's okay, except that they print their opinions sometimes, but then those opinions have a way of becoming fact…when they aren't. Take Morris' statement about the fence for instance. I read the article where Morris said that, the interview he gave to Zeke Handler of *The Sporting News*—the original printed piece. In the sentences they quoted from Morris, he says in there about me, 'He was one of the best hitters I ever saw.' But in other articles I've read where they quote that original article and statement by Morris, they leave that bit out, making it sound like Morris was trying to discredit me, which he wasn't. Heck, Morris himself went six for eight at-bats that day, with one home run and two doubles, if I remember correctly."

"I understand."

"I know I'm not the best hitter. Not even close. But I think Morris was making a point by adding that statement…that he wasn't trying to discredit me by saying the fence was shorter than the posted two hundred ten feet.

"He said as much, didn't he? That's what he said before he said you were one of the best hitters he ever saw. He said, 'I'm not trying to take anything away from old Nig's batting prowess—he was one of the best hitters I ever saw.'"

"I only know that Corsicana had a solid team in o-two—one of the best ever in the minors—and that a bunch of us, not just me, put home run balls over the fence that day. O'Conner got three. Alexander got three. A couple other fellas got two."

"But you put eight up and over, the only person to do that."

He nodded. "But it wasn't about the home runs. Everybody on the Corsicana squad put up big numbers that day. We were like a production line in and out of the batter's box, each batter swinging and hitting the first pitch most of the time. I don't think any of us were in that batter's box for more than a minute at a time. The game went fast. Even Morris said that in that same article with Zeke Handler. Morris said, 'The game rolled along and we made seven to eight runs an inning for several frames.' We had a blast, though, playing that game." He smiled for a moment as he recalled, but then the smile went away. "Still, some days I wish that game never happened, you know? My entire career I've had to answer questions about that game. People don't want to accept the score and home runs as record, what can I do? It all just gets in the way. All I ever wanted to do was play baseball as best I could. Sure I made some mistakes along the way—had my slumps. Show me a ballplayer or human being who hasn't. And I wanted it to be my profession—to get paid for it if I could, just like the other players. I have a wife to support, just like anybody else, a mother that needs care too."

"We all need an income," I said, nodding.

"Like you said, Laird, and thank you for reminding me because sometimes, you know, I forget. I did play hard. I had my moments and gave those guys a run for their money, and a lot of them darn good ballplayers. I stood glove-to-glove and bat-to-bat with them. Some did better than me, sure, but some didn't. That's the way it goes." When I didn't comment, he said, "I'm sorry, fellas. Guess these balls bring back both good and bad memories. But tell your father thank you for me. I sure appreciate the gesture."

"I will. Not sure he'll understand but I'll tell him."

"I never imagined somebody kept these balls. It's funny now but back then...most games, anyway...we used only one ball if we could. But that game so many were getting hit for home runs that they had to keep breaking out new balls. The league ended up sending us a bill later!" He laughed out loud. "Can you believe that? Told us we had to pay for them!"

"You gotta love the early days of baseball," I said, laughing with him.

"Why do you think he wanted me to have these? It's not like they really belong to me. They belong to him. He shagged them, kept them all these years. They're his. So why would he want you to find me and give them to me?"

"I've thought a lot about that, Jay. Believe me—a lot. In my heart I believe this is my father's way...his way of *thanking you*."

"Thanking me? For what?"

"For inspiring him to become a professional baseball player. I don't think he would have ever played professionally had he not seen your remarkable feat of skill that day in nineteen o-two, when you played in his hometown of Ennis. I think he would have gone on to be a preacher like his father, my grandfather. But you changed all of that—you and those eight home run balls there."

"Gee, I hope that doesn't get me into trouble with The Almighty. I'll be seeing him pretty soon, after all."

We laughed at that for a moment. "I'm sure you're safe. My father honored God with the way he lived, in his relationships with people. That's what I've learned. My grandfather believes, as I now do, that God used my father right where he was. Just might be he's using my father still, right this very moment."

"What do you mean? How?"

"I don't rightly know for sure. Maybe these balls my father collected on the field so long ago, maybe they've given you comfort in some way. They have me. I never thought much of my father, never really knew him or wanted to know him until these eight baseballs came into my life. Now I know a lot about him, about the type of man he was, what he cared about, even his struggles. Through it all I've come to love the man in a way I might never have, had you not hit those eight home runs, had he not collected them and then had the foresight to save them for me to return later. Maybe for you they simply serve as a reminder that you were a good ballplayer, Maybe, as you've said, you've forgotten that amid the years of questions about that *one* game with Corsicana—over time, now that you're retired and have a normal day job. Maybe these balls were meant to remind you that you were an important part of this game, just as 'The Greats' were…Ruth and Young and Hornsby…Cobb and Jackson and the others you played with…but maybe in a different way…that a medium-sized guy from a small town in Ontario, Canada could make a big impact on a game so many people love."

"I don't know about making a big impact on the game, as you say. I don't think most people would remember me if you asked."

"My father would. My mother would. My wife would. Billy too. I'm sure Ty Cobb would, Joe Jackson, Cy Young, Nap Lajoie, Babe Ruth, Eddie Collins, all those guys. I'm sure they'd remember you." He thought about my words. "You've made a big impact, Jay, especially on *our* baseball family. We're a better family because of you."

He walked amongst the memorabilia, pondering, I suppose, what I'd just said to him. A couple times he stopped to straighten or dust off pieces he'd saved and had on display. Once I thought I saw him wipe a tear from his eye.

"I'm very glad to have met you, Laird, and your father," He said, turning toward me.

"What about me?" Billy blurted out. "Aren't you glad you met me?"

"You I am especially glad I met," Clarke said, mussing Billy's hair with a hand as he passed, Billy proud and puffed up like a newly elected politician giving a speech to his supporters.

"I'm glad to have met you too, Jay." I stood, picked up my bag and Billy's, handing Billy his before extending my hand to Jay Justin "Nig" Clarke, the man my father admired so much—the man I too admired. "You're a very special man and I won't forget you."

He took my hand in his and looked into my eyes for a moment before bringing his other hand up to wrap it around our handshake. "I won't forget you either, Laird. And I'll be looking for you on the ball field."

Mary heard us walking toward the door and met us there. "Leaving so soon?"

"I'm afraid so," I said. "Thank you so much for your hospitality. Sorry again for barging in on you."

"We enjoyed having you. Can I send some food with you?"

"Thank you, but we're okay. Perhaps you wouldn't mind calling us a cab, though."

"If you walk around the corner to the front of the Ford plant you'll see a line of taxis waiting. Always four or five of them sitting there," Clarke said.

We stepped onto the porch, back into the caustic air, night having fallen along with a light fog.

"Honey, it's dark out. Maybe you should give them a ride," Mary said.

"Yeah, fellas. Give me a minute and I'll get the keys."

"No," I said. "We can walk. Really. It's fine. Thank you again."

"We'll be seeing you!" Billy said, waving behind him as he walked.

"So long, fellas!" Clarke called. "Thanks for coming!"

CHAPTER TWENTY-ONE

Our flight out of Detroit in the morning was at seven so Billy and I found a hotel near Detroit City Airport. The hotel wasn't much to speak of—just four stories, an elevator, and clean rooms with two beds, the stale cigarette smell thrown in for free. And it had a restaurant where we could catch an early breakfast before our flight. I'd told Billy that we were heading back to Hartford, but that we'd have a layover like before, only this time it wouldn't be in Philadelphia; it would be in Cincinnati, Ohio. I hated lying to him, but I just couldn't bring myself to tell him the truth, at least not before we were standing in front of his aunt's home, the pendulum about to drop and possibly sever our relationship forever.

The flight from Detroit to Cincinnati lasted just over two hours and went without a hitch. Billy and I agreed that we both enjoyed the experience of flying, the experience of rapid acceleration, of lifting on air, of ascending toward heaven, of leveling out and descending back to earth, even the occasional heart-stopping drop caused by turbulence. But we also agreed that using the lavatory inflight required a peculiar talent, one that needed to be developed over time. Surely there was a trick that made standing urination a little more accurate. We both supposed we could sit to empty our bladders, but as Billy pointed out, we were both men and men stood.

Once on the ground we headed for the terminal, where I left Billy sitting in a chair, watching our bags while I went to use the restroom. In truth, I had gone to the information kiosk to ask how far Billy's aunt's home was from the airport. All I had to go on was the address Father Michael had given me. The concierge retrieved an area map and determined his aunt's address to be just twenty minutes from the airport by taxi, sending me on my way with a warning not to let the cabbie give me the runaround. "Some are crafty little buggers," the young man with thinning dark hair and Peabody glasses said. "If they suspect you're from out of town, some will take you the long way."

"Thanks for the tip," I said before returning to Billy, who by then had taken to laying across the seats, his head resting on his duffle with his hands behind his head, his feet crossed atop my bag. He looked as at home and comfortable as a woman relaxing in her bubble bath.

I tapped his shoes. "Let's go, sport."

Billy popped up to his feet like he was spring-loaded. "Where're we going?"

"For a ride." I grabbed my bag and started heading for the door, Billy following.

"But I thought we had to catch another plane?"

"We have time."

I tried to stay in front so I wouldn't have to look at Billy, my conscience beating on me like a butcher tenderizing meat. A few minutes later we were sitting in the back of a yellow cab, the driver turning to look at us over the front seat, his arm resting on the back of it, his flat cap half-cocked on his head, his mouth crooked when he spoke, the muscles on one side of his mouth not working. "Where to, pal?"

"Number fifteen, Gosford Lane."

The cabbie mulled the address in his mind for a long moment, but I could sense he was about to pull a fast one on me—or try.

"Yeah, I think I know where that is," he said, turning to put the car in drive and pull out into airport traffic.

"Don't try that with me," I said, acting like a local. "You know where Gosford Lane is. Everybody does."

"Is that the one in the old part of the city, near downtown?"

"That's the one." I hoped that was the one. What did I know?

"Say, pal, you sure you want to go down there? You don't look the type, if you don't mind me saying so."

"What type is that?"

"I don't know…destitute."

"Just drive."

"Aye, aye, Cap'n. It's your funeral."

"Where are we going?" Billy whispered. When I didn't answer he poked the side of my arm. "Did you hear me? Hello."

Looking away and out the window, I said, "Not now. I need to think."

Thoughts swirled inside my head like a destructive tornado. *Destitute? Is that Billy's new fate? Is that what I'm about to do to him, sentence him to a life of want and need? Surely there are good people that fit into that category, right? Just because a person or family is destitute, that doesn't mean they can't love each other, does it? But wouldn't Billy be better off with us? We certainly aren't rich, far from it. But we can give him what he needs—clothing, medical care, and good education, food. He'd never have to beg for a handout, not while I still breathed. Still, Billy isn't ours. He belongs to the next of kin. At least that's the way I understand the law. But what if his aunt doesn't want him? Does that mean he's ours or do we need to turn him over to the state? If she does want Billy, will he be safe living there? He's impressionable at his age. He could follow other neighborhood boys into trouble. Maybe I should tell the driver to turn around? No, I should at least go talk to her. Maybe she's not really destitute, not really that bad off. Maybe I could ask her if I can take him back home for Christmas, then bring him back after. I don't know. I must have been mad to bring him back home on the train. I've ruined his life. No, his life wasn't that good before. Ugh! Why do I do this…to myself...to others?* By the time those thoughts settled, we were there, the neighborhood just as the cabbie had described—destitute.

"Here we are, pal," he said, pulling the car to the curb, the brakes squeaking us to a stop in front of a small dilapidating two-story house, just one in a tight row of approximately thirty houses, the mirror image on the other side of the street, the grass shabby and overgrown in front of the home, the picket fence naked and rotted with several pickets missing, a fat and lazy gray cat laying on the porch rail under the sparse shade of a diseased tree. Up the street I could see a cluster of young men—hoodlums in black leather jackets, t-shirts, and jeans—roughhousing on a corner, hassling a young woman as she tried to pass. Honestly, from the street, things couldn't have looked worse. "Ain't much to look at, is it?"

"Save me the commentary," I said, handing him some money. "We won't be long so if you could wait I'd appreciate it."

"Pal, I wouldn't leave my worst enemy here alone. But I ain't just gonna sit here and get robbed. I'll drive around the block a couple times until you're ready to go. That work for you?"

"He's right," Billy said. "It looks bad. Maybe I could just wait in the car with him?"

"No, Billy, I'm afraid you can't. Yes, driver. That would be fine. I'll just leave my bag in here for safe keeping." I stepped from the car, Billy reluctantly following, his eyes searching about like a soldier waiting for the bombs to start falling. When I grabbed his duffle and closed the door, he looked at me, confused and suddenly scared. "I know I should have told you, Billy, but I didn't want you to get upset."

"Tell me what?" His eyes began to fill with tears. I sensed that in his gut he already knew the answer to his question, but he needed to hear me confirm it.

"This is your aunt's home, Billy...at least it's supposed to be...according to Father Michael."

"But I don't want to live here. I want to stay with you and Janie. You said I could stay through the holiday."

"I know, Billy, and I'm very sorry. It's just that we were so close to here, being in Detroit and all. To come this way and not see your aunt about you wouldn't have been right?"

"You lied," he muttered like the last words of a dying man, turning his hurt face from me, holding his duffle with both hands in front of him and kicking it with his feet as he shuffled through the open gate and up the walk, stopping short just before the steps to the porch.

I walked past and up to the front door, ringing the bell, which to my surprise worked. I glanced back at Billy while I waited for somebody to come to the door. His head hung low, and who could blame him? I'd broken his heart, betrayed his trust. Seeing him downcast like that made me feel ill in my stomach, like I'd just been convicted of a crime, sentenced to a life of imprisonment. Suddenly the door opened and a thin woman stepped into the doorway. Her floral patterned dress seemed handmade and had worn through in places, her sweater missing a few buttons, her brown hair unwashed and shiny, her eyes sunken and dark, her free hand holding a hankie to her red nose. She seemed to be propping herself against the door rather than holding it open, trying, it appeared, to keep from collapsing. I could just see the inside of the home which appeared just as grim as the woman before me, the odor of decay escaping out the front door with the heated air.

"Yes?" the woman kindly asked in a scratchy voice, clearing phlegm from her throat after she spoke.

"Hello, ma'am," I said, somewhat taken aback by her appearance. "Is this a bad time?"

"Well, I don't know what you want, but I'm very sick at the moment, so if it's not important then maybe another time." She began to close the door, suspecting, I suppose, that I was a salesman of some sort, but I put a hand out to stop her.

"Yes, ma'am. It's very important."

Just then she squinted to look past me. "Hello, Billy," she said, unimpressed.

I glanced back at Billy to find him turning his back to us. Right then he dropped his bag and ran, out the gate and down the sidewalk out of sight. I started after him but stopped before the gate, watching him for a moment to see him turn onto the next block, still running at high speed. Going back to the door, I said, "His parents died."

"I know," she said, coughing behind the handkerchief. "But I can't take him." Tears welled in her eyes. "I know he's my sister's child...and I know I should take care of him...but I just can't. I can't even take care of my own children...take care of myself. My husband, he's run off. He couldn't keep a job and has run off. What am I supposed to do?" She began to sob, nearly collapsing before I could catch her and stand her upright again.

"Here," I said as I reached into my wallet, removing the $200 I'd planned to leave along with Billy. "Please, take this." I pressed it into her palm and then started back toward the gate. "Use it to get on your feet again. Don't worry about Billy. My wife and I will adopt and take care of him, if you'll let us."

She nodded, forcing a relieved smile behind the tears, her eyes turning to the much-needed money in her hand.

"We'll write to you."

After those words, I grabbed Billy's bag and ran as fast as I could in the direction Billy had run. I was running down the sidewalk, heading straight for those hoodlums I'd seen when we arrived, when a dog came rushing out a gate after me—an angry bull terrier, with a white body and half his head black, barking and nipping at my heals. I didn't even look back; I just plowed into that ornery group of reprobates, who seemed to be waiting to jump me, scattering them all like bowling pins. They got up to chase me but when they saw the reason I was running so fast—the bloodthirsty dog—they scattered again, this time like rats after the light flicked on.

It seemed like I'd run a mile through the rough neighborhood before I found Billy, leaning against the side of the taxicab we'd ridden in earlier, the driver parked in a way that told me he'd seen Billy running and had cut him off. When I got close Billy began screaming at me.

"You lied! I'm not living here! I don't care! I'll go back to Saint Anthony's! I'll walk!"

"Billy..." I said between gasps.

"No! You'll just lie some more! I hate liars! I hate *you!*"

"Billy, please, I'm sorry I lied to you. It was wrong of me." I stood next to him, bent at the waist to catch my breath. "I made a mistake."

"Then you're not leaving me here?" He asked, settling.

"No, Son, I'm not."

"I can come home with you—forever?"

I stood and nodded. "I'd like that. I know Janie would too."

Right then he ran and leapt into my arms, weeping on my shoulder, holding me as tightly as his little arms could.

"But what if they try to take me away from you?"

"If anybody tries we'll fight them. We'll fight them until we win, until they see that you belong with us."

"And you won't ever leave me?" He leaned his head back, still in my arms, his eyes looking squarely into mine for honesty.

Setting him down, I said, "Come. Lets sit over here and talk for a moment." I led him about twenty feet away from the cabbie and took a seat on the curb, Billy sitting next to me. Looking off ahead, I said, "I do have to go away for a while, Billy, but you'll stay with Janie, help her while I'm gone."

He thought about that for a moment. "But where will you go? With your team? When will you be back?"

The next words were very hard to get out. "The Army is

sending me away for a bit—overseas somewhere."

"To the war?"

"Um hmm."

"No! You won't come back!"

"Billy, I will. I promise."

"That's what my dad said and he didn't! He died! Everybody dies in the war!"

"That's not true, Billy. But yes, some people do die. War is horrible."

"How do you know you won't be one of the people who die?"

"I don't, I guess, but something's telling me I won't be."

"God?"

"I don't know. Maybe. Just a feeling I have."

"But you can't promise you'll come back."

"No, I can't, and I suppose I shouldn't have promised that. But I can promise that I'll do everything in my power to stay alive so I can come home to you and Janie and the baby."

That seemed to satisfy Billy. "I understand, but I don't want you to go. I hate war. It hurts people."

I nodded, putting my arm around him. We sat there like that for what seemed like minutes, both of us quiet, both of us thinking about things. "So, what do we do now, Billy Sunday?"

"Go home," he said with a smile, standing to help pull me up to my feet.

"Sounds good to me."

"Sounds good to me too, pal," The cabbie said, pointing to the gang of greasers running toward us from up the street. "A fella could get killed just sitting here."

Billy and I dove into the back seat while the cabbie raced for the driver's seat, throwing the car into drive and punching the gas before his door ever closed, the tires screeching and smoking, and Billy hollering, "Gee! This is swell!"

CHAPTER TWENTY-TWO

Janie met us at the airport in Hartford later that evening, watching us through the large terminal window as we disembarked the plane on the runway, just as the full apricot sun touched the western horizon behind us, her bright face clear and welcoming behind the glass, her joy in seeing Billy return with me evident in her pacing and exuberant waving. A few minutes later my arms were pulling her against me, her head resting on my chest, her lips reaching for my neck.

"I'm so glad you're home," Janie said.

"Me, too."

"Me, three!" Billy added.

Janie knelt to hug him. "I just couldn't be happier to see you, Billy."

"I know what you mean," he said with a laugh. "Thought I was a goner."

Janie looked up at me and I rolled my eyes. "Well I'm glad you made it back to us." Still looking up at me but talking to Billy, she said, "So are you staying with us for a while?"

I nodded at the same time as Billy blurted out the answer. "Forever!"

Janie rose and took my face in her hands, kissing my lips before whispering in my ear, "Thank you, Laird."

"We still need to go through the adoption process. But his aunt gave us her blessing, so that's good."

"It'll be fine. I just know it." As we walked through the terminal, she asked, "Was she nice? What was she like?"

"Very ill. I'm not sure what was wrong, but she didn't look good. I'll tell you about it later."

"And Nig Clarke? How'd it go with him?"

"Again, later. Let's go."

"So secretive." Janie tickled my sides to make me squirm. "I'm glad you guys are home."

The next morning, while Janie tended to her business, I took Billy shopping in downtown Hartford. He'd need more clothes and some items for his bedroom, which would now be downstairs, his former bedroom next to ours having become the nursery. He'd need things to turn it from a guest bedroom into a boy's bedroom, things like posters and a bookshelf; model trains or planes; sports stuff like a bicycle and a baseball bat; comic books and baseball magazines; encyclopedias for learning; a fish tank for goldfish maybe; a picture frame for the photo of his birth parents; maybe another for the three of us together. But all of that would have to be his decision. It would be his room and he would be able to decorate it how he wanted, within reason. There wouldn't be anything profane; that we would not allow. I found the experience of providing for Billy to be satisfying. I knew that there would be times where Billy would act up or misbehave, but we'd deal with those moments when they arrived. In the meantime, I'd just enjoy learning how to be a father.

In the weeks that followed, Janie and I started the process of adoption, first obtaining support letters from Father Michael of St. Anthony's and from Billy's aunt in Ohio, both letters stating their involvement in Billy's life after the deaths of his parents, and both attesting to our willingness to adopt and support Billy. Father Michael's letter went a step further and actually said that he'd found me to be a man of good character with a genuine concern and affection for the boy, which surprised me given my rough start with Father Michael. He went on to write:

The boy has also expressed a desire to live with Mr. Young and his wife indefinitely, if they will have him. Furthermore, given Mr. and Mrs. Young's recent letter to me, Billy's desire to live with them indefinitely now appears to be mutual. It is my sincere recommendation that this adoption be approved and finalized as soon as possible.

Once we had those letters in hand, we contacted a local adoption agency that introduced us to a social worker. To our relief, she gave permission for Billy to remain with us while we finalized the adoption paperwork. She was a polite and frumpy middle-aged woman named Ms. Parker, about as plain as they come, her sense of humor as gray as her skirt and coat, her hair as dark as the rim on her glasses. Father Michael helped us obtain Billy's mother's official death certificate from the State of Virginia and my mother used her military contacts to obtain Billy's father's death record. Mother also discovered that Billy, being a child dependent survivor of a veteran killed in action, was entitled to a $15 monthly benefit payment from the government until the age of 16, which Janie and I decided would go into a trust fund for Billy, to be used as he saw fit once he reached adulthood.

Meanwhile, we made preparations for Christmas and my forthcoming departure to Fort Benning, Georgia. At Fort Benning I'd complete Basic Training, as well as Infantry Training, after which I'd catch up with the 4th Infantry in England, where they'd be making preparations to enter the war in Europe. Janie struggled to meet the holiday demands of her business as she entered her ninth month of pregnancy, the stress on her body making it difficult to work for long periods of time without getting winded and without feeling the need to sit down. I tried to help, but her patience had withered to a thread.

"Which pie goes into which box?" I asked one day while down

in the basement, Janie hard at work baking, her hair pulled back with a few annoying stands continuously falling in her face, a face streaked with flour, my hands holding two pies out like a candlestick holds candles, ten folded boxes neatly positioned on the table in front of me.

"Laird, they're labeled," she said, waddling over to me, one hand holding her back, the other hand pointing to small colored labels on each box, her belly arriving long before her face. "This one says blueberry...that one apple...this one pecan...this one cherry. Is it really that hard to figure out?"

"It is if you're me. I'm just a dumb ballplayer. I can hardly read, after all. I'm actually surprised I've made it this far in life."

"You're not dumb, just lazy."

"And you're gassy, but am I complaining?"

"I'm not gassy!"

"Oh, you're gassy. Only it's coming out of your mouth right now," I said, waving a hand in front of my nose to clear the stink.

"Laird! That's mean!"

I placed the blueberry and pecan pies in their respective boxes, afterward licking some sticky blueberry filling from my fingers. "Well, I'll put 'lazy' on the list right under 'heartless'."

"Laird, I'm sorry. I don't know why I say those things."

"Maybe it has something to do with that dinosaur you're carrying around inside of you. It growls, you growl. Makes sense, really. I've got the easy part. I just have to wait...and reassure you every so often that you are *not* 'fat and ugly'."

She kissed me, just a peck that barely connected, her face pale and appearing faint as she grabbed hold of the table for support. "I do appreciate your help. I'm just so tired lately—and sore. I guess it's making me cranky."

"Here," I said, leading her to a nearby chair, the skin on her hand soft and clammy. "Have a seat." Right then I heard the phone ringing like a bicycle's bell from the dining room above us. "I'll get that. Be right back."

I ran up the stairs, skipping two stairs at a time, arriving at the dining room telephone by the end of the third ring. "Hello, Laird speaking…Hi, Del. What's the latest?…No kidding?…No kidding?…They said that about me? Really?…No, that's great. Thank you…Okay. Talk to you soon. Thanks for letting me know."

I stood still for a moment, staring at the black receiver like it was an alien spacecraft, my mind trying to determine if the words I'd just heard through the phone line were in fact real or if they were a creation of my imagination.

"Janie!" I called, backing from the phone a few paces before turning to run down the steps to the basement, hitting every stair deliberately like a football player running tire-stepping drills. "Janie! You'll never guess who that was!" I found Janie standing, but cringing in pain. "Janie?"

"It's time, Laird," she muttered.

"Time for what?"

"For our child to be born."

I went to support her as she waddled toward the stairs.

"Now? But I thought you still had a couple weeks?"

"Babies come when they come."

"Well that hardly seems fair."

"I haven't packed anything. I need my travel bag, the one with my makeup and hair stuff…my slippers and my robe. I'm not wearing one of those hospital gowns."

"You're worried about how you look at a time like this?"

"After delivery, silly, while I'm still in the hospital. If I have to walk around I don't want to be exposed."

"Oh, okay. Billy! Come quick!" Billy made it halfway down the stairs before he stopped, unsure of what was happening. "Here," I said, reaching into my pocket before tossing him my keys. "Bring the car around! Quick!"

"But…you want me to drive? Where?"

"He's eight years old, Laird!"

"Oh, that's right. Sorry. Okay," I said, helping her up the stairs one step at a time, pushing from behind and underneath until she made it to the top step. "Billy, bring one of the dining room chairs. Janie, when he brings it, sit. I'll get your things." I was up the stairs and down again with her bag of clothes within two minutes, tossing the bag to Billy on my way out the front door. A few seconds later, after realizing I'd forgotten my pregnant wife, I returned. "Sorry."

"Laird, calm down," Janie said as I led her down the front porch steps.

"How? Do I know anything about delivering a baby? No. I deliver fastballs, and curves, and knuckleballs when I can hold onto them."

"Oh stop, okay?"

"You don't let that baby out until we're at the hospital. I mean it. If it tries to come out you just push it back in. Just push it right back inside." I opened the rear door of the car and guided her as she sat on the backseat, Billy, who'd climbed in from the other side, trying to pull her inside from under her arms. "Under no circumstances are you to deliver our baby in the Buick. I'll never get the mess out of the tuck-and-roll."

"Will you two stop panicking, please?" she said, scooting herself inside along the rear bench seat, still cringing in pain every few minutes.

"Billy, you sit back here with Janie." I closed her door then hopped into the front seat and fired up the engine, giving it too much gas in all the excitement, causing it to scream angrily and kick out a cloud of sooty exhaust.

"Hartford Hospital, Laird," Janie said, as we backed out of the drive, the black smoke of the exhaust passing over us like doom. "Drive slow and easy, okay? Don't go driving like you've lost your mind."

"Too late for that. Buckle your seatbelts and hang on." On that my foot slammed down the gas pedal and the Buick rocketed down the street, one of our pipe-smoking neighbors shooting me a disapproving glance as he reached down to retrieve the daily newspaper from his grass, his burgundy silk robe and matching slippers as out of place as a cow walking down Main Street.

"Laird!"

CHAPTER TWENTY-THREE

By the time my mother and grandparents arrived at the hospital, Janie had gone into full labor. Janie's parents were still out on the west coast visiting her spoiled sister who'd moved out to Hollywood several years earlier to pursue a writing career. They'd gone there before Thanksgiving and weren't planning to return until after the New Year. When I called to let them know Janie had gone into labor, they became excited and offered to come home early, but Janie wouldn't have wanted that, not unless there were complications of some sort. They seemed satisfied when I promised to let them know if anything changed; the New Year was only two weeks away, after all.

I'd always admired and respected Janie's father, a large man in both stature and presence and a judge on the First Circuit Court of Appeals. He chose his words as carefully as one would a fine wine, and he was charismatically loud at times, his booming voice commanding respect. And even though his lot in life sat ten flights up from mine, he never once looked down on me. His wife, on the other hand, seemed hifalutin and stuck on formalities, her greatest concern the gossip columns and whether or not it's proper to drink one's tea with one's pinky raised. To Janie's mother, I was a no-account farmer-jock from low-class parents, a dullard who'd ruined her daughter's chances for happiness, dooming her to a life of mediocrity at best, making her unfit for cultured society—a view not lost on my mother, who on one occasion made it clear to

Janie's mother that the only thing her condescending tongue was good for was licking the grease off her V8. With that in mind, I was glad Janie's parents were out of town; it would have turned our joyous occasion into an ugly affair.

Becoming a father, if I'm being honest, frightened me as much as it excited me, which accounted for why my mother and grandparents found me pacing in the waiting room like a sentry on guard, my Fedora clasped in my hat behind me, beads of sweat trying to cool my forehead. That I was now responsible for the care and welfare of not one, but two children, as well as my wife, who incidentally seemed to be more capable of earning a living than I was, aroused in me a peculiar anxiety akin to leaping from an airplane at an altitude of 15,000 feet, the only thing keeping my body from slamming into the earth at break-neck speed a piece of nylon cloth called a parachute. Both, endeavoring to become a father and willingly jumping from an airplane at altitude, required a certain degree of faith if I hoped to survive either experience. The advantage skydiving has over being a father is that you find out in a matter of minutes if you're going to impact the world; fatherhood, on the other hand, is a lifelong experience, the impact of your efforts never fully known. My hope, though, was that I would be a loving leader to my children—*if* I made it home from the war. If I didn't come home alive, if they shipped me home in a flag-draped coffin or buried me where I fell, my hope and prayer was that Janie would be loving and strong enough for us both.

"Hi, Ms. Emily!" Billy said, rushing over from the window he'd been looking out of to wrap his arms around my mother's waist, the top of his head coming to her upper abdomen.

"Well aren't you an affectionate one," Mother said, rubbing his back.

"Can I call you Grandma now?"

I raised my eyes and cringed when she shot me a violent glance.

"You do and I'll hogtie you," she said. Thinking about it for a moment longer, she said, "Well, I guess it'll be all right, but only if you must."

When Billy sensed something wasn't okay with calling her "Grandma," even though she said it'd be okay, he looked over to find me shaking my head and mouthing the words, "Ms. Emily."

"Think I'll stick with Ms. Emily, if that's okay with you."

"Suits me just fine," she said, pinching Billy's nose.

"Party pooper," Grandmother said to my mother before pulling Billy in for a bear hug. "Well I don't care. You can call me Grandma anytime, Billy. In fact, I'd quite enjoy that."

Mother smiled at me. "I knew you would."

"What?"

"Adopt Billy. Knew it from the first time I saw you with him."

"No you didn't," I said, kissing her cheek.

"Like I said to you before, Grandson," Grandfather said, firmly shaking my hand. "They can read our minds."

"Frightening," I said.

Mother tossed her handbag onto a nearby chair, freeing her hands to rub her own arms. "I've never liked hospitals. They always keep these waiting rooms cold and the smell of denatured alcohol makes it seem like we're all guinea pigs in some hidden experiment. How's Janie? Any word yet?"

"Nothing. Think she's okay?"

"A daisy doesn't grow in a day, Laird," Grandmother said as she made herself comfortable on the sofa, Billy plopping down next to her. "But they're bright little flowers once they blossom." She pulled Billy in close. "Like little Billy here. Isn't he a daisy?"

"How long has she been in labor?" Grandfather asked.

"Since before I called you guys—about three hours. Is that normal?"

Both my mother and grandmother laughed.

"Cowboy," Mother said, "you might as well plant your saddle. It'll be a long evening."

Just then a tall slender graying man came through the double doors that, on the other side, led to the maternity ward and delivery rooms. He wore a white surgeon's gown and had a mask pulled down and crumpled around his neck, the outline of the mask still visible on his flushed and wrinkled face. "Mr. Young?"

"Yes?" I said, walking over to meet him, the others following to hear what we hoped would be good news. "I'm Mr. Young. Is my wife okay?"

"She's doing fine, Mr. Young. Everything went very well."

"That must be some sort of record," Mother said, "three hours."

"It's pretty fast, I'll agree, but fairly common."

"How's the baby?" Grandmother asked, a concerned look on her face.

"About perfect," the doctor said with a smile. "But then most girls are in my experience."

That made my grandmother blush.

"Easy, mister," Grandfather said with a wry grin. "Keep dishing out that sugar and she'll be following you home."

"We have a baby girl?" I asked, stunned.

He nodded. "Six pounds, three ounces. Is that okay?"

I laughed. "Well it has to be! Yes, of course! I'm thrilled!" I hugged my mother and grandparents. "A baby girl! Can you believe it?"

"It's Ripley's," Mother said, grinning and cocking her head. "Thought for sure it'd be a boy. Better get my crystal ball checked, Something's wrong with it."

"Can we see her?" Billy asked the doctor. "I want to see!"

"In a little while. Right now she's being cleaned up and tended to in the nursery. But you can see your mother if you'd like." The doctor motioned for us to follow him.

Hearing the doctor refer to Jamie as Billy's mother struck me at first as odd; yet, I knew it would soon be true, and in our minds it already was.

"Your wife is a bit tired from the delivery," the doctor said, pushing through the double doors and leading us down a bright hallway painted a soft pink on one side, an eggshell yellow on the other. "But I think she should still be awake." He pushed open the hospital room door and poked his head inside. "Mrs. Young, you have some visitors who'd love to see you now, if you're up for it."

From behind the door I heard Janie say in the sweetest voice, "Oh, yes please."

The doctor stepped aside to let us through. There we found Janie lying in bed, the white sheet and knitted bedspread covering only her lower half, her upper half covered by the dreaded hospital gown, her hair wet from sweat and darker in appearance, her face flush and natural, glowing like a rose-colored star. "Hi," was all she said.

"Hi back," I said, leaning down to kiss my favorite lips, which were as soft as flower petals. "You look radiant."

"I feel radiant," she said, her words tender as a feather.

"A baby girl? You were holding out on me."

"My secret's out now. Are you happy?"

"I'm so happy I could cry, sweetheart. I can't wait to see her."

"I'm glad."

Looking up at the room, I said, "I know we're on a budget, but surely they could have done better than this." Her room wasn't much to look at, but at least it was private. The only items in the room bedsides her bed were a corner reading chair upholstered in dark floral fabric, a three-drawer mahogany dresser and a matching nightstand, which gave rest to a pink-shaded glass table lamp, one with a hanging chain to turn it on and off. And there was one lonely window looking out to the parking lot below.

"I like it," Janie said with a shrug of her shoulders. "It's cozy."

"Okay, okay," Grandmother said, gently nudging me aside to lean in and kiss Janie. "Don't be selfish. Let us love on the new mother."

"Have you seen her yet?" Grandfather asked.

"Only for a few moments," Janie answered.

"I'll bet she was just lovely!" Grandmother said.

"She was so red…so messy. But she was darling."

"It'll only take a few minutes with your child before you think it's the most beautiful thing God ever created," Mother said, laughing afterward. "And it only takes a few years before you wish you could give the child back."

"That's mean, Mother."

"Oh lighten up. It was just a joke. But I am glad it's a girl. Finally get to do some girly things."

"You'd better study up on how to be a girl first," I said. "But don't let anybody catch you. It'd ruin your reputation as a man."

"Will she be my sister?" Billy asked, standing at Janie's bedside and taking her hand in his.

Janie raised his small hand to her lips and kissed it. "She will. Are you excited about being a big brother?"

Billy nodded enthusiastically, his head convulsing like a bobble-head doll.

"All you need now is a dog," Mother said.

"Can we?" Billy asked.

"No," I said.

"What does Janie think about you playing in the majors?" Mother asked.

"I haven't told her yet, thank you very much. And how could you possibly know that?"

My mother laughed. "I hear things."

"I'm probably the only guy in professional baseball where my team has to get my mother's permission before anything can happen."

"The Braves called you, honey?" Janie asked. "When?"

"Somewhere between you baking pies and 'babies come when

they come.' Doesn't matter anyway."

"What?" Mother said. "I thought you'd be jumping up and down with excitement. It's been your dream to play for the Braves."

Just then a thirty-something nurse in a white belted dress with matching white nurse's hat and shoes pushed a baby cart through the door. "Hi everyone! I've got a special present for you!" We parted like the Red Sea, allowing the nurse to push the cart up to Janie's bedside, Janie scooting to sit up in bed as the nurse gently lifted our tiny angel from the cart, setting her into Janie's awaiting arms. "Here you go, Mom," the nurse said to Janie. "She's all ready for your love."

Janie began to weep, cradling our daughter close to her breast. "Laird, look at her! She's so small! Isn't she darling!"

She was darling, her flush face round and pillowy, her chin slightly in from her tiny watermelon-colored lips, which seemed to be suckling something that wasn't there, her nose just a small clover-shaped mound beneath eyes that fidgeted under closed lids, her pink knitted beanie covering the top of her head and half her ears, leaving strands of chestnut hair to peek out.

"She's beautiful, like her mother," I said, taking a seat on the bed, leaning back with my arm around Janie as she held our newborn.

Billy came over to have a closer look at her, tickling her face with a finger. "She's so soft!"

"Well, isn't this a precious sight?" Grandmother said. "You're a family!"

"What do I do?" Janie asked the nurse. "I've never done this."

"You just hold her for awhile, bond with her. In a little bit we'll have you feed her. I'll just step outside," she said, pulling a small hand-bell from her pocket and setting it on the nightstand, the bell end down and handle up. "My personal calling card. If you need me just give me a jingle. I'll hear it."

"Thank you," Mother said to her on her way out.

"She has your nose, Grandson," my grandfather said, smiling. "And Janie's hair."

"That could change, though, right?" Janie asked.

"That's the fun of it, dear," Grandmother said. "They always keep you guessing."

"Have you thought about a name yet?" Mother asked.

"Would have been easy if we'd had a boy," I said, "but then there must be some sort of law as to how many Laird Allen Youngs there can be."

"You *honestly* didn't consider the possibility of a girl?" Mother asked, sounding annoyed.

"Oh, we did, we just haven't narrowed our choice of girl names yet."

"We like several," Janie said, gently rocking our namesake. "Delilah was one. Not sure why. We just like it, I guess. Annabelle was another."

"She doesn't look like a Delilah," Mother said. "And Annabelle sounds like a cow."

"This is one thing you don't get a say in, Mother," I said. "And Annabelle does not sound like a cow."

"She looks like a Lillian," Mother added. "Lilly for short."

"There's no way! You can't—"

"That was on our list too," Janie said. "How do you do that?"

Mom laughed. "I've known my son all his life. He's pretty predicable in his likes and dislikes."

"Really? Predicable? Okay, Einstein, give me the last two names on our list."

"Nope. I've said enough."

"Coward," I said.

"Emily was on our list too," Janie said, still rocking our baby, not looking up.

"Bet you didn't guess that one," I said.

"No," Mother said, embarrassed. "That's very kind of you."

"How about Autumn?" Grandfather suggested, gazing out the window. "Autumn Young has quite a nice ring to it."

"I like it," Grandmother said. "Sounds like an artist, or a movie star! Wouldn't that be something?"

"Look," Janie whispered. "She's sleeping. It's so precious!"

"She does look like a Lillian," I admitted.

"Do we need to decide right this minute?" Janie asked, softly. "She'll tell us what her name is, won't you sweetie?"

Just as the nurse poked her head inside the door, the nameless one began to cry—louder than seemed possible given her size.

"Those lungs! Definitely got those from her mother," I said.

"Okay, kids," the nurse said. "Time for Mom to do her first feeding. I'm afraid you'll all have to step out to the waiting room. The cafeteria is open if you're hungry. Fourth floor. Up the elevator and to the left."

IT WAS A small cafeteria by hospital standards, and since we were the last ones to make it through the dinner line before the kitchen closed for the night, there were ample tables available for us to sit and chat, the chairs consisting of plastic seats and backs mounted to cheap metal legs, the table a terrible laminate rendition of oak that felt wet and slick, having recently been wiped clean. The food wasn't bad though. I chose some sort of fresh-water fish in lemon butter, and a creamy spinach creation and dinner roll to go with it, a slice of key lime pie for dessert. Mom, however, didn't eat, reminding me once again how thin she'd become.

"What's wrong, Mother?"

"Nothing, Laird. Why?"

"You're not eating again."

"Oh stop your meddling."

"I'm not meddling. I'm just concerned. You've become so

skinny. You're like a blade of grass when I see you from the side. Can't be healthy."

"My stomach's just a little upset. I'll eat with your father when I get back to the ranch."

"You guys are staying with her," I said to my grandparents, shoveling a fork-full of fish into my mouth. "You ever see her eat?"

"Not that much, no," said my grandmother. "I've been meaning to mention it."

"What is this?" Mother snapped. "I'm fine. Worry about yourselves."

"Loving you, Mother, is like loving a brick. You're so hard on the outside that any caring just bounces off."

"That's not true," she said. "If I recall I've shown you a great deal of love over the course of your life."

"But you don't let me love you back."

"Do you want to love me back, Laird. I never thought—"

"Sometimes, yeah. Sometimes. I mean...I know I haven't been an emotional sap with you, but I am your son. You're my mother. But whatever you want."

"Well, thank you, Laird. I do appreciate that you care. I'm sorry for putting you off. Honestly, I'm fine. I'm just not hungry lately."

"Maybe you should see a doctor," Grandfather said, "next time you're at the hospital with Al."

Mother placed a gentle hand on my grandfather's hand. "Thank you. If the opportunity presents itself, I'll look into it. Now, can we talk about something else."

"Like?" I asked.

"Like why it doesn't matter that the Braves called you up."

"That does seem a little odd, Grandson," my grandfather said. "You playing for your father's team...I thought that's what you've always wanted."

I feared that moment, when I'd have to tell them. Janie and

Billy were the only two who knew I'd be leaving in just a week—and that I may not be coming back. After taking a deep breath, I said, "Because I've enlisted in the Army."

Mother sat expressionless while my grandmother began to cry, my grandfather patting her hand for comfort from across the table.

"I just knew this would happen," Grandmother said.

"He'll be okay," Grandfather said. "If there's one thing Laird knows it's how to fight." His attempt at humor was lost on my mother whose face still hadn't betrayed any emotion. "When do you leave, Grandson?"

"The day after Christmas. Less than a week."

"So soon?" Grandmother said, placing her hands over her mouth, stunned.

"Well say something mother before you burst. I thought that's what you wanted. That is why you gave me Tennyson's book of poems, right? Why you bookmarked and wanted me to read *The Charge of the Light Brigade*? 'Into the mouth of hell rode the six hundred'... 'Theirs not to make reply, theirs not to reason why, theirs but to do and die'... 'When can their glory fade?'... 'Honor the charge they made' and all of that. That's why, right?"

"No, Laird. That's not why I wanted you to read that poem," Mother said, uncharacteristic tears welling in her eyes. "I wanted you to read it because, well, I was hoping when you read those words you'd have more respect for your father, for the sacrifice he made. I wanted you to see that very few God-fearing men would ever *want* to endure the horrors of war, to go and kill other men and in so doing put their own lives at risk...that very few men *want* to charge into battle, into bullets and bombs and chemicals that kill and permanently maim...run headfirst into utter and bloody barbarism. Yet men do. I wasn't asking you to go do it. I was only hoping you'd see the *duty* some men feel in doing so. I was trying to help you better understand your father and how duty could compel someone like your father—who loved you more than his own life, who loved us both more than himself—to leave us, to leave *you* knowing it might cost you your father."

There was a long silence between us; nobody at the table spoke. Her words bore so much weight that they deserved contemplation. Her words carried the weight of armies of men—and women— who had made the ultimate sacrifice, many because their country asked, some because they asked it of themselves, all because of *duty*. Yes, many had succumbed to the draft, but they always had a choice to make. They could have objected, protested, lied and connived to get out of it, as I had tried, as some surely did, but the men that went didn't do that—and many of them died. Many, like my father, went but came home permanently changed.

"Well, I do understand, Mother. I didn't want to, I admit it. But I do now. So thank you."

"Do you mean that, Son?"

"Yes," I said, looking off, once again sensing the gravity of my decision to enlist, once again realizing that, like my father, I may have to give all or part of my life for that sense of duty I now felt, the sense of duty I now shared with my father. "I need to go. I need to do my part."

"Your part in what?" Mother asked, her question more for my sake than hers.

"In defending innocent people against aggressive tyrants like Hitler and Mussolini."

"That's why you're doing this, Laird? Really?"

I thought about her question. "Partly...but mostly, I guess, because Dad was right. You can't let your friends fight alone—your fellow countrymen. Not when the cause is just. Not when many of these boys won't come...no...that would be an ugly mirror to look into."

Just then my mother rose from her chair and walked over, bending to hug me from behind while I sat, saying nothing for the long moment she held me. Before her arms released me she kissed my cheek. "Your father would be so proud of you, Son," she whispered in my ear. "I'm proud of you."

Her words caught in my throat. "So, is it Lillian or Emily?" I asked with an awkward laugh. "Those are my two choices, anyway."

CHAPTER TWENTY-FOUR

My last week at home, the week leading up to Christmas and my subsequent departure for the Army, went by entirely too fast, the way a vacation does when you're away from a job you dread. The hospital released Janie to come home the following morning and since neither of us knew anything about caring for a baby, my grandparents agreed to come stay with us, at least until Janie felt comfortable caring for a child on her own. Janie gave me a list of her customers' phone numbers and I called to let them know she'd be on maternity leave for a while, but that we'd still fill the orders and have them delivered by a hired delivery boy, who happened to be a high school kid from up the block. Meanwhile, I'd spend every moment possible with my beloved wife and newborn baby girl—whom we named Emily, to the delight of everybody, especially my mother—and with Billy, whose boundless joy brightened any room he was in. Of course, to avoid confusion Billy would have to call my mother "Grandma" when she came around, a small sacrifice she seemed willing to make for the team.

I also spent more days with my grandparents during that time, whom I'd always adored. I especially enjoyed conversations with my grandfather, whose wisdom seemed to come from a higher power, from a different age even. His words, though they might seem tired and old-fashioned to the younger generation of progressives and rebels, were to me timeless, as relevant today as they'd ever been. One day, while the ladies baked to fill orders, all us guys went into Boston to do some Christmas shopping, making a day of it. During the drive my grandfather took time to impart more of that wisdom.

"Laird, have you ever thought about what you'd like your legacy to be?"

"No, I can't recall ever thinking about it."

"What about your father's? If he was to die today, and I pray he doesn't, what would *his* legacy be?"

I glanced over at him while I drove, my hands at ten and two o'clock on the steering wheel, my tall grandfather sitting gentlemanly in the passenger seat, his head nearly scraping the headliner, his eyes panning the scenery as it passed. "I'm not sure, really. I'd have to think about it."

"Would you say your father was a righteous man?"

"I think so. That's what everybody says—that he was a man of principle."

"Would you say that he was a loving husband?"

"Mom would have to answer that, but by his war letters I'd say he truly loved her."

"And would you say he was a loving father?"

"Yes. Yes, I would."

"What else could you say about your father, if he were gone and somebody asked you about him?"

"Well, I'd tell them that he played professional baseball."

"Would you say he was a good baseball player?"

"Yes. He had a nice swing...could really hit the ball...had good chops at shortstop."

"Is that it?"

"I don't know, Grandpa. What are you getting at?"

"I'll answer your question by asking you this. What is a legacy?"

"An account, I guess, of what a person does while they're alive." I glanced once again at him, looking for his approval of my answer, which he gave with a nod.

"Yes, but it's more than that, Grandson. A legacy is a living testament to what once was, a composition that brings to mind not just the accomplishments of a person, but their ideals, dreams, desires, failures, their spirit…their soul and heart. To mention only one's accomplishments, well, that would be like recalling a one-dimensional character from a dime-store novel. You leave out the good stuff, the meat that makes the person come to life again before your mind, the stuff that lets another know that this person was a genuine living child of God."

"I still don't understand what you're getting at."

"Grandson, I think part of the reason you've had trouble in your life accepting your father was that you never really knew the man inside. Oh, I think you've gotten a good glimpse of him over that past month or so, and I think you now know he was, and still is, a good man. But do you think you'd have been as angry at the world, at him and your mother, if you'd taken the time early on to discover more about him than just that he was a ballplayer and soldier, more than an invalid?"

"I suppose not."

"Let's try this. Say I came up to you now and said, 'Hey, Laird. I heard your father was retarded!' Would you punch me in the nose, as you have others who have said that about him?"

"Well, I still wouldn't like it. But no, I guess I know enough about my father now to defend him with words."

"What would you say, then?"

"Well, I'd say my father was a hero, and that he'd sustained a head injury in the war. I'd say that my father didn't have to go fight but he wanted to, for all of us who couldn't fight. I'd say my father had fears like the rest of us but that he faced them head on, with God's help, and with the loving support of my mother. I'd say that my father was from Texas and that before the war my father played shortstop for the Boston Braves, when Rabbit Maranville wasn't playing, that he'd known he wanted to be a professional baseball player since he was eight years old, that he batted right-handed and threw right-handed. I'd tell you that my father had a keen sense about things, that he loved people and knew when somebody needed help, that he would always run to be the first one there, even when he had no shoes on his feet. I'd say that my father only ever loved one woman, my mother, and that they'd loved each other since 'they had brown in their britches.' I'd tell you that my father had a profound faith in both God and the goodness of man, though there were times when men, such as myself, didn't treat him kindly. And I'd tell you that my father knew the true meaning of gratitude and took every opportunity to show it…and that he loved me more than he loved his own life."

My grandfather smiled, "Now you know the man that was. When you get home from the war, I hope you'll take some time to get to know the man that still is."

I nodded to myself, thinking that my grandfather was right: there had to be more to my father than just being an invalid. And it made me think of my own legacy, which I believed was my grandfather's intent. What would others say about me—know about me—if I didn't make it home from the war? Would my mark on this world, on the lives of others, be mostly positive or mostly negative? Would they be proud to say they'd known me, or would they be ashamed to say it?

"I want a legacy!" Billy said from the backseat.

"You have quite the legacy already, Son," I said.

"Indeed," My grandfather added. "And a lot yet to come."

After we finished shopping we headed over to Braves Field—home of the Boston Braves—a grand ballpark just off the Charles River and not far from Fenway. I'd promised Billy I'd take him there and I needed to let Casey Stengel, Manager of the Braves, know of my commitment to the Army. Standing on the sidewalk in front of the gates to Braves Field was like standing before the gates of heaven; I stood in awe of not only their size, but also at what lay on the other side.

"Can we go inside?" Billy asked, each of us looking up at the massive walled fortress before us.

"That's what we're here for," I said. "Dad played here, Grandpa."

He nodded as he wiped a tear. "Yes. I know. Hard to imagine, though."

"Can I help you gentlemen with something?" a nearby landscaper asked.

"My name is Laird Young. I'm with the Boston Braves," I said, smiling as I heard myself say it. "A new player. I'm here to see Casey Stengel."

"Laird Young..." he said, his weathered black hand rubbing his old black chin. "Seems to me we had another Young here a few years back...first name Al, I think...nineteen fourteen to nineteen seventeen...shortstop, good hitter when he played."

"Wow! You know your baseball."

"Just the Braves, Son—just the Braves. I've been here since the day they opened. Wouldn't want to be nowhere else."

"He was my father," I said before stating the obvious. "I'm his son."

"Well, Mister Young, my name is Hershel Hawks, purveyor of everything green here," he said, walking over to shake my hand. "Welcome to the team. You'll find Mister Stengel's office through those gates and up a couple levels, right behind home plate."

"Thank you."

"My pleasure, Mister Young. Looking forward to seeing you play this year."

A few minutes later I walked into Casey Stengel's office, two levels up and just behind home plate, right where Hershel Hawks said it would be. Billy and my Grandfather waited outside, finding themselves a couple seats in the stands that overlooked the large green field.

"Laird," Casey Stengel said to me as he came from around his desk to shake my hand, still in his uniform even though it was the off-season. "I've heard great things about you. I like the way you play ball. Think you'll be a great starter for the club."

"Yes, sir," I said. "That's what I've come to see you about."

"Have a seat." He motioned with his arm for me to take a seat in a chair directly across from his desk. After sitting in his chair, he said, "How's your mother?"

I nearly choked when he asked that. "She's fine. A bit pushy, but then you already know that."

"Not at all, Laird. I enjoy talking with her. I'll let you in on a little secret. It was your mother who told me about John Dagenhard. Your mother said he wasn't being coached to his full potential at Hartford."

"Yeah, I know Dagy. We played together. Didn't do much though as a pitcher for Hartford. Six point something ERA if I remember in forty-one. Didn't play in forty-two. Pretty good last season, though."

"Well, the last time I didn't listen to your mother it cost me Dutch Leonard. But I waited on Dagenhard last season to see how he would start with Hartford. By September his ERA was down to three point one so I brought him up to pitch for the Braves."

"I know. He did good."

"The season was almost over by then, but he pitched eleven innings for us with, get this, a zero point zero ERA. Now he wants to go fight in the war. Can you believe that?"

"Lots of guys going overseas. Did my mom tip you off to me, also?"

"No, Laird. That was my call. You're a fine all-around player. And I like the way you pitch. No knuckleballs, though," he said with a chuckle. "No, Laird, you got the call because of how you play the game, and because right now I'm short on pitchers. Like you said, lots of guys going overseas to fight."

"Well, that's sort of why I'm here, Mister Stengel."

"What? You too?" he said, throwing up his hands in defeat. "When will the bleeding stop?" It was a bad metaphor, given the human cost of war, but I understood what he meant. "When do you leave?"

"In three days—just after Christmas."

"So I don't even get one game out of you this season? I'll tell you what, kid. I'm so mad at Hitler and Mussolini for what they're doing to my team—that Tojo guy too! Might just go over there myself! End this stupid war so we can get back to playing baseball!"

I laughed. "Yes, sir."

"I don't blame you, Laird. If I was your age I'd go too. Not much call, though, for a fifty-two year old private."

"If you don't mind me saying so, I think you and the other managers can do your part right here at home, just by keeping this game going. I've been told newsreel of the games is being shown over there whenever possible and that radio broadcasts are being replayed. Newspapers carry the scores and highlights too. They say it really boosts moral when our guys overseas get a chance to watch or listen to or read about the games. Even Roosevelt said it'd be best to keep the game going—in his letter to Commissioner Kenesaw Landis."

He nodded before standing to shake my hand. "Well, Laird, I'm sorry to see you go, but I understand. Let me know when you get home and we'll see if we can work you into the lineup."

"Thank you. Listen, my son and grandfather are outside. Would you mind if we went down onto the field. I'd like them to see it from down there. I think they'd really enjoy that."

"Absolutely. I'll do you one better," he said, coming around the desk and leading me outside. "How about I grab a catcher's mitt and a glove and we'll let them watch you pitch me a few?"

"Really? That would be incredible! Thank you!"

"Go on down. I'll be there in a minute."

Once on the lower level, we travelled the concourse until we found a small walkway out to the field and the pitcher's mound, where I stood, gazing like a star-struck boy at the high bleachers and the diamond all around me.

"I've always dreamed of playing in this stadium," I said to Billy and Grandfather. "See those outfield walls? They're so deep a player has a better chance of hitting an infield home run than one out of the park. These right and left field fences...over four hundred feet from home plate! The centerfield fence...nearly five hundred feet! That's unheard of! Think about it. That's a lot of air a ball has to travel, and a lot of ground to cover for an outfielder."

"It's certainly awe-inspiring, Grandson."

"This is swell!" Billy added.

"Did you know it took seven years and a new type of ball before a batter finally hit one over the fence for a home run—a guy named Frank Snyder with the New York Giants. Just an amazing accomplishment! And look at this place! It can seat over 40,000 fans! When this park opened back in nineteen fifteen it was the biggest ever. Can you believe that?" I shook my head in disbelief. "And Dad played here during the fifteen, sixteen, and seventeen seasons," I added, running over to shortstop and turning to face home plate, my feet spread shoulder-length apart and my hands on my knees—in a fielder's stance, just as my father would have been back then.

"Ready to pitch a few?" Casey Stengel called out as he walked onto the field, stopping behind home plate. "Here, young man," he said to Billy, holding out a brand new leather baseball glove. "Go give this to your old man." Billy grabbed the glove from his hand and ran it out to my grandfather, which made everybody but Billy laugh. "Not that old man," Stengel said. "The other old man. Your father."

There was a brand new baseball inside the glove. Once again I looked around at the mammoth park, this time envisioning my teammates at their respective positions and a runner or two on base. While I looked, I had the glove under my arm, my hands rubbing the ball, the way I always had before a pitch to a tough batter. A few moments later my arm was in motion—a fastball, straight down the pipe, ending with that sound I'd come to love: *Thwack!*

"That's why I called you up," Stengel said, throwing the ball back to me. "You've got one heck of a fastball, kid. Let me see a few more."

I threw him three more fastballs, each over the plate.

"Now show me that curve I've heard so much about."

"Yes, sir," I said, once again rubbing the ball, thinking about my next pitch. A minute later I dropped one in for a strike.

"This time Casey Stengel walked the ball back to me on the mound. "You're good, Laird. Wish I'd seen it sooner."

"Me, too," I said.

"Sure you don't want to stay and play for us? I could make a few calls. I've got friends on the local draft board."

"No, but thanks. This is something I've got to do."

"Okay, then," he said, nodding his respect before turning toward the tunnel that would take him back to his office.

"Here's your glove, Mister Stengel," I said, following him a few steps holding out the glove.

"Keep it. You'll need it when you come back."

"Thank you!" I said. He simply waved behind him and kept walking.

"I like him," Billy said with a smile.

"I knew you'd say that." I tossed Billy the ball and headed to home plate. "Pitch me a couple." When I turned back around Billy was standing on the mound. "Not from there, you silly goose. You wouldn't make it halfway with your arm strength. Come closer. Twenty feet or so." I thumped my fist into the sweet spot of my glove. "Give me your best, Billy Sunday. Preach to me."

Billy giggled before winding up and pitching his first ball, a lazy lob that actually found its way across the plate in the strike zone.

"That's incredible! You've been holding out on me."

"Quite impressive, Billy," grandfather said, his hands clasped behind him as he watched our little upstart. "You're a natural."

"Really?" Billy said, excitedly.

"With practice, of course," Grandfather added. "You've got to put in the hours, but you've got natural talent to build on."

Billy threw a few more to me, the whole experience somewhat surreal. First I'm actually standing on the pitcher's mound at Brave's Field. Then I'm pitching to Brave's manager, Casey Stengel. Then I'm wrapping it all up with my new son pitching to me, my grandfather there to share in it all. *Nothing could ever top this,* I thought, *except maybe pitching to my father in a real game, here at this park. That,* I thought, *would be my idea of the 'perfect game.'*

CHAPTER TWENTY-FIVE

Christmas arrived with a shadow hanging over it—the dark realization that it would be my last full day at home with my beloved wife, my beautiful baby girl, and my new adoring son. The next morning I'd leave for the war, a thought that had me up before sunrise, my clothes and shoes in hand as I silently tiptoed in my pajamas past baby Emily's crib, which Janie had rolled to the foot of our bed so we could easily keep an eye on her in the night. Once downstairs, I did my usual routine of putting the kettle on before peaking out a window to see what the weather was doing. Though darkness still lingered, it had surrendered enough of the sky to dawn that I could see the freshly laid, thick blanket of snow covering the yard, the burgeoning red sky temporarily painting the snow pink.

"Is it time to open presents yet?" I heard Billy say behind me.

I turned to find him ambling toward me, rubbing his eyes and yawning, his hair a mess and angled up on one side like Gumby. As he hugged me, I said, "Not yet. Go back to bed."

"I can't sleep anymore."

"Me neither. How about some hot chocolate?"

"Okay," he said, sleepily, following me into the kitchen to silence the whistling kettle.

Once we each had a mug of hot chocolate—Billy's with marshmallows—we returned to the living room window to watch the sunrise together from two chairs I'd slid close, the lighted

Christmas tree just to our left in the corner, a colorful array of presents underneath like giant seeds waiting to sprout open, its piney scent blending with the aroma of hot chocolate.

"Isn't this something?" I said, referring to the orange orb cracking the eastern horizon, throwing a warm glow over the glassy Podunk River across from our home, the bushy heads of the snow-covered trees lining its banks looking like giant oranges. "This is why we bought this house—the view on mornings like this. But then you probably have bigger things to think about at your age."

"Like what's in my presents," he said with a giggle before taking a careful sip of his hot drink.

"Is that important to you, what you get for Christmas?"

"I'm a kid. What do you think?" We both laughed at that one, before he said, "I'm really happy that you're adopting me."

I nodded. "We're happy too, Billy."

"That's the best present."

"So we can return the other presents we bought you?"

"No!"

As we sat there watching the sun complete its slow rise over the snowy landscape, I couldn't help but think that one day—while I trudged with my platoon across the bloody and pocked fields of Germany or France, while I slogged my way up the mud-plagued rutted roads leading to Hitler's lair—I'd recall this Christmas postcard in my tired mind and it'd bring a smile to my face, that it'd remind me of the life I have waiting for me back home.

"Is this the first Christmas without your mom?"

Billy nodded.

"Think of her a lot, huh?"

"She liked Christmas," he said, remembering. "But we had to make our gifts."

"Nothing store-bought?"

He shook his head. "Mom said it was because making things for each other was more personal."

"But you don't think so?"

"I think it was just because we didn't have much money."

"Well, I like the idea of making each other something as a gift."

"Like carving Janie's face into a piece of wood?"

I laughed. "Okay, not that, but maybe something simpler. We could start next year."

"You won't be here next year," he said, somberly.

"You don't know that, Billy. A lot of guys are gone less than a year."

His silence told me he didn't believe me. I'm not sure I believed I'd be home within a year either. Just then I heard something and turned in my chair to find Janie coming down the stairs in her robe, her morning face sleepy but cheery, baby Emily wrapped in a plush pink blanket and being carried in her arms.

"Well, this is a nice picture," she said, "the two men in my life enjoying a private moment Christmas morning. Anything us girls might be interested in hearing?"

"Just comparing our tattoos and muscles—guy stuff."

"I've seen your muscles," she said to me, batting her eyes. "Delightful."

Janie sat in the nearby rocker, one arm and hand cradling Emily, the other hand snugging the blanket around Emily's body and head to keep out the chill. "This scene would be a lot nicer with a warm fire going."

I popped to attention and gave her a salute. "Copy that, ma'am. I'm on it."

"Billy, honey, would you mind getting me a mug of that hot chocolate? Just set it here on the table until my other honey can hold Emily."

Billy followed my lead and saluted. "Yes, ma'am."

"Isn't this nice, sweetie," she said to Emily. "Our own private army."

"Have you fed her?" I asked, arranging kindling and logs in the fireplace before striking a match and setting the pile ablaze. "Of course you haven't. I haven't prepared the bottle. Should have done that first." I went to the kitchen and put a pan of water on the stove, my eyes searching for a clean baby bottle for the formula.

"What time are your parents and grandparents coming?"

"Early evening, Mom said."

"Why so late?"

"To give us the day together, I guess. That's why my grandparents had me take them back yesterday. They should have just stayed, though."

"It was nice of them to do that."

"I think they're only coming tonight to say goodbye to me."

"And to open gifts."

"They're opening their gifts first, I think."

"Do you think we should do the same?" Janie asked.

"Suppose so," I said, removing the bottle from the hot water and testing the temperature of the formula on my arm. "What do you think, Billy?"

"He's probably wondering why we haven't opened gifts already," she said to Billy, who nodded enthusiastically as he carefully set her hot chocolate on the end table next to her.

"You guys can start if you want," I said. "I'll just be a minute."

"We can wait," Janie said, rocking gently in the chair, baby Emily suckling her finger until I could get the bottle of formula warmed to the right temperature.

"Somebody should invent pre-warmed baby formula," I said.

"Somebody already did. It's called breast milk."

"That's gross," Billy said.

We had discussed breastfeeding Emily, but Janie decided it would be inconvenient, especially when out and about. Breastfeeding at home was easy enough for her, but breastfeeding in public presented too many challenges for Janie. Besides, bottle-feeding allowed me to feed and bond with my daughter as well, something Janie and I both thought was important to her development.

"How do you know you weren't breastfed?" Janie asked Billy.

"My mother wouldn't do that to me."

Billy sure could make us laugh.

"I suppose it does sound pretty gross to an eight-year-old."

"Here you go," I said. "One bottle of baby formula, shaken but not stirred."

"No," Janie said, standing and handing Emily off to me. "Here *you* go."

"Come to Daddy, sweetheart."

I took Emily and sat in the rocker, holding and feeding her while Janie started fishing presents from under the tree, the fire blazing next to her, its flickering orange light reflecting off her face and eyes. Billy stood close to her, playing the middleman as she distributed the gifts, saying to Billy as she handed them to him, "This one's Laird's. This one's mine. Billy, this is yours from us," and so on. Once she had finished, we each had a small stack of gifts, the only ones remaining under the tree the gifts for my parents and grandparents, and two for Carl, one from us and one from Billy. And several gifts for baby Emily sat under the tree unwrapped, things like clothes and baby blankets and more bottles.

Billy opened the first gift. "Wow! A sketch book!" he said, jumping in circles as he does when excited, stopping to flip through the blank pages. "Thank you!"

"You said you were an artist," I said, rocking Emily as I fed her. "Now you can show us."

"I will. And it's small enough to fold and put in my back pocket. Oh…is it okay if I fold it?"

"It's yours, sweetie," Janie said. "If you like to carry it with you and you want to put it in your pocket, then fold it. But be careful not to get stuck by the sharp pencil."

"I will. Thanks."

"You're next, Janie," I said. "Open the small one on top of your stack."

"You mean the one in the shape of a perfume box?" she asked, smiling.

"Maybe it is, maybe not."

She carefully unpeeled the wrapping, as if planning to reuse the paper, something I never really understood. Unwrapping was supposed to be fun, not laborious. "Well, it's not perfume," she said when she saw the plain-looking box. "But what is it?"

"Look inside and find out."

She flipped open the end and slid out the gift. "It's pink ribbon. I don't understand."

"Unroll a bit and read what's imprinted on it."

Janie unrolled it until she could read the silver glittery imprint, which she read aloud. " 'Janie's Pies and Pastries—Homemade & Handmade'."

"I know it's a strange gift, but I thought it'd be a nice thing to wrap around your pie boxes, like the way we wrap ribbon around our Christmas gifts."

"Laird, this is so thoughtful! I love it!" She came over and kissed my lips. "This will look lovely on the boxes!"

"Just wanted to show my support, you know, of you and your business. Maybe sometimes I don't show it but I am really proud of you."

She kissed me again. "Thank you, honey. That means as much as the ribbon."

"You're next, Dad!" Billy said, handing me a gift—from him the tag read. It was a very small slender item, not boxed, only wrapped. And it felt weighty for such a small thing.

"Thank you, Son."

"Here," Janie said, taking Emily from me to free up my hands. "Let me love on my baby girl for a few minutes."

"I hope you like it!" Billy said, now on his knees in front of me as I unwrapped the small package while sitting in the rocking chair. Before I could comment on the gift, Billy said, "It's my pocket knife. I wanted you to have it—for the war."

Janie's eyes immediately filled with tears, my throat choking up. Billy's heartfelt gift reminded us that I would be leaving very soon to go to a place where it was literally kill or be killed, a place where I would need a knife and a gun to defend myself against other men with knives and guns trying to kill me. Giving me his knife, I imagined, was his way of helping me to come home alive.

"Thank you, Billy," I said, swallowing hard and nodding, gazing upon the ivory handled buck knife like a priceless gem.

"Do you like it?"

"More than you know, Son." He stood and leaned in to hug me. I held him with a little more emotion than I might normally have shown. "Thank you. I'll take it wherever they send me."

In the next bunch of gifts, Janie got her favorite perfume—a delicate fragrance that reminded me of a botanical garden. Billy got a collection of new baseball cards from me, one of which was the rookie card for a guy named Stan Musial, a guy so good his first year with the Cardinals that in just twelve games played he hit for four twenty-six with a slugging percentage of five seventy-four. His second year—1942—Musial hit ten home runs and was twelfth in MVP voting. In 1943, just last season, Musial led the National League in hits, runs scored, triples, doubles, slugging percentage, batting average, and won the voting for Most Valuable Player in the National League. Out of all the cards we gave Billy, I told him Musial's would surely be worth something later on.

For my part, I got a new leather billfold, one with a few plastic sleeves in the center for photographs. "Stoke the fire a little, will you, Billy?" I said.

Billy grabbed the poker and started moving logs around a bit, allowing more oxygen to get to the fire, which made the orange flames jump and the wood crackle, the warmth emanating into the room, bringing with it the pleasant smell of burning wood.

"Okay, last ones," Janie said. "You first Billy."

"It's huge!" Billy said as he began to open his gift from the both of us, which we'd wrapped and boxed inside another bigger box, which we'd wrapped and boxed inside an even bigger box before wrapping it. By the time he got to the third box inside, he was laughing so hard that he was crying.

"That's the last one," I said. "Promise."

"I don't trust you," he said, still laughing. "But okay." He unwrapped the last box—one of Janie's old shoeboxes—then removed the lid. "Wow! Tools!" he said as he pulled a brown leather tool belt from the box and unrolled it, revealing some very unique tools.

"Not just tools," I said. "They're your very own wood carving tools."

"All mine?"

"All yours," Janie said, still holding Emily. "Are you excited?"

"Yes! I'll get right to work!" he said leaping to his feet.

"Hold it, sport," I said. "Today's a union holiday. You can start work tomorrow or the next day."

"Okay. Thanks!"

"Your turn, Janie," I said, rising from the rocking chair to take Emily from her, who had finished feeding, now asleep and dreaming, a peculiar odor rising from under the blanket. "I think she needs changing."

"There's the living room floor," Janie said. "Lay a towel down and have at it."

"Uh, are you serious?"

"Yes." She looked at me for a moment. When I didn't move, she said, "What is it about baby poop that makes men cower? Give me a minute. I'll change her after I open my gift." She read the tag on the top of the gift, just under the red and green bow. "To Mom.

From Billy." She unwrapped the gift to see a small wooden wall plaque with a short hemp rope attached. The surface was a natural pine, tan in color with colored calligraphy painted in the center, a flowered wreath painted around the words, which she read aloud. "With God, all things are possible. Matthew nineteen, verse twenty-six. How sweet!"

"Great Grandpa helped me pick it out."

"I figured," Janie said.

"Do you like it?"

"It's lovely, Billy! Thank you! I know just where to hang it!" She walked over to the fireplace. Above the mantle—about head height—was a nail with nothing hanging from it. When she laid the rope over the nail to let the wooden plaque hang, she stepped back and gave it a look. "That's the perfect place for it, don't you think, Laird?"

"Perfect," I said. "Now where's *my* last gift? Come on. Let's have it."

"Wait," Janie said, going over to the dining room table. "It's in my purse." A moment later she returned to stand before me, her hands behind her back. "Pick a hand."

"Right."

"No, but you can still have it," she said as she brought her left hand around, which held a wallet-sized photograph of herself, recently taken. "It's not much, but I thought you might like to take it with you. I'm told all the GIs carry their best girl's picture with them, so they don't forget there's somebody at home who loves them, who's waiting for them to come home."

"Ah, Janie, it's...I don't know what to say," I said, retrieving my new billfold from the end table. "I'll put it in my new wallet right now."

"Is it okay?"

"Sweetheart, I'll look at it everyday I'm away. When did you get this taken?"

"When you guys went into Boston to go shopping."

"Well, thank you. I honestly can't remember ever getting such thoughtful gifts. Usually it's all baseball related—not that there's anything wrong with baseball stuff. But you know what I mean."

She hugged me, careful not to squish Emily whom I still held in my arms, Billy coming in to join us.

"Somebody stinks," Billy said.

"Whoever smells it has to change the diaper," Janie said. "That's the rule."

"Not me," Billy said, bolting up the stairs to the upper bathroom and closing the door. A second later we heard the door lock turn.

"Boys," Janie said. "And men. Give her to me. Go hide with Billy in the bathroom."

THE OTHERS ARRIVED about six in the evening, just as promised, their hands loaded with food and gifts as they entered through the front door, Carl holding my emaciated father in his arms while I lifted my father's wheelchair up onto the porch, my father's eyes still wide and unblinking, his face still void of emotion, his arms still rigid and bent at his side, his fists still clinched. The only thing odd was that he grunted when Carl lifted him, as if he'd felt some discomfort—odd because I wasn't sure he was capable of feeling anything in his stupor. In all the years he'd been that way, I'd never seen him respond to painful stimuli.

"One of these days I'm gonna build a ramp," I said.

"It's no bother, Mr. Laird," Carl said. "He don't weigh much more than a feather."

As Carl sat my father back onto his seat, I said, "Carl, I just want to thank you for all you've done for my father and mother over the years—and for me. You've sacrificed a lot for us. I guess I've never said it before. Felt I should, though."

"Wasn't no bother, Mr. Laird. Y'all have been good to me too."

"I sure wish you could just call me Laird."

"Yes, sir, Laird. Y'all have become my family and family takes care of each other."

"But what about the family you were born into? In all the years we've known you we've only seen you go back to visit once."

"Well, we was never that close, you know? My daddy, he drove us apart with his drinkin'. Just consumed by hate, you know? The bottle was his way to peace, he thought. It taught me that hate ain't no good for nobody. Once I left home I didn't feel much call to return. Besides, I feel useful here with y'all. Ain't much use to nobody just pickin' cotton."

"You miss your mother, though, right?"

He nodded, thinking it over as we stood on the porch, my father in his chair between us. "She's old now, but my sisters look after her. I do wish, though, I could bring her here one day, you know, for a visit. I think she'd really like the beautiful New England countryside."

"You should. I'm sure my mother wouldn't mind."

"Be too much trouble right now," he said, somberly.

"Why? What do you mean?"

"Laird," Mother called from inside the house. "Bring your father inside. It's too cold for him out there."

Carl lifted the front wheels of the wheelchair over the front door threshold as I pushed the chair. "You should bring your mother out, Carl. Mom would want that."

"Maybe so, Laird. Thank you."

After our Christmas dinner meal, which seemed identical to our Thanksgiving turkey dinner, we retreated to the living room for conversation in front of the warm fire and the twinkling lights of the Christmas tree. One of the things we'd do at such times, when we were all together like that, was to have hot chocolate with my grandmother's traditional peppermint bark candy, which she liked to say was one of the easiest treats to make, only requiring a layer of white chocolate over a layer of dark chocolate, and crumbled candy canes sprinkled over the top. It had been one of my father's favorites, I'm told, and had become one of mine too. Biting into a piece of Grandmother's peppermint bark candy felt a little like biting shattered glass, with the sharp edges of the crumbled candy cane harsh against the soft skin of the upper pallet; but the taste of white and dark chocolate and peppermint would soon come alive in our mouths, melting into a sweet and creamy, crunchy breath mint. Sometimes we'd add a piece to our hot chocolate too, watching as the white and dark chocolate melted into a floating swirl on top.

"So are you ready to go?" Mother asked from the loveseat, her arm around Billy who sat close to her, staring into his cup as if waiting for something to happen, my father in his chair between her and the fire.

"I think so," I said, sitting next to Janie on the sofa, baby Emily asleep in front of us in a small cradle I rocked with my shoeless foot, a cradle that reminded me of the manger of Christ. "Picked up my travel uniform yesterday from the Army depot. Fits pretty good."

"He's so handsome in it," Janie added, trying to put on a happy face.

"I'll bet he is," Mother said, smiling, recalling some image in her mind. "Your father's fit pretty nice too."

"Emily!" Grandmother said, shaking her head, but smiling to herself.

"Look, Grandma," I said. "I think she's blushing."

"Stop," Mother said, patting my father's leg. "That's just the fire light playing tricks."

We all had a good laugh after that.

"Have you given any thought to our offer, Laird," Grandmother asked.

"What offer?" Janie asked.

"I've been meaning to talk to you about it. I guess with Billy and going to Detroit I forgot."

"Talk to me about what?"

"They want to leave us their ranch in Texas, but they'd like us all to live there—Mom and Dad too."

"We'll build you another house," Grandmother said.

"By 'leave us' you mean when you die?" Janie asked. "Don't talk like that."

"That's what I said."

"I think it's a great idea," Mother said in a way that told me she'd already been made aware of the offer.

"Me too!" said Billy. "I could be a cowboy!"

"We'll see how things go over the next year," I said. "How do you feel about it, honey?"

Janie said, "I could live in Texas...on the ranch. It's so pretty there."

"But what about your business?"

"Pies taste the same in Texas as they do here, I suppose." Then she smiled. "Be nice to see you strutting around in tight jeans and a cowboy hat."

Mom laughed. "Now who's blushing?"

"I could get used to the idea. But after baseball—and the war, of course."

"Here," Mother said, handing me a brown, rectangular leather pouch. "It's from all of us." I opened the flap and pulled the contents out partway to reveal a nice pen, some parchment paper, and some matching envelopes. "So you'll write," Mother added.

"Yes," said Janie.

"Small enough to carry in your rucksack," my grandfather said.

"I'll make good use of it. Thank you."

"Heard you went and saw Casey Stengel," Mom said. "Said he wasn't too happy about losing you—tried to talk you out of going."

"Yeah, but he had me pitch a few balls to him down on the field. Dad, you should have seen me. I thought about you the whole time." Right then my father grunted and thrashed violently in his chair—only for a brief moment, but enough to make everybody take notice. "Dad?"

My mother smiled lovingly. "That's the first time I've ever heard you talk to your father as if he could hear you."

"But did you see that, Mom? Did you hear that?" She nodded, seemingly unaffected. "How can you be so calm about it? He heard me!"

"I know."

"But…what do the doctors say? Is he coming out of it?"

"They don't know enough about the causes of stupor to say one way or the other. Just a watch and see."

I shook my head. "Did you tell Dad that I went to see Nig Clarke—that I returned the baseballs and met him?"

My father thrashed and grunted again.

"No, but you just did," Mother said.

"This is crazy!" I said, excited and leaning forward on the sofa, facing my father. "Dad, I met Jay Justin Clarke—Nig Clarke—the guy who hit those eight home runs, those eight balls you gave me to return. I met him. He said he remembers you from the war. He said you were one of the greatest hitters he ever saw! Can you believe that?" This time my father just grunted. "He said he looked for you after the war! Said he just knew you had to be a big league ballplayer, but that he couldn't find you! Dad, can you hear what I'm saying?" This time there was no response. "He said to tell you thanks for thinking of him, that he'll cherish those baseballs more now that he knows who you are." I looked at my mother who smiled behind a flood of tears. "Mom?"

"I'm fine—just happy. I've been praying for this day for the last twenty-five years, the day when the two of you would have a conversation."

"Does he know about tomorrow?"

"Yes," Mother said, wiping her eyes. "We've had that talk already."

"Did he...I mean...?"

"No. There was no response, Laird. But he heard—I know he did." She stood and walked over to the coat rack near the front door. "It's getting late. We should go." She gathered up hers, as well as my grandparents' coats. "It'll be a slow drive with the snow and ice on the roads."

"They've probably cleared them all by now," I said.

"Your mother's right," Grandfather said. "It's time to say our goodbyes."

A few moments later we were all gathered on the front porch. The air felt cold on the skin, but clear and refreshing to warm lungs, and the night seemed exceptionally dark, brightened only by the quarter moon's light reflecting off the snow-covered ground.

Carl stepped up to hug me and shake my hand. "Laird, you keep your head down over there—your butt, too. See you when you gets home."

"Thank you, Carl."

My teary-eyed grandmother hugged me next, bundled up to the chin in her long coat and knitted scarf. Holding me close for a long minute, she said, "I don't have the words, Grandson."

"You don't have to say anything, Grandma."

"You know we love you and we'll be praying for you every day."

"Thank you," I said as she stepped from the porch, crunching her way through the snow to Mom's woody wagon.

"Grandson," My grandfather said, extending his hand, pulling me in close when I took hold of it. "I'm about as proud of you as a grandfather can be. You're a special man, Laird, with qualities unique to you, like your toughness. I have no doubt it'll serve you well in battle."

"Yes, sir," I said, my throat tight. "I'll do the best I can for you."

"Do it for yourself, Grandson—and for your fellow soldiers who'll be depending on you, as you will them."

"Yes, sir."

"Most of all, when things around you are chaotic and you're afraid, remember, Grandson, there is at such moments a peculiar peace…a peculiar comfort that comes from prayer."

"Yes, sir."

He patted me on the shoulder, gave me a nod of respect, and then took a step down off the porch before stopping and turning to say, "I'm looking forward to the day when we can say our hellos to you again. Praying it'll be soon." On that he went to join his wife and Carl at the car.

"Help me with your father, will you, Laird," Mother asked, wheeling him to the edge of the porch steps. Carl saw us and ran back to help lower him to the ground. As Carl started to wheel my father toward the car, I stopped him. "Wait," I said, walking around to the front of my father and leaning down to hug him goodbye. When I did, he seemed to moan, the way an animal does when it's hurting. "I love you, Dad. I know I haven't been a good son, but I promise to do better. I'll miss you and think of you a lot over there."

When I pulled back to look into his normally dry and wide eyes, they were wet and only half open, and he breathed slower than normal. I kissed his forehead before returning to the porch and my mother, Janie standing near her, both in tears.

Janie kissed my cheek, saying, "I love you, Laird," before turning and going back into the house, taking Billy with her.

"So this is it," My mother said, turning her downcast face from me.

"Guess so," I said, unsure what else to say.

Looking back at me, she said, smiling, "I really would've liked to see you pitch at Braves Field."

"Yeah, me too. But there's always next year."

She looked hard and deep into my eyes. "There better be." Then she grabbed hold of me and pulled me to her, holding me tighter than ever before, kissing my neck once and whispering in my ear before walking off, "Give 'em hell, Son, then you come home—you hear?"

I stood alone on the porch and watched as they drove away, the red taillights of the car growing smaller and smaller until they were nothing but a memory in the night. I wondered to myself if I'd ever see them again. I imagined they were all silent in the car as my mother drove, each of them wondering the same thing. I wondered if I'd ever have another conversation with my father like I'd had that Christmas evening, if I'd ever have another chat with my mother about baseball and the Braves. I wondered about my grandparents, about who would take over their ranch if I didn't make it home alive. And I wondered how they'd remember me— about my legacy.

SOMEWHERE IN THE early morning hours of December 26, 1943, I found myself unable to sleep any longer and rose from bed momentarily to retrieve my precious daughter from her crib at my feet, returning to lay back with her asleep and bundled on my chest, her tiny face turned to the side and resting on my neck, her silky hair brushing the underside of my chin. Janie turned and I lifted my arm to wrap around her, Janie's head now on my chest also. We laid like that until the sun rose and light pierced the bedroom curtains, all the while Janie and I listening to the whimpers our sweet daughter made while dreaming, my eyes fixed on my pressed Army dress uniform hanging from the top of the closet door by a hanger.

"We should get up, honey," Janie said. "Your taxi will be here in a half-hour."

I nodded, carefully lifting Emily off my chest as I sat up, Janie still lying on her side in bed, her eyes red and swollen from crying in the night. I laid Emily next to her and kissed them both. "Don't get up."

"No, I want to make you some breakfast before you go."

"Please don't," I said. "I want to remember you both just like this, not on the porch crying as I drive away."

"But honey," she started to say.

"Please, Janie. I can't imagine a more beautiful way to remember you both than the way you are right now."

I kissed her again before heading to the bathroom for a quick shower. Ten minutes later I was putting on my uniform before a long, wall-mounted mirror in our bedroom, my eyes watching the reflection of Janie watching me from the bed. I smiled to her through the mirror before she diverted her sad eyes away. Once I buttoned the last button on my Army jacket, I grabbed my duffle bag and went to take a seat next to Janie and Emily on the bed, the fingers on my left hands gently moving strands of Janie's hair from her tear-stained face.

"You look very handsome, Laird."

"I know," I said, grinning.

"Two stripes. What does that mean."

"Corporal."

"Is that good?"

I shrugged. "Gives me a little authority, but not much." A moment passed in silence. "Will you be okay?"

"I'll have to be, right?" When I didn't respond, she said, "We'll manage, but it won't be the same around here." I nodded and she began to sob, sitting up and throwing her arms around my neck, burying her face in my chest. "I'll miss you terribly, Laird. I'll be so worried."

"It won't help to worry, sweetheart. Try to just go on like

normal—like I'm just on the road with the team again."

"Only now you're dodging bullets instead of high fastballs."

"Stop, please." A few moments passed in silence. "I'll write you as soon as I get to Fort Benning in Georgia. Send money when I can."

"You'd better write. Those letters will be all I have of you while you're gone. Where do you go after that?"

"Wherever The Fourth is."

"Oh, Laird, please be careful," she said, kissing my face all over before I stood and headed for the bedroom door.

Looking back at her in bed lying next to baby Emily, my duffle bag at my side, I said, "Loving you is the best thing I ever did, Janie." On that I walked out, the sound of Janie's sobbing following me down the stairs, burning my gut like a hot poker. Before walking out the front door I stopped to say goodbye to Billy, who sat on the bottom stair with his head resting on his hands, his face solemn. "Hey, sport."

"Hi."

I saw through the window the taxi pull to the curb out front. "Time for me to head out."

"I know."

I sat next to him. "Can you promise me something?"

"Um hmm."

"Can you promise me you'll look after Janie and Emily until I get back?" I asked, putting my arm around his shoulder.

"Okay."

"I mean it. They'll need your help. It's a big responsibility I'm trusting you with, but I know you can do it."

"But what if you don't come back?"

"Don't talk like that. I'll be back before you know it."

He handed me a folded piece of sketch paper, the drawing side folded to the inside so it couldn't be seen. "I made this for you. But don't look at it until you drive away, okay?"

"Thank you. I promise, I'll wait."

Billy stood and hugged me goodbye while I sat on the stair, putting his face level with mine. "I love you, Dad."

"I love you too, Son," I said, choking on my words. "The taxi's waiting. I need to go."

After Billy released me, I walked over to our dining room, removed a sealed, letter-sized envelope from my inside breast pocket, then set it in the center of the dinner table, leaning against the vase of pink and white lilies I'd bought Janie the day before Christmas. I turned and took a few steps before stopping to look back at the envelope, the outside of which read:

If I don't make it home…

"What's that?" Billy asked, now at my side.

"A letter."

"Who's it for?"

After a long moment, I answered, "Janie," and then walked out without looking back. As the taxi sped away, I thought about the solemn purpose of that letter and the loving words therein, words meant to comfort and sustain a grieving widow, and words meant to give a daughter a glimpse of a father she never got a chance to know. Then I remembered Billy's drawing still in my hand at my lap. I glanced down and unfolded the paper. When I saw the caricature of me pitching in my Braves uniform—on the mound at Brave's Field, my leg raised in front of me in an exaggerated way, my cleated foot longer than normal, my face focused but my lips contorted, with my cap askew on top of my head and falling over my eyes, Billy and Grandfather admiring me from behind the mound in similarly humorous caricatures—I smiled, thinking immediately of Norman Rockwell and his famous baseball images, the ones seen regularly in *The Saturday Evening Post*. I honestly couldn't believe how talented Billy was at the age of eight. He wasn't as skilled as Rockwell—not yet—but Billy *was* an artist—just like he said.

CHAPTER TWENTY-SIX

After spending thirteen weeks at Fort Benning doing both Basic and Infantry Training, the Army shipped me off to England to meet up with the 4th Infantry, who'd arrived January 24, 1944, in anticipation of a large and secret amphibious offensive into Europe, codenamed *Operation Neptune*—to be undertaken on a day termed *D-Day*. For five months the 4th Infantry trained with allied forces on the bases and shorelines of England, until the early hours of June 6, 1944, when the order came from Command that the weather had broken and we could finally commence operations—our goal to take and secure the beaches of Normandy, France, which were controlled by the Nazis. It would not be easy, we were told, and with mined beachheads and seaside cliffs defended by hundreds of German machine guns fortified in concrete pillboxes, there would be heavy Allied casualties— including some of us from the 4th Infantry Division.

During that time in England, our communication with our families and loved ones had been cut off. They did, however, allow us to send one letter back home explaining why we would not be able to write, though each letter was heavily redacted by Command before being mailed, and our address or location could not be given. This, I imagined, must have been hard on my family, especially Janie. I imagined her worrying herself awake nights, crying to herself so as not to alarm Billy, possibly even lying to him, telling him she'd heard from me and all is well—that I'm safe. I imagined my domineering mother making angry phone calls to Army brass, trying to shame them into telling her where her boy was and if he was alive. And I imagined my grandparents on their knees in prayer, "The best position to mount a defense," my Baptist grandfather saying.

Operation Neptune would turn out to be the largest naval invasion in history, with eight different navies contributing nearly 7,000 vessels of varying types, including the 4,100 landing craft that would carry me, my fellow infantrymen, and Allied forces as close to the heavily defended shore as possible; we'd have to wade the bloody shore break—German bullets killing and injuring some of us—to get on the beach itself. Once there, we were told, it'd be a fight for survival until the beachheads could be secured and heavy armor and medical could come ashore. For my part, I was part of 21,000 Allied troops slated to take *Utah* beach—the westernmost beach of the Normandy assault—and as it turned out, my platoon was in the lead landing craft, standing and packed tighter than bottles of nitroglycerin in a box, waiting to go off.

Officers barked a lot of orders as we boarded our landing craft from a troop carrier hiding in the fog two nautical miles offshore; once the landing craft pulled away from the ship, however, an eerie silence fell upon us. Nobody spoke as our mostly plywood boat motored through the fog toward the unknown, the heavy flat-bottomed personnel carrier fairly stable in a turbulent sea. A few of the men got sick—the flaxen-colored, putrid remnants of last night's dinner splattering on our uniforms—but nobody made fun of them or said even a word. We would need each other very soon; it was no time for banter, no time to make more enemies than already awaited us onshore.

Suddenly we broke through the fog into early morning light to get a glimpse of the beach and fortifications before us. What I saw and heard sent a chill up my back and I could feel my hands begin to tremble as they clinched tightly around my M1 Carbine rifle, which I held erect in front of my body, as everybody did. Along the long beach, which was now only seven hundred yards in front of us, were large steel stars and rolls of barbed wire. The large steel stars were meant as landing craft barriers and there were hundreds scattered about the sand like enormous jacks thrown by a giant hand. Along the top of the cliffs, German soldiers fled and dodged our naval bombardment, which had commenced an hour prior to our landing. And there were the infamous German pillboxes, at least ten of them at equal intervals across the top of the cliff—large concrete bunkers with slits cut into them, looking like ten sets of evil eyes staring down on us, slits that suddenly came alive with muzzle fire from a whole heap of MG 42 machine guns, bullets spraying our landing craft a second or two after the flashes, sounding like a thousand hammers smashing our wooden boat into oblivion. We ducked as best we could but we were packed in too tight and a deadly bullet violently struck the shoulder of a man in front of me, splattering blood and bone across my face as he dropped to his knees in agony. I felt myself about to puke and prayed for God to get me out of there alive. That's when everything went silent in my head; the silence lasted no more than five seconds but it was five seconds of utter peace. Then the armor-plated front landing craft door dropped like a rock into the water, exposing us to deafening German fury. Men in the back began to scream at men in the front, "Move!" and "Get out!" and "Go, you idiots!"

Our Captain yelled from the front as he leapt into the water. "Don't stop on the beach! Move up to the cliffs, underneath those machine guns or you're all dead!"

There were forty men on my boat and I stood in the last third of the cluster. By the time I jumped into the chilly water, several other men had been wounded by machinegun fire. One guy was floating near the front, and with the help of the surging sea, I shoved his bloody body back onto the landing craft before wading into the fight. Some of our guys were firing back at the cliffs, so I hollered, "Move! Save your ammo until they're in range!" The German machine guns had an effective firing range of 2,000 yards, our infantry rifles only 300.

I glanced to my left and right and saw that we were the spearhead of the assault on Utah Beach, the others only then beginning to leap into the choppy water from their bobbing boats. "Move! Come on!" I yelled, grabbing one scared-stiff soldier by his rucksack and pulling him with me toward shore, the water now only up to our knees, bullets whizzing past and zinging into the water near us. "Move up! You wanna die, soldier?"

Once on the sand I ducked behind the first landing craft barrier I saw, pulling the other soldier down beside me. The sound of gunfire echoed off the cliffs and the water, and wounded men were crying out in agony on the sand and in the shore break. Looking at his pale face, I could see the soldier I'd grabbed was only about nineteen years of age, ten years younger than me. He was scared and wet and cold—and about to be killed if he wasn't more aware. "Listen, Son," I said. "Look at me! Are you hearing me?"

"Yes," he muttered behind chattering teeth.

"I know you don't want to be here right now! Neither do I! But you've got to focus on the objective, which is first to keep yourself alive, second to help keep the rest of us alive! Understand!"

"Yes, Corporal."

I looked him square in the eyes. "You can do this, okay? You can!" He nodded. "Okay! Here's what we're gonna do! We stay out in the open too long and they'll pick us off like chickens, so we're going to zigzag through these steel stars, keeping our heads low, make them earn their shots! Got it?" He nodded again, so I pointed to a shallow cave 300 yards up the beach, saying, "Our destination is under that cliff over there! That's the safest place we can be right now! Follow my lead!"

I patted his shoulder and started running, my head low, bullets pinging off the metal barriers I used as shields. A long two minutes later I slammed my body up against the cliff, as tight as I could so as not to get shot from the guns above, my rifle pointing upward and ready to fire at any German bold enough to poke his head out. A few seconds later that scared soldier slammed his body next to mine against the cliff. When I looked at him, he smiled awkwardly. "Good, Son!" I said.

A few minutes later, twenty-two of the men in my landing craft were beside us against that cliff—including our captain—every man exhausted.

"We're off by about two thousand yards in my estimation!" the captain said over the noise of gunfire and exploding artillery, his intense eyes scanning his pocket map.

"Sir?" I said.

"We've drifted! We're supposed to be over there!" He pointed.

"Well if we had come in over there, sir, we'd all be dead! Look at those fortifications! We'd have been ducks in a pond, sir!"

"Divine providence, maybe!" the captain exclaimed with a wry grin.

"Roger that, sir!" I said. "We're on their flank now! If we move before some of them can reposition, we can take out those pillboxes—minimize our casualties, sir!"

And that's just what we did. While the Germans focused their guns out to sea, on the landing craft bringing in more Allied troops, our platoon scaled the cliffs above us by shimming up a protective crag I'd found, a washout created by time and heavy rains, I figured. Once on top of the cliff, we began clearing those pillboxes and other German fortifications, though it wasn't easy. Those brave and determined Germans could fight, and they knew how to use their guns. As we went along, there were less machine guns firing on our inbound troops and more and more men made it ashore to help us. It was an ugly affair and men died, some of which I killed—one with Billy's knife.

We'd just burned out a pillbox and I'd gone in to make sure there were no survivors inside. There were five bodies lying in smoldering heaps on the concrete floor and one man splayed out on a chair, the smell of charred flesh sickening. As I walked through I saw no movement and yelled, "Clear," slinging my rifle over my shoulder afterward. That's when the partially burned German soldier on the chair leapt at me, grabbing me around my neck from behind and pulling me to the ground on top of him, my front facing up. He fought hard to choke me out and I struggled to breathe as I tried to squirm free. The German soldier was amped up on adrenalin, though, and too strong for me. I tried to reach the Army-issue KA-BAR fighting knife I'd kept strapped to my rucksack chest strap—upside down for quick release—but it had fallen out during the scuffle. That's when I remembered Billy's buck knife. My right hand managed to get it free from my pocket and I flipped it open, stabbing him repeatedly in the thigh until he released me. Once he let go, I quickly rolled over and instinctively buried the knife into his heart, holding it there until he took his last breath. I got to my feet, gasping for air and reaching for Billy's knife, but when I saw it sticking in the dead man's chest, I couldn't bring myself to pull the blade free. How would I ever be able to give that knife back to Billy after it'd been used to kill a man? So I left the knife in his body and returned to my unit outside, nearly in tears having just experienced the true horror of war.

It took us less than an hour to clear those fortifications. While we worked up on the cliff, heavy equipment began clearing those enormous steel stars from the beach, which would allow landing craft to bring heavy armor and more personnel up onto the beach itself. But we still had to contend with defensive artillery being fired at us from far off, as well as sniper fire coming from a German marksman perched somewhere along the cliff, possibly in another small cave. Sand exploded all around us, but it wasn't nearly as terrifying as the hail of machinegun fire we'd experienced coming ashore. Still, the artillery fire took the lives of some of our men as we cleared the beaches—nearly killed me, also.

Once we'd opened a few slots along the beach, boats came ashore in droves, so many landing craft running up on shore that unseen bodies floating along the waterline were being crushed. I knew then that something needed to be done. Our captain had been wounded clearing bunkers, as had our platoon sergeant; that left me in charge.

"Stop and gather the wounded around these barriers so they don't get run over! Stack the dead over there!"

In my mind, it didn't matter that they were dead; they were still our guys and they deserved a proper burial, not to be run over in a rush to get supplies and equipment ashore. So we began carrying wounded men first. On my way back across the beach to look for other wounded men, artillery exploding all around me, I heard a man call out to me from behind a steel star, not too far from the cliff we'd taken earlier.

"Soldier!" he called out. "Can you give me a hand?"

When I looked behind the barrier I saw that the man was actually a major, tangled in some barbed wire, and he wore a medical insignia on his chest and a white band with a red cross on his arm. "Sir?"

"My leg," he said, wincing as he tried to stand.

His right pant leg at the thigh had been torn open and there was already a bandage in place, but the blood on his pants told me that his injury was serious. "Is it broken, sir," I said, kneeling at his side, ducking and covering him as an artillery shell exploded about fifty feet from us. "Sorry, sir," I said, climbing off of him and helping him sit up again.

"No, it's not broken, but the shrapnel took out a big chunk of flesh."

"All right, sir. Let's get you untangled and up." I pulled the barbed wire off of him and as I helped him stand on one leg, I slipped myself under his shoulder, his arm around me. "That's rotten luck, sir."

"You're telling me. I just got here ten minutes ago. I'm supposed to be treating you, not the other way around."

"You're accent. You from New England somewhere, sir?" I asked as we hobbled and ducked our way toward the shoreline.

"South Boston. You?"

"Lynn. Looks like we're neighbors." I waved my arm and whistled sharply to flag down a landing craft that had just unloaded a tank and was about to pull offshore, its door partially raised. When the door suddenly reversed to lower again, I knew he'd seen me. Just as I laid the major on the floor of the boat, something slammed into my left ribcage, harder than any punch I'd ever received; then another hit me, only this one lower, closer to my hip. I started gasping for air and suddenly felt weak, my knees buckling, everything starting to go black. The last thing I felt were a pair of hands pulling me aboard the boat.

WHEN I AWOKE I was in a hospital bed somewhere, people in Army uniforms standing over me and saying my name.

"Corporal Young," a man said. "Can you hear me?"

"Corporal Young," a woman repeated.

"Where am I?" I said, my throat dry and sore, my words hoarse, my eyes trying to bring the faces above me into focus. "Who are you?"

"You're back in England, Corporal," the man answered. "My name is Colonel Roberts. I'm an Army surgeon."

When my vision sharpened, I could see two middle-aged men and an older woman—one of the men leaning on a cane. I gathered the woman was a nurse, probably with some authority given the shiny silver captain's bars on the collar of her white nurse's dress. She handed me a cup of water and I took a big sip from it before handing it back to her.

"Surgeon?" All around me were various medical staff tending to injured and convalescing GIs in white-blanketed beds, some guys with their limbs in traction, others with bandaged nubs where limbs used to be. A lot of men had obvious head injuries. "What happened to me?"

"You were shot—twice. You don't remember?" Colonel Roberts asked.

"Last thing I remember was helping some major into a landing craft on Utah beach. I felt some pain in my side and everything went dark."

"You were aiding me," the man with the cane said. "Major O'Brien. I'm in your debt."

"That pain you felt came from two, seven-point-nine millimeter bullets fired from a German K98 sniper rifle."

"Thought we lost you," the major said. "Glad to have you back with us."

"Southie, right?" I said.

When the colonel gave Major O'Brien a curious glance, the major said to him, "South Boston. He and I are sort of neighbors. He's from Lynn."

"Hartford now, but I grew up in Lynn."

"Just the same," Major O'Brien said.

"I feel like I got broadsided by a Mack truck."

"The first bullet struck your middle left ribcage, breaking two ribs and puncturing your left lung, and barely missing your heart by the looks of it. The second bullet entered here," the colonel said, gently touching my left side, about four inches above my hip, "but it zigzagged inside, nicking your descending colon and liver."

"That's pretty bad," I said. "Will I be okay?"

"We were able to suture your liver and colon—repair your lung. But we need to watch you closely for signs of infection. Anytime the colon gets pierced, infection is a concern."

"When can I get back to my platoon?"

"Son," the colonel said, "I don't think you understand. You're out of this fight."

"You mean I'm going home?"

He nodded. "Eventually. You'll convalesce here for a while. When we're sure there's no infection, and when you can get around well enough on your own, then you can go home."

"How long have I been here? Does my family know?"

"You've been here six days."

"Six days?" I said, surprised. "I've been out all that time?"

"With our help, yes," Colonel Roberts said. "And yes, we notified your family by wire the night you arrived. We'll wire them again with the good news that things are looking up. Now get some rest." Colonel Roberts turned his attention to the nurse. "If anything changes or you see any signs of infection, let me know."

"Yes, sir," was all she said before they left me there alone.

As I lay in my hospital bed—the throbbing pain in my ribs ever present—my mind returned me to the horrific scene inside that German pillbox—the burned men inside, the fight to the death I had with one of them, the ivory handle of Billy's buck knife sticking out of the man's chest as he lay there dead. I felt my body begin to tremble as tears formed in my eyes. *Lord, have mercy on me,* I prayed. *Forgive me for what I had to do. Forgive me.*

TWO DAYS LATER Major O'Brien came to see me in the ward, taking a seat at my bedside as I sat up in bed, my back resting against some pillows and the metal headboard.

"How are you feeling, Corporal Young?" he asked, leaning his cane against my bed and extending his injured leg out, rubbing his thigh through his uniform trousers.

"Better, but still feeling weak."

"You'll get stronger. Your body went through a lot. Give it

time."

"How are you, Major? How's the leg?"

"A little sore. That's what I came to see you about." He handed me a letter. "Before I forget, this came for you this morning."

I looked at the return address on the envelope. "From my wife," I said with an excited smile." I opened the letter and started reading while trying to listen to the major.

"I won't keep you then," he said. "Just wanted to say one more time how grateful I am to you for getting me off that beach. Without you I probably would have been killed."

I stopped reading when I heard what he said. "But somebody grabbed me too. I remember now. It was you. You pulled me onto the boat—saved my life."

"We helped each other. But you wouldn't have been such an easy target if it wasn't for trying to help me."

"Still, Major—thank you." I started reading Janie's letter again as Major O'Brien explained that he was shipping out that day, back home to Boston. His injury had ended his tour of duty.

"Good news from home?"

"My baby girl," I said smiling. "She just started teething, my wife says."

"That's painful. But she'll be fine."

"You have kids, Major?"

"Three. One boy and two girls. The boy's in college now. Hard to imagine sometimes."

I sat up suddenly after reading the next few lines of Janie's letter. "I gotta get home."

"Hold it, Son," the major said. "You're not going anywhere. Not right now."

"My mother. She's ill. My wife says she's in the hospital!"

"Calm down. Easy does it. Does your wife say what's wrong with your mother?"

My eyes scanned the letter until I found the answer. "Says here, 'systemic lupus erythematosus.' What is that? You're a doctor, Major."

"Wow. Systemic lupus. That doesn't just show up. She must have had symptoms for some time."

"How serious is it? Will she…is she dying?"

"Hard to say from here. I'd have to see her records—examine her. But yes, systemic lupus is very serious. It's an autoimmune disease."

"What does that mean?"

"The immune system, for reasons we don't know, begins attacking healthy tissue throughout the body causing painful systemic inflammation. That's why I said she would have shown symptoms long ago."

"Not my mother. She would never let anybody know she was hurting."

"She must be very tough. Inflamed joints. Inflamed myocardium, pericardium, and endocardium of the heart. Inflammation of the lungs—called 'pleurisy.' Kidney failure. It'd be very hard to hide the pain from those things."

His explanation of my mother's disease brought to mind a suffering animal trying to carry on for its master's sake. "Well, is there a cure? Can anything be done?"

"No, Son. I'm afraid there is no cure for systemic lupus. Not yet."

"But…how long does she have?"

"I couldn't say without examining her."

"You're going home today, you said! You could go see her! Maybe help her!"

"Corporal Young—Laird. I'm sure she's got good doctors already."

"You don't know my mother, Major. She *never* goes to the hospital, except to take my father to his appointments. The doctors she has are the ones on duty when they brought her in. Maybe they don't know about Lupus like you." Thinking back for a moment. "I knew something was wrong with her before I left. She was so thin—and tired. I tried to get her to go see a doctor, but she wouldn't."

"What's wrong with your father?"

"Head injury—fighting in the first war. Left him in a stupor."

"I'm sorry to hear that." Major O'Brien thought about things for a moment before asking, "What hospital is your mother in?"

"Says here she's in the Intensive Care Unit at Massachusetts General. Intensive Care? Major, I've got to get home. Can you get me out of here?"

"I'll see what I can do," he said, rising at my bedside, leaning on his cane while he placed a caring hand on my shoulder. "Let me go see her first. I'm flying out," he looked at his watch, "in two hours. When I land in Boston I'll go straight to your mother. If it's that serious, I'll see if I can get you home sooner. Deal?"

"Thank you, sir," I said, extending my hand in friendship.

Shaking my hand, he said with a smile, "For now, just try to focus on something happier, like that sweet little girl of yours."

"Yes, sir."

As he walked away I recalled the conversation my mother and I had on the porch of my house the day she brought me the tin box and baseballs. I recalled her face and the worry, and how she said some mornings she just didn't know. I thought she meant that she didn't know if my father would be alive when she woke, but it was her she was talking about. That's why she gave the baseballs to me early, before my father died. She wanted to try and mend our relationship before *she* died. She knew my father would need care and she knew she was dying.

The next day, about noon, my nurse brought me a telegram from Major O'Brien, along with an official looking manila envelope. The telegram read:

Your mother's condition is grave. Your orders to come home will arrive shortly.
~ Major Patrick O'Brien, MD
Army Medical Corps

CHAPTER TWENTY-SEVEN

Major O'Brien sent a driver and car to get me from Boston's Logan International Airport on June 16, 1944, the day after I received his wire in England. He must have known my injuries would make it difficult to get around on foot because he had the driver bring a wheelchair with him up to my terminal. To be honest, the long, turbulent flight from England to Boston had caused me considerable discomfort, so the wheelchair was a welcome sight. Thirty minutes later I was standing outside my mother's hospital room in the ICU, trying to muster the courage to go inside while brushing the wrinkles from my Army dress uniform—wincing from the pain whenever my torso rotated even slightly.

"Are you all right, Corporal?" a man said behind me.

I turned and felt relieved when I saw it was Major O'Brien, only he wasn't in uniform; he was in a suit and white smock, embroidery over his breast pocket that read:

Dr. Patrick O'Brien, M.D.
Chief, Neurosurgical Services
Harvard Medical School

"No, sir, I'm not."

"The pain?"

"No, sir. The nerves."

"Ah," he said, nodding with pursed lips.

"You're a Harvard neurosurgeon?"

"When I'm not playing soldier," he said, grinning.

"How is she? You said in your wire her condition was grave."

"She's in bad shape, Corporal."

"Laird. Please call me Laird."

"Okay, Laird. The primary problem right now is your mother's heart. It's slowly shutting down."

"I felt my throat tighten as tears began to fill my eyes."

"Be strong, soldier," the major said.

"Yes, sir," I said, sucking my emotions back down. "How long does she have?"

"Two weeks. Maybe less."

"Has my father been here to see her? She wouldn't want to be away from him for long."

He placed a hand on my shoulder and said, "We'll talk about your father after. Now go. She's been waiting for you."

The varnished natural wood door had a lever-type knob, which made it easier to open quietly, and was large and wide enough to wheel a bed through. Inside I found my mother in bed on her back, the covers tucked under her exposed arms, her eyes closed and face flush, her long hair unkempt and covering much of the white pillowcase, her wheezing breaths labored. As I closed the door behind me, the hinges squeaked and her eyes opened, searching for the culprit. When she saw me standing there in my uniform, a concerned look on my face, she smiled and patted the bed where she wanted me to come sit.

"Hello, Son," she barely managed to say. "Janie was right. You do look handsome in uniform."

Sitting next to her on the bed and taking her clammy hand in mine, I said lovingly, "Mom, why didn't you tell me?"

"Would it have done any good?" She coughed intermittently, her hoarse voice straining.

"I wouldn't have gone had I known."

"I know."

"You wanted me to go, even though you were sick?"

"I wanted you to become the man your father hoped you'd be. If going to war was part of it, then so be it."

I shook my head. Never had I known a person so hard to understand, yet somehow wise in their confusing ways. "I'd laugh if all this wasn't so sad."

"Let's not argue. How are your wounds? Are they healing?" I nodded but didn't speak. "Laird, don't shut down on me. Not now."

"What am I supposed to say here, Mom? Am I supposed to act like everything's okay—that you aren't..."

"Dying?"

"Yes." I felt more tears rising but forced them back by closing my eyes.

She squeezed my hand. "It's okay, Son. I'm ready to go now."

"How can you say that? What about us? What about Dad?"

She smiled, which struck me as odd. "I know now you'll look after him."

I looked at her gaunt face for a long moment. Death seemed close, yet she had a pleasant aura about her, a strange peace. When a tear escaped from one of my eyes, I lay my head on her chest, the way I had many times as a child when my feelings had been hurt somehow. She stroked my head for a few moments.

"This crew cut suits you."

"What do I do now, Mom?" I said, my head still lying on her chest, her laboring heart beating a fast *thump-thump* in my ear.

"You go on living, Son."

"How? You've always been such a strong presence in my life." I sat up and wiped my tears. "On my own I'll just fail, like always."

"You never gave yourself enough credit, boy. Did you fail over there without me?"

"I was in the fight just four hours and got shot—twice."

"But I'm told your actions and leadership saved many lives in those four hours. It's not the time, Son, it's what you do with that time that matters."

Just then somebody pushed the door slowly open. At first there was nobody there in the doorway, but then my father rolled into the room, being pushed by Major O'Brien. "Somebody else wanted to see you, Corporal."

"Hi, Dad!" I said, rising and going to hug him. He grunted and thrashed in his chair, this time visibly happy. "He's still doing that? Amazing!"

"That's what we're here to discuss with you, Laird. Your mother thought," he said, looking to my mother, who nodded for him to continue, "that, given her limited time with us, we should discuss your father's condition and some new treatments available to him."

"New treatments? Like what?" I asked.

"Well, perhaps you've noticed over the years your father's muscles atrophying. They're shrinking from lack of use, the cause his stupor and inability to function properly. But you may have also noticed improvements, however slow, to his responses to stimuli."

"Yes, like the grunting and thrashing becoming more frequent," I said. "Why is that?"

"It's hard to say without looking at his brain, but my theory is that his brain is atrophying also, like his muscles, though at a much slower rate."

"I don't understand."

"I had a look at your father's war records, including his medical records. When he suffered that blast injury in the first war it fractured the back of his skull."

"I know. That's why he's the way he is."

"Yes, but field medicine back then was sort of rudimentary. It wasn't like it is now."

"You're telling me that somebody just patched my father's skull like a flat tire and sent him on his way?"

"Sort of, but with a little more skill than that. What I think they did was piece his skull back together as best they could in those conditions back in nineteen eighteen on the battlefields of France, and I think what they may have done was set the fragments of skull too far in, which put pressure on that part of the brain as it healed and scarred. I think it's possible also that a fragment of skull may have been lodged in his brain and not been removed, with the same result, interrupting normal functioning. But now that his brain is shrinking, so to speak, the pressure caused by the repaired skull is easing. That may be why he's starting to respond to things a little now. It's only a theory, but if I can get a good radiological image of his brain, I may be able to confirm my suspicions."

"Is that possible?"

"I think so. There's a new radiological imaging technique being experimented with whereby a dye is used to highlight abnormalities in the brain during x-ray."

"You mean like tumors?"

"And bone fragments, bullets, even abnormal skull pressure. Up until now we had to open the skull without knowing. To use a military analogy, sort of a search and destroy approach, hoping in the process we didn't cause collateral damage to brain tissue and quality of life."

"Is the surgery dangerous? Could my father die?"

"The dye and x-ray aren't dangerous, but anytime we cut into the skull we risk doing further damage. We've made great progress in that regard, but there is still risk to life, yes."

"Mom, what do you think?"

"I think I'd love to hear my husband say hello to me one more time before I say goodbye." She loved my father more than her own self and the thought of getting to talk to him again, hold him and kiss him, have him hold her and kiss her, that thought must have brought her great joy.

"What about Grandma and Grandpa? They're his parents. Don't they get a say in this?"

"They think we should try—that we owe your father that much."

My sights turned to my father, sitting stolid in his chair. I wished at that moment he could speak, that he could tell me what *he* wanted to do. That we were about to make a decision that would put his life at risk without his consent didn't set well with me. Still, it had to be made if we hoped to restore my father to some semblance of the man he was before the first war.

"What if he dies, Mother?"

She thought about my question for a moment before saying, "Then God will get us both—together."

"Okay," I said, glancing first at my father, then my mother, then at Doctor O'Brien. "When?"

"Now. I've got an operating room and staff on standby. All I needed was your consent. First we need to get the scan of his brain. If that proves my theory, then we go from there."

"What's the goal here, Doctor?"

"If I see what's causing the problem, and if I can remove what's causing the problem, I don't see why your father couldn't live a fairly productive life again, with rehab, of course. But time will tell to what degree all of this has caused permanent brain damage."

"Could you wheel him closer, Doctor?" Mother struggled to ask. When he did, Mother used all the energy she could muster to sit up and kiss my father's lips. "I love you, dear husband. I'll see you soon."

After she lay back down, I went over and hugged my father again, kissing his cheek and saying, "Love you, Dad. We'll be here when you get out of surgery."

"I'll let you know as soon as I know anything," Doctor O'Brien said as he wheeled my father out of the room and out of sight.

"Pray for him, Laird," Mother said, coughing. "He'll need it."

I nodded. "I need to go call Janie."

"She's already on her way. Your grandparents, too."

"They're staying with her and the kids?"

"Um hmm."

"That's good. Did they ever go back to Texas?"

"Yes, but they came back a few days ago, when they heard you got shot and might be coming home."

"They didn't come back for you?"

She smiled. "That too, I suppose."

"Um hmm. Thought so." I removed my jacket and threw it over the back of the corner chair.

"You're bleeding, Son—your ribs."

I looked under my arm to see a small red stain. "Guess some stitches must have pulled loose. I'll get it taken care of later." I sat gingerly in the chair that I'd thrown my jacket over, leaning back and stretching out my crossed legs in front of me. "Right now I'm exhausted."

"I'm glad your home, Son," Mother said.

"Me too, Mom." On that I closed my eyes, the stress and lack of sleep over the last ten days sending my mind and body into a deep slumber. When I woke, it was to the sound of Billy giggling.

"Dad," Billy said, one of his fingers teasing one of my closed eyelashes. "Oh Dad, are you in there?"

Suddenly I slammed open my eyes and yelled, "Boo!"

Billy jumped back about two feet in fright. "That's mean," he said as I grabbed his hand and pulled him in for a hug, still laying back on the chair, wincing a bit at the pain the embrace caused me.

"Careful, Billy," Janie said, her pretty face overjoyed at seeing me again. "He's hurt. Remember?"

"How long have I been asleep?"

"About an hour," my mother said.

"Help me up," I said to Billy, who came under my arm as I

stood. Once on my feet I enveloped Janie in my arms, her face buried in my chest as she sobbed, I closed my eyes and breathed in the familiar fragrance of her shampoo that I'd remembered in my dreams while at war. "Why are you crying?"

"Just happy...happy your home alive...happy I didn't have to read that letter you left me."

"Me too. But I told you I'd come back alive."

"Yes, but you almost didn't. I was so worried when I got the telegram from the Army. I thought it was one of those letters, the kind that starts with, 'We regret to inform you that your husband is dead.'"

"Well, it wasn't," I said, smiling and kissing her one more time before greeting my grandparents. My grandmother held baby Emily in her arms, and I said, "Here, let me see my little girl." She handed Emily to me and I cradled her in my arms, tickling her tiny nose with one of my fingers, causing her to smile and giggle. "Isn't she the most beautiful thing you've ever seen? And so big now."

"I weighed her when we came in," Janie said, tossing the baby bag on the chair where I was sitting earlier. "She's doubled her birth weight already."

"Oh, a porker, are you?" I said sweetly. "Where's Carl?"

"At the ranch," my mother said, her voice still hoarse, "taking a well-deserved break. That's one thing I wanted to talk to you about." She let a moment pass before saying, "I want Carl to have the house and property...if your father and I pass together...or if the surgery leaves your father in the same state." Then she watched me and listened for any sign of protest.

I nodded, still gazing at my daughter's sweet face. "Yes. He deserves it."

"There's fifteen thousand in our savings account. Give him two thousand to get started. Use the rest to care for your father."

"How is Dad? Any word yet?"

Mother shook her head and looked off, closing her eyes as if praying.

My grandfather stepped to her bedside and took hold of her hand. "He's in good hands, Em."

She turned her head and smiled. "I know."

I wondered if my preacher-grandfather meant Doctor O'Brien's hands or God's hands. Perhaps he meant both. "You must be very tired, Mom. Maybe we should go out to the waiting room."

"Yes," she said, clearing her throat after a short coughing fit. "A little."

We each kissed her before leaving the room. From the doorway I looked back at her as she lay there, her eyes closed, her body so weak and frail, only half the woman she was when I left for the war. As I looked at her, one thought kept going through my mind: *Will she live long enough to see her beloved husband one more time?*

LATER THAT DAY, while we ate in the hospital cafeteria, Doctor O'Brien came to see us, still in his surgical wear, a cup of steaming black coffee in his skillful hands. As he sat, he removed his surgical headdress. None of us said a word as we anticipated news of my father. Would he tell us the surgery yielded no results? Would he tell us my father's surgery went well and all was good? Or had he come to give us the worst news of all—that they'd done all they could but my father had died during the procedure?

He took a careful sip of the hot coffee before saying, "Never did like this hospital's coffee." When none of us commented, he said, "He's doing fine."

"Thank goodness!" Grandmother exclaimed.

"Praise the Lord," Grandfather happily added.

"Did you find what you were looking for?" I asked.

He nodded. "The imaging showed both a small bone fragment still lodged in his brain tissue, and pressure on the brain from the skull repair done so long ago. To be honest, I'm surprised he had any function at all."

"Will he be back to normal now?" Janie asked, cradling and bottle-feeding Emily.

"It's hard to say at this point. Fixing the skull repair was easy enough, but digging a bone fragment out of live brain tissue has its risks. Our hope is that we didn't cause further damage to any neural pathways while extracting the jagged bone. Time will tell on that."

"Does my mother know?"

"Yes. I've already spoken to her, though I'm concerned she may pass before your father regains some level of consciousness."

"Oh, she just has to see him," my grandmother said.

"To be honest," Doctor O'Brien said. "I think that's why she's holding on."

"She's a fighter, Doctor," I said.

"That's *one* thing she has going for her," he said with a forced smile.

"When can we see him?" grandfather asked.

"He's in recovery at the moment. Give it about two hours. I'll come to the waiting room and get you." He stood and walked off, placing the full cup of black coffee on top of a trashcan on his way out.

Two hours later, just as promised, Doctor O'Brien led us to the recovery room to see my father, who was lying on his back on a surgical gurney, covered by a white blanket, with his arms exposed, his upper torso and head slightly raised, the crown of his head wrapped loosely in gauze bandage. And a glass IV bottle hung high on a stand next to his bed, the tube leading to one of the veins in his left arm. We approached his bedside slowly, as one would approach the crib of a sleeping baby, gazing down on him with adoring eyes. Grandmother gently took one of his hands in hers and bent to kiss it, light as air so as not to disturb him.

"We've got him sedated for now," Doctor O'Brien said. "But if his vital signs remain stable, we'll remove the sedative and see how he does."

That's when I noticed the color of my father's face—red and flush rather than its normal pasty white color. "He looks good," I said to the doctor. "His color, I mean."

"Do you know where he'll go after here, Doctor?" Grandfather asked.

"He'll have a room in ICU."

"Where Mom is? Maybe they can share a room?" I said, excitedly.

"That would be grand!" my grandmother added.

"I'm afraid not," Doctor O'Brien said. "The ICU rooms aren't designed for two patients." After gazing upon my father for a few moments more, the doctor said, "I think we'd better go. I'll let you know when he wakes."

It was getting late and Janie needed to get Emily and Billy home to bed. They'd return, they said, first thing in the morning. For my part, I'd stay at the hospital in case any sudden developments happened with either of my parents, opting for a sofa in the waiting room rather than the compact chair in my mother's room. Besides, she needed her rest and I was still having violent flashbacks from my fight with the charred German soldier, flashbacks that, had she seen them, might have given my mother a fright. I didn't want that, not in her fragile condition. As it turned out, I slept pretty well on that waiting room sofa, and I don't recall having any nightmares. Though the couch cushions were vinyl-coated for easy cleaning, they were soft and comfortable. And I used my rolled Army jacket for a pillow. The only thing that stirred me awake was the smell of breakfast being wheeled past me in the morning on a squeaky food cart.

After sitting up and rubbing the sleep from my eyes, I made my way down to the bottom floor and a coffee kiosk I remembered seeing on my way in the day before. I'd never much liked coffee and made a distasteful face at the first sip, but I needed something to drown the fatigue I felt. That's when I saw Janie and the kids coming toward me down the main floor corridor, my grandparents and Carl following closely behind.

"Any word yet on your father?"

"Not yet—no."

"How's your mother?"

"I was just about to go check."

We went back upstairs and were greeted at the ICU entry doors by a polite nurse who said we had to wait to see my mother, that she was being bathed and that it'd only be a few minutes longer. So we waited, and we waited. An hour later, Doctor O'Brien came out to greet us.

"Good morning," he said. "I've got some great news. Your father—he's awake and talking, though he's having a difficult time of it after twenty-five years."

"That's fantastic!" I said, Billy bouncing enthusiastically in circles next to me.

"Thank you, Doctor!" Grandmother said, hugging the doctor, a big smile on her lips. "We're overjoyed!"

"Can we see him?" Grandfather asked.

"Yes, of course, but go in one at a time. His mind is just waking up, after all. We don't want to overload it too fast."

"You go, Laird," Grandmother said. "You should go first."

"Yes, Grandson," my grandfather added. "It should be you."

I kissed Janie's cheek and followed Doctor O'Brien into the ICU toward my father's room, which, I was told, sat right behind my mother's. Had she known that, there would have been no stopping her from getting to him.

"We've got him sitting up in a wheelchair. I'll warn you, though. He's having muscle control issues. They were tense for so long, now they're loose. The nurse is trying to get him to eat."

I felt as nervous and unsure as a mischievous kid being led to the principal's office by his teacher. "Wait," I said, stopping before my father's closed hospital room door. "I think my mother should see him first."

Doctor O'Brien looked at me for a moment and then said, "Okay, Laird. Maybe you should stay here then, turn around so your father can't see you. I'll wheel him into your mother's room, leaving the door open. After a few minutes, you come inside."

I nodded and then waited for Doctor O'Brien to wheel my father out of his room. Every part of my being wanted to rush over to my father when I saw him, but I turned my back as instructed, waiting for the sound of my mother's hospital room door opening. That's when I turned back around and quietly stepped near the open doorway, eavesdropping on what I was sure would be a very emotional reunion.

I watched as Doctor O'Brien wheeled my father as close to my mother's bedside as possible, and I watched as my father took my mother's hand in his shaky hand, her head turned away, seemingly asleep. But when she felt his touch, my mother turned her head in his direction and opened her eyes.

"Hello, Em," I heard my father say, his voice deep, just as I'd imagined, but weak. When she realized who was holding her hand, she suddenly sat up, like she wasn't even sick, throwing her arms around his neck and sobbing on his shoulder, twenty five years of lost love pouring out on him at that moment. "Don't cry, Em," he muttered, but she cried and cried as he held her for several more minutes.

Tears rolled down my cheeks as I watched and listened to a beautiful love story come to life again.

"I've dreamed about this day so many times," she said, my father stroking her hair, her head still on his shoulder. "But I'd begun to lose hope." Leaning back and looking at the chocolate colored eyes that had captured her heart so long ago. "Still, I prayed. I prayed and God answered." She kissed his face all over before falling back on the bed in a coughing fit.

My father held her hand and then leaned forward to remove some strands of hair from her face with his fingers. When she finished coughing, and the pain had left her, her eyes turned to him again. "The doctor tells me you're sick, Em."

She began to cry again, nodding and saying, "It hurts."

"Your illness?"

"No," she muttered behind the sniffling and tears. "This...us. I thought...I thought if I could just see you again I could die in peace. But now...I can't imagine leaving you...and it hurts, Laird," she said, pointing to her heart, "right here."

"Oh, Em," my father said, softly kissing my mother's hand. "If this had happened and you weren't here..." He just shook his head, his hand rising to—I assumed from behind him—wipe some tears from his cheek. "I wouldn't have wanted that."

She smiled adoringly at him. "You were asleep for so long—so, so long." They must have heard me crying because my mother leaned her head to look around my father's shoulder to the doorway where I was standing, my father turning his head also. My mother smiled and waved me inside. "Come in, Son." I hesitated, part of me feeling like I was treading on hallowed ground, the other part just scared to meet my father. "Please," Mother added.

"Is this...?" my father started to ask, his weak arms fighting to turn the wheelchair around.

"Yes, Laird," Mother said. "This is our son—your son."

I wiped the tears from my cheeks; my father wiped his. For a long moment we just looked at each other. Then my father shook his head slightly, glancing at my mother before turning back to me with a smile. "You've grown a lot since the last time I saw you."

I laughed awkwardly. "Yes, sir."

"Christmas night. You were just three years old."

"Yes, sir."

"And now...you're a soldier," he said. "It's strange, but

somehow I knew that."

I glanced at my mother. He heard us, all right. "Yes, sir...well, I was a soldier...Fourth Infantry," I said, holding up my jacket and showing him the Fourth's diamond-shaped, ivy insignia patch on my sleeve's shoulder. "I got shot."

"The Fourth..." he said, closing his eyes to search his memory. "What was it we used to say?"

" 'Steadfast and Loyal.' "

"Yes," he said with a nod. " 'Steadfast and Loyal.' " Just then my father set the brake on his wheelchair and with all his strength, stood and held out his arms to me, his legs shaking under the strain. Like a little boy who'd just come back from summer camp, I rushed into his awaiting arms, weeping just as my mother had—on his shoulder. His bones were prominent in his back as I held him, the result of the atrophying muscles Doctor O'Brien spoke about. It felt good to hold my father for the first time, and I felt safe in his arms, as a boy should. "Guess we have a lot to catch up on, you and me." I nodded, glancing at my mother who was smiling and wiping her tears of joy. After our embrace I helped him sit again in his wheelchair. "Are you married?"

"Yes. She's out in the waiting room."

"Any kids?"

I nodded and smiled. "Two. An adopted son and a newborn daughter...named after Mom."

Mom raised her eyes to him, as if to say, "What's a girl to do?"

He smiled back at her before saying to me, "Bring your family in. I'd like to meet them."

"Should I bring in Grandma and Grandpa...and Carl...or should I wait until after?"

"They're here too?"

"We've all been waiting a long time for you," Mother said.

"Please, bring everybody in. Are my teammates here too?"

"You haven't played baseball in twenty-seven years, honey,"

Mom said with a laugh.

"Oh," he said, deflated.

"Go get the others, Son," Mom said to me, her voice betraying fatigue, her face wincing from some unseen pain. "I'm sure they're all chomping at the bit to see him."

My father took hold of her hand again, his eyes concerned for her. When I returned with the others, he was still holding her hand—and she was crying again. All I heard as we came into the room was my father telling her, "I'll be there before you know it, Em, and then we'll have forever together." When they heard us come in my father turned and said, "Mother!"

My grandmother hurried to his side, bending and holding his face in her hands, kissing his eyes and telling him how much she loved and missed him. When my grandfather approached, my father tried to stand out of respect, but my grandfather put a hand on my father's shoulder and said, "No, Son. I'll come to you." My grandfather bent over and hugged his son—my father—in his wheelchair, saying, "I've missed you, boy."

"I've missed you too, Dad," he said. As my grandfather stood, my father looked at me and cocked his head, as if to say, "Introduce me to your family."

"Dad, this is Janie, my wife."

"So pleased to meet you, Janie." He offered her a warm smile but Janie handed Emily off to me and went to kiss his cheek instead. "Oh, I could get used to these," he said to her. "And who is this young man?"

"This is our son, Billy."

Billy walked over and extended his hand. "William Bradford Sunday-Young, sir. Glad to know you."

My father laughed. "Such a polite, boy. Well, William Bradford Sunday-Young, I'm Laird Allen Young the second."

"I know," Billy said. Pointing to my grandfather, he added, "And he's the first Laird Allen Young." Pointing to me, Billy said,

"And he's the third."

My father said with a smile. "I like him."

I walked over to my father and laid baby Emily in his arms. "Dad, this is your granddaughter—Emily."

He looked at her adoringly for a long moment, wiping a tear from his cheek. "I'm overwhelmed," he said. "So much joy in one day." A moment later, he glanced up at my mother and said, "Emily is the perfect name for this child."

His comment made me wonder if he was thinking the same thing as me—that one Emily would be going out of this world, another having just come into it. I couldn't help seeing the blessing in that coincidence, if it was a coincidence at all.

"And who's this?" Father asked, looking at Carl who was standing in back of all of us, trying not to intrude.

I motioned for Carl to step forward. "This is Carl, Dad. He helped Mom take care of you for the past twenty-five years."

Carl seemed to blush as my father reached a hand out to him. When they shook hands, my father said, "I'm indebted to you, Carl."

"We all are," Mom said. "We couldn't have done it without him."

"Well, I hope you'll stay on another twenty-five years, Carl," Father said. "Only I promise you won't have to work nearly as hard."

"It's become my home, Mr. Young," Carl said. "Happy to stay on as long as you'll have me."

"Call me, Al."

"Yes, sir," Carl said.

Just then Doctor O'Brien poked his head into the room from the doorway. "Could you keep it down? You're making the nurses cry out here." He stepped inside. "Everything okay?"

"Wonderful, Doctor," Mother said, coughing after she spoke.

"Just a few minutes longer," he said, before leaving us. "They both need some rest." Catching sight of my bloody Army shirt, he said, "Come see me after and I'll fix those stitches."

"Yes, sir," I said, throwing him a lazy salute as he left.

We sat and chatted for a little while longer, catching my father up on some things he'd missed over the years. After each reference he'd simply shake his head in amazement. Mother told him about *The Great Depression* and how hard things were, and she caught him up on the Boston Braves. That's when my father, who still held baby Emily, asked my mother, "Does our son like baseball?"

Everybody laughed.

EPILOGUE

My mother died two days later, in the early morning twilight—alone, except for my father who sat at her bedside, holding her hand as she passed. My father said her last words to him were spoken with her last breath. He said my mother took a deep and labored breath, then upon exhalation whispered, "'My cup runneth over.'" With those words my mother passed into heaven. Doctor O'Brien, who'd been watching from the doorway, said my father laid his head on her breast and wept—for an hour he said, until they had to wheel his wife's body away.

At her memorial service—which was held at the historic First Baptist Church of Boston three days later, on June 22, 1944—people shared anecdotes from their encounters and friendships with my mother, many of them baseball players and coaches, all of them saying how much they respected her knowledge of the game, but also how much of a nag she was. That made me laugh. Casey Stengel said she was the greatest baseball statistician he'd ever met.

After the funeral we travelled by train to Texas with her body and casket, where we buried her on my grandparents' ranch, under a large oak tree on a hill overlooking the neighboring ranch where she'd grown up. Dad said he couldn't think of a better place for her. We stayed in Texas for a month. While there, my father and I rehabbed, sometimes just tossing the baseball back and forth with Billy while my grandparents, Janie, and baby Em watched. I cherished those catches with my Dad, as I know he did.

When my side had healed and my pitching arm had regained its form, I put a call into the Braves' front office. Casey Stengel was gone and no longer managing the club. His replacement was a Hoosier named Bob Coleman, who'd managed for more than twenty years in the minors before the Braves hired him. The Braves were on the back end of another losing season and Coleman said he could use all the help he could get on the mound. He said when I get back to Boston to come throw him a few, just to confirm what Casey Stengel had already told him about me. So in early August, upon our return to Lynn, Massachusetts, my father and I paid a visit to Bob Coleman at Braves Field in Boston. And just as I'd done with Casey Stengel, I pitched a few to Coleman who squatted behind home plate, the entire Braves team working out in the outfield for the afternoon game against the Pittsburg Pirates, which they would lose by a score of 8-13. After he caught a few for me, Coleman said he'd see about working me into the lineup—that he'd call me later that day and let me know.

That night, while at home with Janie and the kids, Coleman called, telling me to come in the following day to get fitted for a uniform, that I'd be starting in a home game on the 25th of August, against the Phillies. When I called my father to tell him, we both wept. It was the culmination of a family dream, led largely by my mother. That she wouldn't be there to share in the experience saddened us, but we knew she'd be watching—and she'd be smiling.

There was one thing I wanted to do, though, something that would make the occasion even more memorable for my father— for all of us. So that night I mailed a letter to Jay Clarke, telling him the good news about my father, and telling Clarke that it'd mean the world to my father to have him there, sitting beside him as he watched me make my major league debut. In that letter I included my telephone number and a check for airfare, telling him he could stay with us at our house while he was here. Then I waited. Five long days later the phone rang; it was Jay Clarke. He was so excited for me—especially for my father—and said he'd be overjoyed to join us for the game.

When we picked Clarke up at the airport, he said to my father, "Hello, Al. Nice to see you again. Boy, you sure can hit!"

My father smiled. "Thank you. You aren't so bad yourself."

When my father asked Clarke about the eight home run balls I'd returned, Clarke smiled. "Some guy named Mel Fisher called me. Offered me three thousand dollars for the set. Autographed, he said. I told him, 'Call me back when you're serious.'"

So on the afternoon of August 25, 1944, I took the mound at Braves Field, warming up for my first major league game—against the Philadelphia Phillies. In the stands, in the first row behind the Braves' dugout, sat my father and his boyhood idol, Jay Justin "Nig" Clarke. When I glanced over at the two of them after making my last practice pitch, the catcher throwing the ball over my head to the second baseman, they where chatting it up like old pals. I imagined them talking about that day in Ennis, Texas, so long ago, the day that, years later, changed all of our lives—mine, my father's, my mother's, Clarke's, my wife's, Billy's, my grandfather's and grandmother's, Carl's, and even baby Em's. It made me think about the game we all love so much, about how our shared love for the game healed us—made us all better in some way.

Just then the infielders gathered around me on the mound—first baseman Buck Etchison, second baseman Connie Ryan, shortstop Whitey Wietelmann, third baseman Dee Philips, and catcher Clyde Kluttz. Somebody tossed Kluttz the ball and he handed it to me, saying before they all returned to their respective positions on the field, "All right, rookie. Show us what'cha got."

"Play ball!" the home plate umpire hollered, bending for a moment to brush off home plate, the leadoff batter waiting patiently outside the batter's box for the catcher to return.

I looked up to heaven and whispered, "This is for you, Mom."

The next sound the crowd heard was a loud *Thwack!* when my fastball hit the sweet spot of the catcher's mitt.

"Steeeerike!" the umpire called.

The next pitch, the same result. And that's how it went for the first three innings. I was on fire—unhittable. But in the fourth, after throwing nothing but fastballs and curves, I got a little cocky. When the catcher signaled for my fastball again, I shook him off. When he called for the curve, again I shook him off. In frustration, he called for a changeup, a pitch I rarely threw. When I shook him off again, he simply threw up his hands as if to say, "Throw whatever the heck you want!"

And that's when I did the unthinkable—I threw my knuckleball.

I threw my knuckleball...*and my father was there.*

NOTE FROM THE AUTHOR

"Nig" Clarke and how I came to write this story...

After ghostwriting non-fiction books for several other authors, I decided to take a break and write a novel that revolved around the early days of baseball—a game I played as a kid and a game for which I hold great affection. With that in mind, I went searching for an interesting event in the game's history I could build a story around, which led me to Jay Justin "Nig" Clarke and his eight homeruns in a single game back in 1902.

The more I read about the game and the controversy around the score and size of the field, the more intrigued I became. After learning more about how that controversy shadowed Clarke throughout his major league career, and literally to his grave, I found myself sympathetic to his plight. The account of that game is fully documented and supported by ample evidence, including sworn testimony from the scorekeeper and others present, yet there were, and still are, many skeptics. In his later interviews, Clarke seemed reluctant to answer any more questions about that game. He'd grown tired of them and seemed to want to talk about his other accomplishments, like catching the perfect game for Addie Joss in 1908, or playing baseball during a few off-seasons in Cuba. But the press wouldn't let it go.

In Clarke's last known interview with Watson Spoelstra of *The Sporting News,* published on October 22, 1947—less than two years before his death—Spoelstra writes, "He [Clarke] had to be prodded into talking about his eight homeruns....It wasn't until many years later that baseball gave his epic slugging some recognition. The late Al Munroe Elias came across a box score of the game in 1902." You think that would have put an end to it, but it didn't. That article has generated subsequent misinformation attributed to

Clarke, namely that Clarke couldn't even remember the date of the game. But in reading the *original* article, the game's date is inserted into Clarke's dialogue in parenthesis, right after Clarke says, "We were playing Texarkana that day," and before he says, "I remember it as though it were yesterday," which tells me that Spoelstra or the editor inserted the date for clarification to the reader; only the date inserted is July 14, 1902 rather than June 15, 1902, which is believed by most historians to be the actual date the game was played, supported by a dated box score I have in my files. The reason the game was played in Ennis, Texas that day instead of Corsicana was because it was a Sunday and Corsicana, Texas had "blue laws" in place which prohibited games on Sunday. June 15, 1902 is a Sunday; July 14, 1902 is a Monday.

So with those things in mind, I asked myself:

"What if somebody found those eight baseballs—those eight homerun baseballs hit by Clarke in Ennis, Texas in 1902? And if somebody did find them, how would that impact 'Nig' Clarke's life and the life of the person that found the baseballs?"

That is how this story came to be.

Noah McCaffrey

NOTE: If you'd like to share this book at no cost to you, please take a moment to leave a review on one of this book's online retail pages. Books that get reviewed more get promoted to potential readers more by online retailers; thus, your reviews are important and will play a big part in this book's success. Thank you so much!

ABOUT THE AUTHOR

Noah McCaffrey lives in the eastern U.S. with his wife and dogs. He studied storytelling and film production long ago at a university out west. After a few years living and working in Hollywood, Noah moved away and began writing. Much of the past 15 years has been spent ghostwriting for other authors. Now he's writing for himself—and his gracious readers, of course. He played baseball growing up, pitching and catching mostly, and is a member of SABR—the Society for American Baseball Research. One thing he feels passionate about is writing inspirational family fiction that serves to help build character in men.

www.ingramcontent.com/pod-product-compliance
Lightning Source LLC
Chambersburg PA
CBHW031544240626
47153CB00002B/376